OUTBACK DESIRE

He stared at her for a moment. A warmth and a desire that had always been there rushed to fill him with an unbearable craving more torturous than pain. Finally, with a slight gesture which cast aside years of denying in his mind what his heart had always known, he said softly, "Come here, Jessica."

She rose and went to him like a moth to a flame, went down on her knees beside him.

"You undressed me and bathed me," he said, amused. "You, a very proper lady. Weren't you shocked?"

Jessica felt her face flush. "Of course not. I'm a doctor. My thoughts were only on your wound and its treatment."

His eyes searched her face and his smile deepened. "You lie, Jessica."

Suddenly he pulled her, gasping, down to him, her softness pressing against his chest. With a swift movement, he had her beneath him, her lustrous hair spread over his pillow.

Her eyes, wide with surprise, went dark with some other emotion as Eric gazed down at her. "Jessie . . ." he said, struggling with the last vestiges of his confidence and propriety.

"No," she whispered, her hands going to the back of his head. "Don't stop now."

She drew him down to her, and her lips parted beneath his—warm, moist, and inviting. . . .

WILD FURY

GINA DELANEY

ZEBRA BOOKS
KENSINGTON PUBLISHING CORP.

ZEBRA BOOKS

are published by

Kensington Publishing Corp.
475 Park Avenue South
New York, NY 10016

First printing: February 1987

Printed in the United States of America

Part I

1850

Chapter I

The parched early summer landscape, which Jessica had viewed as distressing only that morning, had suddenly changed. The new grasses having painted the plains in hesitant shades of green in spite of the drought, along with the monotonous distant blue-green hills, had all at once taken on a dreamlike quality. The environment had become almost ethereal. Even the meaningless clouds in the opal sky resembled angels of a sudden, and Jessica could almost hear them sing above the soft trod of Summerfield's hooves on the beaten track.

As she held the old horse's reins while he drew the carriage eagerly for home, she was certain her life would never be the same. One's life never is, she thought, once one has seen a miracle. And today, Jessica had seen a miracle. For the first time in her life, she had witnessed the birth of a child. At that moment when her stepfather, Aaron, had taken the tiny miracle in his hands, Jessica had felt the glory of being a woman. When they had watched the infant gasp and take his first breath, Jessica and the mother, Betty Schiller, had exchanged a special glance. Woman to woman. That moment, at least, was one a man could never share.

Jessica tossed her head and flicked Summerfield's reins to hurry him along, though the horse needed no hurrying. No man could feel the triumph of birth that a woman did, though his hand did the delivering. Jessica blinked and for a moment the angels above became only clouds already vaporizing, and the dreamy plains about her became the dark gray-green plains of thirsty grass again. For Aaron as a man could heed the calling of his desires. She could not. He was the physician which she, as a woman, could never be.

Still, she could assist him, even though assisting was like watching others swim in the cool water of a creek and not being allowed to go into the water oneself.

When Karl Schiller came to say that his wife needed Aaron's help in delivering the child, Jessica had gone first to the Schiller's farm southeast of Bathurst, and Aaron had come later on his horse after finishing a visit with a patient in Bathurst. The Schillers had nine other children delivered by Karl himself. But this child hadn't wanted to come so easily and Karl had come for help. After the child was delivered and Betty Schiller had been made as comfortable as possible, Jessica had set out for home while Aaron stayed to drink a toast with Karl Schiller and his grown sons. Jessica hadn't wanted to wait for her stepfather to finish his toast, not with the silly Schiller twins there with their mocking eyes and insolent grins and the taunting looks of their wild friends. Youths. Brigands was what they were, wild colonial boys.

Just then Jessica became aware of the sound of horses approaching from behind the carriage, and a glance back told her that the rowdies were there, as if her image of them had conjured up the real things. White teeth flashing delightedly in their tanned faces, the Schiller twins were approaching with four of the district's wildest youths. She pressed her lips together and gave Summerfield another flick of the reins. But the unwelcome escort soon rode up beside her, three men on either side of the gig.

Jessica's eyes, the color of the indigo waters of Sydney Cove, flicked over the young men on their cantering mounts. They were all in their early twenties, several years younger than Jessica. Though the men in the district dressed much alike, one could distinguish the Schiller twins from the rest even at a distance. For they were taller and more broad-shouldered than most, and if they happened not to be wearing their hats, their hair shown gold like ripened wheat. They sat their mounts now in an insolent slouch, but even then they rode tall.

It was Reginald who shouted above the clatter of the gig's wheels and gear. "What's the hurry, Miss Jessica?"

Jessica didn't answer. She had learned years ago that one of the easiest ways to manage the Schiller twins was to ignore them.

"Me and Rube wanted ye to celebrate with us. Celebrate the new brother," Reginald went on.

Half brother, Jessica corrected him in her mind. The Schiller twins had been born in Sydney before Betty Schiller was even married.

"Tell her, Rube," shouted Reginald to his brother. "Tell her it don't show much courtesy runnin' home like this without celebratin' such an event."

Jessica glanced at Reuben, the other twin, riding beside the carriage on her left. Reuben, the exact likeness of his twin, did not smile. He touched the brim of his

9

cabbage tree hat and observed her from hooded lids. Nor would Rube reply. He seldom did. It was as if what Rube lacked in cheer and speech, Reginald made up for by being too generous with both.

Jessica concentrated on the track ahead, not very distressed by the silly lads. An angry glance from her was usually all she needed to dissuade the taunts of the twins and their friends. She did not know why unless it was because the Aylesbury family enjoyed the respect of everyone they knew. Her stepfather, Aaron Aylesbury, was not only one of the wealthiest and most successful station owners west of the Blue Mountains, but he was also the only certified physician. Jessica's stepmother, Penelope, still a district beauty even though she was in her forties, was wealthy in her own right, a breeder of fine Merino sheep, the daughter of one of the most influential exclusionists east of the Blue Mountains. James, Penelope's brother, owned a large cattle station adjacent to the Aylesbury property. Jessica was surrounded by family which the people of the colony respected—and she commanded respect herself.

Tall and graceful as a young eucalypt, full bosomed and round armed, Jessica was the most desired woman west of the mountains. Her blue eyes were her pioneer mother's—her real mother's. The mocha and cream lusciousness of her skin, which was a mystery to everyone except her own family, came from her Aboriginal grandmother.

"Aiyee, Jessica," Reginald called. "I say, whoa, lass." Reginald drew a bottle from inside his shirt and held it up. "A toast, Miss Jessica, a toast to help us celebrate the new baby. Hold up, Miss Jessica."

Jessica had no intention of stopping the gig. "Go away,

10

Reginald," she shouted and gave him one of her glares.

Reginald flinched, but only briefly, and laughed. "Just one moment. It's a happy day." When he saw the stubborn set to her chin, though, and that she had no intention of reining Summerfield in, his own jaw hardened and he spurred his mount and rode to catch at Summerfield's bridle and bit.

Like Reginald's shadow, Rube did the same on the other side, and it was only seconds until Summerfield stood halted on the track, jerking his head and stamping his hooves, with the dust of the track wafting ahead of them all on a northern breeze.

Leather creaked and horses snorted as quiet, somber Rube stayed at the horse's head, and his twin turned his horse about to approach Jessica again. The other lads were grinning and touching their hats to Jessica more out of good-natured admiration than any malice. Jessica sighed and leaned back against the carriage seat.

Jessica hadn't decided yet whether she liked the Schiller twins or not, though she'd known them for years. They were rowdies, always into mischief. They had taunted her as far back as she could remember, Reginald with his good-natured grins and hoots and Rube with his quiet impudence.

"Come on, celebrate with us for just five minutes," Reginald said, reining his horse beside her again. He leaned on the saddle and grinned down at her. "It's not every day ol' Rube and me gets a new baby brother or sister."

"Only every nine months," one of Regie's friends drawled.

The lads guffawed and then looked sidelong at Jessica to see her reaction.

11

Reuben had Summerfield's bridle firm. The carriage was going nowhere. Jessica couldn't get away this time, so she rested her hands in her lap and leaned back against the carriage seat and smiled wryly, prepared to endure the harassment until Aaron came along, which he would do shortly. Besides, she was still in a glorious frame of mind and was determined that even the Schiller twins weren't going to ruin it.

Reginald's face was aglow as he watched her, his blue eyes sliding from her lips to her bosom and back up again. "Ah, Miss Jessie. I'd name the new babe for you if I had my way. But I can be content just knowing you set your pretty feet inside our house."

"What else did she set inside, Regie," spoke up one of the other lads.

The mob laughed hilariously, while Regie ignored them. "You should be a doctor and set up a business of your own." Regie went on: "'Cause then I'd be sick all the time and let you doctor me."

One of Reginald's friends, Howey Dobbs, bent over clutching his abdomen and groaned, "Oh my stomach. My stomach. I've been poisoned. I need a doctor."

The youths laughed and Johnny Coleson said, "Women can't be doctors, Howey, but they can be nurses." Johnny grinned hugely and looked around at his gawking friends. "Anybody here know where there's a nurse?"

Jessica kept a grimace painted on her face and let her boredom with them show. Better to endure this than to act perturbed. Not only had she put up with these young men since her childhood, but her brother Eric had fought these same rascals often because of their crude attempts to get her attention. But Jessica figured she could do more with her arrogance than Eric could with his fists. She glanced up at the sky with its half-angel clouds and drummed her fingers on the side of the carriage.

"Hey, Miss Jessica," Johnny said. "Can you nurse ol' Howey. He's terribly sick."

"She can nurse me anytime she likes," Howey guffawed as his eyes went to Jessica's bosom.

The young men howled with laughter as Jessica settled deeper into the carriage seat and listened for other hooves on the track.

"Don't mind them," Regie said to her. "Since they've grown up they've gotten rude."

Jessica merely sighed with infinite boredom.

"Say Regie," Howey Dobbs said grinning and showing his big front teeth. "Maybe Jessica don't think we've grown up. Least ways not like *she* has."

"Howey, if you'd grown up like she has I wouldn't be running around with Regie and Rube. I'd be running off with you," said Johnny.

The lads howled again with laughter, and it was then that Jessica realized that the exuberance of their hilarity had been fueled earlier, probably with some of Karl Schiller's own vintage wine while she was assisting Aaron with the birth of the child. Her fixed smile ceased slowly and she resisted the urge to glance back again to see if Aaron was on the track behind her. If the boys were sober, she could manage them. If they were drunk, she wasn't sure.

"Please ignore the lads. They are not gentlemen," Regie said. "Now me, I'm a gentleman. And I therefore invite you to have one swallow of my father's best wine under the shade of that gum tree." Reginald pointed to the one lone gum tree which stood at the side of the road.

13

At that moment Summerfield happened to toss his head and jerked the bit from Reuben's hands. In a flash Jessica had gripped the reins and the carriage lunged forward. Better to keep moving, she thought. Stopped on the empty track she was more vulnerable to their insolent stares and barbs. And moving she could at least get closer to home.

Feeling the grit of dust in her teeth and perspiration on her brow, Jessica kept Summerfield at an easy gait. The lads whooped and laughed and shouted hilarious quips at each other, and all the while bits of Reginald's pleas came to her on the breeze.

"Now, I'm mortified, Miss Jessie . . . Didn't mean to make you mad . . . You going to tell your father? I didn't mean no harm . . ."

Jessica glanced at him from time to time and guessed he intended to escort her all the way home.

"Please Miss Jessica. Can I call on you? You ain't got a steady beau, have ya? Why not me?"

No, she didn't have a steady beau. People said that was odd for a girl of twenty-eight. She should have been married and had three or four children by now, they said. She had gentlemen callers, all right. Had even been proposed to by "Uncle" James, her stepmother's brother who owned the property next to the Aylesbury's. But she'd declined every offer. She knew people wondered why Jessica Aylesbury never married. She didn't understand why herself. Not that she didn't have dreams of love. It was just that in every dream when a man took her in his arms, the man was always tall, with dark eyes and hair, and he always, always looked exactly like—

"That's right, Miss Jessica," Reginald said, no longer smiling. "Don't speak to the Schiller lads, they're bad.

14

They're poor and they're wild. I don't blame ya. No, not at all. A pretty lady like you with rich parents."

Jessica glanced at him just in time to see the fleeting look of pain on his face before he grinned again.

"That's what I admire about you, Miss Jessie. Everything you do is so-oo ladylike. From the tip top of your beautiful head to your tiny lovely toes. Not to mention everything in between." He laughed aloud and cried to his companions. "Look at 'er, lads. She even drives like a lady."

Something snapped in Jessica's well-ordered mind. Perhaps it was the earlier euphoria of the afternoon, or perhaps it was the soft silence of the summer day itself. Or perhaps it was Reginald's challenge, that she drove like a lady. Ahead the road was wide and straight, and about here was where Summerfield always picked up his pace, anticipating his own stall four miles ahead. Jessica suddenly grabbed the buggy whip from its holder and half rose off the seat with a wild, high, "Hi yi, Summerfield!" and flicked the whip expertly just over the gelding's right ear.

In a flash Summerfield bunched his powerful shoulder muscles, arched his neck, and he was off, shod hooves beating the dust of the track, and the carriage fairly flew.

With a surprised, "Yee-ee *hi!*" Reginald Schiller spurred his horse.

The carriage thundered and jolted beneath her, and the horses racing on either side were blurred in her peripheral vision. The reins in her hands vibrated with the tension and force of the race, and Jessica's bonnet strings pulled at her throat.

Reginald, laughing, shouted delightedly, thundering beside the carriage. His identical brother raced on the

15

other side with a grim smile, their comrades left slightly behind, still caught in the paralysis of surprise.

"Hi yi!" Jessica screamed at the horse, and as the wind roared in her ears and tore at her bonnet, blurring her eyes with tears, a great sharp thrill rose from her breast to fill her throat and burst from her wide-open mouth in a high-pitched shriek of laughter.

Summerfield took the challenge. He was a quarter horse and had been a trotter in the races in Sydney for years in his younger days. Even yet in his retirement, he never let a horse muzzle ahead of his own if he could help it.

Jessica laughed again, threw back her head and laughed, for Summerfield, in spite of the burden of pulling the carriage, was pulling slowly ahead of the brothers. Reginald, in a wild delirium, whipped off his hat and beat his horse, whooping, his golden hair blowing back in the wind.

Jessica shouted again and glanced at Rube. His expression had not changed, and she found herself wanting him to laugh, to shout, anything. This quiet almost menacing twin—what was he thinking? Were his glances as sinister as she imagined?

She flicked the whip again over Summerfield's ear. Every woman in the outback could drive a carriage, and most could ride like a man, in spite of the handicap of the sidesaddle. Jessica could do it all and well.

The race was filling her with a wild abandon. The world was suddenly hers for today she had witnessed a miracle. She was suddenly like the wind. Free. Free to laugh and shout and cry out. To love—no, not to love. Somehow not to love. She bit her lip, and the wind carried away her tears of joy.

16

Then he appeared like an apparition in her side vision, a man on a bay horse riding down a hill toward the track. He raced like the wind, and the rest of them might have been standing still. She saw his angry startled face as he came close to the track ahead of the carriage, mouthing her name. They raced past him, but he joined the race and pulled ahead. He rode like a demon, like no one else. A horse beneath him was never a steed but a wild fury.

Jessica laughed at her brother's grim face and shouted, "Hi yi, Summerfield." She shrieked with delight as her bonnet strings loosened and her hat went flying away from her.

Howey Dobbs dropped behind, but the others continued the race beside the carriage even as her brother reached for Summerfield's bridle. He caught it, jerking, and Jessica saw that he meant to stop her. She pulled back on the reins and stomped on the brake as the dust fogged, and the rumble of the wheels on the track slowed, slowed, and clattered at last to a stop.

The dust still fogged across them as their sweating, snorting steeds stamped, and the Schillers and their friends laughed, mopping the perspiration off their faces with their sleeves.

Coughing and trying to catch her breath, Jessica spread her hand over her breast, and through the loose tendrils of her blue-black hair watched her brother ride to the side of the carriage. He did not look at her at first, though, and the mouth beneath his newly grown mustache was grim. It was to Reginald he spoke:

"Schiller, you bloody rake," he said tightly with barely controlled anger. "Are you trying to get Jessica killed? What in hell were you trying to do?"

Reginald replaced his hat. "It was a race, Eric. And it

17

was Jessica's own idea, not ours."

Eric did not take his eyes off Reginald. "I don't believe you."

Reginald, grinning said, "Ask Jessica."

Eric studied Regie's face a minute longer, then turned his dark glittering eyes on Jessica. He said nothing.

She smiled and nodded. "It's true."

"Why?"

"I felt like it."

"*Felt* like it?"

"Today I watched Father deliver a baby boy. Mrs. Schiller's baby, and I feel wonderful."

Jessica watched the deep tan of Eric's face go paler for a moment, his astonished eyes deepen in color. "You watched—" Sudden perspiration beaded his forehead, and Jessica smiled secretly to herself. Eric was tall, broad shouldered, hard muscled, and lean, with a strong, handsome face, his father's dark-brown eyes and hair, the kind of man women dreamed of and swooned over. The hands holding the reins of his horse were strong and deeply tanned like his face and neck, and he sat his horse like a man on a throne. Women also loved Eric's smile and vied with each other to elicit it. Jessica could usually bring a smile to Eric's face with just a tilt of her head. He wasn't smiling now, though. The thought of birth, especially if there might be blood involved, had turned her hot-blooded, strong, handsome stepbrother to stone. Cold stone.

Eric Aylesbury, the grandson of a well-known Parramatta surgeon and the son of the district's only physician, hated medicine. He loathed it. Medicine treated wounds and wounds meant blood. Birth was no miracle to him; it was an atrocity. He gestured now at the

18

carriage, anger making his voice stern in spite of the pallor of his lips. "For that you risk your life to race in Father's old gig?" Before she could answer he looked at Reginald. "You caused this. If you had caused the gig to overturn, Schiller, I'd have had your head on a platter."

Reginald knew of Eric's phobia. "Not if you had to do the cutting yourself," he said grinning.

The other youths chuckled cautiously.

At that moment Howey came riding up to the carriage wearing Jessica's dusty bonnet. The youths cackled with laughter but cut their hilarity short when they saw Eric was not amused. Eric reined his horse with easy grace, rode to Howey and jerked the hat off his head, rode back to the carriage and handed it to Jessica.

When she took it, he finally smiled, his eyes taking in her hair which had come loose in long spiraling strands, and the smudge of road dust on her face. "The devil take you, Jessie," he said. "Look at you. What will Mum say?"

She snatched the hat from him. "Mum won't notice. She'll have eyes only for you. Because you haven't been home in so long." Her hand had brushed his when she took the bonnet from him, and the sensation the touch caused startled them both.

"It's only been eighteen days," he said.

"Nineteen."

His black brows shot up, and Jessica could feel her face blushing. "Well," she said to cover her embarrassment, "you only come home when you know Father is away."

"And speaking of the devil . . ."

Eric's gaze had gone to the track behind the carriage and, leaning to the side, Jessica looked back to see a rider coming at an easy canter. Aaron, her stepfather. She saw

Eric about to move away. "Don't go."

He paused. "I'm in no mood to see him."

"Then why were you this close to home?"

"I was looking for James."

"Perhaps James is at our station. He visits us often even if you don't."

Eric fixed her with a steady gaze which said more than it meant to. "I know."

The Schiller twins and their friends sat their horses and watched as Dr. Aaron Aylesbury approached. The doctor cantered up to the gig and reined his brindled gelding, looking first at Jessica then at Eric, then at the mob of ruffians surrounding the gig. When his gaze came back to Eric he said simply, "Well?"

Eric's eyes snapped as he indicated Jessica. "My sister will tell you."

Aaron at forty-eight still sat tall in the saddle like his son. He still had the same straight, unruly hair as his son, but with full sideburns now threaded with silver. His brown eyes had softened with the years and narrowed from the habit of squinting across the sun-drenched landscape. Aaron was still trim from many hours in the saddle, and at the moment one sun-browned hand held the reins of his American thoroughbred while the other spread almost protectively over the saddlebag which held his medical supplies.

"It was all in fun, Father. A celebration for the baby's birth," Jessica explained, and even while she explained, she knew the excuse was feeble. For how do you explain explosions of joy?

Aaron didn't understand. "How . . . did you celebrate?"

"We raced."

20

Aaron stiffened visibly and turned back to Eric. "You raced? Knowing that the creek's ahead?"

"If you'd built the bridge over the creek that I suggested years ago," Eric answered, "there wouldn't be any danger."

Aaron's face went vermilion under his tan. "That— that's beside the point!"

"Eric didn't race, Father. These young fellows and I did," Jessica put in quickly.

Now Aaron stared at her. "Jessica, you could have overturned the carriage at the creek and killed yourself."

"I know. That's why Eric stopped me."

Aaron frowned at his son who had made no effort to explain his own innocence, then looked around at the six youths. None of them would meet his gaze except Reginald who smiled without much humor. "Well, Mark?" Aaron said to Reginald.

"Sorry Dr. Aylesbury," Reginald said. "But it was mutual consent. And we wouldn't have let the gig turn over." While Aaron continued to stare angrily at them, the others moved away, and Reginald touched his hat murmuring, "It was all in fun. We meant no harm. Sorry, sir. Good-bye, Miss Jessica. Uh . . . guess we'd better go now. See you about, Eric. G'day." He trotted to his waiting companions. Then with whoops and shouts the young men rode off down the track in a cloud of dust.

When Aaron's eyes came back to Jessica she said steadily, "You called Reginald Mark."

Aaron colored again. "Did I?"

"Yes, you did."

To hide his embarrassment, Aaron dismounted and walked his horse to the back of the gig where he began to tie him. Jessica's and Eric's gaze met. They knew why

21

Aaron had called Reginald Schiller Mark. The same reason that Eric disliked both the identical Schiller twins. For the twins looked exactly like Aaron's half brother, Mark, dead now twenty-two years. Neither Jessica nor Eric had to say anything. They read each other's thoughts. Having grown up together as siblings, they had shared the telling of each Aylesbury family tale and of the secrets told, as well as the ones not told.

The carriage tilted as Aaron climbed into it with a soft grunt and took the reins from Jessica's hands. He shifted in the seat, then looked up at Eric getting ready to ride away again. "Coming home for tea?"

Eric said, "My home is James's station now, remember?"

"Your home is with your mother, Jessica, and me. Your work station is with James," was Aaron's curt reply.

Eric's eyes snapped and he turned his horse about to ride away, but he hesitated when Jessica reached toward him. "Eric. Please do. For a little while." It had indeed been nineteen days since he visited, thirty-four before that.

Eric moistened his lips and nodded abruptly. Aaron flicked Summerfield's reins and the carriage lunged forward.

As Eric turned his horse about on the track and set him at a canter, pulling ahead of the carriage going toward home, Jessica leaned back on the carriage seat with a sigh of relief.

Chapter II

Annoyance rode with Eric on the track going home. Annoyance at his father for reminding him that the Aylesbury station was his real home, as if he didn't remember. And beside annoyance rode something soft, something he could not bring to the front of his mind, something that made him smile. The picture of gentle Jessica with her hat blown off and her hair mussed and her face smudged with dust. Even more than he missed home and his mother, he had missed his sister, Jessica.

Ever since he and his father had had the enormous disagreement over what he should do with his life, Eric had stayed away from the Aylesbury station, taking a job at Uncle James's station, where he had perfected his skills as a stockman. When on occasion he heard that his father was away, he would come to visit his mother and Jessica. That fight over his not wanting to go to England for a formal education was only the second big one they'd had. The first one had been when he and his mother had sat him and Jessica down to tell them that Jessica wasn't really his half sister.

23

It was a bloody-hell experience for Eric when his mother and father had sat him and Jessica down and told them plainly and without embarrassment their story. They told how his father, Aaron, had come home from England where he had obtained his formal education, had visited his childhood sweetheart, Penelope, several times before he had gone exploring across the mountains and had become lost. They told how Penelope had married Aaron's half brother, Mark, because of some misunderstanding. Then, after Penelope had married Mark, Aaron had returned from his expedition and had married another childhood sweetheart, Annabelle. The child which Annabelle had been carrying at the time was Jessica.

Eric remembered well his early years at the station south of Sydney, thinking that he was Mark's son, seeing the hate in Mark's eyes when he looked at him. Eric remembered Mark's death at sea, then a year later going with his mother across the mountains to the Cranston station where Aaron was head stockman. Jessica was just a month younger than Eric, both being six years old when he and Penelope came with their sheep from Penmark to make their home with Aaron. Both Eric and Jessica had grown up thinking that Aaron was their father, and were shocked and hurt to find out that he was not Jessica's father at all. She was the daughter of Eric's half-Aboriginal uncle.

Well, well, life was a spiderweb of woven intrigue, wasn't it? No harm done, though. All came out right in the end, did it not? No one but himself counted the cost of spending the first five years of his life being hated by the man he had thought was his father. Of seeing Mark strike his mother. No, everything had come out fine and they had lived happily ever after.

Eric's smile went bitter but not for long. From the top of the hill he looked down at the Aylesbury station, an expanse of acreage mostly cleared of bush now, stretching west and south as far as he could see, with the house below surrounded by dogleg fences and cross fences, green paddocks with grazing cattle in the meadows and sheep on the hillsides.

Chickens scattered in the yard when Eric rode into it, and hired hands paused in their work about the station to shade their eyes and wave in recognition to him. He waved back and swallowed back the hurt of no longer being part of the place.

In the sparse, dappled shade of the big gum tree he dismounted, and when his father's new black-fellow groom came grinning to take his horse, Eric said, "Just water him, Toby, and tie him to the fence. I won't be here long."

"Aye, Mr. Eric. I'll water ol' Red sure enough."

As Toby took the reins, Eric pushed his hat away from his forehead and jerked his head toward the bay stallion tied to the fence under the gum tree. "Mr. James is here then?"

"Aye," Toby said. "He come about ten minutes ago, Mr. Eric. Came to see the doctor, he did."

"Oh?"

"Came wi' something important to say, seems to me. Wanted to go look for the doctor but Miz Penelope, she made him stay for a cup o' tea."

Curious and slightly apprehensive Eric looked toward the back door of the house. He'd been out on the east run of the Cranston station all morning and hadn't seen James since daybreak. He wondered what made his uncle head in to the Aylesbury station to see his father this time of day. Eric scratched his chin. Getting set in my ways, he thought. Anything in the least out of the ordinary and I wonder what's gone wrong.

The sound of the gig made him turn and watch his father and Jessica riding into the yard, Summerfield picking up his hooves in an old show-horse's prance, anticipating his cool water and grain. The big smile on Jessica's pretty face made Eric smile, too.

Aaron Aylesbury took his time handing Summerfield's reins to Gomer, the black-boy stable hand, and then he sauntered over to Eric, but Jessica gathered her skirts up and hurried to him, smiling. She opened her arms, and brother and sister, who were not brother and sister at all, embraced. Eric was surprised and then embarrassed when he felt her softness against his chest. He held her away from him and looked down into her face, more beautiful because of the dust and disarray. Her eyes always startled him, for their deep indigo blue was almost unnaturally beautiful. The smooth mocha and cream skin was the only hint that she was part Aborigine.

"There. You're properly greeted now," she said. "Welcome home."

Eric grinned. His own brown eyes went to her figure in spite of himself, and he shook his head. "I thought you were as beautiful as you could get, Jessie, but I see you're looking better than ever."

She laughed. "You talk as if you've been away for years."

Jessica felt Eric's fingers dig into the flesh of her arms and saw his eyes going dark with all the old hurts and disillusionments, and she glanced at Aaron, who was coming to stand beside them. "Look, Father, did you see? James is here," she said to distract them. She took both men's hard-muscled arms in hers and walked between them toward the house. She wanted desperately for the two to get along, to not fuss and spoil Eric's visit. "What a nice surprise. Both our favorite fellows here at once. We should kill a beef and make them stay for supper."

"How about a fatted calf?" Aaron said sardonically as he let her lead him to the veranda.

"Not until his prodigal son has offered to be a servant in his father's own house, though, Jessica," Eric quipped. "Which I won't."

Jessica's lips tightened at their bickering, but she refused to be dismayed. "Mum will talk you into staying. Mum and Mrs. Chun."

Eric tried to pause and frown, but she tugged him onto the veranda. Suddenly she was frantic with the fear that her brother would go away. She must make him stay.

Both men stepped upon the veranda and stood aside to let her enter the door. She looked from Aaron to Eric to see if indeed they meant to follow her inside. That seemed to be their intent, though they were looking at each other with the same dangerous lights dancing in their eyes.

The Aylesbury station house sprawled in a fat rectangle which was almost a square, and though the house was built on two levels, the square footage of the ground floor amounted to more than many of the prestigious two-story Georgian houses in Sydney, Parramatta, and Bathurst. It was a combination of Georgian uniformity and Australian practicality, with the central hall running the full breadth of the house from front door to back door, with three rooms on each side of the hallway, one behind the other. But there was no wasted space anywhere. Every wall, nook, and cranny had a purpose for being.

When Jessica, Eric, and Aaron entered the familiar hall through the back door—the front door was seldom used even by visitors—they followed Jessica through an oversized doorway into the large, square kitchen. Against the far wall was a fireplace built of stones hauled from the Blue Mountains, with a firebox large enough for a man to stand up in. Bending over the jack with its kettle of boiling water was Mrs. Chun, who piped, "Aft' noon, doctor. My, Jessie love, looks like you tangled with a bushranger sure. And my, my, look who else is here. Eric."

From the long rectangular kitchen table, Eric's mother rose when she saw them. James was sitting at one end with a china trade teacup between the palms of his big hands. He rose when his sister did.

Eric's mother, Penelope, was beautiful even yet, a slender woman with emerald-green eyes and dark, chocolate-brown hair, now frosted softly with threads of silver. Her naturally white skin had been tanned by years of exposure to the sun to a delicate ivory. The green eyes were, as Jessica had predicted, first on Eric's face. "What a surprise." Then her eyes went quickly to her husband. "Aaron. You look weary." Taking his arm, she smiled at Jessica. "And you look radiant, Jessie. He must have let you see Mrs. Schiller's baby. How is she?"

"Next time I might let her deliver a baby," Aaron teased. "There are such things as midwives, you know."

"Don't you dare, Aaron. Don't you dare add to Jessie's frustration of wanting to be a doctor. If I hear of you doing such a thing, I won't allow you to take her along again. She's a gentle lady. Now all of you. Come and sit down and have tea." Penelope glanced at her brother

28

James standing at the table with his tea. "James has come with some unwelcome news, but everything will be all right. You men will think of something, I'm sure."

Aaron let his wife lead him to the kitchen table where he smiled and shook James's hand. As Penelope's younger brother, James was a favorite in this household. Aaron had taught James all he knew about raising cattle while they had all lived together on the Cranston station which was now exclusively James's.

But Jessica had detected a slight tremor in Penelope's voice in spite of her lively chatter and self-assurance, and she sensed that Uncle James's visit was not a social call. The sudden tension in Eric's arm added to her apprehension.

James Cranston fixed his eyes on Jessica and gave her one of his slow smiles, and she was compelled, as she had been all her life, to embrace him briefly. "There now," she said desperately wishing that all was well and Uncle James and Eric would stay for dinner and laugh and sing and play Penelope's father's old lute as they had done before Eric went to live on the Cranston station. "You'll have to stay for supper, Uncle James. Eric's already agreed to it."

Eric laughed in spite of himself. "I didn't. She's playing games again."

"I'm not. He did agree. Father will vouch for it, won't you?"

Aaron pulled out a chair for her. "No. Eric's a grown man now and can vouch for himself. He said so."

Everyone's smiles were strained as Penelope turned away to take the tea things Mrs. Chun handed her, and the men took their seats at the table. There was a forced smile on Eric's face for his mother's sake, but his angry eyes proved the smile was a lie.

"Well, James. You look like a man with a mission," Aaron said, his deep voice ringing true in the room where the silence had become uncomfortable.

All eyes were on James Cranston now. As usual, he took his time answering.

James Cranston was the best stockman in the Bathurst district. Nobody doubted it. The fact that Cranston money was behind him and that his father, Oliver, had started the station with Aaron's help years ago didn't alter the fact that James had become a superior grazier in his own right. He had invented some of the equipment now used by every stockman in the district and had developed stock breeding methods implemented by graziers throughout the colony. He was like Jacob of old. His cattle multiplied even in drought years when other graziers' cattle didn't. His calves gave more multiple births than any of the others in the district. Sam, James's head stockman, had a habit of saying, "Them that 'as, gits. And them that ain't got it, don't." Sam swore an American told him that once.

James was as handsome as Penelope was beautiful. Nothing unsettled James much. "He's like a tom cat who's found the only spot of sun on the porch," Aaron had said once. "Poke him and prod him and he won't even blink. He'll just roll over and wait for you to go away."

But tension showed in James's face now in the crinkling at the corners of his eyes, in the muscles tightening and loosening in his jaws. He took his time answering Aaron, as he took his time doing everything else. But finally he tilted his chair back until it rested on its two back legs. "It's Ben."

Aaron's face showed no expression but Jessica saw his lips tighten. Ben Crawford, Jr. was Aaron's cousin who owned the cattle and sheep station just to the north and west of the Aylesbury station. He was a smiling nondescript man, who had defied his own father to become a stockman in Bathurst.

James went on: "Remember the two convict workers who escaped from Webb's station last week?"

Aaron nodded.

"The mounted police found them camped out on Ben's place. Had Ben arrested for harboring bolters."

Aaron gasped in exasperation. "Ben? Arrested?" His hands clutched the arms of his chair. "Ben never did a dishonest thing in his life."

Horror-struck, Jessica said to Aaron, "Surely they'll release him. They have no evidence to hold him."

"No," James said. "But they will have."

She looked to Eric to dispute James's assertion, but Eric said, "If they don't have anything now, they'll figure something out. So now somebody's got designs on Ben's property? *Damnation!*"

His curse startled Mrs. Chun, who gave a chirp and dropped her bowl of dough onto the worktable.

Jessica had her hand at her throat. They all knew what had happened to Ben—the same thing that had happened to several other settlers in the district during the past year. Every one of them honest people. The police had barged in to arrest them on some charge or other that had never been proven.

The troopers had the law behind them. It was a result of Governor Darling's proclamation some twenty years ago which gave the police power to arrest on mere suspicion and to enter and search a private citizen's

31

premises without a warrant.

Aaron stood up, forgetting his tea, fury flushing his tanned face and setting his hands to trembling. "Where's Ben now?"

"Bathurst jail. Awaiting his hearing." James let his chair back down.

"They can't make a charge like that stick against Ben."

"They can if they hire some bludger to witness against him. Say that he saw Ben and the bolters conversing friendly or something. You know how it's been going, Aaron. No settler has won his hearing yet."

"If they find him guilty, we'll appeal. We'll demand a trial."

Jessica was remembering how the settlers had been fined so exorbitantly that they couldn't pay their fines and had ended up having to sell their land.

"Same scoundrel is behind this as is behind the others," Aaron breathed. "Same underhanded tactics to get land cheap. You'd think Livingston would be smart enough to think up other ways. This particular method's getting stale."

Jessica exchanged looks with her stepmother. Until now nobody had actually voiced who they suspected of being behind the land scams. Everyone knew, but nobody had said. They didn't dare. The great scourge of fraud that had come to the district a year ago had now touched them. She was horrified and worried, but she realized there was additional intrigue in the fact that now Judge Livingston had dared defraud a member of the Aylesbury-Crawford-Cranston clans.

For Judge Livingston had once been in love with Penelope and had always had a personal vendetta against the Aylesburys because both Aaron and Mark had married her. Livingston, now a widower with a son, was one of the most influential magistrates in New South Wales. The judge had nothing against the Crawfords, especially easygoing Ben, but the family knew that he would go to great lengths to make trouble for Aaron Aylesbury, even if it meant making innocent people suffer.

Like a magnet, Penelope drew everyone's eyes to her. They all seemed to be thinking the same thing as Jessica. Shocked, Penelope stood with the china trade teapot still in her hands. She breathed, "Oh Aaron. Perhaps we should talk to the judge—"

"No, dammit," he roared, causing Mrs. Chun's hand to fly to her mouth and powder it with flour. "Talk? Talk to Rodney Livingston? I'd rather confer with the devil in hell. And anyway, talk about what?"

"Then what are we going to do? Ben is your cousin. There must be something some of us can do. What about your father? What about Ben's father?"

Eric had been quiet, listening and thinking. And Jessica knew him enough to know the silence was ominous. He let out a low hiss now like a steam kettle coming to a boil. "I've a feeling the judge and his marionettes are going to try something funny at Ben's station, so I'm going to go over there to make sure he doesn't."

Jessica was studying Eric's face, seeing his quick mind working in the changes of his eyes and mouth, and her horror turned to panic. "No, you can't go there, Eric," she said standing. "You can't. There's bound to be trouble."

"I'll send some of our men over to Ben's station," Aaron stated flatly.

Eric looked at his father. "I don't want your men."

"But you can't go there alone," Penelope protested.

"I won't be alone, Mum. Ben has seven hands."

"But are they loyal? Are they reliable?"

Eric shrugged. "I don't know. They're emancipists. As long as things are going smoothly at the station they'll be loyal. But if trouble comes, who can say?" His glance went quickly to his father, because Aaron's father, Matthew Aylesbury, was an emancipist, a pardoned convict. "But I can handle 'em. I'll go now before someone duffs his livestock."

"You can't go alone," Aaron said steadily.

Eric raised his brows. "I'll take Sam, if James agrees."

"You're just looking for a fight, aren't you?"

For once Jessica was wishing Eric would back down rather than bicker with his father. Instead, to her horror, he smiled slowly and replied, "Maybe."

While Aaron's eyes went blacker with anger, Penelope went to her son, caught him by the arms, and looked up into his face. "Surely you wouldn't take the law into your own hands. You'll be regarded by the authorities as an outlaw." She drew her breath in shakily. "Let James and your father send over some of our men to Ben's."

Eric briefly put his arm around his mother's shoulders. "Mum, I'll be all right."

But Penelope, studying his face, shook her head slowly. "No," she mused aloud. "No, you won't be all right."

"I don't like it!" Aaron said coming around the table to stand before them. "I don't like you going to Ben's station even with James's hands. I'll send Stringybark Joe over." Aaron turned to James who had, characteristically, remained silent and out of the fray. "Can't you send your station boss for a few days, James? Without Eric? I can spare a few hands too and—"

"I don't want your station hands, Father," Eric said. "If there's trouble I want to know my men. I know James's ringers. They'll fight if they need to."

"I won't allow it."

Eric stared at his father, his eyes level with his own. "I think, sir, now that I'm twenty-eight, the time is past for your disallowing anything I do." Eric turned on his heel and strode from the room with Jessica just steps behind him.

Tears blinded her as she snatched up his hat from the hook near the back door and dashed outside after him. Why did it always have to be this way? Angry words that sent Eric away. Always away. Eric bolted off the veranda, and Jessica had trouble keeping up with him as he strode across the sun-bathed yard toward the big gum tree, his boots stirring up the yellow-brown dust as he went.

By the time she caught up to him, he was untethering his horse from the paddock fence. As she approached, her mind working with a mixture of disappointment, anger, and hurt, he looked up at her, and she could see his face flushed in anger. As if he had been speaking his thoughts all along he blurted, "Who is *he* to tell me I'm looking for trouble, Jessica? The old men around Windsor and Parramatta still talk about Mark and Aaron Aylesbury who used to lead the emancipists' sons against Livingston's crowd in bloody street brawls. When they were young Father and Mark even fought *each other*. Grandfather Cranston says they got their fighting habits from Grandfather Aylesbury. Says both Father and Mark were brawlers. And he accuses *me* of wanting a fight."

Without waiting for Jessica to reply, Eric put his boot

35

in the stirrup, getting ready to mount. "Father always makes a fool of me in front of you," he added between clenched teeth.

"No one can make a fool out of you but yourself, Eric."

He turned to look at her. She stood with the west wind stirring wisps of her dark hair which was caught at the back of her head in a chignon. Her voluminous skirts whipped against her legs as she squinted at him and handed him his hat. The hat was battered and dirty, a sweat-stained, broad-brimmed hat woven from the fronds of the cabbage tree, the standard hat of graziers throughout New South Wales.

Eric let his foot drop from the stirrup, took the hat from her, glancing at her through his dark eyelashes.

"You're going to Ben's, aren't you?" she said studying him. His face softened as she took the reins from his hands and tied them to the fence again. "Stay. For once stay and cool off."

"I can't."

When she turned back to face him the hat was jammed down over his head, shading his handsome face. Something stirred in her heart. Something she didn't understand. Perhaps affection for the little boy he used to be. Perhaps admiration for the strong-willed man he had become. "The toads have hatched down by the billabong," she said, knowing he didn't need an explanation. As children it was the favorite event of the early summer, and they used to catch the tiny ugly creatures and pretend they were cattle and sheep. They had made little paddocks for their tiny livestock out of twigs, and station houses and sheep runs, and had buried in great solemn funerals the tiny toads who hadn't survived their handling.

Sometimes she wished they were children again. Life then had been so uncomplicated. It had seemed she and Eric would always be companions. She took his arm. He resisted only for a moment. Then he came along with her toward the pond and into the grove of gum trees, his tense arm folding her long, delicate fingers in the crook of his elbow.

Neither spoke. This moment together seemed somehow too sacred for words. They were silent until the gum trees and wattle had closed the house from their sight and had come to the banks of the muddy creek. She had always respected his moments of silence, his privacy, even as she was doing now. She waited for him to speak as she stripped the last faded yellow blossom from a wattle bush. He looked at her and smiled again. "Jessie, you're the only sane person in my life besides Mother," he said finally.

Jessica did not laugh at him. "Uncle James is sane."

"Yes. Uncle James is, but he belongs to that older generation who thinks we should leave law and order in the hands of a few, even if that few are corrupt."

"He believes as Father does, that we can right our wrongs by electing our own officials, by appointing our own legislators and judges, and you know, Eric, that they are right."

"Aye. They are right. Only it takes too long. It will be years before we have full rights as citizens. In the meantime, Jessie, what do you think we should do? Let people like Ben serve their time in prison for something they didn't do, see their land taken for fines they can't pay? Watch these kangaroo courts set up to arrest and convict decent men so that English capitalists can buy up acres and acres of land?"

Jessica knew that Eric had always felt passionately about vindicating the wrongs done to the settlers, but because this recent injustice was directed at Ben, it must seem to him that the time had come to act. It was Ben who had taught twelve-year-old Eric to drove, muster, and brand cattle when Ben had worked here on the Aylesbury station. His father had been too busy managing the station and treating patients to teach Eric. It was easygoing Ben who had taken young Eric under his wing and taught him the intricacies of using the catch rope, too.

The billabong was a widened place in the creek bed where in wet years the swimming was good. Now it was stagnant and shallow. Jessica pulled him down beside her on the grass and began to weave long stems of grass, just as, when a child, she had made necklaces and bracelets and had pretended she was his princess. "I don't know what the answer is, Eric. But violence can't be it."

"I hope to avoid violence."

"Then why are you taking Sam and Coolabah and Jacky with you? Those are rough fellows."

"Somebody's sure to duff Ben's stock if somebody isn't there to oversee his place. And if the police or any of Livingston's crowd show up, well, I aim to protect Ben. That's all."

Her eyes came up to meet his. She was startled and so was he by the impact of their close gaze. They looked away. "How?"

He was silent for a long moment. "I don't know."

Jessica nodded, pressing her lips together, and said nothing.

A magpie chortled in a tree overhead. A breeze stirred

the surface of the billabong, green with rotting vegetation. Overhead the cloud-angels had vanished and the sun had already bleached the opal sky almost white. "Then you *are* looking for trouble."

He looked at her quickly. "You and Father. I am forever bedeviled by you both."

"You are bedeviled by your own restlessness."

"It's this country. It's still raw and untamed and nobody seems to do anything about it. Every advancement we make takes forever. Even our first colonists, my grandparents included, were pinned to the east coast by a chain of mountains no more than eight-thousand feet high for twenty-five years before somebody finally found a passage through them. And we'll take decades to have complete freedom, more before we have law and order. It takes us decades to accomplish what takes the Americans merely years."

"The Yanks accomplished their freedom from foreign governments by going to war."

"Perhaps I should have been a Yank."

"Perhaps. If you could come to peace with yourself, though, you could fight other battles then."

Eyes flashing, Eric clambered to his feet. "You really don't approve of me anymore, do you?"

"Of you, always," she replied rising. "Of your rebellion, no. I wish you'd use your anger as your Uncle Mark did. He led men in political battles, struggling for the emancipists' rights to vote, to serve on juries . . ." She paused seeing the fury in his face.

Leaning toward her, his eyes flashing, he said, "Don't ever mention his name to me again." When he saw the hurt look on her face, he relented. "Mark led and what did it gain him? A watery grave. A memorial service along

39

with hundreds of men who died with him on the ship. A wife who turned away from him and a stepson who hated him. That was twenty-three years ago and we still don't have full rights as a colony."

It was true and she dropped her stubborn gaze from the intensity of his glare. "Promise me you won't go to Ben's. Let Father send—"

"No!"

Eye to eye they stood, this brother and sister who were not brother and sister at all. "Then you'll let us know how you are doing, won't you?"

"Not likely."

"Then I shall come to see for myself."

His hands shot out and gripped her arms painfully. "No you won't, Jessica. I won't allow it."

"I think, Eric, now that I am twenty-eight, the time is past for your disallowing anything I do."

Eric stared angrily as his eyes roamed over her face, and the grip on her arms vibrated like the strummed strings of her stepmother's harp. A slow hiss came from between his teeth as he released her and stepped backward, suddenly pale, as if he had just discovered that she was a ghost.

"Oh Eric, aren't we still friends? Nothing has really changed between us."

"Yes. No." He stood, arms spread as if to keep his balance, a stricken look creasing his handsome face. "But hell, Jessica. We're not the same. We're—we're—" He paused. "We've *grown up*." For a moment he looked at her, slowly raised his finger and shook it in front of her face. "And don't you follow me again." Then, as if to escape her, he abruptly turned and rushed away through the trees.

Jessica felt as if she had been struck. The atmosphere was charged with electricity as just before a thunderstorm. It seemed that lightning had crackled between them and had left the earth trembling beneath her feet.

But looking up, she saw only the pale blue sky, cloudless and clear. And the only thunder she heard was the gallop of Eric's horse as he rode away.

Chapter III

Eric had been at Ben Crawford's for three days when Jessica mounted her mare, Chelsea, and set off down the Bathurst track. Women were always waiting for their men. They waited for them to come home, to leave, to act, always something. And she was sick of it. She was sick of the worry and the tension in the atmosphere at the station, of Penelope's troubled thoughtfulness and Aaron's quiet anger.

It occurred to her that if she acted, even though she did not know what she would do or say, that something, something would change, would happen. So here she was on the Bathurst-Melbourne track, letting the spirited mare walk for awhile, at least until they came to the smaller track which would lead to Ben's station.

It was mid-morning and the air had that clear, static quality that promised neither rain nor wind. The Bathurst plains was an island of clearings in a boundless ocean of undulating blue-green bush country. The bush surrounding it on all sides was thick and mostly impenetrable, consisting of dozens of species of eucalypts and undergrowths of wattle, vines, and scrub. The plains looked like a park in comparison, with rolling, grass-covered land with only occasional groves of cedar and eucalyptus, ideal country for cattle and sheep. The track led north from the Aylesbury station for several miles, then angled east. Mostly, it led through open plains, but occasionally through stands of forests where the ancient trees grew forty feet or more in height before it branched out and grew slender willowlike leaves so sparse that the shade was never dense beneath them, allowing grass to grow lush even on the forest floor.

At the moment, Jessica rode with the forest on either side of the track, and even in her unsettled frame of mind, she noted the sparkling brilliant color of the various birds as they flitted across the track and in the branches of the trees. Aqua blues, sapphire, bottle greens, and scarlet reds flashed among the trees, and only the parrot and parakeet chatters and squawks reminded the romantic of heart that these were birds, not gems cast to earth by the hand of God.

Overhead a wave of snowy cockatoos with yellow crests flew, and she knew they would settle in the grassy plain beyond the grove of trees. Wildlife abounded on the plains, but progress had pushed back the primeval animal into the bush. Often in the evenings, Jessica had seen gray kangaroos coming out of the eucalyptus forest to forage in the tall, waving grass, but the cattle and sheep, rivals for the rich grasses of the plains, had driven the hapless animals farther and farther away to the west, and she did not see them as often as she had when the Aylesburys first settled the plains.

Jessica resisted a momentary urge to rein Chelsea, dismount, and scour that forest for medicinal plants.

Perhaps this was a tap on her shoulder from some dark brown arm from her heritage, reminding her that she was the great granddaughter of a medicine woman.

When Jessica had turned twenty-one and Aaron and Penelope had revealed her heritage, Jessica had asked to meet her grandfather, Buck Crawford. Buck still made his living trapping and leading hunting and exploring expeditions in the bush. Aged like petrified wood, Buck had been curious to meet his granddaughter, but his general disinterest in the human race had prevented his becoming attached to her or anyone else.

From Buck Jessica had learned that her Aboriginal great-grandmother was still living. Dandaloo was her name, the Aboriginal tribe word in New South Wales for beautiful. Dandaloo lived near Parramatta, in a small, lusterless, nomadic native village far enough from civilization for some privacy, yet close enough to towns and settlements to beg if necessary.

After Buck's visit, Aaron had gone to Parramatta and brought Dandaloo back with him. The old woman was like a rotting log, crumbling, with blackish-brown skin like old bark when the life's gone out of it. But snow-headed Dandaloo had a winning toothless grin, and her delight at finding out she had a great-granddaughter who was part white and beautiful pleased Jessica immensely. During her three month's visit she and Dandaloo had roamed the woods and the hills near the cattle station. And that's when Jessica had learned about the native cures.

Dandaloo was a medicine woman, and during those three months she taught Jessica everything she knew about native medicine. There was a wealth in the various kinds of eucalypti. From the gum of certain eucalypti one could extract cures for respiratory ailments, rheumatism, and diarrhea. Some produced a resin with an astringent quality which closed wounds and stopped the flow of blood. The gum of the green wattle cured dysentery and diarrhea. From the leaves of a kind of trefoil one could concoct a solution to prevent scurvy. In the bush the sarsaparilla yielded a tea which made bad boys good by cleaning their overcrowded blood. The bottle brush soaked in water yielded a syrup for sore throats and colds. Wattle bark could be made into a tanning lotion for unbroken cuts and. scalds. The smoking dried leaves of the blue gum could ease attacks of asthma. Clean mud was the best poultice.

Old Dandaloo taught Jessica which specie of gum trees—or eucalypt—could be used to treat what ailment, and which part of it, leaves, bark, or resin, was used and how to prepare it. Jessica had learned to love Dandaloo, and she had savored and memorized everything, including the native myths, which the old woman had taught her. Her entire family, indeed everyone she knew, looked upon her desire to become a doctor as a passing fancy, but Jessica believed that if she listened to old Dandaloo and to Aaron and assimilated the knowledge of both cultures, somehow, someday, this would be of use to her.

Jessica had never met her father. Deenyi, her half-native father, was part owner in a whaling enterprise and now lived on Van Dieman's Land. Someday, Jessica wanted to go to him.

Because Jessica was bemused, it was Chelsea who heard the sounds first. The mare tossed her head and pricked her ears forward, causing Jessica to become quickly alert. Though she was never afraid to ride the tracks or the plains alone, Jessica was always aware that

45

bushrangers roamed the country, and there was always the danger of meeting with a convict who had escaped from some nearby station. But as she frowned and listened, the whooping and laughing settled over her like a familiar shawl. She touched her mount's flanks gently with the heels of her boots, and Chelsea picked up her pace to a gallop.

But as Jessica topped a hill, she reined the little horse to view the scene below. She sighed and shook her head, slapped Chelsea with the reins and trotted down the track toward the noisome young men and a wagon which trundled toward her.

As she drew near, she was amazed to notice that the wagon around which the Schiller twins and their friends were riding sat full of young women, and that on the wagon's seat, staring at her from beneath her old-fashioned coal shuttle bonnet sat a formidable-looking woman.

Reginald, Rube, and their friends were trotting their horses beside the wagon, whooping and shouting quips at each other just as they had done with her the day she drove from the Schillers after seeing the baby delivered. Now when they saw her approach, the youths reined their horses in the road looking sheepish, but Reginald rode toward her.

"It's a gold mine," Regie shouted. "Look, Miss Jessie. Twelve *girls*. And a woman."

Jessica's eyes went to the girls in the wagon. Indeed. In a country where men outnumbered women ten to one, the wagon load of young women was a gold mine. "And what are you doing, Regie Schiller? Harassing them?"

"No-oo, escorting 'em."

"This doesn't look like escorting to me."

"It's Mrs. Chisholm. You know, that lady over in Sydney who takes in immigrant girls and sees they get jobs? Well, that's her, and she went to Scantlin over in Bathurst to ask for a police escort down the Melbourne road and he refused. So me and the lads thought we'd come along. Make sure the Riley gang doesn't come swooping down and carry 'em off."

Jessica studied his young face. He was ecstatic. And when Regie was ecstatic, he used very poor judgment. "Well, why are you behaving like larrikins? Why can't you just ride along and behave?"

Regie looked crestfallen, but Jessica ignored him and turned Chelsea to ride along close to the driver's seat, where the famous Carolyn Chisholm still drove her four horses resolutely on.

"Good morning," Jessica said. "I hope these scamps haven't been annoying you too much. I'm Jessica Aylesbury. And you are Carolyn Chisholm?"

The woman nodded and smiled. "Pleased to meet you, Miss Aylesbury. And yes, I am Mrs. Chisholm. And yes, these young men have been very annoying. They have bedeviled us all the way from Bathurst. The girls are distraught. Their dignity has been insulted, and they are all near tears."

Jessica glanced at the distraught girls. All twelve of them were sitting on seats which had been built into the bed of the dray, holding their bonnets with one hand and the sides of the wagon with the other. But their shy smiles and coy glances at the young men riding beside them belied their insulted dignity at the moment. Howey Dobbs was handing one young woman a flower which she took and brought to her nose.

Howey, grinning said, "Not many of our flowers smell

good, miss, they're just for looking at." Besotted with awe, he added coloring, "Like you."

"There, you see?" Mrs. Chisholm said. "Here I've driven over one hundred miles from Sydney with sixteen girls, and I've been able to place only four in positions. Your settlers outback aren't very prosperous, I must say. And instead of help or interest, I have been constantly besieged with larrikins, old and young. I am fortunate indeed that my girls haven't demanded to return to Sydney. Though in Sydney they will starve. Convict girls are much cheaper to employ, and Sydney's full of them, as you must know."

Jessica was amazed that this handsome woman could be the famous Carolyn Chisholm who had taken immigrant girls under her wing. The government had offered free passage to anyone in England who would migrate to New South Wales. The men who migrated could find employment, but the young women could not. They had accumulated in Sydney like so much driftwood, in a new country where they had been promised honest employment. They had escaped the poverty and slums of England to sail to New South Wales, only to find that they could not find jobs. They had lived in doorways, under boulders, along the shore, until Caroline Chisholm had taken pity on them. She had bought a rundown house in Sydney, restored it, and made it a home for the girls. Then she had set to to find work for them.

Regie had lost interest in the immigrant girls and was riding beside Jessica now. "But there ain't one girl prettier than you, Jessica," he said, touching the brim of his hat.

Jessica rolled her eyes. "Regie. You must leave at once. Take your young larrikins and go away. If you don't, I shall report you to the police."

"Aw, but Miss Jessie—"

"Did you hear me, Reginald? At once!"

Regie glanced back at the wagon load of girls and sighed. Reluctantly, he turned his horse about and trotted back to the young men following the wagon.

"Aylesbury," said Mrs. Chisholm. "You must be related to Dr. Aaron Aylesbury."

"He's my—uh—father."

"Ah. Excellent. It is to the Aylesbury station that I'm traveling. I placed one immigrant girl with an elderly Aylesbury family on the Hawkesbury."

"My father's parents," Jessica said. Her mind was already going over the possibility of hiring one of the girls. Actually, they did not need another domestic. Old Mrs. Chun, who had been Aaron's housekeeper when he was head stockman on the Cranston station, was their housekeeper now. And though she was getting on in years, she was still healthy and strong.

"Wonderful. Your father's father, Dr. Matthew Aylesbury, said that you would definitely hire one of my girls."

Jessica had to smile. "He did?"

"Yes. He said that I must tell his son, Aaron, that his father insists that he hire one."

Jessica laughed. That sounded like her grandfather, all right. Giving commands to Aaron as if he were only nine years old. Rather like Aaron was doing Eric these days.

The Schillers and their friends were trotting away, looking over their shoulders, and the girls were waving and sighing and casting disgruntled looks at Jessica, as Mrs. Chisholm turned about and looked at them. When she turned back, she adjusted her bonnet with one hand.

49

"There, you see. The poor dears have been in constant fear of bushrangers and are relieved that these no-good young men have left them at last."

Jessica opened her mouth to say that she wasn't so sure about that, when the thud of hard hooves on soft ground caused her to turn irritably around, thinking that the Schillers were coming back. Instead, from the forest on the left side of the track six men dashed, their teeth bared in evil grins, their bodies leaning forward as they wielded rifles and pistols.

The girls in the wagon shrieked in fright as two men surrounded the Schiller bunch and the others surrounded the wagon, causing Mrs. Chisholm to rein her horses.

In horror, Jessica saw the men for what they were. Bushrangers. Dressed in flannel shirts and moleskin trousers, they were bearded and unkempt, with the savage appearance of desperate men. With shock, Jessica recognized one man from a picture that had been sketched in the Bathurst newspaper. Jacob Riley. *Oh my Lord*, she thought, *It's the Riley gang.* The most desperate gang that the Bathurst district had seen since its establishment.

Riley trotted up to Mrs. Chisholm and doffed his cabbage tree hat. Then he bowed low to Jessica. "Ladies," he said, flashing uneven yellow teeth. One glance showed Jessica that his men had surrounded the wagon and were gawking and grinning at the whimpering girls, and that two still had the Schillers and their friends held at gunpoint.

If Carolyn Chisholm was frightened, she didn't show it. "Now see here, my good man," she said with a lift of her chin. "I've not got long to be on the road today, and

50

you're hindering my progress. What is the meaning of this?"

Riley bowed low from the waist. "Mrs. Chisholm," he said. "'Tis wounded to the core I am, for ye've caused me to lose me faith in womankind. Five years establishing a reputation for villainy I've been, and you cast it aside with this one little venture. Tell me what I've done wrong, madam, that ye feel safe enough to travel in this country alone and unescorted with a wagon load of girls?"

"God, my young man," Mrs. Chisholm replied. "We have faith in God. And He will protect us. And though we drive through the valley of the shadow of death, we have no fear."

Riley looked wounded. Still pressing his hat to his heart, he looked around at the forest of eucalypti, then up at the watercolor painting of pink-breasted galah winging southward against the azure sky. "The valley of the shadow of death?" he asked. Sweeping his hat to the side to indicate the countryside he went on, "This? Madam, 'tis fairly paradise."

As Jessica stared amazed, she was remembering that bushrangers had, from the beginning of their existence, captured the hearts of Australians. Since New South Wales had been a convict colony from its inception, its citizens had distrusted authority from the beginning—rather like Eric—and the bushrangers had become the embodiment of every Australian's desire to thwart that authority. That many raped and killed and most robbed and stole did not lessen the romantic thrill that the colony felt toward these adventurers. And Jessica recognized that Riley was playing his role to the hilt.

As if her thoughts drew his eyes to her, Riley brought

his gaze to Jessica. His gray eyes moved up and down her form, and a slow smile split his bushy beard from his mustache. "Now. In paradise there's always angels. What be your name, miss?"

Jessica glanced at the wagon load of girls. "What has that to do with anything? You must realize that we are near the Crawford station and that the station has several hands on it, and all I have to do is scream and they will be down upon you in seconds."

Riley raised his brows. "Miss Aylesbury, ain't it?" He nodded. "Aye. Miss Aylesbury methinks." He turned in his saddle and motioned with his hat for one of the men to come to his side. An older man rode up beside him, sober and half angry. "Now tell me, Schultze, would this beautiful lady be one of the Aylesbury clan?"

Schultze looked Jessica up and down. "It's Dr. Aaron Aylesbury's daughter."

Riley straightened as he looked at her. "Now we thought we had a payload in the wagon, Schultze, but this here lass, now that's something else." He looked at his friend. "See what I'm thinkin'?"

"Ransom."

"Aye." He looked at Jessica. "And a right pretty ransom she'll be, too. Aylesbury is worth a few pounds. Yes, indeed."

Schultze dully glanced at the girls in the wagon. "What about them?"

"Schultze, ye've lost all yer imagination. How often do the men get this kind of chance? There's two girls for each of us and—"

"Now see here, you scoundrel!" Mrs. Chisholm interrupted. "You wouldn't dare abscond with these young women. I won't allow it. Now you be gone this minute, you loathsome creature." She raised the reins to slap the horse into motion, but one of the bushrangers had the lead horse by the bit.

"I don't think so, ma'am," Riley said.

"Well what about those young men back there?" she demanded. "They'll be bringing the police, and every man in the district will be chasing you in no time." For all her bravado, Mrs. Chisholm was becoming pale under the bonnet, and Jessica was casting about desperately for a way out of this. Her beautiful morning had become a nightmare. This country she had grown up in was suddenly full of menace. *But if she could break away, race into the trees close enough to Ben's station house, scream, and call for help—*

Suddenly she did break away, digging her heels into Chelsea's side, and the little horse lunged forward off the side of the road. In a flash, she could hear a horse behind her, and she knew that it was Riley. Sunshine filtered like bridal veils through the leaves of the gum trees overhead as the little horse carried her in her desperate attempt to run for help. She heard screams from the girls behind her, heard the unmistakable shout from Reginald Schiller. Vines tore at her as she raced, tore her hat from her and clutched at her hair and her shirt. But Chelsea could not out race the bushranger's long-legged horse. She remembered that bushrangers always stole race-horses, maintaining the fastest horses in the colony. The roan stallion came abreast of her, and Riley, with teeth bared, reached for Chelsea's reins. She dug her heels again into Chelsea and beat the bushranger with her reins. Then the bushranger's horse bumped Chelsea, and the little mare went down. Jessica pitched into the dried gum leaves and brambles, but scrambled up running. She opened her mouth for a scream for help, just as her head jerked back. Riley had her hair in his hand, but she jerked it loose. She had always been a fast runner, and for a moment, she thought she could outrun the man on foot. But suddenly something hit her legs from behind and she fell, plowing up the mat of leaves with her chin. Riley was lying on his stomach beside her, panting and grunting. "Little girl," he gasped. "Ye run like a native."

Jessica tried to scramble up, but Riley pinned her to the ground. "No you don't, milady." He flipped her over on her back and caught a knee in his side for his trouble. "Oomph," he said. "I hadn't planned no harm to ye, but one more of those and ye'll get what my men are goin' to give to the girls in the wagon." He jerked her to a sitting position beside him. "Now remember that." He panted in her face. "One more attempt to get away and I'll do what my manhood desires and not what my pecuniary interest dictates I should do with ye. Understand my meaning?"

Jessica stared at him with contempt. Never in her life had she been in danger. This was an insult to her and to every woman in the world, to every settler who had struggled and fought to clear the outback settling this wild country. She spit in his face.

Riley wiped the spittle off with the arm of his sleeve. His face registered anger, but he said with a wry grin, "Now I ask ye, was that nice?"

Just then they heard gunshots. A second later a horse came tearing through the forest, and Jessica looked up in time to see Regie Schiller, his hair flying back in the wind, his face a study in frozen rage. "Miss Jessica! Don't worry. I'm coming." But his horse ran under a low-hanging wattle branch and with a thump and a groan, he was knocked from the saddle and landed with a sickening thud on the ground, flipped twice backward, end over end, then lay still, face up, on the forest floor. He did not move.

Stunned, Jessica merely stared at him as Riley winced and said, "Now ain't that a shame. Your rescuer will be in slumber land for awhile. We'll tie the rest of the lads up. Then it's bye-bye to the track and off to the bush for us and our new lassies. Come, miss."

Jessica tried to jerk away. "Let me go to him. He might be killed." But Riley held her and lifted her up into the saddle, in front of him on his own mount. He held her firmly as he turned the horse about and headed back the way they had come while Regie Schiller lay with a peaceful smile on his face on the gum leaves.

Jessica was never one to submit to anything she didn't agree with, and she was constantly looking for escape as Riley held her close, and she felt his hot tobacco-tainted breath on her ear. On their short ride back to the track, she was remembering with dread that bushrangers were men who had escaped into the bush and made their living robbing stations, occasional banks in town, and conveyances on the road. They were a constant menace and had been since the first convict had escaped the cruelty of a settler on the other side of the mountains. The average man could not survive in the bush. So the bush was the desperado's greatest ally. It sheltered him and hid him, while resisting other men's attempts to pursue. Bushrangers had learned to live in the bush because they had to. It was many a convict's only vestige of freedom.

When they arrived back at the road, Rube and the other three lads of the Schiller mob were tied together, back to back, sitting on the side of the road. Hands were tied behind them, and kerchiefs had been tied over their mouths. The girls were being held at gunpoint lest they scream again, and Mrs. Chisholm was standing in the road, screeching at Schultze who had taken her place on the wagon seat.

When Mrs. Chisholm saw Jessica, she pressed her lips together and strode to Riley. "Now you let that young woman be. And tell your ugly men to leave my wagon be, too. I'll have every policeman in the colony after you, you wretch from the gutter. You abominable serpent."

Riley ignored her. His hand had found Jessica's small waist, and his fingers were digging into her side. Jessica was not wise to the ways of men, but she knew that his hands, which had held her firm at first, had begun to tighten. His fingers had inched upward towards her breasts, and his breath had become quicker against her ear. Without a doubt she knew that he had changed his mind about not harming her. Even his voice had become soft as he shouted to Schultze. "All right, the trail is only a mile away. Take it when you get to it and go as fast as you can." Then to the other bushrangers who sat their mounts beside the wagon, he commanded, "Go ahead of him and make sure the trail is clear."

One of the men said, "What are we going to do about Mrs. Chisholm, boss?"

Riley looked at the furious woman in the track. "We'll leave her."

"You don't want to take her, too?"

"No."

"Want us to tie her up?"

"No. Leave her be. I don't want her harmed." Jessica heard Riley take a slow deep breath. "She reminds me of me mother."

The wagon had just begun to move when, suddenly,

the gang's horses began to turn about and Jessica became aware of the thudding of hooves. "Damnation!" breathed Riley. "Another day, Miss Aylesbury." Unceremoniously, he dumped Jessica to the ground and was off with a shout, a clamor, and a cloud of dust.

Sprawling on the ground, Jessica watched as four men brandishing rifles swooped down on the track with shrill cries. She recognized men from James's and Ben's stations and also Eric. The three men pursued the Riley gang out of sight, shooting as they went, but Eric was off his horse before it had come to a full stop and knelt beside her, grasping her arms in his hands. "Jessica!"

The little girl in her turned loose, and Jessica began to cry in seeing Eric's horror-stricken face.

"Did he hurt you?"

"No," she sobbed and held onto his arms. "Oh Eric, I was just coming to see you when all this happened."

He held her to his chest, and she could hear the steady thunder of his racing heart. "Damnation, Jessie. That was the Riley gang."

"I know."

His hands were caressing her back, and his breath was stirring the hair on the top of her head. "We heard screams and shouts. We expected trouble, but not this kind." He held her from him and looked at her. She watched his eyes studying her face and saw his expression soften. Then he cleared his throat and released her abruptly. He moistened his lips and glanced at the wagon. "Who the hell are they?"

"Carolyn Chisholm and her immigrant girls. Oh Eric, the gang was going to take them away."

"I'll bet." He helped her up. "And you, too."

"For ransom."

"Uh-huh. And no telling what else." Suddenly Eric was angry. "Bushrangers. Another pestilence in this country. And the police are helpless to stop them." He removed his hat and beat the dust out of his trousers.

By then Eric's friends were trotting back and in the next few moments, they had released Regie Schiller's friends and had brought Chelsea and a stunned Regie from the forest. Within fifteen minutes, the immigrant girls were again riding down the track with Mrs. Chisholm, only a bit shaken, driving them. But this time, Schiller's young men and Eric's were escorting them.

After Jessica had ridden beside Mrs. Chisholm for awhile, she rode back to Regie Schiller, who sat quiet and morose upon his horse. "Thank you for trying to save me," she said to him.

But Regie just hung his head and shook it.

"Are you all right? You have a nasty lump on your forehead."

"I'm fine," he muttered without looking at her.

Finally, Jessica rode beside Eric while Mrs. Chisholm began to regale Sam, Eric's friend, about the terrible brigands in this country, and the immigrant girls continued to giggle and cast shy glances at the men.

Jessica and Eric rode in silence for awhile, Jessica waiting for him to speak first, knowing he was angry with her for being on the track alone and getting into trouble.

"You had no business coming for me, Jessica," Eric said, finally.

"We hadn't had any reports from you," she replied.

"That's because there hasn't been anything to report."

"Still, you should come home and relieve our worry."

"There's nothing to worry about."

"Father thinks there is."

"Father has been wrong before."

"And so have you. And you are wrong now, Eric."

"Yes, you said that."

They exchanged glances. Eric looked away.

"You behave as if you hate me now, Eric Aylesbury, but ten minutes ago, you acted like you cared."

"Of course I care. You're my sister."

"No. I'm only a distant cousin."

"Doesn't matter. But if you don't care about yourself, then I don't either."

"Yes you do."

"Go about following me and get in trouble then. I don't care."

"Don't you?"

"No."

She saw the flush of scarlet beginning somewhere beneath his shirt and rising up his neck to flood his face. It was the phenomenon that always happened when Eric was lying. "You are lying, Eric Aylesbury."

They had come to the rise where they could look down on the Aylesbury station now. Eric cast her only one glance when he raised his arm and called, "Okay, men. We'd better get back to Ben's." He looked at Regie. "Schiller, now that it's perfectly safe, you can take them on in." He looked at Jessica. "Jessie . . ." He paused, and his face was still angry as his dark eyes darted over her face. "Damn you, don't come looking for me again. Do you hear?"

"No," she said.

Eric shook his head and turned his mount about. Then, with a clatter and thud of hooves, he and his men tore off back up the track.

*　　*　　*

Penelope received Mrs. Chisholm with delighted surprise. She fretted over the women's ordeal on the track, but was able to get control of her fears in order to concentrate on hiring one of the immigrant girls. While Mrs. Chun served the girls stew outside under the gum tree, Penelope sat presiding over the tea things in the parlor, and Mrs. Chisholm read the qualifications of each girl. Emotions still awhirl, Jessica sat near her, listening. No girl's qualifications stood out from the rest, but Jessica was remembering the behavior of the girls in the wagon when they were being threatened by the bushrangers. She had barely time to observe the girls individually during the ordeal, but she had noticed one girl who had not screamed or whimpered. Instead the girl had calmed the frantic ones and had stared with a steady gaze at her tormentors. Jessica had noticed this just for a second, but she remembered the girl's face.

At last, when Carolyn Chisholm had exhausted her list of qualifications, Penelope had turned to Jessica. "What do you think, Jessie?"

They did not really need a servant girl. But Mrs. Chun was getting old and bedeviled with rheumatism and surely would welcome help. Besides, Aaron's father had demanded that they hire one. Jessica said, "Mrs. Chisholm, who is the girl with the white embroidered collar? Pretty, with curly brown hair. Is always mothering the others?"

Carolyn Chisholm smiled and bobbed her head as her cup clattered into her saucer. "That would be Carrie. Carrie Crocker. A sweet lass, indeed. No special qualifications, but she can help cook and clean. Sews a mite, too."

Jessica looked at Penelope. "I would like to have

Carrie as our domestic."

And so Carrie Crocker was hired. Although Penelope attempted to convince Carolyn Chisholm to remain the rest of the day before going down the track, she refused, saying time was short. She loaded the wagon once more, and she and the immigrant girls resumed their trek, going south toward the next station. Escorted by six eager, well-armed station hands.

Carrie Crocker was a quiet, smiling girl just five years younger than Jessica and so grateful to have a place to work. In the next few hours while they chatted and relived their dangerous adventure of the day, Jessica helped Carrie settle into the small empty room across the hall from Mrs. Chun's room, unpacking her one valise which held only two frocks and two nightgowns, a few undergarments, and a small box of keepsakes brought from home. The room was under the back staircase and had once served as a pantry, but Penelope had recently put a small trundle bed in it. It had proved to be a handy place for Aaron or Penelope to take a nap without having to go up the stairs to the bedchambers. Later they would bring more furniture from the attic. It pleased Jessica that Carrie seemed happy with the station and with her room. The rest of the afternoon and evening passed quickly. Jessica was excited about Carrie's employment, and before dinnertime came, they had been sitting on Carrie's bed while the gentle but lively girl talked about her home in England, the death of her parents, and her decision to leave, taking her small inheritance to pay for passage to the promised land of Australia.

Jessica, in turn, answered Carrie's questions about the Bathurst district, who the Aylesburys were, and finally, with a secret smile, who those handsome rogues were—

the blond-headed twins who had taunted them, then ended up escorting them.

When night came and still Aaron had not returned from Bathurst, she and Penelope went out onto the veranda to sit in the wicker rocking chairs. Carrie soon joined them, taking her mending with her.

Jessica looked out over the yard. This was the part about being a woman she hated the most. Waiting. Waiting to see what the men would do next. She wondered if Eric had reported the bushranger's attack on the women and if the police would respond. Besides that, she was back to wondering if anything would happen at Ben Crawford's place. And if trouble did come, what would Eric do?

And Aaron. She wondered if the hearing had gone well for Ben. If so, why wasn't Aaron home?

As Jessica rocked, her hands idle in her lap, she pressed her lips against her teeth. Resolved: As of tomorrow, if Aaron's not home, I shall go into Bathurst and find out what's delaying him. And this time, I'll go well armed.

The rockers made faint creaking sounds on the veranda boards as the two women rocked.

There was no long twilight in New South Wales, Australia. There was only day, and then night fell like a slate-gray curtain on a stage and stirred the night insects alive. Flying and crawling insects tuned up their instruments, and soon a loud, primeval rhythm band was playing in full swing. There were steady clicks and rasps in different tones, pitches, and cadences, with the prehistoric shrill of cicadas in the gum trees surrounding the yard and along the creek. And from the creek came the jungle cry of the kookaburra, laughing, and he was joined by others calling, laughing hysterically as if at the rhythm band of the insects.

In the distance a cow bellowed, and Jessica's ears picked up the tinkling sound of the bell on one of Penelope's favorite merino ewes.

One of the hired hands in one of the cottages near the paddocks laughed and whooped, probably having won a hand at cribbage or some other favorite game.

Jessica strained her ears for a sound of hoofbeats on the track. But all she heard were the usual night sounds, the sounds she had known since infancy.

Chapter IV

It was the fifth day since Ben had been arrested. Eric reined his horse and as he looked around, wiped his mouth and chin with the sleeve of his blue broadcloth shirt. For four days Ben's ringers had been mustering the cattle on the west run, had drafted, roped, and branded all the clean skins they could find, had driven the bullocks to the yards near the house. The yarded bullocks would be driven up the track to Bathurst for slaughter.

Eric removed his wide-brimmed hat and scratched his unruly thatch of dark brown hair. The cabbage tree hat was usually cool, but when a man worked up a sweat in the merciless sun, his body steamed, and some of that steam invariably got trapped under his hat.

He replaced the hat, his narrowed eyes scanning the yarded cattle. Ben had three cattle yards, large paddocks near the house. Someday he would have many large yards, but for the time being, his ringers had to muster and draft the cattle on the open runs. Ben kept a neat place and had good ringers, eight in all. Some of them were black native boys. Eric's parents and grandparents, along with their contemporaries, had always called them natives or blacks. But the scholars were calling them Aborigines. They made excellent ringers, and a native ringer was a high-class citizen among his tribe.

Ben's station spread over two hundred acres of prime grazing land in an area adjacent to the Bathurst district called the Evans' Plains. To the south of the Evans' Plains Eric's own father had wandered lost for four months. Now most of that wilderness was settled, either by legal land holders or by illegal squatters. This plain was, perhaps, a little barer of trees than the Bathurst Plains where most of the Aylesburys' and the Cranstons' stations were located, and most of it was still wild and untamed. The plains in the area consisted of rolling hills of grass sprinkled with stands of gum trees. And where the creeks ran at the foot of many of the hills, the trees were thick, a respite on a summer day like this—if the creek held water.

In the distance, high hills rose blue-green; overhead the sky was almost always bleached out by midday. Flocks of white yellow-crested cockatoos flew chattering over the trees near Wilson's creek. A flock of green, yellow, and red parrots were settling in the gum trees.

Eric's gaze came away from the distances and focused on Ben's house. Since Ben had never married, he never had built anything better for himself than the slab hut. Like a squatter who didn't figure he could stay long on the land, Ben had built his hut of rough-hewn slab walls and roofed it with wooden shingles which Eric's great-uncle, Owen Crawford, had hewn in his shipyards on the Hawkesbury River. The shingles had been carted by dray over the mountains. Inside the hut the slab walls and ceilings were covered with lathe and plaster. The floors were sawn boards butted together. Ben's house had a good chimney of handmade brick. There were only two rooms in the house: the large living room which served as parlor, kitchen, and dining room, and a bedroom with nothing in it but a bed with ticking filled with gum tree leaves, and a mirror on the wall. Ben had added a lean-to in the back of the hut for storage, and a veranda all across the front. In the whole house there were only two windows: one in the living room and one in the bedroom, and only last year had Ben gotten enough glass to put in them.

Ben's hired hands' huts were made of slabs of stringy bark nailed to upright posts driven into the ground and were lined up in a neat row like the servants' huts on his father's station. These huts on Ben's property were made of the same stuff as Ben's house, except Ben's walls were slabs of wood and plastered over. Such huts didn't look much better than the brush huts the natives threw up when they settled in a place for awhile, but they were typical of settlers' dwellings, especially the squatters. The huts were breezy in summer, and in winter, when the winds blew and the temperature sometimes got down to below forty degrees fahrenheit, you could throw kangaroo hides over the bark and make it cozy enough. And there wasn't much upkeep to such a house.

A whoop brought Eric's attention round to a black man driving a bellowing mickey—a young bull—toward the yards, and his grin stretched under his mustache as he watched. It was Jacky, one of the best stockmen, attempting to drive the young bull into the bull yard. The mickey kept dodging the gate opening, though the other ringers now on foot were doing their best to urge him in by whoops and yells and waves of their hats.

The mickey turned suddenly and charged Coolabah Cecil, who went springing just ahead of his nose and leaped a fence into the horse paddock.

The young bull blew, snorted, stopped at the fence, and pawed the ground. Then, unexpectedly, he turned and eyed Eric's horse.

No time to think about it, Eric had his stock whip in his hand and spurred his horse forward in an attempt to bluff the bull. But he knew if the bull kept charging, his horse would likely turn tail to him and kick the daylights out of the mickey. Such an antic could crack a good cow's skull and ruin a good animal. That's why the stockmen kept their stock horses mostly unshod.

But the mickey seemed to be less inclined to charge than to escape. With his tail toward the gate he made a move to lunge on around Eric's right side, but Red, the intelligent, well-trained stock horse under him, anticipated the bull's move and lunged at him. The bull bounced to the left just as the horse did, then to the right again, but the little horse headed him off again. Back and forth, back and forth, the bull's front quarters went, while his back quarters barely moved, with Eric in the saddle gracefully leaning with every move of the horse until the bull lost heart, wheeled and ran into the yard kicking up his heels as he went.

Grinning, Eric let the little stock horse trot up to the gate where the animal blew into the yard as if to say, "And *stay* there."

The ringers had missed this young bullock out on the run somehow, so now they were going to have to brand him in the paddock with the calves. He watched as Coolabah chased him with the catching rope, a noose on the end of a forked pole, which he slipped over the mickey's head. Coolabah's horse braced his hooves and pulled the noose tight. Three other ringers ran to the mickey and wound ropes around his front and back legs. Then Sam ran over with the branding iron and branded him. Eric barely noticed the odor of singed flesh and hair as the bull bellowed. But Jacky did the worst. With his trusty knife he did his gruesome operation, turning the mickey into a bullock by castrating him. Since the bull was already more than half grown, all his growth had gone to making him a reproductive animal instead of a good market animal, so probably the mickey would end up being a bullock for pulling a dray. The mickey bellowed furiously. The dastardly deed had been done and Sam and Jacky released him, then rushed out of the yard before the bullock could exact his revenge on them.

All done. Eric looked up at the sky. A man learned to do that often outback, looking for clouds, and if there was a cloud, to assess it. Was it drifting west to east? Was it white on the top and dark on the bottom, a harbinger of rain?

No clouds. The sky looked like faded blue calico, with its white and multicolored sprinkling of galah, cockatoos, parrots, wild pigeons, and crows. The sun, becoming more and more like a ball of white-hot light as it slid toward the western horizon, was still hot.

Sam rode up to Eric. "If 'ambone has tucker ready I'll forever be in 'is debt. I'm so 'ungry I can't wait another bloody minute." Sam removed his cabbage tree hat, a wide-brimmed, dome-crowned thing with the usual kangaroo-hide band, and looked up at the sky. "No clouds. Wilson's creek is dried up today. Another week of this drought and Crawford's creek will be dried up, too." Sam scratched his bristling jaw. The man was twenty-four and hadn't gotten any closer to growing a beard than having cornsilk wisps on his chin. Eric didn't want to grow a beard, though it was the fashion for ringers. His father hated beards. His grandfather Matthew Aylesbury raved and ranted about the young rapscallions growing beards and mustaches. In his father and grandfather's young days the fashion had been for men to have their faces clean shaven.

Eric was remembering the tale of when Aaron had gone on the exploration expedition with Jessica's grandfather, Glenn Moffett, and several other men. They had met natives who had never seen white men before and thought they were women because they did not have beards. The expedition party had to draw straws to determine which of them would demonstrate his maleness in the only irrefutable way. Aaron had drawn the short straw. And he had never gotten over it. To this day, he got furious if anyone mentioned it.

"You see, Father?" Eric had said once. "If you'd had a beard you wouldn't have had to expose yourself."

Aaron's mouth had tightened, his face reddened, and he hadn't replied.

"Done?" It was old Hambone calling from the only real building on the station, a kitchen hut, which contained a rock fireplace big enough for him to cook a meal on for eleven men and then some.

"Done," Eric called.

"If he has beef stew and has plenty of tomato sauce, I'm going to kiss him on the cheek."

"You do and you'll have a free passage to England through the bloody air," Hambone said. He was old, older than Grandfather Matthew, perhaps about seventy-five, but he was still strong as an ox and could cook better than any woman. He had been on his grandfather's prison ship, had been assigned to Penelope's father's farm, and had just six years ago come over the mountains to the outback station to work for James, seeking a change. James had lent him to Ben until the mustering was over.

Just as Eric reined his horse around, he caught movement out of the corner of his eye. Over the ridge they came. Riders. For a moment he thought of the Riley gang, of Jessica. But no, these were the troopers they had been expecting. He raised his arm and whistled, tucking in his bottom lip, curling his tongue. The other men stopped what they were doing and took up their rifles. Sam had an old musket, the others the new breech-loaders. All had pistols strapped to their waists held by a thick belt over their tight moleskin trousers.

"Is this it, boss?" Sam asked.

"This seems to be it."

Sam hitched his pants up, ready to do battle, and Eric stayed on his horse. His hand went to his holster and adjusted it on his hips. Then he pulled the breechloader from the scabbard attached to his saddle, slid a bullet into the chamber, and lay it across the saddle in front of him.

All right. Let 'em come. A great surge of excitement went through him.

Six decent landholders had lost their legally owned land, through a subtle force. There was a man behind this wickedness and everyone knew who it was, but no one knew how to stop him. The man wielded his influence and caused the only law enforcement in the colony of New South Wales to do his bidding. The settlers on the plains were angry men. Angry and afraid. That's why Eric differed from the settlers. He was angry, but he wasn't afraid. He had nothing to lose.

The troopers came clattering into the yard on sweaty, dusty steeds. As Eric sat watching, he noted that over half the troopers were natives. The black fellows were all good trackers and once they learned to ride a horse, no man could ride better. He smiled sardonically when he saw that the captain himself, a hulking, vulgar emancipist, had led the troopers to Ben's. The troopers came to a dusty halt before them, and Scantlin's small pig's eyes took in the scene around him: The station house, the cattle in the yards, the men sitting and standing in the yard, and at last Eric and his rifle. A slow, yellow grin spread the stubble of a beard around his mouth.

"Y'er young Aylesbury, ain'tcha?"

Eric's horse moved restlessly under him, but he never took his eyes off Scantlin. "Eric Aylesbury. Can we be of service to you?"

Scantlin snorted. "Naw. We just came to take possession of Ben Crawford's property. By order of the court of New South Wales, of course, and hold it as security until Crawford pays 'is fine. For ya see, 'e was found guilty of 'arboring bolters."

"That doesn't surprise me. Who was the witness against him? Or was it the color of Ben's eyes that our honorable magistrate took a dislike to."

Scantlin eyed Eric with suspicion a moment before he replied, "The colony of New South Wales 'ad two witnesses who saw Crawford feedin' the bolters and directin' 'em to a 'iding place."

"Uh-huh. And who were the witnesses?"

"Don't know 'em. Two swagmen, I think." Scantlin's smile ceased. "But it don't make no difference, Aylesbury, because the magistrate made 'is decision, and I'm here in the name o' the law to do my duty."

71

"Over my dead body."

Scantlin's small eyes darted from man to man in the yard, then came back to Eric. "I don't think you understood, Aylesbury. I've come wi' my men and aim to station some 'ere to see nobody duffs cattle or tries to make off with any o' the property. Because this property is bein' held for the colony of New South Wales until Crawford pays 'is fine."

"Crawford can't pay a fine and the magistrate knows it."

"Then you understand better 'n I thought you did. Crawford can't pay so this is the colony's property and I'd advise you now to—"

Eric's hand went to his rifle and rested there. "No, I understand even better than that, Scantlin. Ben can't pay. He might have to sell his property, and your good friend Livingston over in Sydney just happens to be looking for a piece of land. Go back and tell the magistrate that Ben isn't going to sell, that somehow, someway we'll see the fine is paid."

Scantlin's face was reddening now. "Can't do that. I got orders."

"You know what you can do with your orders. Now get!"

A sudden shot rang out from among the troopers, which startled even Scantlin. Jacky's hat spun off his head. Eric raised his rifle in one smooth gesture. Scantlin grabbed his own rifle, and Eric pulled the trigger.

Scantlin's face folded in wrinkles of agony like a dried apricot as he grabbed his ear. The sound of the ringers pulling back the hammers of their rifles made the troopers pause in reaching for their own rifles.

Scantlin's hand came away from his ear, and his face

was purple with rage. "Ye shot me ear off!"

The blood dribbling down the side of Scantlin's head sickened Eric, but he never batted an eye. "Just the lobe," he said.

The big police captain's hulking frame had begun to vibrate with fury as he turned to his frightened troops. "Well, ye jack o' knaps. *Arrest 'im!*"

The troopers looked at Eric, at the ringers, then at each other.

"I said arrest 'im in the name o' the law!" Scantlin screamed.

The troopers moved hesitantly forward on their mounts. Eric gestured with his rifle, suggesting he might shoot Scantlin if they tried to arrest him, but the men knew the Aylesburys: honorable people, not murderers, and so they moved forward. Eric spurred Red in the flanks, but the horse shied at the approach of the troopers. Someone fired a shot into the air. As Eric was jostled about a rifle butt grazed his head. Stars sprinkled the sky in his head amidst the clatter of gear, the shouts, and the shuffling of feet and hooves. When the numbness in his head subsided he was still sitting on his horse, but his rifle was gone and Scantlin was before him, his ugly face twisted with a mixture of agony and rage while he held a kerchief to the side of his head.

"Ye'll be sorry fer this, Aylesbury," he roared. Then to the troopers, "Take 'im away."

A trooper poked him in the back, another prodded old Red and, surrounded by mounted police, Eric was forced to ride out of the yard. He was fearful and alert now. A glance around showed him that two troopers were remaining on the premises and held guns on the ringers who were gathering their horses.

Fury filled his soul. How his father would rage and mock his efforts! At least he had resisted. No one else in the district had ever resisted. What now? As he rode, feeling the great lump swelling on the side of his head, his thoughts dwelled on his father. He could just see him shaking his head at his son's shortcomings. Eric thought of his mother, how shamed she'd be by his arrest. He thought of Jessica and felt the blood returning to his cold face with a rush. How embarrassing! Jessica, who believed in him, who thought as he did.

He raised his head and saw the low foothills to the Great Dividing Range in the distance to the east. The foothills. The bush was still a wilderness, still a siren song to a troubled soul.

Suddenly he kicked Red with such force that the horse bolted, jolting against the side of the trooper's horse beside him. The trooper's horse whinnied and the others shied and pitched. There was only time enough for one trooper to get off a frightened shot, which caught Eric like a mule kick just beneath his right collarbone, before he plunged from amongst them. Hands still tied loosely behind his back, he was off.

He rode like the wind toward the Bathurst-Melbourne track. Like a native spear he dashed across the plains of tall gray-green grass with the policemen behind him and the wind whistling in his ears. One hand came loose from the rope, and he had the reins now. With the rope tied about his right hand, he flayed Red's flanks, and the horse pulled ahead of the troopers as if they were standing still.

Pain blinded him, but not too much to see the forests in low-lying hills ahead. If he could just get there he could gain enough time to decide what to do before they

74

tracked him down.

The hand with the rope had gone numb. Shots spattered and fell short behind him. The trees were ahead.

Crash! He was into the thicket, a dense growth of wattle, vines, and scrub. Limbs tore at his clothes, slapped his face, but Red plunged on bravely, sensing his master's desperation. Towering gum trees rushed past now. Minutes flew by, then an hour. And finally, when Eric felt the horse lunging up the slope to higher ground, he reined him and listened.

There was no sound in the bush now except for the chattering of parakeets in the trees overhead and the mournful chortle of a crow in the distance.

When Penelope Cranston Aylesbury left her first husband's home south of Sydney, she brought with her nine drovers, four of her assigned convict servants, and her son Eric. The drovers had been hired to drive the sheep over the mountains to the Cranston's cattle station over which Aaron Aylesbury was station boss. Although their employment had been only temporary, six of the nine drovers had stayed to work on the Cranston station. Years later when young James Cranston took over the running of the station, Penelope and Aaron went to their own land farther south and west from Bathurst. The six drovers had gone with them.

Drovers came in two distinct types. There were sheep drovers and cattle drovers, and although most stations ran sheep and cattle together, the duties of the ringers and the sheepmen were often diverse. Normally a shepherd wouldn't touch a bullock or cow, and a cattle stockman wouldn't be caught dead herding sheep. And when the washing, droving, and shearing of sheep had to be done, the shepherds did it while the ringers tended to their mustering, droving, drafting, and branding of cattle.

Aaron was the owner but he had hired a station boss named Zachariah Bodine as "station boss," to oversee the cattle. Penelope had hired her old sheep station boss, Hiram Blackmon, to oversee the sheep. Aaron saw to the cattle part of the station and Penelope the sheep. At the moment, Penelope was watching the washing of her precious Spanish merinos, a hot, tiresome, frustrating task.

The sheep drovers had mustered the sheep on the open run and driven them to Wilson's creek, where the sheepwash platform was set up. Penelope stood on the edge of the run just out of the hands' way near the creek below the yard of the house, smiling into the western breeze while her keen green eyes were on the sheep, calculating how many bales the mob would bring this year.

Jessica was beside her. Though she had never taken to women's menial work such as sewing and mending or cooking, neither did she care much for the management of sheep or cattle. Since she was twelve years old, she had wondered what she did care about. Her grandmother Moffett had been an excellent horsewoman. Aaron's grandmother Aylesbury managed the farms on the Hawkesbury better than any man. Her stepmother, Penelope, managed the sheep like a seasoned shepherd.

Jessica knew that she appeared serene. Her poise, cultivated in Penelope's "pure merino" household, was unruffled. But inside she was a frustrated woman. Inside she trembled at her future, wondering what it held for one who had but one interest in life—medicine, a man's profession.

Aaron recognized her dream and dismissed it with a smile. Penelope thought it a passing fancy. James listened to her dreams of practicing medicine with the indulgence of a special admirer, and Eric wouldn't even let her talk about it.

Now she watched the bleating, foolish sheep which her stepmother loved, pouring into the creek, driven by the darting, nipping, barking sheep dogs. The dogs knew their job well and were guided by the short, long, low, or high-pitched whistles of the drovers. Each type of whistle communicated a different instruction to the dogs, who responded instantly with no mistakes. They drove the bleating sheep into the creek to be washed, then out the other side to dry, in preparation for the shearing which was scheduled to begin in two days.

"How many does that make us now, Jessie?" Penelope asked pleasantly with a glance at her stepdaughter.

Jessica straightened her spine. "I—I wasn't counting, Mum."

Penelope turned her head to look at her, her green eyes narrowed against the brilliant sun even under the brim of her cabbage tree hat. She studied Jessica for a moment, then said, "Jess, don't worry. Aaron will come soon, I'm sure. And don't forget that if anything has happened to Eric, we would know by now."

Jessica smiled. "You have just proven to me that you have your mind on Eric too, Mum."

Penelope smiled. "Yes. I admit it."

"And the worry line in the middle of your forehead hasn't left since *he* did."

Penelope looked away. "Aaron's on his way home. I

77

feel it. He's on his way."

Jessica turned her face toward the track to the north and east. It was empty, shimmering in the heat waves coming up off the parched dry plain. She kept her eyes on the track, knowing that her stepmother and stepfather were so close that each knew what the other was thinking before a word was spoken, and that sometimes no word had to be spoken at all. Then she saw them. She recognized Aaron and also James. "Here they come, Mum."

Penelope turned, squinting at the track. "Ah. Aaron has bad news. I can tell by his posture."

As they waited for the men to see them, Jessica noticed that Penelope had removed her hat to fan her face, the knuckles of her hand white as she gripped the hat tighter than she needed to.

They remained watching as Aaron and James came close and dismounted. Aaron pushed his hat away from his brow, and James came to stand beside Jessica before either of them spoke. Together the four began to move toward the yard, the men leading their horses in silence, the women waiting for the news which would surely affect all of them.

"Ben was found guilty and fined five hundred pounds," Aaron said finally.

Penelope said nothing.

"How could they have found him guilty?" Jessica demanded.

James's dark Cranston eyes narrowed slightly as he answered, "Scantlin, the police captain, came up with two swagmen who claimed they saw the bolters chopping wood at Ben's station. None of Ben's men were called as witnesses in his favor. Ben will remain in jail until he can pay the fine. Of course, he'll have to sell part of his land to pay it."

"And guess who's ready to buy that land," Aaron growled.

"Judge Rodney Livingston," Penelope said, her mouth tightening.

Jessica glanced at her, fascinated because this was the woman Livingston had loved in his youth. It was Aaron and his brother, Mark, whom Livingston had sworn to destroy when they were young.

Jessica looked at thirty-nine-year-old James. He and Penelope were the offspring of Oliver Cranston who lived near the Hawkesbury near Aaron's grandparents' Aylesbury. The Cranstons had been friends of Rodney's parents, but James had always disliked Rodney as a child and liked him less as an adult. Rodney Livingston had been admitted to the bar and became one of the most influential judges in New South Wales.

Aaron took a deep breath. "An agent from an unknown buyer came to Ben in jail and told him he had a buyer for Ben's land, just as we expected, but of course he did not say who the buyer was."

"What did Ben say?" Penelope wanted to know.

"Not much. Just shakes his head."

"Poor, quiet, uncomplicated Ben," Penelope said. "And what of Eric? Have you heard anything of him?"

"Only that he and some ringers chased the Riley gang away from a wagon load of women." Aaron glanced at Jessica. "And that Jessie was along. Let's go inside. I want to hear more about that."

But as they came just under the big gum tree at the edge of the yard, they recognized James's stockman, Sam, riding up the track toward them. Jessica clutched James's

79

arm when she saw the look on Sam's face and the blood on his shirt. "Oh dear God," she breathed, and barely felt James's hand grip her shoulder.

Sam lost no time stopping before them. Panting he wiped his mouth on the sleeve of his shirt and barely nodded to them before he blurted, "The police came." He caught his breath and went on, "at noon." He went on to tell the story of Scantlin's demands, of Eric's resistance. "Eric told them to get off the land. Scantlin said he wouldn't. There was words and someone in the police force took a shot at Jacky. Next thing we knew Eric had raised his rifle as easy as you please and shot off Scantlin's ear."

Aaron's face was crimson. "Ear!"

Sam pulled at his own ear. "Well, just the lobe. But it didn't set well with the captain, so he ordered Eric's arrest. That caused a standoff. Words were said then, the men got into a fight with the police, and after all was said and done, Scantlin had Eric tied up and hauled off."

"Oh bloody hell," Aaron breathed and passed his hand over his face. He looked at Penelope, whose face had gone pale. "I knew it. I knew he was going to get into some kind of trouble. I told you that, years ago, the boy was always running away." Aaron took another deep breath. "Where did they take him, Sam? To Bathurst jail?"

Sam ducked his head and scraped the dust with the toe of his boot. "He didn't go to jail, sir."

Aaron frowned.

Sam looked up. "Eric . . . took off.

Aaron stared at him. "He what?"

"Escaped," Sam said. "They tied up his hands and set off down the track with him, surrounded on all sides, with all of us lookin' on. And all of a sudden, Eric spurred

80

his horse, sir, broke from amongst the police, and took off down the track." Sam couldn't help but grin as he continued, "The police chased him, they did, but after an hour or so, Jacky and me trotted along, and met the police coming back. They lost him in the bush, sir. Last we saw of him, he was headed east toward the mountains. One bloody thing that bothers us though. They did get a shot into him."

Aaron's face had gone from crimson to a kind of bluish-white under his tan. Penelope looked almost faint. "What now?" Aaron was barely able to ask.

Sam's countenance fell. "They aim to hunt him down, sir. Captain Scantlin says he'll find him. For you see, sir, Eric's considered a bolter now."

"A bolter. And a bushranger," Aaron said steadily. Penelope leaned against him and his arm went around her. Jessica saw his hand on her arm tremble, but he jerked his head toward the house. "Come in the house, Sam. I'll see to that wound in your arm."

Jessica stood beside James as Penelope, Aaron, and Sam went into the house. Her stepparents were shaken, just as she was, grieved and frightened, but she had not missed the look of pride in their son's stand for what he thought was right. It was just a glimmer through their shock and fear, but it was there.

She looked up at James, and before he was able to conceal it, she saw a gleam in his eye. It was almost a pleased look she saw on his face before he composed it. What did it mean?

James was a tall man, dark eyed and dark haired like his father, a slim, extremely handsome man who had never married. James had been invited to more balls and had been offered more bribes to marry various settlers' daughters than any man in the colony. Yet, he had steadfastly worked on his station, building it up, acquiring the respect of every settler. When she, Penelope, Aaron, and Eric had lived on the Cranston station before James was old enough to take it over, she had loved him, called him Uncle James. James had always been a good-natured, easygoing man who would take her up on his horse and give her a ride. It was James who had taught her to ride when she was older. And James who had been the first to propose marriage to her, though he was twelve years older than she.

They were great friends and she had often teased him. "James, why don't you get married and settle down?" she had asked once.

James had grinned and said, "I'm as settled as I can be, Jessie, and the reason I haven't married is because I'm waiting for you."

But of course it wasn't possible that James was glad Eric was in trouble. He, too, was proud of Eric, she knew that.

"Oh you men!" Jessica said suddenly furious. With eyes blazing she gathered her skirts and stepped off the veranda and strode toward the stable. James, grinning, fell into step beside her.

"What have we men done now, Jessie, that displeases you?"

"So pleased that Eric took a stand for Ben. Even though it cost him his freedom and no telling what else." She stopped and turned to James suddenly. "Don't you men realize that he will be hunted like a criminal? Possibly killed?"

James smiled. "Possibly. On the other hand . . ." Bemusedly, James scratched his chin, and his black eyes drifted east, toward the mountains. "I wonder where Eric would go," he said.

"I haven't any idea," Jessica replied, but already her mind was going over the possibilities. And what if his gunshot wound was serious? Eric knew nothing whatever of caring for wounds. He detested medicine. She realized that James was studying her, and she made her frown smooth out. "I only hope he hasn't gotten himself killed."

James smiled at her. "Would you worry about me like that, Jessie?"

She said, truthfully, "Yes."

James nodded. She knew he was going to leave, because he pulled the brim of his hat down over his forehead. "I've got to be going, lass. Tell your mum and father good-bye for me. I'll see them tomorrow."

Jessica only nodded, for she could see James's thoughts were elsewhere at the moment. She hoped he had a plan for saving Eric somehow.

She watched James take the reins of his horse and swing into the saddle. She waved to him as he turned his mount about and rode off, and she remained standing, watching him ride down the track toward the north and east. His station was closer to Bathurst and only a few miles off this very track toward the east. Her own eyes went to the mountains, not even visible from here because of the nearby low hills. As children she and Eric had played together on the station which was now James's. Knowing Eric as she did, where would he go? What would he do?

Took off toward the mountains, Sam had said. Toward the mountains.

"It's a secret. And if I ever run away from home, I'll send

83

for you to cook for me," twelve-year-old Eric had said. *"Here's where you'll find me. You know Sorrenson's Peak? On the west there's lots of white cliffs and rocks . . . you follow the creek up until it gets small enough to jump across. Then you start looking for them."*

"Looking for what, Eric?"

"Caves."

Caves. To her knowledge, no one had yet discovered those secret caves of Eric's, if indeed they were real. If—

Suddenly, she knew they were real.

The next morning Aaron set off down the Bathurst track. He had told the women his plan to go on over the mountains to Sydney to speak with Mark's old friend, Stuart Mays, who was one of the most influential solicitors in the colony. Mays had as much reason to hate Livingston as Aaron did. He would know what could legally be done for Eric. And Penelope, still pale, was determined to oversee the shearing, in spite of her horror and worry. When she was gone, Jessica left a note on her pillow. Then, carrying a large bundle under her arm, she mounted her mare and rode out of the yard. When she came to the small bark outbuilding beyond the grove of trees, she dismounted and went inside where she quickly changed from her cumbersome dress to a pair of moleskin trousers and a blue shirt, and tucked her hair up under a cabbage tree hat. Then she rolled her dress up into the swag and remounted the mare.

She rode off the track into the brush, following a little-used path that followed the border between James's property and Aaron's. She looked over her shoulder frequently as she rode. Surely the police had spies out, thinking that the Aylesburys would know where Eric had gone and would attempt to follow them. But as she topped the hills and looked about, she saw nothing. The blue-gray hills of grass undulated like ocean waves frozen forever. The sun was bleaching out the sky already, and the flies were thick around her face. But she saw nothing, heard nothing.

She leaned the reins of her horse to the right again and headed him east.

James lowered the glass and smiled. She might fool somebody with the man's shirt and trousers, but no man, *no man* had a turn of a thigh like that nor such a beautiful behind. She could wear a baggy shirt and hide what was up front for awhile, but not for long, not for long. He had guessed right. Neither Aaron nor Penelope nor any of Eric's friends would know where he had gone. But despite the four years Eric and Jessica had lived apart, if anyone would know where he had gone, Jessica would.

James watched her. As soon as she was out of sight again, he would follow. She would lead him to Eric. Once he had located him, he'd have to ride into Bathurst to the police and lead them to him. His plan was working out better than he had thought. There were a lot of ways to skin a cat, and all his ways had failed so far. But this time he had a feeling the plan was going to work. It might take weeks, months, or even years, but the plan was going to work this time. How fitting that his only love would be the key to it.

Chapter V

Eric had said that it was a half day's ride from the Cranston station to the caves. From the Aylesbury station it should be less. Jessica knew that it was easy to get lost in the bush, especially if there were no landmarks, but there were landmarks here; Sorrenson's Peak, just a small rounded hill with an outcropping of stones on its summit which reminded her of a woman's breast. And ahead was the double-peaked foothill which was the easternmost boundary of surveyed lands. Beyond them, the ground turned rocky, hilly, with limestone bluffs and ridges where no cattle and few sheep could graze. No man had yet claimed that land between here and the mountains.

Jessica knew that there were still natives running free and wild who had learned to hate the white intruders with good cause. She also knew that the bush harbored bushrangers, desperate men, mostly escaped convicts. But it never occurred to her to be afraid.

She had ridden for several hours across the plains: Undulating hills of grass with few breaks, dotted with occasional stands of gum trees, their crop of leaves characteristically sparse enough to let dappled sunlight through so that grass could grow beneath them, and yet they could shade the cattle and sheep from the sun.

Jessica followed the forest of gum trees and wattle and twining vines, following the dry creek bed toward its source because she knew she could not get lost, because the source of the creek was near the point to which she must ride.

The forest was noisy. Even in drought it was noisome, with the colorful parrots screeching and chattering overhead, flashing their brilliant colors among the branches. Occasionally a kookaburra laughed and since laughter was catching, it set dozens of others laughing like ribald men at a bawdy play, their cries echoing among the trees, back and forth. Chelsea snorted once, causing Jessica to become alert, but it was only the chortling of a magpie that had disturbed the mare.

The forest soon opened out into a wide creek bed, which she followed, Chelsea's shod hooves clopping on white stone in the creek bottom. Jessica felt the need to hurry, but hurrying in this instance could cause her to be detected if someone was watching and so she moved at a slow but steady pace. Occasionally she looked back over her shoulder. Someone could be following and probably would in time. Natives could track Eric easily, and many of the mounted police were half native. Eric would know this, but if he was hurt, he would try to gain time by hiding until his wound healed. She winced, hoping his wound was not bad. Then she smiled again, remembering that Eric hated anything to do with medicine or wounds or human blood. Poor Eric.

When the creek makes a wide arch to the west, you climb

up out of it onto the bank and you will see a large pile of boulders which look like someone piled them there, only they're too large for humans to lift, Eric had said. Jessica couldn't remember all his instructions. After all, it had been sixteen years ago, but she was hoping she could remember enough of them to get her there. But what if he wasn't there?

Chelsea lunged out of the creek bed, and Jessica paused to look around her. Dense bush all around, but to the east the stone cliffs, the foothills of the mountain range. Then she saw the pile of stones and knew she had remembered right.

While she sat, she looked up at the sky. Light blue with curling veins of high meaningless clouds. A flight of pink-breasted cockatoos, called galah by the natives, winged overhead squawking and disappeared into the forest. It was then that she heard the rustling in the grass.

Frozen, she looked about her, her hand going to the small pistol that she carried in a holster on her saddle. But the sound was coming from the side of the creek bed. Jessica shook her head. It was only an anteater having breakfast.

She moved on. Now, she headed straight for the twin peaks. It would take most of a day to get to the caves, if she found them at all, and another day to return home. But she had left Penelope a note telling her she was going to find Eric, that she might not return for two or three days, and for them not to worry. They would worry, but they knew that Jessica had a mind of her own, a will of her own "like a man," Aaron had said once. And it occurred to her time and again that Eric might not be in the caves. He might have gone into the bush instead, or down the track to Port Philip, to the town called Melbourne.

Oh, Eric. You've caused us all so much consternation so many times with your rebellious ways. How you've worried Mum and grieved Aaron, and yet you've done nothing wrong; only had a stubborn will of your own— and a terrible rebellion against authority.

Jessica rode on and the sun reached its zenith in the opalescent sky. Now that she had left the forest, she was amazed at the stillness, the silence. This silence was what Aaron had described when he was lost in the bush years ago. This terrible silence, this lonely melancholy land. To the Europeans, this land called Australia was strange, primitive, foreboding. To Jessica it was home, and she would never dream of going anywhere else.

The closer to the mountains she became, the lonelier she felt, and she wondered desperately now if Eric felt as alone as she.

Whoever thought he'd be eating kangaroo rat? Eric moaned and poked the pitiful wisps of smoke coming from his cooking fire. He had to use the driest wood he could find to keep the damned fire from smoking and revealing his whereabouts. He was lying on his side, too spent to sit up, and poked at the sizzling rat skewered on the gum stick and propped over the coals on two forked sticks. He had ridden fast to the caves, obscuring his trail as best a man could when he was bleeding from a wound he shouldn't have had. He glanced down at his blood-covered shirt and felt the cold prickles on his face spreading over his body. His vision dimmed momentarily. Agh. He hadn't been able to bring himself to even look at the wound, but he knew it had stopped bleeding long ago. Not much of a wound probably, but it *had* bled, and that thought was enough to make him sick. If he could just get up the nerve, he could wash it or something.

He looked around him. The limestone caves which he had discovered years ago were ideal hideaways. They were extensive, going probably for miles underground, with tunnels and chambers reaching to God only knew where. His cave, though, had hot and cold running water, with air holes through which his smoke could exit, a natural draw like a chimney. The floor was soft with thousands of years of sifted dirt. The caves were in the sides of the mountains, white, limestone cliffs, on which stunted gum trees, wattle, and other bush grew. You couldn't see the caves until you were upon them, but he could climb up above this very cave and see for miles, almost to the very edge of the occupied plains.

Eric looked up at the sky outside his cave. If it would only rain, he could leave here, work his way south to Melbourne. What he would do there, he didn't know. He did hope that somehow, someone would clear Ben of his accusation. Father Aaron would try. He would go to Stuart Mays in Sydney. And he would go to Matthew, his father, who pulled some considerable weight with the governor. As for himself? Had he done right to defend Ben's property against the police? Had he done right to escape? He thought about that for the hundredth time and decided he had done the only thing he could do as an honorable man. He had escaped in order to be free to do more. It was like Aaron always said: You have to begin righting things at their source. And Eric intended to get at that source as soon as he could.

Bloody hell. It was taking the rat too long to cook. He reached one hand out and knocked the sizzling animal off into the coals. Swearing, he fished it out and took his knife from the rock and cut small pieces from it, ignoring his burning fingers. The meat was surprisingly good, had a wild taste like kangaroo and wallaby. If you didn't think about its being a rat, you could—

Suddenly his stomach seemed to close off. He swallowed back the nausea that threatened him and froze, not moving a finger until the nausea passed. Finally he thought, so much for kangaroo—

Eric retched silently into the dust of his cave. Once he had stopped he lay back on his swag and shut his eyes. It was all his father's fault. All his careful descriptions of wounds and sickness and dying which he had written down in his bound papers. They had all made Eric sick to death when he was just a lad, and he'd never gotten over it. Never gotten to where he could watch a man bleed, be sick, or die. Another wave of nausea went through him, but it passed. And now that he was wounded himself, the very thought of sickness and—and blood— He retched again, this time louder. Methodically he wiped his mouth on his neckerchief, so out of breath from his effort to empty his stomach, which was already empty, that he panted.

Then he heard the sound of a hoof striking stone. Eric forgot his nausea and the blood on his shirt, and was on his feet in a flash, out of the cave. He did not know when he had grabbed his rifle but it was in his hand as he scrambled up the rocky slope to the place above his cave where an enormous rock jutted out of the cliff, shading a flat area, the place from which he could view the countryside for miles around.

He squinted against the glare of the sun on white rock, his eyes sweeping the bush country below the foothills, then to the more sparse vegetation below. He heard a horse below. He crouched. There was only one horse coming then. It couldn't be Jacky, who was the only one who knew where the caves were. A native tracker? Probably. But he had thought it would take the trackers longer to track him. There!

He spotted the rider coming through the draw that led up to the caves. Eric strained his eyes to make out who it might be, but he did not recognize him. All men in this country dressed alike, so you couldn't tell by their clothing. The rider came steadily toward the caves, glancing up periodically, but mostly looking about as if expecting someone to jump him. Well, you bludger, you are about to get jumped, all right.

Trembling with weakness after his climb up to the ledge, Eric crouched, laying his rifle aside and loosening the holster at his hip. He drew the pistol carefully. As crazy as his vision was, he might miss if he shot, and he didn't intend to kill anyone anyway. The only way was to overpower him. He watched, trying to identify the rider as he passed below. There, the rider was reining the horse because he had seen the cave. Whoever he was he was young and trim and inexperienced.

A damned tracker, all right, but the hands on the reins were white, not black. He'd have to jump him. The jolt would probably make his wound bleed again—his wound bleed—

The earth undulating beneath him and the dense forest across the brief clearing wavered. He shook his head to clear it, but gray and black spots danced before his eyes.

Suddenly night descended, and Eric had only one impression before unconsciousness overcame him. The thighs on the horse were not a man's, and the horse itself was Jessica's.

He tumbled through the soft night in slow motion and exploded in a shower of stars.

Jessica shrieked and Chelsea reared and screamed. She fought the reins until she got the horse under control. Trembling violently, she looked down at the still form of Eric just inches from Chelsea's hooves.

He lay face up and perfectly still, his face pale as the moon.

"Eric!" she cried and dismounted hurriedly. Beside him she knelt and patted his face. He did not move. She felt for the carotid artery at his neck and felt the quick, faint pulse. Her hand rested on the bloody shirt and she shook her head. He had fainted and no wonder. He had bled and had done absolutely nothing for the wound. "Oh Eric," she said, more disgusted than afraid. She looked about her at the white limestone world. The ground was white, the rocks white, the cliffs white, and only the density of the brush broke the monotony of white. In her panic, she saw the opening of several caves, but the nearest one was the largest. She placed her hands under Eric's arms and dragged him. He was heavy, dead weight, they called it, and with much moaning and grunting and pulling and stops to rest, she finally pulled him into the cave.

Her first impression was coolness, a breeze coming from within the cave, of dripping water somewhere, of a small campfire and the odor of burned meat. She could see where he had been lying: an indention in the dust and his swag. She dragged him to the fireside and lay his head on the swag, felt his face again, his pulse, still weak and rapid. She noticed the uneaten meat nearby and shook her head, smelled the rancid odor of his sickness, too, and

93

scraped dust over it with her boot before she hurried to Chelsea again.

The little mare had discovered Eric's horse, and after making his acquaintance, had begun to crop the virgin grass under the gum trees. The horses would have to be hobbled soon, but right now she had to see how bad that wound was. She took her medicine bag from her swag and hurried back to the cave.

Kneeling beside him, she unbuttoned his shirt. His face was still deathly pale, his black mustache making it seem even whiter. His dark lashes, which were long enough to make a woman envious, lay on his pale cheek. His black brows had white dust in them from his fall. His hair was in its usual disarray, and she couldn't help but smile.

Now she had his shirt open. His deep, muscular chest generously covered with dark hair was matted with blood just below the right collarbone. Jessica caught herself staring at the chest, a man's chest. And this was Eric, the little boy she had grown up with. And how he had grown! She stared unbelieving at Eric, the man. She took a deep breath, blood rushing to her cheeks. She remembered his sudden confusion of five days ago when he had held her arms. *But hell, Jessica. We've grown up.* Yes, we have. Now she understood his confusion. One doesn't feel like this toward a brother.

Stunned she stared at his face, remembering that Eric was not her brother at all. Finally, coming to her senses, she looked about her for the source of the dripping water and saw it coming from above. Water was seeping from a seam in the rock of the cave's ceiling and dripping into a pool of clear water the size of a washtub. Jessica went to it, whipped off her neckerchief and dampened it in the pool. The water was clear and cold. She went to Eric again and cleaned the crusted blood from the wound and examined it carefully. It was only a flesh wound and not very deep at that. He must have lost some blood, but certainly not enough to cause him to lose consciousness. He had fainted, pure and simple. Fainted at the sight or thought of his own blood. She smiled and shook her head. With a tentative probe of her fingers, she satisfied herself that the musket ball, though small, was still inside the wound, just under the surface of the skin. Well, it was just as well he was unconscious, for if he hadn't been, he would be soon.

From her bag, Jessica took her instruments. They were crude—Aaron's old ones—but too valuable to throw away when he had bought new ones. Lately he had taken to washing everything in spirits, believing that some sort of invisible organism caused disease and that infection was transmitted by the use of dirty instruments. He believed that the alcohol in the spirits killed such infectious organisms on the instruments. Jessica opened the corked bottle and poured the rum over the forceps. Then bent to the wound.

She parted the edges of the wound gently, then reached in with the forceps. Eric offered a soft moan and Jessica bit her lips, kept probing until metal touched metal. Extracting the ball wasn't as easy as she had thought it would be, but she had soon drawn it out. A trickle of blood came from the wound, and she tucked the clean linen into the wound until it had stopped. Carefully she uncorked her bottle of eucalyptus oil and sloshed it on the wound. Aaron believed the oil was also a disinfectant. Following his instructions, Jessica had made a bath of the oil by boiling a pound of eucalyptus leaves in a pound of hog fat, straining it while it was hot, then storing it in tightly corked bottles. The pungent, pleasant smell of eucalyptus filled the cave as she applied it to the seeping wound. Now for the dressing.

When she had placed the linen pad over the wound and sealed the edge with the resin from the red gum tree, she sat back on her heels and allowed herself to notice that the shadows from the gum trees outside the cave were lengthening. Night would fall soon. She was weary from the worry and fear of the day, from the ride, from the heat, from her efforts to help Eric. She must yet hobble the horses and put something on the fire to cook. Wearily, she rose and went outside the cave.

Outside she found a spring just a short distance from the cave on the edge of the clearing and let the horses drink, then she hobbled them where they could graze just at the edge of the clearing under the shade of the gum trees. She relieved herself behind a boulder, then went back into the cave. Eric was still unconscious. She shook her head, a little worried now, hoping desperately he would not take a fever. If he did, she would have to bleed him, which really didn't make much sense to her since the bleeding was why he was unconscious.

As she took a stew pan from her own swag, filled it with water and poured jerked beef and dried vegetables into it, it occurred to her that perhaps—perhaps a doctor should use some common sense in treating a patient and not be so dependent on treatments of the past. Perhaps some of those treatments were wrong.

When the stew had just begun to simmer, Jessica wet the rest of her neckerchief and went to Eric again. Smiling she bathed his face, noting that he did not seem as pale as before. Without giving it a thought, she leaned over and kissed his chest, just above the bandaged wound. His soft, slow breath did not pause. She watched him, smiling, wanting to touch him, to place the palm of her hand on his chest, but instead, she stroked his cheek tentatively with her fingers. Her eyes were drawn to his lips, so innocent in unconsciousness. She had the sudden urge to kiss them, but shook herself out of the desire just in time and made her mind come back to her business. He was resting well, and she needed to tend now to herself.

She rose and went to the pool. The water was cool and with only one backward glance, she unbuttoned her shirt and pulled it off, leaving her bare except for her trousers and chemise. She dropped her handkerchief into the water and bathed her face and neck. Then dipped it into the water and washed her bare arms and chest above the chemise. She sighed and felt the stiffened muscles of her arms and back loosening. Sleep would come easy to her tonight.

Through a blackness Eric emerged into consciousness. His eyes focused first on the ceiling of the cave. Cave? He blinked. The light from the fire danced on the ceiling of the cave, the cave where he had come to escape the police. He frowned. But somebody came. The rider. He turned his head slowly. Outside the shadows of the trees were long. He could see two horses grazing. Two? Yes, his and— That was Jessica's mare.

He remembered crouching, ready to spring onto the rider below the ledge when everything went black. Eric held his breath and turned his head the other way. There was a form. A form beside the cave pool. Her back was to him. Eric smiled. It had to be Jessica, for nobody's hair was as luxuriant. No woman's hair escaped the chignon at the back of her head and spiraled down her neck quite like Jessica's.

He was remembering now that he had told her about the cave years ago, but how could she remember that and the details of how to find them after all these years? His hands came up slowly to touch his bare chest. He smiled and lifted his head to look at his wound. *Mistake.* Spots danced before his eyes, so he lay his head back down until they went away. Then he looked at Jessica again.

Her shapely back was toward him and in this secret moment, he let his eyes dwell on it, the tiny uncorsetted waist, the delicate spread of her hips, the rounded buttocks in the tight trousers. Her blemishless arms. Her hands went up to her hair to take out the pins. He watched fascinated as she shook out the dark tresses which cascaded in curls and waves over her white shoulders. He took a slow quiet breath. Jessica.

He swallowed and blood rushed to his face. He watched as she smoothed her hair, then caught it in her hand, preparing to twist it round her hands and pin it up again. He shook his head.

"Don't."

With a jerk, she turned toward him, her eyes wide, giving him a view of her breasts, round and ripe as melons beneath her chemise. Her surprise vanished. "Well, good evening," she said, her fine dark brows arching as she reached for her shirt and clutched it to her bosom. "You spied."

Eric ran his fingers over his bare chest. "So did you." Two spots of color touched her cheeks. Their eyes held for a moment. "You followed me again dammit," Eric said, sitting up.

Her eyes never left his. "I did. And I'll do it again if I have to. Where would you be if I hadn't come?"

"Lying here casually eating supper," he snapped.

"You'd be feverish by morning, though, from an infected wound."

"Bah!"

"Who would tend to you then?"

He waved her away and looked at the fire. "What if the police followed you?"

"They didn't. From the mountainside I could see for miles behind me. There was no one at all."

"Why did you come?"

"I knew you were wounded."

"Always playing the doctor," he growled. "You'd risk your life to play doctor."

"I don't play anymore, Eric."

Slowly he looked up at her. The embers of the fire crackled, and a small flame leapt up, fanned by a breeze, filling the cave with an amber glow. She was kneeling, sitting on her heels, and she had slowly lowered the shirt from her bosom. They knew each other well, knew what they both were feeling, knew what each other was thinking, that they drew each other like the earth draws the lightning.

He stared at her for a moment. A warmth and a desire that had always been there rushed to fill his body with an unbearable craving more torturous than pain. Finally, with a slight gesture which cast aside years of denying in his mind what his heart had always known, he said softly, "Come here, Jessica."

She rose and went to him, went down on her knees beside him.

He reached a hand toward her.

"You need rest, Eric," she said softly, taking his hand. "Soon the stew will be finished and I'll brew up real

English tea."

His hand went up her arm. "Just like a woman, thinking of food at the damndest moments." Her flesh beneath his hand was soft and achingly smooth and warm. The blood pounded in his head. "You undressed me and bathed me," he said amused. "You, a very proper lady. Weren't you shocked?"

Jessica flushed. "Of course not. I am a doctor. My thoughts were only on your wound and its treatment."

His eyes searched her face, his smile deepened. "You lie, Jessica." Then he pulled her down to him, felt her soft breasts press against his side, even as his lips sought hers. He stretched his legs out and raised up over her, bringing her down beneath him. He raised his head and looked at her face.

Her hair was spread over his swag. Her eyes had grown dark, and her lips parted to show the tips of her perfect white teeth. "Jessie . . ." he said, as he fought the last vestiges of his conscience and propriety.

"Don't bother me now," she whispered as her hands went to the back of his head, "with words." Then she pulled him down to her, and her lips opened beneath his, warm, moist, and inviting.

Chapter VI

She parted her lips and welcomed the thrust of his tongue, feeling the rush of heat through her. She moved beneath him until her breasts pressed against his chest. Even as their passion grew, Jessica tried not to touch his wound. But he crushed her to him, his want and need going far beyond any pain his wound could bring. He drew her tongue out and sucked it as his hand slid from her shoulder to her breast. When he caressed it, a moan came from deep within her. She opened her mouth to him, and her hands went to his side and slid to his back.

Every movement he made sent deeper thrills through her body. Reason abandoned her, and all she desired in the world was to open herself to him, to give, to let him have her, all of her. As if reading her mind, he brought the straps of her chemise down, until he had bared both her breasts, and with a groan he cupped first one, and then the other. Then with a gasp, he took his mouth from hers and looked at her. His eyes were dark with desire, his lips damp. His breath was hot and quick on her face. Almost savagely, he kissed her neck and then the hollow of her throat. Her hips moved beneath him, and her hand went to his waist. She wanted more, wanted to give more. He paused in his lovemaking just to look at her, his eyes going to her breasts. She knew that, like most young men his age, he must have had women before. She waited, suspended in a vacuum of breathless desire, watching his passion-darkened eyes going over her breasts and throat and lips.

The nostrils of his slender nose flared and beads of perspiration formed on his brow. His breath was ragged.

"Don't stop," she whispered. "Please don't stop."

Trembling, Eric pulled her chemise off over her hips and legs, the wrong way, but he didn't seem to remember how to do it, only to get it off. Then while she studied him with misty eyes, he unbuttoned her trousers, and with only a brief hesitation, began to pull them off over her hips along with her pantaloons. When he saw her bare abdomen, he paused and gazed at the beauty of her. He bent down and kissed her navel, kissed the curling hairs beneath as he pulled the trousers down, then off.

Eric jerked his trousers and underdrawers off, flinging them to the side. Her eyes went down from his chest to his waist to his loins. He hesitated until she smiled and held out her arms to him. He lay beside her then, half on, half off her, and pressed his mouth on hers again, moving his lips until she became restless beneath him. She wanted him to touch her. He cupped her breasts and kneaded them, then took his lips from hers, leaving a trail from her chin to her neck, to her breasts. Then he took a nipple into his mouth and teased it with his tongue. She caught her breath. As perspiration slickened his body, Eric's hands went all over her, stroking, caressing, loving. She moaned and his hand came down to cup her between her thighs.

There she was moist and ready. She caught her breath, but desperate desire made her writhe against him. Jerking her mouth from his, she glared at him from passion-darkened eyes and said huskily, "I need you. Please, Eric."

He raised his hips over her and lowered them onto her. One shake of her head and she reached down and guided him inside.

He gasped, pausing when he felt the barrier within her. And then slowly he penetrated it as she watched his face. Her eyes widened and her breath ceased as he began to move in her slowly, gently, letting her open to him. Jessica groaned with a mixture of pain and pleasure and finally spread her thighs wider for him.

Instinctively, her hips joined in the rhythm of his movements. Suddenly a hot flush crept through her, drawing all sensation from her fingers and toes, through her hands, arms and legs, rushing to that place where he and she were one.

When she wrapped her legs around his waist, Eric gasped, stiffened, and she could feel him throbbing within her. Her womanhood grasped him, pulling, pulsating with him. As she thrust her breasts against his chest, her legs and hips jerked with explosive release. He made one final plunge, then lay on top of her, breathing his hot breath into her ear as she continued to emit tiny moans again and again.

At last she lay still and wrapped her damp arms around his waist. He smiled and nuzzled her neck. Her love for him was overwhelming, and she rocked him gently in her arms as tears of joy slipped from her eyes.

They lay for a time, and then Jessica sat up, pulling on

her shirt saying, "The stew will boil away if we don't eat it."

Eric sat up and watched her as she took the billy can from his swag and went to the pool and filled it with water. She stepped outside the cave just far enough to take five gum tree leaves from a nearby tree and put them in the bottom of the billy can. Then she stirred the coals and added some kindling until the fire was a small blaze, and set the can on the pole across the forked sticks. Eric rose tentatively and stood, pulling on his pants while she politely kept her back to him.

"I'm going to see to the horses," he told her.

She looked up at him now. Locks of dark brown hair were falling over his forehead, and his eyes looked slightly glazed with pain, but he grinned. "I've already seen to them," she said. "Watered and hobbled them."

"Well, I need . . . to make a trip to the bushes."

"Oh." Jessica marveled at herself for blushing as he went out.

Once they had eaten the stew and drank the tea, they banked the fire and stretched out on their blankets for the night. As Jessica came to him, he pulled her down beside him, and they lay without speaking for some time in each other's arms.

"Tomorrow . . ." she began.

"Let's don't think about tomorrow tonight," he told her and pulled her close to his side.

Together they listened to the familiar sounds of the bush, and the less familiar sounds of the high country. Over all was the rasp of the cicadas and the beetles, a steady racket overplayed with swells and crescendos. The hoot of an owl sounded just outside the cave's entrance, and they heard the mouselike squeaking of bats as they flew about in the dark outside. The sounds were loud but steady, and the blankets spread on layers of soft sand were almost as comfortable as any mattress, not that it mattered. For soon they became lost in each other's touch, each other's warm smell, and he was nuzzling her hair while her hand massaged his shoulder.

"You must sleep. You're weary from your ordeal, Eric. And please don't feel that you must make love to me again tonight. I understand if you can't."

His nuzzling stilled. "Is that a fact?"

Her hand went into his tousled hair. "Remember Father's books? His medical books?"

Eric gave a soft sigh. "How could I forget? When I was a young lad I used to leaf through them and look at all the sketches of nude women."

She smiled into the blackness, barely lit by the soft glow from the coals of the fire. "I have been looking through them, too. And not long ago I read the anatomy and physiology of the male organs."

He snorted. "For shame."

"And I read that in order for the male to ejaculate, many things have to be just right. The organ is a muscle, you know, and all muscles must have a rest period. A man cannot have one orgasm right after the other because the sperm supply must be replenished in the scrotum first, and the musculature of the er—you know—which is part of the ejaculation force must have time to become engorged with blood. And none of this can take place when a man is very, very weary, or is ill."

Eric had ceased to move and lay very still with his face against her neck. "Jessica. Must you be so clinical?"

"I'm sorry," she said. "I just wanted to tell you that I understand why you might not be able to make love again. We can just hold each other, can't we, Eric?"

His hand crept slowly under her shirt, found her bare breast and caressed it gently. His thumb went round and round her nipple.

"Because your loving me like this," she said with a quick intake of breath, "is almost as good as what we did earlier."

He made a softly grunting sound and came up over her, bending to find her mouth. His warm lips worked on hers, sending great spasms of thrills through her. His hot male smell caused her to want to pull him close, so that she could feel his body as well as smell it. "And I do love you," she whispered, shutting her eyes against the ecstasy of his body against her.

His hand savored her breasts and massaged her abdomen, then went again to that place between her thighs. She caught her breath. He lifted his lips from hers and smiled at her.

"You mustn't try to please me if you can't . . . if it tires you."

His hand stilled again.

"I understand, you see. That the male organ cannot recover so soon after—" He kissed her mouth. "Tomorrow, perhaps . . . In your condition it should take several hours before you can . . . before you can do it again." He stilled her chatter with his kiss, and when he lifted his lips from hers again she said, "I . . . I guess."

She felt his heart pounding against her own chest as he took her hand in his and guided it to that place which had indeed recovered miraculously. "Guess again," he said softly.

She squeezed his erect manhood and guided it between her thighs. "Love me then," she whispered.

Eric slid into her slowly. She was open to him, and he began to move gently inside her until her hips undulated beneath him and her breath came in quick, desperate gasps. She thought his passion had reached its pinnacle, but when she raised her legs and pulled his thighs against her, he cried out. Gritting his teeth, he pulsated in her again and again, until the insides of her thighs responded, pulling, pulsating.

Shortly, when they were both spent and lay against each other, legs entwined, damp bodies molded together, she heard the soft, even breathing of his sleep and she smiled. No, she did not want to think of tomorrow yet, just of tonight.

The night sounds cascaded around the mouth of the cave and lulled her. Jessica sighed and caught his hand and folded it against her cheek.

Jessica rose before Eric woke. Smiling down at the innocent, little-boy look on his face as he slept, satiated and peaceful, she pulled on her undergarments, shirt, and trousers and went out into the trees to relieve herself. Then she checked the horses who nibbled her shoulder gently, trying to bribe her with soft horse kisses to unhobble them, but she only laughed and rubbed their muzzles.

She had never witnessed a twilight or dusk or predawn light. In this vast, predominantly unexplored country, dark changed almost suddenly to light as the sun made an unheralded appearance in the eastern horizon. She could not see it today because of the mountains rising abruptly above to the east, studded with tangled, stunted wattle and brush, but as she sat down on the ledge from which

Eric had fallen the day before, she could see the vast plain below. As she watched entranced, the grassy, hilly plain changed from slate gray to fawn brown, and then to bronze. The tops of the gum tree forests turned from gold to bronze, then to olive-green. Warblers chuckled musically in the bush. Nearby three kookaburras flushed a morose crow from a tree and chased him down the ravine to the south through the brush.

Within minutes the indigo sky became azure, and the shadows of the mountains shrank on the gold and green plain below, drawing back toward the mountains like souls returning to giant bodies.

Dawn had never been more beautiful to Jessica. She was seeing every tree, every shrub, every exquisite hue more acutely than she had ever seen them before. It was as if she had been seeing them all before through a thin veil. Love had lifted the veil, but she knew that if Eric had been beside her, the dawn would have been only ordinary, for his beauty as a man would have outshown it. Eric had always been her first love. Her country, the land in which she lived, her second.

A horse snorted, and Jessica turned to look down at the edge of trees. Eric, with saddle over his shoulder, was approaching the horses and speaking softly. He rubbed his horse's muzzle and threw the blanket and saddle over his back. He glanced up at the ledge where she sat and, grinning, raised a hand to her. Alarmed she rose.

"Where do you think you're going?" she called to him.

He motioned for her to come down off her ledge, which she did with ease, marveling at how easy it was to get about without the cumbersome burden of skirts. Once she had reached the level of the cave opening, she strode to him as he was cinching the saddle under the horse's belly. "Where do you think you're going?" she demanded again.

"South."

"But you can't ride yet. You're . . . wounded."

Eric pulled the cinch tighter and glanced at her. "But not very. Dr. Jessica Aylesbury said so. Anyway, you know as well as I do that the trackers will be on my trail by now."

She touched his arm. "But wait. Don't rush. Let's think about all this first."

"I have to go."

"I wanted to talk to you. About what you should do. Aaron has gone to Sydney to consult with Stuart Mays about what can be done for you."

Eric had finished saddling the horse and turned to her. "Stuart Mays can't do anything. Nobody can. Certain branches of the police force are manipulated by men in power, and they'll see me in prison, or worse."

"You're not that important to the police, Eric."

"I am to Scantlin, my love."

"But you will have a hearing, and when the magistrates hear you were just protecting Ben's property—"

Eric took her by the arms, his dark eyes playing over her face. "Jessie, I've no intention of serving a prison sentence I don't deserve. I did assault a police officer, remember."

She nodded. "I wanted to ask you about that. Why did you shoot off the lobe of his ear?"

"So he'd have something to remember me by," he said and released her.

"Oh, Eric," she said exasperated. When she saw that he was adamant about leaving today, she asked, "Well, what will you do? Where will you go?"

He stood with his hair falling in his eyes and looked down at his boots a moment. "I hope to go south, to the Port Philip district."

"Melbourne?"

"The Port Philip district is trying to legislate for separation from New South Wales, and if that comes about, the New South Wales police force will no longer have jurisdiction in the Port Philip district. I won't be in danger of being arrested there."

"But it may be months before they are a separate colony! What will you do in the meantime?"

He looked at her and smiled. "Go bush."

Jessica sighed audibly. "Go bush. Something you've threatened to do since your childhood." She raised her hands and let them fall to her sides. "Eric," she said. "Sit down please."

He stood tall, broad shouldered, towering over her, three locks of his straight dark hair falling over his forehead, a smile touching only one side of his mouth, his dark eyes looking deeply into hers, and then, like a small child, he looked around him, found a large white boulder just at the edge of the line of trees and sat down. As she stood, hands on her hips, watching him, he smiled and spread his arms. "Here I am."

She went to him and stood close. "Now tell me, what makes you so rebellious?"

His eyes darkened, but only for a moment. "You know why."

"That was years ago. Are you going to spend your entire life running from the hurts of the past?" He clamped his jaw tight and watched as she sat down beside him. "Mark Aylesbury is dead, Eric."

Mark Aylesbury. He had married Penelope when Aaron had gone to the bush and did not return. Eric had grown up thinking that Mark was his father, Mark who hated him because he was not his, because he represented a union between the wife he loved and the brother he envied. Eric spent the early years of his life under the glare of jealousy. Mark had never dared show that jealousy to him, until toward the end. He had simply ignored him, ignored him as if he had not existed. As Eric grew and saw the love and concern other fathers had for their children, he did not understand, and a hatred began to simmer in him for the handsome blond man. Along with the hatred came the guilt for that hatred. Envy was there, too, of other lads whose fathers cared for them. One smile. He would have treasured one smile. He had never had that smile.

Before Mark left for England, he had begun to strike his mother and Eric, too. His explosive temper became unleashed, and he could no longer hold back the hatred he felt toward Aaron's son. He had shouted that hate from his eyes, and so Eric had learned to resent Mark, who was the first person of authority in his world.

Then Mark had died at sea. A year later Penelope had gone overland to Aaron, then boss of the Cranston sheep station. "Aaron is really your father," Penelope had explained to Eric, a small boy of six.

As Eric sat now, remembering those bitter years, he remembered the great, wonderful delight he had felt at learning that Aaron was his real father, though he did not understand all there was to know about it then. All the guilt was gone, all the hatred. He had grown up being taught to respect his elders, especially his mother, his father, and James. Later it was other people, the minister

111

at the church in Bathurst, Mr. Simms, the public school teacher at Bathurst. The governors, the legislators of New South Wales. The police. All authority. All the rulers, the makers of the law, household law, district law, colonial law. But Mark had made his indelible impression on him. Mark, the solicitor, the legislator, the *authority*.

He clenched his fist on his knee. Was this the reason he had a chip on his shoulder, daring any man to knock it off? Was he, indeed, still allowing Mark to influence his life?

Jessica placed her hand over his fist. "A long time ago."

He looked down into her upturned face. "But my inner turmoils don't change the fact that the authorities are attempting to take Ben's land from him, does it?"

"No," she had to admit.

"Nor that they have managed to move in and take up other men's property for fines, fees, taxes—"

"But why must you take it upon yourself—"

"To defy them? Because nobody else is."

"There are other ways of defying them, and Aaron and the other settlers are attempting to persuade the legislators—"

"Too slow, too uncertain, and ineffective."

"And your way is better?"

"It will be. In time."

"In time, the pirating of the land will be stopped by legislation and police reform."

"Will it, Jessie? Will it truly?"

He was right. It was too slow, years away. Meantime men were losing their sheep and cattle stations, their farms. Their land was being eaten up by land grabbers in Sydney. Young men like Eric were becoming disillusioned and angry; older men were becoming angry and afraid. If Eric had not made a stand, some other man would have, soonerer or later. Probably soon.

His eyes were fixed on hers. "Just because I am running away doesn't mean I'm beaten, Jessica. Not in the long run. And in the months to come, remember that whatever you hear about me, if you hear anything at all, that I want what's best for you and Mum and Father and Ben Crawford and men and women like them. Can you remember that, Jessie? No matter what?"

"Eric . . ." She reached out to him, and he enfolded her in his arms and held her for a long moment. Then his kisses moved from her hair to her forehead, her eyes, to her lips. When he lifted his lips from hers he said, "Now see what you're making me do? I can't get caught up in you again. Not now. I have to be going. I have to hurry."

She could not keep the disappointment out of her face and voice when she said softly, "Well, if you must go bush, come have some breakfast first." She did not know whether to detain him, talk him into going back home and into trying to work out whatever sentence he may be given, or encourage his departure. She needed time, time to try to understand what it was he wanted, needed to do.

They ate boiled salted beef and damper. Damper was a mainstay of explorers, hunters, settlers, anyone on the track. Deep in thought, Eric watched her make the damper. First she made the fire hot, then cleared away the ashes in the middle. Sweeping the fire area clean with a tree branch, she put the damper in the center. The damper was a dough made of flour, salt, and water, which she now covered with hot ashes. The damper was done in minutes and proved to be the best he had ever eaten. With the billy tea she made to go with it and the beef, breakfast was hearty and would stick to his ribs. They ate in silence. Finally she spoke: "I'm going with you."

He stopped chewing and looked up at her. "No you're not."

"Yes. I must."

"Jessica. I'm considered a bolter now, an outlaw. You can't go with me."

"But I can."

"I won't have it. I mean it, Jessica." His face was full of fury, and she took her eyes from his.

"Then what will I do?"

"Go on as before."

"How can I?" She made a sweeping gesture with her hand to indicate the cave. "After yesterday?"

Eric rose and went to his swag and picked it up. "We made it harder for each other," he said. "Jessie . . ." He took her by the arms as she stood and held her to his chest. "Jessie, let me get established in the Port Philip district, in some business. When I do I'll send for you."

Jessica knew she could not go with him. She would hamper him in whatever he had to do. He would be a bushman, live for several months, perhaps several years in the bush until Port Philip district became a separate crown colony. Then he would find a way to make a living, establish himself in the new district and send for her. Years.

"But what do you know about the bush?" she demanded. "Nothing. Many men have died there—"

"I've hunted with Father. He taught me what he learned about survival in the bush. And he taught us both the things he learned from your father and grandfather. And—"

"Words. Not experience."

114

"Knowledge, Jessie. Not just words."

The bush. She shut her eyes and saw the bush. Miles, hundreds of miles of rolling hills and flats and river bottoms covered with dense forests of eucalyptus trees, wattle, vines, brush, all of it alike and no landmarks. Aaron, stumbling in the wilderness coated with mud to keep the insects from eating him alive, making a weapon out of the tongue of his boot, wearing kangaroo and wallaby skins. Eating what he could kill. Squeezing water from toads to keep from dying of thirst. Water. That was the most frightening thing. The lack of water. There had been a drought the year Aaron was lost in the bush, and there was a drought now. Bush fires. When her father and her grandfather had found Aaron, overcome from the smoke of a dying bush fire, he was clad in skin clothing, and the exposed parts of his skin were covered with mud. His beard was a tangled mess of matted and frizzled wool, and he looked so wild and fearsome even the natives were afraid of him. A man never quite recovered from being lost in the bush.

Now Eric lowered his face to the top of her head. "Jessie. I've got to go. And you've got to stay."

She shuddered and said nothing.

"In time, I'll send for my money. Father can withdraw it for me from the bank and somehow get it to me."

She drew away from him. "I need to see to your wound," she said reaching toward him.

His hand clamped over his wound through his shirt. "No," he said.

She saw that he was white around his mouth. "I won't hurt it, just look at it and—"

"No," he said with finality. He slung the swag which contained his blue blanket, his two stew pots and billy

115

can, his knife and his flint, the dried beef and tea leaves and damper onto his back. "There's no time for it. Scantlin will have had time to ride to Bathurst and receive orders to track me. He should be on the trail by now, and if he rode all night, he could be close. I have to go, Jessie."

She followed as he strode out of the cave, noticing that the muscles in his jaw were working with emotion. He was leaving the place of his youth, his home, his family, the woman he loved. Wordlessly he tied the swag behind his saddle as she watched him through her tears.

Suddenly, like an apparition, a hulking form appeared on the slope above their cave. *Scantlin.*

Jessica's eyes flew to her scabbard attached to her saddle where she had left the little pistol she had taken from Aaron's gun chest. Eric froze, his hair seemed to be standing on end. And while they stood aghast, troopers materialized out of the bush surrounding them. Speechless, Jessica watched one of them lift her pistol from its scabbard.

There was a lifetime of despair in Eric's eyes now, but he did not let it show in his face.

Scantlin grinned. "You shouldn't have stopped here, Aylesbury. Should have gone on down in the bush. And your sister shouldn't have followed, either." His evil eyes rested on Jessica and ran up and down her form.

Scantlin was a big man pushing fifty in years and sixteen stones in weight. He had an unconscious habit of giving the front of his pants a quick scratch every few minutes. His small gray eyes fastened on Jessica, and his yellow grin widened as he touched his scabbed ear. "Per'aps she ought to tend to me wound. Per'aps she has some soothin' ointment to rub on it. What do ya say, miss? Do ya 'ave—"

"Scantlin, you have me," Eric snarled. "I just didn't think your trackers could do it this fast."

Scantlin smiled hugely. "Trackers didn't have to track you. I 'ad me an informer. You mought know 'im."

Scantlin's eyes went to the bush below the cave opening. From it emerged a man who stood facing him. Eric's face registered shock. Jessica's gaze followed Eric's.

James.

Chapter VII

Carrie liked the room under the stairs with its sloping ceiling where the staircase went up. It was every bit as large as Mrs. Chun's, and like hers, the room had two windows, one which looked out toward the backyard facing south, the other which looked to the side of the house facing east. Carrie liked her room better than the other housemaid's because with her east window, she could watch the sun come up in the morning, though she was usually up before sunup.

The little room, which was only ten by twelve feet, had once been the pantry and storeroom for the kitchen, before the outside kitchen was built with its own storeroom. The fragrance of gumwood, with which the entire house was made, still lingered here in this room along with the scents of the herbs, spices, fruits, and vegetables which used to be stored there.

When they hired Carrie five days before, they brought an armoire out of the attic to go with the old-fashioned bed, which had been Mrs. Aylesbury's when she was a girl. Both were made of gumwood by Owen Crawford, a relative. Dr. Aylesbury had brought a washstand from Bathurst which he placed beside the bed, and Mrs. Chun had cheerfully brought in a cream-colored pitcher and bowl for it. After six months on a ship, the room was paradise. And to Carrie, it was paradise compared to the attic room she had grown up in as a girl with its single, small dormer window over the door.

At the moment, Carrie was smoothing back her hair from her face. Soon, she and Mrs. Chun would be preparing high tea. Or, as they called it here in this desolate land, "supper."

The pounding of horses' hooves outside caused Carrie to run to her back window and peer out into the yard. A dun-colored stallion was coming to a dusty stop in the yard. She pressed her lips together when she recognized two of the young men who had harassed her and the others the day they had arrived on the dray. They were the twins. One of them was shouting something. Since Jessica had disappeared, leaving a note on Mrs. Aylesbury's pillow that she was going to search for Eric, the entire family had been expecting to hear something. Mrs. Aylesbury had been upset when Jessica left, and even more upset when she could not locate her brother, James Cranston, at his station. Carrie hurried out of the room, not wanting to miss anything exciting that might happen. And she hoped it wasn't any bad news about Jessica.

She hurried the few steps out into the central hall to the back door, just outside her room door. The back door was open, as always, to let the breezes through. On the veranda stood Mrs. Aylesbury and Mrs. Chun. The twins remained on their horses.

"Troopers are bringing Jessica to the station, but Eric's being taken to jail," one of the twins was saying.

119

He had not removed his hat, and his manner did not seem particularly unhappy that Mrs. Aylesbury's son, Eric, had been discovered.

"Is he badly wounded!" Mrs. Aylesbury's question was more of a demand than a question.

"Not that I could tell. He looked kinda sick, though. Jessica looked . . ." Reginald grinned. "The same as usual, only . . ."

"Well?"

"Only she was wearing a man's clothes."

Penelope's chin came up when she saw the gleam in Reginald's eyes, knowing that he was mocking as usual, the scamp.

Reginald's eyes then rested on Carrie. He grinned and touched the brim of his hat. "Evening, miss. I heard the Aylesburys had hired you. What luck."

Carrie muttered a thank you. She didn't want to seem too friendly because Mrs. Aylesbury wasn't. She had heard what scamps these young men were. Mischief makers. Rowdies. And whose luck was he talking about? Hers? Or his? Her blue eyes went to the other twin, who was looking at her without smiling, his expression completely inscrutable.

Reginald nodded to Mrs. Aylesbury, to Mrs. Chun, then to Carrie. "Just thought I'd prepare you." With a jerk he reined his stallion around and, followed by Reuben, rode out of the yard with the same rapidity with which he had come.

Mrs. Aylesbury watched them go for a time, then she turned frowning toward Mrs. Chun. "And the doctor's not back from Sydney, and no one knows where James is." She looked out over the yard where the stockmen were beginning to move toward the house, probably

120

wanting to learn the latest news about Eric and Jessica.

Carrie knew she should be frightened by the strange, unsettled happenings in this place. People spoke with fear about bushrangers; they were wary of their own police. And wild natives abounded and still threatened farms and homes. There weren't many people about, and there was always a sense of urgency, of danger. Yes, she should be frightened, but she wasn't. She had chosen this country and come what may, she would live in it. It was *her* country now. What little fear she had was overshadowed by the sense of adventure—and of wanting to help make her new country better. Rather like the way she made her plain frocks prettier by adding extra lace and embroidering designs on the collars.

Carrie liked her new home and the people with whom she had cast her lot. She had vowed to help them any way that she could. She would start now by fixing Mrs. Aylesbury some tea.

"Excuse me, Mrs. Aylesbury, mum, but if you'd like to come inside I'll fix tea. We've nought to gain standin' here, have we," Carrie said.

Penelope's misty eyes rested on Carrie for a moment. "No," she said smiling. Then she gathered her skirts and went inside.

Wordlessly, Carrie and Mrs. Chun set the long trestle table in the kitchen with the crockery plates which the family used when there was no company. They didn't know when Jessica would arrive, or who would be with her, so all they knew to do was set the table for supper and wait.

Before long, Jessica came riding in, tired, disheveled, and as Reginald had said, wearing a blue shirt and moleskin trousers. With her hand over her mouth,

Carrie watched her dismount, for she had never seen a woman in trousers before. And they fitted her tightly, as they did the men, revealing the curves and outlines of her body. The two troopers who delivered her watched her behind as she came toward the veranda, taking off her hat and dusting the trousers. Penelope stood wordlessly watching her, until Jessica came to stand before her. Jessica's startling violet eyes were steady. "I asked the troopers in but they were ordered to return immediately to Bathurst." She only glanced back at them as they turned their mounts, and with a wave of their hands, rode out of the yard.

Jessica studied her stepmother's face for the anger that might be there. "Eric had a deep chest wound, Mum, but it was only in the muscle. I did the best I could with it." She avoided Penelope's eyes then, knowing what she would ask next.

Penelope said, "Come inside, Jessie. We've supper fixed and you must be famished."

Grateful tears sprang to Jessica's eyes, and she followed Penelope inside.

"Mrs. Chun will have it all on the table by the time you wash up," Penelope said.

Jessica hurried up the stairs and pulled off the men's clothing, and put on an afternoon dress, washing her arms and face and smoothing back her hair. A soaking bath would be in order later, a not too rare luxury in this household, for Penelope had a propensity for bathing as often as she did.

For supper Mrs. Chun and Carrie served "squatter's stew," a succulent concoction made from bits of pork, cabbage, carrots, turnips, potatoes, tomatoes, and onion, boiled together and served with fresh hot bread. As

Jessica and Penelope ate, Jessica told the story of finding Eric, omitting nothing except their lovemaking and the fact that Eric had planned to go south toward Melbourne. Jessica wondered if her new status as a woman showed. Surely something as wonderful as her love for Eric must show on her face. She told of James's part in capturing Eric at the last. And when she finished telling it, Penelope's face was ghostly white.

Penelope rose slowly, her hand going to the neck of her dress. "There is a reason," she said softly. "James loves Eric, has always loved him as a nephew."

Jessica could not look at her. She did not want Penelope to know her suspicions. The troopers had surrounded Eric there in front of the cave, had tied his hands behind his back and made him ride between them all the way to the Bathurst track. She had not even been able to talk to him, but riding between two other troopers, she had tried to reason why James would have allowed this to happen to his own nephew.

James had spoken to her, but she had not responded, and he had ridden on ahead of the others to Bathurst, leaving her to the leering glances of the white troopers. It was just as hard for her to believe he had left her for the police to escort home as it was for her to believe that he had led them to Eric.

"James . . ." Penelope shook her head in bewilderment. "James must have thought that Eric was better off in jail than roaming the bush. Certainly Aaron thinks so. Oh Jessie, I wish Aaron were here. He might know why James would do such a thing."

Jessica sat, weary, her mind a jumble, marveling that life, which could go on smoothly for years, could then suddenly change. She looked up. No, not everything. For here we are again, we women. Waiting on the men to determine our destiny.

"Sooner or later, Rodney Livingston's secretly manipulated enterprises will be found out, Aaron. In the meantime, I think just you and I and Jory McWilliams are the only ones who suspected the judge of any wrongdoing. That's because we know him better than anyone else."

Aaron nodded, his gaze going past Stuart's head out his clean, multipaned window which faced Sydney Cove. For a second his mind went back to another time, twenty-eight years ago, when Stuart and Mark were assistants to different town solicitors, Mark's office located in a wing of the Rum Hospital just down Macquarie street. Eighteen twenty-two was the year he and Mark had graduated, Mark from Cambridge after taking courses and reading for solicitor under a solicitor there, and Aaron from medical school in Edinburgh. They had returned home to find Sydney changed in the five years they had been away. They had been amazed at the carriages, few as they were, which plied the streets. When they had left, the only carriages belonged to the governor and a few high officials in the colony. They could walk the streets of Sydney for days without seeing a carriage, but when they had arrived home from England, they had delighted in seeing two or three in one day.

Now gothic structures of concrete and stone lined Macquarie and George Streets. Carriages, gigs, and hacks plied the streets constantly, and coaches carried the mail from town to town this side of the mountains. The ships with sails billowing crowded the port, and in The Rocks area, where Aaron's father had stumbled ashore in 1801, brick buildings were jammed together, housing taverns and bordellos, now the slums of Sydney. A man did not dare go there at night anymore, where he and Mark used to meet their friends to drink stringbark in Foster's tavern. Foster's was now a house of ill repute, where sailors of the ships went for hard liquor, opium from the East, and hard women. A man could get shanghaied in The Rocks area.

Clothes had changed, too. The slim, delicate dresses the women wore had disappeared, and now they wore voluminous skirts and petticoats with hoops and corsets and absurd hats with feathers, fruits, plumes, and birds. And men were wearing beards. He shook his head, wondering what the world was coming to. His own father staunchly refused to grow either mustache or beard, but Penelope's father, Oliver Cranston, was more stylish with a mustache.

Aaron's eyes came back to focus on Stuart's face. Even Stuart wore a beard, now neatly trimmed as befitted an important solicitor and legislator. Stuart and Mark had fought for the right of the emancipists, convicts having served their sentences and pardoned, to be represented in government. Mark had died while carrying just such a proposal to England. Stuart had taken his place as the spokesman for the emancipists and their sons, the "currency lads." As a result of much legislation and controversy, Stuart, at last, had been given a place on the legislative council of New South Wales. Stuart was a fanatic, like William Wentworth, but Aaron had supported his cause all the way.

"If the police do find Eric and he is taken to jail, is there anything we can do in his defense?" Aaron asked.

Stuart tapped his finger on his chin. "You know for a fact that I can exert some pressure on the judge there, but you also know that Livingston just about has the district judges in his hip pocket. The tactic which I will use, though, will be to downplay Eric's importance in this; that he was only defending his uncle's property as any decent Australian bloke would do." Stuart paused and smiled quickly. "Forget about the Australian part. The magistrates are exclusionists for the most part, pure merinos. English to the core. Um. Let me see." He picked up his pen, actually it was Mark's pen which Penelope had given to him after Mark's death. "The facts which will be against him is his resisting arrest and—" Stuart looked up at Aaron and his deep frown smoothed out. "He shot the captain's ear off?"

Aaron sighed. "Just the lobe."

"Just the lobe." Stuart sighed also. "That isn't apt to please the judge much."

"I know."

"Furthermore, he resisted arrest by escaping."

"Yes."

Stuart clicked his tongue. "What does he plan to do now, I wonder."

"You know Eric. He's always wanted to go bush."

"Yes, but as a bushman, not as a criminal."

The two friends just looked at each other. Stuart had avoided using the word, "bushranger." In the colony when criminals escaped, they could always take to the bush which was wild, uncharted, untamed, and unexplored, where, if they knew how and few did, they could live off the land—and off the cattle and horses and sheep they stole. Eric was an honest man, even if he was a bludger. Aaron shook his head again. "Well, he's now a criminal, so I figure he thought it was better to be a free criminal than a jailed one."

Stuart smiled. "I'll do my best, Aaron. You know that. I'll, of course, take the case myself."

Aaron rose, followed by Stuart, and offered his hand across Stuart's littered desk. "Thank you, Stu."

"Don't mention it." Stuart grinned and said, "Say, mate, you still have some of that Pomey twang in your speech you picked up while you were in England."

Aaron nodded. "Once you catch it, you've got a bit of it for the rest of your life. Like the pox."

Australians had formed their own unique dialect. Aaron had watched it evolve. The lower classes of men from the streets of London with their cockney accents and men from the upper classes in England had mixed and mingled in New South Wales and had stirred their accents together, added a pinch of Irish, a dram of Scotch, a grain of Yank, seasoned it with some spicy slang, and behold—the Australian language. Aaron was accustomed to it, but listening to Stuart now, he could contrast his speech with that of a pure merino Englishman.

"Well, don't warry, mate. Somehow somedie, we'll see those wowsers up a gum tree, we will." Stuart shrugged. "And who knows but whot Eric's case, if he's tried fair dinkum, might be a test caise. Don't worry. We'll get 'im off one wie or another."

Aaron remembered a time when Stuart's accent was more English than Australian. Things change. Aaron replied, "You think like I do then, eh? That Eric's better off comin' to trial? They could hang him, you know."

"Nay. Never a chance of that. Not an Aylesbury." Stuart clapped Aaron on the back. "Not even Livingston would want ya father on his back, or you either. And remember, Oliver Cranston is Eric's grandfather, too, and he was old Livingston's best friend. Judge Livingston was Cranston's own solicitor before he became judge. So you see? If Eric comes to trial, we can get 'im off. I'll bet my beard on it."

As Aaron stepped out into the glaring sun he rubbed his own smooth chin. He felt better about Eric, though he was having mixed emotions about his situation. If the police found him, it was even possible he could be shot. In the past, on occasion, the police had shot bolters before they got them to jail. And the captain would not be happy with Eric for shooting off his earlobe. But if Eric were safely brought into Bathurst and jailed and taken to trial, Stuart seemed reasonably certain he could get him pardoned.

Aaron looked up at the sun. Noon. Must get on down the track to his parents' farm where he'd spend the night. And then, tomorrow morning, he'd set out for home.

"Visitor to see ya," the prison guard said.

Eric was lying on the cot in his cell in Bathurst jail, his head resting on his hands. He looked over at the form which was but a dark image framed in the opened door of his cell. He sat up and swung his legs over the side of the cot, his eyes focusing on the visitor's face. When he recognized him, his mouth stretched into a grimace.

"James," he hissed. Then he raised his head and called to the guard, "I don't want to speak with this man, damn you."

But the guard shut the door with a bang, and the keys turned in the lock. Seething with fury, Eric's eyes came slowly from the door and focused on the face of his Uncle James.

James removed his hat and, with a slight smile, indicated the stool near the cot. "May I?"

"I've got nothing to say to you, James."

"I don't wonder. But I have something to say to you, Eric."

Eric stared at him. James was a tall, slender man even at the age of thirty-nine, a result of his working his own station right along with his ringers and jackeroos, tailing horses, mustering, droving and yarding cattle. He was a handsome man, too, and it had always amazed Eric that James had not married. For every widow and single lass in the entire district had fluttered their eyes at James, inviting courting at one time or another. Eric knew damned well who James wanted to court: Jessica. And as he had ridden, under arrest, with the troopers to Bathurst, in his confused and pain-smothered brain, he had figured out that James wanted him in jail out of the way so that perhaps he could court Jessica— But no, Jessie had been free to encourage his courting for years. His eyes followed his uncle as he sat down on the stool and hung his cabbage tree hat on his knee.

Fury overwhelmed him. Eric jumped up and strode to the door, caught the bars of the door window in his hands and called, "I say, I don't want to visit with this man. Guard! Guard!"

"The guard won't come, Eric."

Eric turned to face James. So! His beloved uncle had seen to it that the guard was paid so as not to interfere! Fury shook him. He stood trembling, hands clenched at his sides. "Then that's unfortunate for you, James. Because I'm going to beat the hell out of you for leading them to me."

James was solemnly undaunted. He looked up at Eric and indicated the cot. "Sit down Eric. I've come to help you escape."

Eric's dark eyes narrowed. "Escape!" When James nodded, curiosity got the better of his anger. "Why get me arrested and then help me escape? That doesn't make sense."

"Of course it doesn't. And it never will unless you sit down and listen to me."

Eric moved slowly to his cot, keeping his angry eyes on his uncle. When he sat down on the cot, he rested his fist on his knee.

James glanced once at the door of the cell, then rested his hands on his knees and leaned toward Eric. "I bought one of the finest and fastest race horses from Tad Crawford I have ever seen," James said smiling slightly. "He's a stallion, black, full of meanness and fury. And he's yours."

Eric's dark eyes flashed from the dim light coming from the window. Then he twisted his face and said, "Mine!"

James nodded. "Yours. I have a vested interest in seeing that you escape. If you're game."

Eric sat on his lathered steed and looked down from the heights onto the plains below. He wiped the perspiration off his forehead and lips with the sleeve of his shirt and grinned. "Thankee, uncle," he said.

Below the Bathurst plains stretched far and wide, surrounded on all sides with mountains. Eric had headed for the heights to the east where stony ground hid the passage of a man better than the dust of the plains. He'd run this bedeviled horse for three hours or more. According to the sun, he had escaped Bathurst jail just before dawn.

The guard, smelling strongly of rum, had shuffled to the front of his solitary cell that morning with his breakfast, had shoved it through the door and turned to go away. In a flash Eric had the guard's head pinned to the bars of the cell by the crook of his arm. With a finger in the man's ribs he'd said, "This is a pistol, you bloody bludger, and if you've got a brain in your head you'll be very still and quiet."

The guard had been so frightened he'd broken wind loudly, but he hadn't moved while Eric extracted the keys snapped to his belt and, after only four tries, had found the one that fit his cell door.

He had ordered the guard inside his own cell, locked him in, and made his escape. But just as he started to bolt from the corridor in front of the cell, the guard had grabbed the bars and stared at him, whereupon Eric had waved his lethal finger, which the guard had mistaken for a pistol, and grinned. Then he'd bolted out of the corridor, through the empty captain's office, and out the door. As James had promised, the black horse was waiting impatiently across the street under a gum tree.

Eric had ridden out of town in a flurry of dust, shouts from the jail, and a shower of feathers from the scattering squawking chickens in the street.

James had been right. This horse was a fury, ran like a streak of lightning, and wasn't ready to quit yet. At the moment he was blowing and stamping, and kept turning around to look at Eric out of the corner of his plum-shaped eye. Once, he had peeled back his lip and shown his teeth.

"If I didn't know better, ol' mate," Eric said to him now, "I'd swear you were offering to bite me."

His eye caught movement below. There they were, the police. On his track, perhaps four miles away. And there'd be no going back to the caves. Not the ones where he and Jessie— But there were other caves farther south, according to James's stockman, Jacky. Eric patted the stallion's neck. "Best be going on, friend," he said aloud. "The time has come for us to go bush."

With a jerk of the reins, Eric turned the restless stallion about and tore down the hill heading toward the forest of eucalypti below. The police would be hard on his heels, he knew, but he had three advantages over them. Surprise, this fast horse, and the fact that their trackers were, at the moment, so inebriated that they wouldn't be able to get out of bed, much less see a track in the forest. James had said he would tend to it, would give Jacky enough rum to distribute among the native trackers. Naughty, naughty, Uncle James. Father would disapprove of giving the natives rum.

Eric had descended the hill now in a shower of shale. He raced across a dry creek bed, reined the horse and jumped down to brush away the tracks in the creek bottom with a gum tree branch. Just when he backed up to view his hasty job, he felt a nip on his arm and jumped aside. The stallion had a mean look in his eye, and Eric lost no time in delivering a blow to his muzzle. "You bloody bugger," he cried. "No wonder Tad Crawford sold you." He did not want to examine the bite; it might have broken the skin. He didn't need that. The wound in his chest was already aching again. So he mounted the horse, placing his hand over his chest wound, and kicked the stallion's flanks as hard as he could and reined the animal into the forest.

Eric whipped the horse with the reins, though he didn't need much encouragement to run. Dodging wattle branches and vines and young eucalypti, he raced the horse, going steadily south. He *hoped* he was going south. In the forest, even though gum tree leaves were sparse, a man could go in circles and not know it. In this bush country there were few landmarks, and where there were landmarks, you couldn't see them for the thickness of the bush.

And the bush went on and on. He passed huge trees with the bark hanging down from their trunks. He passed the river gums with their white trunks, the scribbly gum with the squiggly designs on their trunks. He saw a white gum with its snow white bark, rare in this part of the country, and wattle, wattle, and wattle. It seemed that he tore through the same tangle of wattle and pea vines over and over. He kept catching the aromatic, medicinal scent of crushed gum leaves and some rare scented flower over the odorous sweat of the horse. Most flowers in New South Wales did not have a fragrance.

The sweat foamed and flecked off the horse now, and Eric slowed him and came into a clearing. He reined the horse and stood up in the stirrups to get his bearings. Ah. He *had* been going south, according to the sun. To the east some three or four miles away rose the foothills where the limestone caves were, where he and Jessie—Better not think of that. He had to head south and a little west, paralleling but staying well away from the track to Melbourne. Almost due west now was the Aylesbury station, and if he were on a high enough hill, he might be able to see the house. The police would look there.

They'd pass here, too. Eric nudged the stallion and moved on, keeping to stony ground as best he could, but a good native tracker would be able to find even one overturned stone within several miles' radius. Or a horse apple.

"Hope Uncle James didn't feed you much, you blood sucker," Eric said to the horse. He was at an easy lope now. No problem finding grass here when he decided to stop, but finding water was another thing.

Once you make your escape, you're on your own, James had said to him in jail the evening before. *Your survival will depend on what you've got within you.*

Twenty-eight bloody years I should have something helpful in me, Eric thought.

He rode all day. The sun rose high in the sky and attempted to burn through the gum trees to the forest floor, but all it managed to do in its efforts was to dapple the leafy floor with spots of light, enough light to allow grass to grow, but not enough to burn a man.

Eric's pace was slower now. He was entering rougher country, unpopulated, and for the most part, unexplored. No wonder his father had gotten lost in it. It was a sea of hills, vales, and forests with a network of creeks. He hoped they ran water.

He found one just after noon, a deep creek running crystal-clear water. He dismounted and gave himself and his horse a short rest and a drink of water. His chest wound was throbbing and sending shooting pains up to his shoulder, but he wouldn't let himself think about it. After a moment's rest, he and his horse moved on.

At dusk he sat atop a high rocky hill and looked down on the country below. Vast, deep and silent, it spread in varying shades of green, blending into grays and blues.

There was no sign of settler, station, farm, or creature. Only the all-pervading silence. He looked up at the sun, setting toward the western hills, and decided he'd best find the caves.

He found them just before the sun slipped below the hills, just where Jacky had described them to him over a year ago. Limestone caves, three of them. Big as rooms and dry, located in the side of blindingly white bluffs amidst a maze of tall rough hills, thick bush, and deep, winding creek beds.

On a shady ledge before the caves, he rubbed down the black stallion, keeping a wary eye on him, then he unpacked the swag James had packed for him. Only the necessities. *Can't pack more than what a swag will hold,* James had told him. *You'll have to travel light to travel fast.* There was a rifle in the holster behind his saddle, and in the swag was flint and iron pyrite for making fires. Jerked beef, dried fruit, flour. One tin pan and a billy can. Tea. And a pistol. Eric picked up the pistol, wrapped carefully in felt, and examined it. He smiled. It was a revolver. A Yankee-made Colt 45, by God. Very rare in Australia, indeed. He turned it over and over in his hand and lifted his eyes west. He could probably have found quartz for flint and iron ore himself. He could have trapped wallaby and other creatures in order to have something to eat. But what he couldn't do without were the weapons. They were the necessities. For what he had to do.

Chapter VIII

"Do ya ever get the urge to run off to sea or somethin' Rube? Or are you content to be a cocky all yer life?"

Reuben Schiller was just bringing the ax up from the log and slid his left hand down to the ax head, pausing to look at his brother. "Pa needs us here," he said.

Reginald sneered. "Pa needs us, eh? D'ya believe that? He's got Ludy and Palmer comin' on. They'll be seventeen and eighteen next month, and there's the others, too. How many cockies does it take to grow hops and vines, tell me that?" Reginald wiped his dirty sleeve under his nose. "'Sides, he ain't our pa, and I don't feel we owe him nothin'. We've worked for our keep ever since we were four years old. Remember when we used to run errands in Sydney when he and Mum first got married?"

"Aye. I remember." Reuben brought the ax up over his shoulder and came down on the log with all his might. The split in the log widened and, with a great snapping sound, split in two.

Reginald looked up at the bleached sky. Unless it

rained soon, the whole country would be a tinderbox waiting for the first spark to ignite it. There was nothing more hideous than a bush fire. It could wipe out lots of people in just a few hours. One of the Sydney newspapers, *The Australian*, claimed that the districts here west of the mountains were sparsely populated, but as far as Reginald was concerned, it was overly populated. Just down the track toward the south coast, toward Melbourne, though, the bush got thicker and the sheep and cattle stations fewer. Not a hundred miles south, a man could ride for days without seeing another human being.

Rube looked at him. "Pa said a cord of wood before dark, Regie."

"Pshaw. He needs a cord of wood like he needs another wife. And he don't need another wife with the way Mum is."

"Mum was a whore."

"Now, Rube, are you wantin' to fight about that again?"

Rube lowered his ax slowly, his eyes narrowing at his brother, his mouth tightening.

Reginald wasn't in the mood for one of their fights, so he changed the subject. "It's just that I'm sick of all this hard work." He sighed and said, "I wish I was rich. You know what's the first thing I'd do if I was rich?"

Rube shook his head.

"I'd ask Jessica Aylesbury to marry me."

Rube's cold gray-blue eyes slid to the track going south of their farm, then came back to rest on his brother's face, but he didn't answer.

"And you could court the Aylesburys' new servant lass, couldn't you?"

"No."

Reginald shook his head. "I don't understand you, Rube. She's a pretty little thing. And you never do much rovin' for girls, just enough to satisfy your lust once in a while. Don't you ever dream of having a pretty woman?"

Rube reached down and picked up the two logs and tossed them aside as if they were two potatoes. "Aye."

Reginald grinned. "Who, Rube. Who do you dream of?"

Rube, without smiling, pointed to Reginald's ax. "Chop," he said.

Reginald shrugged his broad sun-browned shoulders and hefted the ax up over his shoulder, whistling a bawdy tune. The brothers' *chop, chop, chop* rang in the gum forest, drowning out the thunder of hooves on the track, but they heard the clanking and clattering of gear, then paused and listened. Reginald's eyes met Rube's. "Troopers," he said.

The brothers left their axes and began to run through the eucalyptus forest that surrounded the west vineyard. When they reached the vineyard, they could look across it for half a mile to the house where, indeed, mounted troopers in their ragtag blue uniforms were crowding the yard of the Schiller house. They ran on, and when they came to the yard, heard their father say, "No, ve ain't zeen him. And I ain't zeen nobody else comink along ze track."

Captain Scantlin was barely able to keep his spirited horse still as he looked down upon Karl Schiller. "You'd bloody well better be sure of that, Schiller. Because if you're coverin' for 'im, I'll put you in jail quicker'n you can skin a cat."

Reginald went to stand beside his father, looking

138

quizzically at him.

"You, dutchy," the captain said, pointing his horse whip at Reginald, "'ave you seen Eric Aylesbury about today?"

Reginald and Rube looked at each other, then back at the captain of the police. Reginald said, "No. I thought he was in jail."

"Was," the captain said, hitching at the front of his pants. "He escaped. Early this morning. Somebody outside jail saw 'im going south. Some say 'e was on a black 'orse; some say the 'orse was dun colored." The trooper studied the twin brothers from his slitted eyes. "I'm tellin' ye bastards if you seen 'im, ya'd better speak up."

Rube narrowed his cold eyes and said, "My brother said we ain't seen 'im, Captain."

Captain Scantlin studied Rube, decided he didn't want to press the matter. He bobbed his head. "Very well. But if you see 'im and don't report it, you're as guilty as 'e is. It'll be jail and a fine fer ye. Mind now what I say." Then, with a jerk of his reins, he turned his horse, gave a command to the troopers, and the mounted police thundered out of the yard in a cloud of dust.

No one moved in the Schiller yard for some time. Schiller's attention turned to the twins. "Now ain't zat a shame. I'm feelin' plenty zad for ze doctor. He's such a goot man. And Eric, he ain't such a pad poy either. Und hiss own uncle against him, leadin' the troober to him like he done. What do you subbose is going to happen to him, eh? Out there in ze bush." Schiller placed his hand on Reginald's shoulder. "Ah mein hemmel, such a shame, eh Regie?"

Reginald's eyes had gone down the track with the

troopers where they were already disappearing through the trees of the forest. "Aye," he said bemusedly, "such a shame."

When Aaron turned grimacing to face the women, his teeth seemed extra white, gleaming in his deeply tanned face, which was covered with the brown dust of the yards. Behind him the six cattle yards had just been emptied by nine of his stockmen. Beyond, the cattle were bellowing. With bobbing heads they were being driven up the track toward Bathurst, for sale and slaughter. Spring mustering had been detained this year because of Ben Crawford's problems, and because Aaron had gone to Sydney to seek help for him and Eric.

Now Aaron turned about in his saddle to watch the ringers droving the cattle up the track, then swung off his horse and led him to where Penelope and Jessica stood, squinting against the sun, watching the cattle.

"How many head finally, Aaron?" Penelope asked shading her eyes. Both women were wearing wide-brimmed cabbage tree hats made for men, but nothing, not even the shade of the veranda, could protect them entirely from the glare of the afternoon sun.

"Two hundred twelve," he replied.

Jessica watched as Aaron gave his wife one of those looks, his brown eyes crinkling at the corners, saying *I love you*, even as his mouth stayed closed with a smile. New South Wales men did not make any outward show of affection for their wives, but Aaron did not have to; it showed every time he looked at his. Jessica smiled to herself and folded her arms across her breast. Aaron came to stand beside them, turned to look down the track again. He had just arrived home from his trip to Sydney and to his parents' farm yesterday evening. Neither he nor Penelope had slept much since Eric's capture and imprisonment. Both were despondent. "I've a feeling I'd better get the cattle sent north. Eric being in trouble and Father not looking good at all," he had said.

Aaron had visited the farm on the Hawkesbury on his way home from Sydney, had been easy in his mind about the health of his mother, but his father, now seventy-three, had seemed drawn and pale, and when Aaron had checked him over, with Matthew shouting his objections the entire time, he had discovered a heart irregularity. Aaron had told Penelope, "It's the first time I ever shouted at my father. I told him to stop being childish and to listen to me. I ordered him to rest, stop walking through the fields. I told him about his heart irregularity, but he pooh-poohed that and was more concerned with the regularity of his bowels."

Now, as Aaron stood staring down the track, Jessica could see the creases in his forehead deepening and didn't know which he was thinking about: Eric's capture or his father's health. His hand went automatically to his left rib cage. He had broken his ribs three years ago while drafting cattle on the west run. He had tossed the loops of the catching rope over a mickey's head, and, at that moment, his horse stepped in a wombat hole and fell, causing him to flip over his head and land on his ribs.

"Ribs hurting you?" Penelope asked, now smiling. "All that fuss just to manage cattle." It was an old feud between the two of them, Aaron pretending still that he hated sheep and Penelope that she hated cattle, when actually each of them had come to terms with both animals long ago.

141

Aaron turned to her, and Jessica saw that gentle look in his eyes again. "Aye. I must have gotten soft during my trip east. And speaking of soft you should see Stuart Mays these days. Beard and all. I'm getting quite used to seeing beards now."

"Aaron Aylesbury, don't you go to thinking about growing one. I like your face just as it is."

"The better to read my thoughts, my dear?"

"Nonsense. I can read your thoughts without looking at you."

Jessica was still gazing down the track, watching the cattle, which had begun to bellow and part. As she squinted, she noticed that horsemen were moving against the cattle coming toward them down the track. "Father?"

Aaron turned to look at Jessica, then followed her gaze to the track.

The troopers came forward through the parting cattle on the track until they emerged from the mob and rode into the yard. Penelope and Aaron glanced at each other, and Jessica could see the worry in their glance. Was it Eric?

The troopers reined their horses and Captain Scantlin touched his cap, nodding to Penelope, Jessica, and Aaron. "G'day, Dr. Aylesbury," he said. While his eyes searched the house, the yard, the stable, the barns, he said, "I don't suppose you know that your son, Eric, has escaped jail?"

Penelope placed her hand on Aaron's arm, but Aaron narrowed his eyes at the trooper. "No, I didn't."

The trooper studied Aaron carefully, then grunted. "Some bloke aided 'is escape, doctor. The guard said 'e 'ad a pistol." The thought of a pistol caused Scantlin to glance around again.

"That's not possible," Aaron said softly, agonizingly.

The captain's searching eyes came back to fix on Aaron's face. "How else could 'e 'ave escaped?"

"No one's visited Eric in jail."

"No one but James Cranston. And it weren't 'e who gave 'im the pistol. I am a very careful man, doctor, an' I had Cranston searched well before 'e went in to question 'is nephew. About a 'orse 'e thinks 'e stole, by the by."

Aaron and Penelope glanced at each other. They must have been thinking the same thing Jessica was: that James would never suspect Eric of stealing a horse.

"Nay. I don't trust nobody, even Cranston." The captain's eyes went to Jessica, and he hitched at the front of his pants. "Well, we will have to search your premises, doctor."

Jessica knew what Aaron was thinking. The exclusionists had forced through a legislation that gave the police permission to search one's premises without a warrant.

Already the troopers were dismounting. Captain Scantlin slapped the dust from his trousers with his gloves as he approached the veranda. "We'll be gettin' on wi' it, then," he told Aaron.

Aaron said, "Be sure, sir, that you do the searching carefully. And if anything is broken or stolen, I'm holding you personally accountable."

The two men stared at each other. Dr. Aaron Aylesbury was a reasonably wealthy man and a respected one in the district. No man had ever crossed him as far as Jessica knew. And Captain Scantlin was not comfortable about it, either. But he smiled mockingly. "Aye," he said. Then his shifty gaze went to Jessica. Her skin crawled when his gaze dropped briefly to her breasts.

Penelope, Jessica, Aaron, Mrs. Chun, and Carrie stood

in the kitchen while the men went over the house, looking in all the rooms, under the beds, the pantry. Outside, they peered and poked around in the summer kitchen and storeroom. The stables and barns were searched by the men. When all was thoroughly gone over, the captain came to stand on the veranda where the family and their servants had gathered once more.

"Well," he said, "'e don't seem to be 'ere." He smiled again. "But don't worry. We'll find 'im." His eyes went to Jessica, and he gave that slight gesture to her when Aaron's eyes had gone briefly elsewhere. The gesture of a hand cupping her between her thighs; a gesture so slight that no one would have noticed had it not been for the fact that Jessica had endured it before, when she had ridden with the troopers from the cave after Eric's capture. The captain turned away, gave an order for the troopers to mount, and when he had mounted his horse himself, he looked down upon the family on the veranda.

Aaron caught the bridle of Scantlin's horse and said, "When you find him, then what?"

The trooper shrugged. "I don't know. Depends on whether 'e resists arrest again or not." He grinned, showing yellow teeth. "I have orders to shoot to kill, if 'e resists."

While the captain's eyes fixed on Jessica, Aaron said, "Captain, be sure you don't kill him." When the captain's eyes came back to rest on Aaron's face, Aaron continued, "Because if you do, I'll kill you."

Captain Scantlin's smirk faded as he saw the truth in Aaron's eyes. His eyes narrowed, and then, without a word, he reined his mount about, gave a wave of his hand to his men, and the troopers rode out of the yard toward the track to the south.

144

As they watched the troopers tearing down the track, Jessica was feeling sick. In her mind she was going over again where Eric might escape to this time. He had spoken of going south, possibly all the way to Melbourne in time. Although, as long as Melbourne was part of New South Wales, the troopers could track him there.

Jessica and Aaron exchanged looks, but it was Penelope trembling with anxiety who asked, "Do you think Eric can survive in the bush?"

Aaron's face was somber as he put his arm around his wife. Perhaps he was remembering the months of torment he had spent in the bush alone as a young man: the lack of water, lack of food. But he was also remembering that he had taught Eric how to survive in the bush. Even when Eric was only a lad of six, he had taken him on horseback into the bush and taught him how to find edible plants and how to find water. He had taught him how to make spears, slings, how to make a fire from flint and iron ore. Eric had even gone on a hunting expedition with his great Uncle Buck, the greatest bushman New South Wales had, even yet. "He'll survive," he said aloud, "even though he escaped no doubt without provisions of any kind. No weapons, no food, nothing."

They were just about to turn around and go back into the house when they saw a rider coming down the track from Bathurst. They paused when they recognized James. Jessica clenched her teeth. It was James who had caused all this. Penelope set her hands on her hips as she watched him ride into the yard, and Aaron's jaw set.

But James, solemn and easy as always, rode to the veranda, touched his hat, and dismounted. The three stared at him as he came to the veranda and propped his boot on the step. "The troopers just left?"

"Yes, and no thanks to you," Penelope snapped. She had never said a cross word to her brother in her life. And even now she softened under his benign gaze. "I don't know what's happening here, James."

Aaron had ridden to James's station when he had arrived from Sydney, to talk to him, to try to find out why he had betrayed Eric, but James had been away. *No tellin' how long he'll be gone, doctor. Maybe three, four days,* James's head stockman, Sam, had said. *Where did he go?* The stockman had shrugged. *Don't know. Sydney, I think.*

"I don't know why you led Scantlin to Eric, James," she said, her voice barely above a whisper, her face showing her pain, the pain of betrayal. "Eric is your own nephew."

"Penny, what do you think Eric's chances are in the bush alone?"

Jessica saw her stepmother frown, looking out on the track, pondering. "Better than in Bathurst jail, I suppose. Sooner or later I fear Scantlin is going to harm him." Penelope looked at her brother again. "And when he does, I'm going to hold you accountable."

James had his hat off and motioned with it toward her. "Penny, Eric's crime of resisting arrest would have brought a small fine at most, or a short jail sentence. Shooting a police officer is another matter, I grant you, but he could have worked it out, or we could have appealed. That's why I had him jailed. You know how I regard Eric. Don't you believe I wanted the best for him?"

As Jessica studied her Uncle James, the man she had adored all her life, she listened to his words and recognized only half-truths. His expression showed a lie.

His actions, his expression, his words, and his voice was a conglomeration of truths and lies, mixed up in a quiet, orderly man. She shook her head and turned to follow Penelope inside, but just before she did, she caught a look in Aaron's eye, a certain look of disbelief. And it occurred to her that perhaps Aaron had seen the real truth in James's eyes.

In the ensuing weeks, Penelope did not invite her brother into the house, but neither did James appear again on the place. The family heard no word from Eric. It was as if the bush had swallowed him whole.

Bathurst wasn't really a town. It was a settlement with scattered buildings, police headquarters, Government House, and on the outskirts of the town were the sheep and cattle stations of the pioneers who had followed the surveyor over the mountains and claimed the land. But Bathurst, located in the bowl of a lovely plain, at least had a market and a dry goods store where Penelope and Jessica were shopping while Aaron attended the auction of Ben Crawford's cattle.

The auction was being held in the cattle yards north of town. The agent who represented the mysterious buyer of Ben's sheep had not wanted to buy the cattle. Ben had thought it better to sell them to his neighbors anyway, who found it cheaper to buy his cattle than to go to Sydney to buy them.

Everyone in the district knew that Ben, like the rest of them, had invested all his capital in land and livestock, and had no ready cash with which to pay his fine. Since the fine was so high, Ben had to sell his livestock and most of his land to pay it.

147

Aaron had come to Bathurst to the auction. He didn't want to increase his stock of cattle this year because of the drought, but he intended to buy any stock Ben's neighbors didn't, to help Ben every way he could. There was no helping Eric. No one had any idea where he was, and to break the devastating gloom around their home, Aaron had allowed Penelope and Jessica to come along with him. But because men's language tended to be rough and drinking to be hard at these Bathurst cattle auctions, Aaron had suggested they not attend. They had decided to shop instead.

The dry goods store was a warehouse-type building made of slabs of wood and roofed with bark. All the goods in it were laid out on tables with no semblance of organization. Saddles were placed on the tables along with saddle blankets and tin kitchen utensils. Bolts of fabric gathered dust on the same tables with small farm tools. Penelope would pick up a bolt of fabric and moan with displeasure at the hole in the fabric which an awl had made, but she did not complain. Jessica had been raised in the Bathurst district and was not as distressed as Penelope over the lack of proper stores. But Penelope had been raised near Parramatta just fifteen miles from Sydney. Its shops were small but fairly well supplied with goods. And only a few hours over the track from Parramatta was Sydney where one could buy almost anything.

Penelope was shaking the dust from a bolt of blue broadcloth when Jessica heard the shouting outside the warehouse. Hurrying to the door, along with two other lady customers and the sleepy storekeeper, she and Penelope looked out at the dusty street and saw six riders galloping toward the store. As they came near, Jessica saw that they were the Schiller twins and four of their friends. Jessica stood on the boardwalk in front of the store, trying to make out what they were shouting about. The young men dashed by, glanced at her, and then reined their horses and came trotting back to her.

Jessica shaded her eyes and said, "What is all the shouting about?"

Reginald touched the brim of his hat and said, "Wanted to be the first to tell the news, Miss Jessica."

"What news?"

Reginald's horse danced under him as he thumbed the hat up away from his forehead. "Bushranger held up the stage near the inn on Mount York up in the mountains."

The ladies looked at each other and murmured. Men and women who had heard the shouting began to gather on the boardwalk, which was why Reginald and his friends had shouted and raced their horses in their hope to attract attention.

Mount York Inn was on the decent side of the pass over the mountains.

"Was it a government mail coach?" asked a man who had hurried up to join the ladies on the boardwalk.

Regie shook his head. "Nay, just a stage."

"Was the bushranger alone?" the storekeeper asked.

"Aye."

"He was dressed all in black," said Howey Dobbs. "Black everything."

"Face covered with a black neckerchief," Reginald said delightedly.

"How is it you know about it? We ain't heard nothin'," another man said, suspicious that the young rowdies were making the entire story up.

"Jim Webb came over the mountains on horseback.

Said he was at the inn when the coach stopped there right after it happened. Jim raced on ahead, and we saw him over close to Kelso where his horse went lame. He told us, so we came on ahead."

"Well, what happened? What did the highwayman take?" a woman demanded.

Reginald shifted in his saddle. "He rode up on a black horse, called out, 'Stand and hold!' The drover of the stagecoach stopped." Reginald went on to tell about how the highwayman had ordered the passengers out of the coach at gunpoint. As they lined up with their hands held high, the bushwhacker made the four men hand over their valuables. He examined their papers, too. "But funny thing, he didn't take anyone's valuables except Mr. Wallace's. Mr. Wallace was from Sydney and was carrying considerable coin and bank notes."

The crowd murmured among themselves.

"Bushwhacker took Wallace's money, then made all the men drop their trousers, so they couldn't chase him, I guess. Then he got back on his horse and rode off." Reginald touched the brim of his hat and grinned at Jessica. "Excuse me now. I best be gettin' on to the police station to alert the police."

"Yee-hi-i!" yelled Howey, and the four young men spurred their mounts and left the crowd on the boardwalk in a cloud of dust.

Jessica looked at Penelope, who sighed. "Dear heaven," Penelope said. "Just when we think we're civilized around here, we find out we're not. The pass over the mountains is heavily patrolled. You'd think it would be safe."

Jessica watched the Schiller twins come to a halt before the police station at the end of the street.

"We'll have to be going over that pass soon to the ball in Sydney, and to visit the Aylesburys. Aaron worries about his father. I hope they've caught the rogue by then," Penelope went on. "Well, come, Jessie. I did find a bolt of silk I can live with, so will you help me pick out some lace for it?"

Some feather of an idea, some phantom suspicion was teasing Jessica's mind, and she did not move for a moment.

"Wallace. Wallace," said a farmer on the boardwalk to another man as the crowd began to disperse. "Ain't he the agent that bought Ben Crawford's sheep?"

Jessica grabbed Penelope's arm. They looked at each other. No, their expressions said; no it couldn't be Eric. James then?

They met Aaron an hour later outside the church where they had parked their carriage. He came to them solemn and grumpy. It was not until they had climbed into the carriage, with Penelope on the driver's seat beside him and Jessica in the back, and had started back down the track for home that he told them, "Well, Ben's cattle were all bought by settlers." His sheep had already been purchased and most of his land by the land agent. "Now ol' Ben's right back where he started. Only a few acres of land, and no livestock. He lost the acreage that had the spring on it and is isolated on land with not one running creek."

"You saw him, Aaron?" Penelope asked, laying a hand on his arm.

"At the auction." Aaron shook Summerfield's reins. "I tell you, Penny, the graziers around here are up a gum tree. They're furious, going to have a meeting in town tonight about the high fines and these kangaroo courts

151

that are filled with exclusionists."

"You heard about the bushwhacking?"

"Aye."

"The bushwhacker took only one man's papers and valuables."

"Oh, say what?"

"A man named Wallace."

Aaron frowned at the road ahead, then looked at her. "Wallace is the name of the land agent who bought Ben out."

"Yes. I know."

He stared at Penelope for a long moment, then faced ahead again. "Heeyi, Summerfield," he said.

And Jessica did not fail to notice the lilt in his voice.

The agent who had represented the land purchaser in buying Ben's sheep and land had been robbed of monies with which he had planned to pay for stockmen for the new Stone Sheep Company (Ben's old station) but he was able to hire men anyway, mostly natives, as stockmen. Within a week after Ben's auction at Bathurst, Stone Sheep Station was abuzz with workmen. Paddocks, yards, and a wool shed were being built in preparation for a shipment of sheep to be overlanded from the other side of the mountains.

Meantime, Jessica had had enough of waiting and donned her royal-blue riding suit—impractical for the track, but attractive—and rode to James Cranston's station.

This station near Bathurst was where she was born to Annabelle Moffett Aylesbury. Here Jessica had grown up. Here Penelope and Eric had come from over the mountains with their sheep to join Aaron forever. Jessica rode into the yard. Outbuildings were everywhere now, stables, cow sheds, convict's huts, a blacksmith shop. In the outback a station had to be self-sufficient as there were few trades in the district even yet. The yard was a foot deep in foot-pounded, drought-starved brown dust. Chickens pecked at invisible seeds and dashed about after insects along the fence near the big gum tree. The sound of hammer on anvil came to her, and the distant sound of a native stockman calling, "Coo-oo-ee."

She nodded and waved to the ringers who greeted her and reined Chelsea beside the mounting block. As she dismounted, she saw James striding toward her, his brown moleskin trousers tight on his thighs, his blue shirt open at the neck, his hat pulled low over his brow.

"Jessica," he called, flashing his white teeth.

She said nothing, but waited, holding Chelsea's reins.

"Morning," he said touching his hat.

"Good morning." Her eyes flashed as she glanced about her. "The place seems busier each time I visit."

James put all his weight on one foot, propped the other on the mounting block, and looked about him. "We just finished muster."

"Oh yes," she said looking at him squarely. "You are late this year with your own muster because you lent your ringers to help Ben."

James's dark eyes studied her a moment before he said, "Aye. That's true."

"Mm. Aaron came to see you a few days ago. Sam said you were away. To Sydney, he thought."

"Aye, Sydney."

"It's a wonder you weren't bushwhacked," she said with a smile. "There's a bushranger preying on the

153

coaches on the road over the mountains. But I guess you heard about that."

James grinned. "I heard." He took his boot off the block and fell into step beside her as she led Chelsea toward the shade of the gum tree. Christmas had come and gone quietly. It was January and an ungodly hot midsummer. Once she was in the shade, she removed her hat and fanned her face, unaware that her eyes were very blue in her summer-tanned face. That her lips were full and moist, that the curling tendrils of her hair framed her cheeks, touched pink from the heat of the track.

James didn't take his eyes from her face as she stirred the stew of thought around in her mind. Suddenly she looked up at him. "Have you a black horse, James?"

He smiled. "No. And Jessie, I'm not the bushwhacker. Not a bushranger either." He grinned. "Come inside for a cup of tea. Hambone always keeps a pot—"

"I'm not here on a social call."

His grin ceased. "No?"

"Is it Eric?"

"Who?"

"The bushwhacker." She studied his expression for a sign of the truth. But James's face was as inscrutable as ever. "I tell you, James. If it is, we should know."

James shook his head. "Jessica, you're not making sense. Why would Eric bail up a coach, and why would I know about it if he did?"

The ideas and suspicions stewing in her brain were still an unorganized mess and she shook her head. "I don't know." She turned away from him. "It's just that suddenly there are so many unanswered questions. About you, about Eric. But if you know anything at all—"

Ku-ku-ku-wah-wah-wah, laughed a kookaburra in the trees overhead.

She looked back at James whose face had gone completely blank. "I'm confused about what you're asking me, Jessica." He spread his arms wide. "I'm just the same as ever. Busy is all. I told you why I had Eric jailed. For his safety."

She pressed her lips together.

Suddenly a spark leapt in his eye. "Marry me, Jessica, and you'll know everything I do, everywhere I go."

Jessica turned and put her boot in Chelsea's stirrup. James aided her a little as she swung into the sidesaddle.

"Does this mean no?" he said, a smile tugging at the corners of his mouth.

"You know it does, James." She started to rein Chelsea away, but paused. "Something strange is going on with you, James, and if it involves Eric, I— Tell him—"

James spread his hands over his chest and shook his head. "Jessie, I swear to God. I don't know where Eric is."

She swallowed when she saw the truth in his eyes and turned Chelsea toward the track. As she set the mare at a lope down the track, which wound across the flat, grass-covered plain, sprinkled with stands of eucalypti, she realized that she was more confused now than ever.

But one thing was clear to her. James had proposed marriage to her before. But this time, it seemed to have been a parry, a thrust to distract her mind from pursuing the mystery of whatever was happening with him—or with whatever was happening to Eric.

There *was* something strange going on. And again the men were playing their games.

And again the women were waiting.

In the weeks that followed, the family still heard no word from Eric. Troopers passed the Aylesbury station occasionally on forays into the bush. Jessica could hardly believe that the black trackers could not find Eric.

155

In the meantime, the identity of the unknown buyer who had bought Ben's land and sheep overlanded eighty prize merinos to the Stone Sheep Station. Aaron raged. But soon his rage turned to tentative amusement.

Peter Mayo left the hot, stuffy, bark hut which he and the ringers had built on the new station. He had to relieve himself. He and the others had been playing a new game, poker, and he'd dropped out of the game because he'd kept losing hands. He could hear the others laughing and hooting inside. A faint glow of the whale oil lantern shown through the window, but just a few feet from the hut, the yard was dark.

Over to the north was the stream which trickled out of the hill where the spring was, and he could hear the toads croaking there, even above the clicking and churring of the night insects.

His shepherd's ear listened for the bell of the lead sheep grazing in the paddock as he sent a copious stream against a gum tree. But he didn't hear the bell. When he had finished, he frowned and turned his head toward the paddock. No moon tonight. Couldn't see anything. But a man ought to be able to see sheep, as white as they— He started limping toward the paddock, and the closer he came to it, the more alarmed he became. His eyes widened in his fat face and his mouth opened. The gate of the paddock was open, and there was not a sheep inside.

He turned suddenly, but halfway around an arm clamped over his throat, and he heard the breath of a man in one ear and the click of a pistol hammer in the other.

"One sound, mate, and the crows'll have station-boss brains for breakfast."

156

Mayo gagged and rolled his eyes. "Who—"

"A man gets hungry, mate, so I took the liberty of skinning one of your merinos. Got me enough meat for a week."

"Them are valuable animals. The judge— What I mean is, y'er a bloody bushranger."

The bushranger released him suddenly and with pistol in hand, motioned toward the paddock. "The ewe I skinned is there. Pick it up and put it on my horse."

Terrified, Mayo did as he was told, thinking he had surprised the bushranger while skinning the sheep. He did as he was told, because he didn't have any loyalties to his employer. Hadn't even met his employer. Besides, the bushranger had a desperate look in his eye and would probably just as soon kill him as not. He wrapped the skinned animal in the canvas it was lying on and tied it on the back of the bushranger's horse. There was another bag on there, too, stamped Sydney Mercantile.

"Say now, fellow," Mayo said. "That's our bloody bag."

"I took the liberty of relieving you of some of your flour and a few other dainties for the palate. Now get over there." The bushranger motioned toward the post where the station bell hung.

Mayo rolled his eyes. "What er ye going to do?"

"Go on, move!" The bushranger poked him in the side with the pistol, and Mayo stumbled to the post.

In ten seconds he was firmly tied to it with his own belt and was relieved to see the bushranger mount his horse.

"One thing before you go," Mayo said. "Where are the bloody jumbucks?"

The whites of the bushranger's eyes flashed. "No telling." Then he reined his horse about and thundered out of the yard.

Gone. All of his employer's merinos. Run off the hills, no doubt. The bushranger had caused a breakaway. Sheep would be dashing wild and scared over a cliff somewhere. And he, Peter Mayo, would be fired sure. When he no longer heard the hoofbeats of the bushranger's horse, Mayo bawled out for the others: "Breakaway! Help! Breakaway! Breakawa-aa-ay!"

Chapter IX

Aaron, Penelope, and Jessica had worried about whether Eric could get along in the bush alone. Now they were almost certain he was managing very well.

The prize merino sheep on Ben's old acreage were duffed one night in early January by a bushranger on a black horse. The mob of eighty jumbucks disappeared without a trace. The graziers in the Bathurst district were worried. They knew that the outlaw Riley gang was about, but they had not thought that the gang would come back to the district so soon after being chased into the bush after the episode with the Chisholm girls. But Boombinny, the police's crack tracker, followed the tracks of the stolen sheep from the Stone Sheep Station and scratched his head in bewilderment. For their tracks simply disappeared when they came to the road. Besides that, there was only one set of horse tracks with them. While the graziers set extra watches on their own livestock, another disturbing thing happened. Aaron was having a glass of stringybark beer with Dick Lawson on his station when the Schiller twins rode into the yard surrounded by their usual crowd of dust and friends. Aaron and Lawson went out onto Lawson's veranda and squinted out at the twins.

"Highway robbery, highway robbery," Reginald shouted with delight.

Aaron and Lawson stepped off the veranda at the same time, thinking that the Riley gang was at it again, but Reginald said, "You know the man who's boss at the new station over on Crawford's old land? What's his name?"

"Mayo," Aaron said irritably. "What about him?"

"Well, Mayo had ordered goods to build a wood shed with, and it was coming down the track early this morning by dray. When all of a sudden out of the bush came a single rider, held up the driver, made him step out of his trousers. The robber stole his trousers, turned over the dray, set the horses loose, took what goods he needed and set fire to the rest, then disappeared into the bush again."

Reginald was breathless with his speech, and the longer he talked the more excited he became.

"My God," Lawson said and caught the bridle of Reginald's horse which was tossing its head and turning, feeling the excitement, too. "You say it was only one man?"

Reginald nodded.

By this time Aaron was near the horse, too, and demanded, "What did the man look like?"

Now Reginald's face really lit up. "The driver, man named Criswell, said he was dressed in a black shirt and black broadcloth trousers, and a black felt hat. And he had a black kerchief over his nose and mouth. Rode a black horse."

Aaron and Lawson stared at the Schiller twin,

unbelieving. Few bushrangers dared operate alone. Most were in gangs. Aaron did not let his thoughts focus on anything, but he felt his scalp crawling. He shook his head visibly at the suspicion that kept begging entrance into his brain.

The next day Aaron and Jessica were returning from the McKenzie station, where old Mrs. McKenzie had been suffering a stroke but had become conscious in the morning. They met Rosco McKenzie, who had been to Bathurst for supplies on the track leading toward the Aylesbury house. Aaron drew the carriage to a halt when he saw Rosco.

"How's me Mum?" Rosco asked first, his horse dancing under him.

"She's conscious, but there may be paralysis on the left side, Rosco."

Rosco nodded, and it became clear that he had something else on his mind at the moment. "You'd better watch out on your travels on the track now, doc. There's that bushranger around, you know."

Jessica glanced at Aaron and he nodded. "Yes, I know."

"It's getting serious now. Judge Livingston from over in Sydney was visiting Bathurst lately. Just this morning when he was riding down the track from Bathurst to look at some land, he and his entire party were held up. It was that bushranger again. Made Livingston give him all his money, his rings, and everything. Didn't bother the rest of the party, but he made the gentlemen give him their trousers, even in front of the ladies." Rosco blushed.

Aaron struggled to keep his face straight. "How did Livingston take it?"

"Folks say he's mad as a bull in ruttin' season—er,

beggin' your pardon, Miss Jessica. Went into the police station and gave the captain what for, he did, for not being able to catch the bloke. So you be careful, doc. You, too, Miss Jessica. For there's no telling where the bludger will strike next."

Aaron nodded. "We'll be careful, Rosco. Thank you."

When they were moving again, Aaron glanced at Jessica, and she met his glance. But neither of them spoke their mind. Because their suspicion was not yet full blown.

Summer heat was searing and dry, but fall was just a month or so away. Already the sheep in the high pastures were wooly again. The rams and the ewes were copulating with vigor this season, an event which brought smiles to Penelope's lips. For Aaron, the hardest work with the cattle was over, and the ringers spent most of their days riding and mending fences. Olif, Aaron's horse tailer, spent his days breaking brumbies and training them for stock horses. But mostly the men were idle.

Jessica helped Mrs. Chun and Carrie can vegetables and fruits for a few days, but most of the days she wandered aimlessly about. For the first time in her life she felt restless, useless, as if she were waiting for something big to happen, but that something never came. She thought often of Eric. She thought of how she loved him, reliving over and over again their night in the cave in the mountains. Surely, surely, she reasoned, some good could come out of this, that he would not end his days hunted and jailed like a common bushranger. In her most secret thoughts, she wondered if the bushranger in black was Eric. She had realized, after a few reports of his escapades, that the daring bushranger had not bothered anyone in the district but Mayo, who was station boss on the Stone (Livingston?) station, the land agent, and Livingston himself. Retaliation for what Livingston had done to Ben Crawford? It sounded just like Eric. The bushranger was considered daring by the men and dashing by the women. She did not know how much his escapades fired the imaginations of the women until she went to the birthday ball in Sydney.

The colony of New South Wales was sixty-three years old this year. On January 27, 1788 Arthur Philip set the first British flag on the soil where Sydney town now stood, claiming the land for Britain in the name of the king. He had been captain of the "First Fleet" which had brought the very first eight hundred seventy-one prisoners from the jails and hulks of England to the shores of the mysterious southern continent then called New Holland. Every year since, someone had given a party in honor of that day. This year, the Aylesburys were invited to an enormous ball given by Aaron's old solicitor friend, Stuart Mays, who owned Penmark, south of Sydney. The large rectangular home had belonged to Penelope and Mark Aylesbury, but Penelope had sold it to Judge Mays when Aaron's aunt, Franny, who had been living in the house and keeping it up, moved to her own smaller home upon the death of her husband, Rolph.

Jessica had turned down several young men's offers to escort her to the ball, most of them from around the Bathurst district who were friends of Mays, but had accepted the invitation of Jory McWilliams, her father's bachelor friend, who was at least twenty years her senior and a friend of Stuart Mays.

The Aylesburys' trip to Sydney began as a family holiday. The family had been worried and depressed over

163

Eric's situation for weeks, and Aaron had decided that they must go on to the ball as they had done every year since he and Penelope had married. Penelope was getting thin and haggard, and Jessica was short tempered. Aaron reasoned that he had better do something before both his own worry and the women's moods drove him mad. Besides, he couldn't delay checking on his father any longer.

Jessica packed her trunk and had Stringybark Joe take it down to the veranda. The ringer grunted and moaned, pretending that the trunk was so heavy he could barely lift it, and Jessica, smiling and pulling on her gloves, followed behind him down the stairs. Outside, the sun, still low in the eastern sky, was already hot.

Ringers were placing Penelope's trunk and Aaron's valise in the dray which would accompany the Aylesbury carriage across the mountains to the Hawkesbury district. Jessica was experiencing a mixture of emotions. She was feeling excited to see her grandfather and her grandparents who lived in the Hawkesbury area, but uneasy, somehow, about leaving home. She turned and looked toward the west, then as far south as she could see. The hills rolled, dotted with blue-green gum trees; rolled to a horizon, too blue and too hazy to see. Out there was the bush, and somewhere, Eric. She was certain now that the dashing bushranger who had plagued the district was Eric. She looked at Aaron, who was watching her, and wondered how much he guessed about Eric.

Aaron spoke. "When I was lost in the bush twenty-eight years ago, I had walked and struggled for miles until I came to a hill. I saw a horizon that looked much like that does this morning," he told her. "It looked like water there, and I thought perhaps I had been near the sea. I know now that it was the Murrumbidgee, that the haze was caused by the river and its plain." He smiled at her and offered his arm. "I only guessed that the land there was good pasture and perhaps well watered. Eric can find water no matter where he is."

Jessica walked with him to the waiting carriage where Penelope sat, also staring south. The frown smoothed out on Jessica's forehead as she smiled. "Do you think he has gone south then?" she asked.

Aaron paused beside the carriage and took her elbow in his hand, looked down into her face, his brown eyes steady on hers. "No," he said.

Jessica climbed into the carriage with Penelope and settled her skirts around her. Both women were dressed in drab colors for travel and had left off their crinolines for the trip. Penelope's dress was dark green broadcloth with a plain V neck bereft of ruffles. The long slender sleeves would keep her arms from sunburning, even under the canopy of the gig.

Jessica was dressed for the ordeal in dark blue which matched her eyes, and the coal shuttle-shaped bonnet tied securely under her chin. Both women's bonnets were straw so that air could circulate through them to keep their heads cool. They had removed the flowers and bird ornaments and had left only the ribbon.

Penelope looked at Jessica's costume and approved. "Well," she said, "we aren't very stylish, but we'll be more comfortable."

"Lucky for us we really don't need corsets," Jessica replied. They laughed. No one would know that neither of them were wearing corsets. They would don those when they got to Aaron's parents' farm and not until. As

Aaron mounted the carriage seat in front and picked up the reins, Jessica was thinking again how fortunate she was to have a stepmother who was more like a friend than a parent. She and Penelope had always gotten along, but she understood that Penelope had liked her mother, even though she had married Aaron.

The carriage moved forward. Bart Simms would follow them, driving the small cart which held their luggage. Two other ringers were following on horseback armed with weapons, in case of encounters with bushrangers or natives. The stockmen would enjoy a holiday, a drunken one, probably, in Sydney, while the family attended their ball.

The women rode in comparative comfort down the track to Bathurst. Much of the track stretched over flat land, but other parts of it climbed hills and descended into small vales, bare mostly, save for the tall waving gray-green grasses and occasional clumps of gum trees. This was called the plains, and the bush could be seen in the distance, covering the hills and following creek banks. They would ascend into the foothills this very day and camp somewhere on the Macquarie Plains.

The family rode near the Schiller farm, and Jessica could see Aaron shaking his head. The vines were withering in the fields from lack of rain. Schiller had located his farm near a creek, but it had never occurred to the German that in this new, strange country, creeks did not always run water. Not even in his most depressing imaginings did it occur to him that not every river ran all the time, nor every creek. Grapevines needed high, dry ground, and Schiller had been delighted with his high acreage. Someone had reminded him that droughts were all too common here in the outback, but Schiller had said pshaw to that. "I vill get my sons to dig irrigation ditches from ze creek," he had said. Now the creek was dry, the irrigation ditches caving in, and Schiller's carefully tended vines were almost dead from the drought.

As they came abreast of the farm, Jessica could see the Schiller twins chopping wood. The lads paused and raised a hand in greeting. Now it was Jessica who shook her head, wondering what would become of those two young men.

Penelope was fanning her face and waving away the torturous flies by the time they went through Bathurst. On the street vendors were selling fruits from their orchards. "The peach crop seems pitifully small this year," Penelope said.

Then the track turned almost due east. Ahead, the foothills to the Great Dividing Range loomed high and sapphire colored. Jessica noticed Penelope's entranced bemusement at the hills, remembering that, as children, she and Aaron had pretended they were exploring the Blue Mountains which Aaron had sworn to find a way through. But Blaxland and Wentworth and Lawson had beat him to it, finding a way through them before Aaron was old enough to.

They camped the first night on the plains. The second day they climbed into the mountain range. The road was still rough, hewn out of the sides of the mountains by convict labor in the year 1813, and the view was spectacular. Except for the clanking and clattering of gear, the horses' hooves, the rattle of wheels on the rocky road, there was no sound. When they paused to rest, the quiet was awesome. Jessica had crossed the mountains four times before, but they never ceased to astound her with their beauty, their wildness and grandeur.

On the fifth morning after they left Bathurst, they came down out of the foothills of the Blue Mountains and beheld below the flood plain of the Hawkesbury River, now checkerboarded with farms and orchards. Here, the drought had not been so severe, and Jessica was enamored by the green.

Down the well-worn track from Windsor, they rode and at last beheld the Aylesbury farm.

It was enormous, spreading nine hundred acres across some of the most fertile country in New South Wales. The house, now painted white, was surrounded by orchards and wheat fields. A pumpkin patch lay to the side of the road. Beyond, Jessica knew that Great-Uncle Thaddeus Crawford had his horse farm. Down closer to the river Great-Uncle Owen had his landing and furniture manufactury. To the west and south was the elder Ben Crawford's dairy farm. And to the west, over that ridge where a stand of gum trees grew, was Penelope's father's farm, where she had been born and had grown up. After the ball was over in Sydney, they planned to spend some time with Oliver Cranston as well as with the Aylesbury clan.

Family. Jessica was so exhausted from the trip that the rest of the day was a blur to her. The greeting in the yard by Milicent, Aaron's mother, a slender handsome woman despite her years, with her snowy hair neatly smoothed back from her face and caught in a bun at the back of her head. Her back was as straight as the day she had taken over the running of the farm at the age of eighteen. And Matthew came out onto the veranda, smiling, waving, bent over a little with arthritic complaints, and for all of his seventy-three years, he was handsome still. Jessica swore to herself that he had the bluest eyes and the whitest hair she had ever seen, and though he tended to be a bit gruff, she liked him. Milicent and Matthew Aylesbury were actually her great-grandaunt and uncle, but Jessica had grown up calling them Grandmother and Grandfather.

Milicent embraced Penelope and then her son, Aaron, then Jessica. Matthew embraced his daughter-in-law, Penelope, shook hands with his son, then embraced Jessica. As he held her at arm's length, he studied her face. "Ah, Jessie," he said. "Tell me, do you still want to be a doctor, lass?"

Jessica sighed within herself. Matthew had always thought it amusing—and perhaps a little fascinating— that she, a woman, had such aspirations.

Now Jessica looked up into his laughing, crystal-blue eyes and replied, "Very much so, Grandfather."

He looked a bit taken aback for a moment but recovered and asked, "Have you heard anything more about Eric?"

Aaron had had to tell his father about Eric when he had come through earlier in the month. Now Aaron shook his head. "Not that we're sure of."

Jessica watched the lines in Matthew's face deepen. "Ah, I had hoped I would see him again before . . ." Jessica also saw Aaron's head snap around to look at his father again. But Matthew was ushering them all upon the veranda, shouting orders for his hired help to put the ringers up in the cabins and take care of the horses. And Milicent was showing them into the cool house which smelled pleasantly of baking breads and cakes and pies, ham, and roast turkey. And soon Jessica was shown her room, a pleasant room which looked east.

Sleep came early to them all that evening after an

enormous meal. Next morning, they climbed into the carriage again to head down the track for Sydney. It was about a three hour trip, so they started early. Matthew and Milicent had been invited to Stuart's ball, but they had sent their regrets. It was too long a trip, they said. Too long a trip for Matthew and Milicent? Jessica wondered about that, and she could tell that Aaron was wondering, too.

The Aylesburys had sent word ahead to reserve rooms at the Milton Tavern, a prestigious hotel, where they rested and changed clothes in preparation for the ball that night.

While Jessica and Penelope helped each other into their hoops and crinolines, they talked and laughed like sisters. "When I was your age," Penelope said, "fashions were altogether different than they are today. We wore those slim dresses with the low bosoms and slim skirts which were supposed to look like clothes that the Greeks and Romans wore. Now look at this. Skirts are so heavy and full that it takes a cage of wire and crinoline to support them. At least we don't have to wear as many petticoats as we would have to do to get this fullness. Can you imagine what that would be like?"

They giggled while Penelope helped Jessica pull the full billowing skirts down over her head. Jessica bit her bottom lips as she tried to catch her breath from Penelope's having to tie the corset so tightly. And now she hoped the dress fit as well as it had last year when she had Aunt Fran Danbury make it. She put her hands on her hips, took in her breath and held it while Penelope buttoned the bodice in back.

"Perhaps we should have brought Carrie with us to help. But I am so used to doing things for myself now that

I didn't think about it. Do you suppose she thinks it odd?"

Jessica shook her head. "No. Carrie has no attachments for Sydney, or anything else in New South Wales, for that matter."

Penelope arranged the voluminous skirts over the crinoline and wire cage which the women called hoops. "I do hope Milicent and Matthew will forgive us for attending the ball, with Eric in such straits. But Aaron and I decided to take Stuart's advice, to behave as if our son had done nothing wrong, which he hasn't. Had we refused to attend the ball, Stuart said, it would be almost an admission of Eric's guilt, for we have never in all our life not participated in the anniversary ball in Sydney. To behave as if Eric is just away on a trip, as if there was nothing amiss, was best for Eric's sake. You do agree, don't you, Jessica?"

Jessica by then was making attempts at repairing the curls, which had become disarranged when she pulled the dress over her head. "I feel guilty to even pretend to have fun when Eric's in trouble. But you're right. If he is apprehended and goes to trial, the jury is much more apt to be lenient if we, his next of kin, take what he did lightly and not make a terrible thing of it."

Jory McWilliams arrived for Jessica at the tavern at half past seven. Jory was a redheaded Irishman, one of the colony's currency lads, but he had made his mark in the East India trade and was considered "well-off" by those who knew in Sydney. He was indeed twenty-one years older than Jessica but still handsome in his way. Standing barely taller than Jessica, still redheaded, with red mutton chop whiskers, he arrived for her dressed in a fashionable dark-blue broadcloth frock coat with match-

171

ing trousers, and contrasting waistcoat of ivory and a gleaming white shirt ruffled down the front. He wore a tall black beaver hat and carried a cane. They made a striking couple riding down the streets of Sydney in the hour just before dark.

The carriage was a gig drawn by one white horse and driven by an Aboriginal whom Jory called Happy. While Jessica arranged her skirts on the seat she frowned to herself, wondering why men found it so necessary to give the natives nicknames which made them sound like naughty children rather than men and women.

Sydney, New South Wales, the largest town on the continent, had grown since she had seen it last. The streets were packed dirt and rutted where the drays had passed. The Victorian gothic structures which were the courthouse and the long Rum Hospital still stood on Macquarie Street as they passed. Carriages much like Jory's plied the streets, and elegant ladies and gentlemen sat in them or walked along the walks, going to their own balls and parties. Hogs and geese no longer roamed the streets, nor did the convicts. Jessica remembered in her youth the convicts in chains roaming about in their yellow or gray jackets.

"Tell me, Jessica, have you heard from Eric of late?" Jory asked now as the carriage passed through a neighborhood of tall white houses. The little wattle and daub huts had mostly vanished now, and the tall rectangular, European houses painted white, mostly, sporting red tiled roofs, had taken their places, surrounded by picket fences with imported European flowers, hollyhocks, geraniums, and roses planted in the yards.

"No. We've not heard of him lately," she replied

simply. But he was on her mind constantly. And inside she wept for him, for his plight, that she could not see him, be with him. Oh how she wished that it were Eric in this seat beside her this night. Yet here she sat, not knowing whether he had gone to Melbourne or remained in the Bathurst district. In her rational mind, however, she knew. She knew Eric was the one who harassed Livingston and duffed his sheep. She did not know what a legend he had become until at the ball that evening.

Penmark. Jessica wondered what thoughts were passing through Penelope's head as she approached the rectangular, white-painted brick house with its veranda all across the front and its white columns. This had been the home, new then, to which Mark Aylesbury had brought his bride, Penelope. Here they had lived, wept, fought, and here Eric had been born. The house hadn't aged much, but the gum trees in the yard had grown much larger, and behind the house the paddocks stretched, surrounding the wool shed Penelope had bought and paid for with her inheritance.

Tonight the house was alight with lanterns and bedecked with flowers and banners for the ball. As Jory's carriage pulled into the yard, it seemed that the entire town of Sydney had come, though Jessica knew that only Stuart's "crowd" were in attendance: currency lads, sons and daughters of emancipated convicts, or poorer free settlers. The exclusionist crowd still, after sixty-five years, did not deign to mix socially with them.

Jessica's heart lightened somewhat and she danced five dances before she chose to sit with several other ladies in a circle at the edge of the dance floor in the large reception room. Penelope was the center of attention, because she had been popular here in her day with the

173

currency lasses, now matured and dowagered. These ladies had grown up wearing the Greek and Roman dresses Penelope had described earlier, and having to wear hoops and volumes of material made them uneasy.

When Jessica took the punch Jory had given her and joined the ladies, they nodded and smiled politely to her and made room for her amongst them. The dowagers and older women remarked about how lovely her dress was, how lovely she was, and Jessica knew that not one of them had forgotten that she was Annabelle Moffett and Aaron's *illegitimate* daughter. Only Jessica sipped her punch, smiling to herself, because they did not know that she was not Aaron's daughter but Deen Crawford's. She did not miss their probing eyes, going over her features looking for Annabelle's. They did not see any of Annabelle's features in Jessica at all, and certainly— their eyes made a pass over her full bosom and tiny waist—not her mother's figure. However they did see a resemblance to Aaron. In the darkness of her complexion. Her tendency toward tallness. Yes, they saw Aaron in her certainly. And Jessica smiled, knowing if she resembled Aaron, it was as his cousin, and not as his daughter at all.

Mrs. Reese leaned toward Penelope. "You must tell me about how the station is doing these days, Penelope. Are your sheep prospering as you had hoped?"

"Oh yes. Better," Penelope replied.

Jessica listened and exchanged smiles with the girls her own age and was amazed how the ladies wanted to ask about Eric but did not dare. Instead, their conversation did a little dance around it, hoping either Penelope or Jessica would offer information about Eric's plight. But they did not. Jessica meantime saw Penelope's eyes roaming the room, going perhaps up the stairs to the bedrooms. Was she remembering? Two spots of high color appeared on Penelope's cheeks. What did it mean? Her green eyes snapped and then grew soft. There must have been awful moments spent here with Mark, but perhaps better ones, too.

Jessica's own eyes roamed the room. Here, Eric had spent the first six years of his life. Jessica caught herself choking back tears as she imagined Eric as a child in this place.

But her attention was brought back when Mrs. Farnsworth, dressed in black frock and shining white pearls, leaned forward and said, "Tell me, Penelope, what is the latest on the bushranger in your district?"

Penelope pretended puzzlement. "Bushranger?"

"Oh you know, the *new* bushranger, the one who dresses all in black and appears and disappears like magic."

Penelope shook her head. "Nothing lately."

Young Miss Fry leaned forward. "Tell me. Have you heard whether or not he's handsome?"

Mrs. Pickle said, "Tut, Emily. How can anyone tell if he's handsome if he has a neckerchief tied over his face."

The ladies giggled.

"Well," began Stuart May's mother, shaking her head. "I for one hope the police don't catch him. Stuart heard just today from a farmer who came over from Bathurst that the police have captured the Riley gang. Can you imagine? After all this time. Somehow, they located the gang's hideaway in the mountains south of Bathurst and the Bathurst police slipped up on them."

"Oh dear, were any of them killed?" queried Miss Fry.

"There are nine in the gang, or I should say were.

175

Three were shot to death, Stuart tells me, and the rest were taken to Bathurst jail."

"There'll be a quick trial for those men, let me tell you," said Mrs. Pickle. "That gang of cutthroats doesn't deserve to live."

"Aye. They've committed every crime including . . ." Miss Tanner's fan paused, and the ladies exchanged meaningful looks.

This irritated Jessica and she said, "Rape."

All the ladies drew in their breaths except for Penelope and Mrs. Mays, who nodded sagely.

"But that's not like this new bushranger," Mrs. Tanner said. "He's gallant to the ladies. And I'm quite sure, by the descriptions of him, that he's young and quite handsome."

"That's what I heard," said Miss Fry, suddenly fanning rapidly. "I heard that he has black hair and black eyebrows and dark flashing eyes. That he's the perfect gentleman to the ladies. And he never takes from the poor, only from the rich."

"Bosh," said old Mrs. Castlemaigne. "The only reports I've heard is that he has taken only from the exclusionists."

Jessica met Penelope's gaze, and she realized suddenly that Penelope knew. At that moment, the question was settled in Jessica's mind, too. Eric was the "new" bushranger. "Oh dear God," she said aloud.

The ladies looked at her quickly. Jessica covered her mouth with her fan, for ladies did not swear. She smiled quickly at them and said, "It just occurred to me that Eric was born in this house."

"Indeed. I remember when he was born," replied Mrs. Farnsworth, whom Jessica knew had been infatuated

176

with Mark in her day. "He was rather premature, wasn't he, Penelope?" Fanning rapidly, she smiled sweetly.

"Rather," Penelope replied with a smile just as sweet.

Though the older women's conversation turned to other things, the younger ones still talked about the dashing, daring bushranger, the modern day Robin Hood, and all the while Jessica was in a daze. Eric. Oh Eric. When will I see you again?

Jessica was dancing a reel when the messenger came. She saw him approach Aaron, and a few moments later she caught a glimpse of Aaron bending over Penelope, still seated with the circle of ladies. Next she saw his eyes roaming the dance floor seeking her out. The reel came to a halt then, and Jessica went directly to him.

Aaron caught her sleeve, his face twisted with worry. "Jessie, we've gotten word that Father is very ill."

Jessica felt her scalp prickle, and no more needed to be said. Aaron made his apologies to Stuart for leaving early, to Jory for Jessica, as Jessica and Penelope gathered their wraps from the parlor suite.

Then the Aylesbury carriage hurried through the black night toward Sydney. Trunks would have to be hurriedly packed, and the family would ride all night toward the Aylesbury farm.

No one said anything, but all were thinking the same thing. If anything happened now to Matthew Aylesbury, Eric could not be there. It would be a terrible blow to Aaron. Jessica knew that he was weeping silently in the night.

Chapter X

Already exhausted from their four-day journey over the mountains, and the three-hour trip to Sydney, Penelope and Jessica were barely able to make the thirty miles back to the Aylesbury farm that evening. Aaron for once was relentless. If he thought of their comfort, or their exhaustion, he gave no indication of it, driving the poor horse down the road, giving no rest to it or to the ringers who had accompanied them across the mountains and to Sydney. They were disgruntled anyway for having to cut their time in Sydney short to accompany the Aylesbury carriage back to the farm. Aaron feared that his father might be gone before he arrived.

But when they drove into the Aylesbury yard, they were greeted by the servants and hastened inside where Aaron, Penelope, and Jessica could tell by looking at Milicent's face that Matthew was still alive.

Aaron rushed into the door ahead of the women, unable to wait for them to gather skirts and reticules and fans, and he had just met his mother in the entrance hall saying, "Mum?" when Jessica stepped inside.

Milicent's face was lined with worry but remained serene. "He is resting," she told Aaron as she gripped his arms and looked up into his face.

"What happened, Mum?"

"Come into the parlor, Aaron, and you, too, Penelope and Jessica." Milicent led them into the parlor and ordered the native woman to bring tea, as they sat down in the parlor suite. Quietly she sat down and folded her long slender hands in her lap. She looked first at Penelope. "Do not blame your father, whatever happens, Penelope. I don't. For it wasn't his fault."

Jessica saw Penelope's face pale even more and remembered how Penelope's father, Oliver Cranston, and Matthew had been enemies for years. It was Oliver who had caused Matthew to be transported from England back in 1801.

"For you see, Penelope, some of your father's cattle wandered into our wheat field near the ridge."

Jessica remembered the ridge, an upheaval in the land which ran along the property between the Cranstons and the Aylesburys.

"Matthew took his horse and drove the cattle back over the ridge at the same time that Oliver was tracking the cattle, and it seems they met on the Cranston side. They had words, angry words, I fear. And when Matthew suddenly toppled from his horse . . ." Milicent's voice caught, but she swallowed and kept her head up. "Needless to say, Oliver was frightened. Brought Matthew home unconscious. Since then Dr. Bryant has been with him, and he has regained consciousness." She looked at Aaron. "It is his heart. Some irregularity."

Aaron's face was etched with fear. "Pain?"

"Yes. In his chest. But Dr. Bryant has given your

179

father a pain medication, and it has helped him rest."

Sick at heart, Jessica was watching Aaron's face because she had learned to study his expression when patients related their symptoms and could tell if they were serious or not. Aaron's expression remained worried.

The native maid brought in the tray with the silver tea service and set it on the center table in front of the mantel. Milicent said no more as she poured the tea, but Jessica noticed that her hand shook. She had never seen her great-aunt's hands shake before.

Aaron rose without touching his tea. "I want to see him. Where's Dr. Bryant?"

"He's gone back to Parramatta but will return tomorrow morning."

Some of Aaron's worry left him then, for if the doctor had stayed the night, it would mean that his father was near the end. Milicent rose and clasped Aaron's hands. "Son, what do you think?"

Aaron shook his head. "I don't know. I haven't seen him, haven't examined him."

"He wants you. He asked for you." Milicent smiled. "He even called Dr. Bryant a horse doctor and told him that you could doctor rings around him anytime."

When Aaron smiled sadly, she went on: "But Dr. Bryant is a friend of your father's and knows he's cantankerous, and doesn't take him too seriously."

"The very fact that he is giving Dr. Bryant a little trouble sounds encouraging. Many people live through these heart attacks, Mum."

She nodded. "I know." But her face plainly showed the others that she was afraid, terribly afraid for the man she loved more than anyone in the world.

Aaron turned and said, "Jessie? Penny? Shall we go in?"

They had put Matthew in the downstairs bedroom, which was at the front of the house. Because of its windows on the north and east, it was a sunny room by day. Tonight it was lit by lantern light which threw a yellow glow over the bed where Matthew lay, leaving the corners of the room in shadows. As they entered, a figure emerged from the shadows, and Jessica recognized Aaron's Uncle Owen Crawford.

"Owen?" Aaron said offering his hand.

Owen Crawford took the hand, said nothing, nodded to the women and went out.

Their eyes turned then to Matthew. He lay propped on three pillows, his full head of white hair whiter than the linen of the pillowcases. Jessica made her evaluation of him automatically, something Aaron had taught her to do recently. She noted his pallor, that perspiration stood in beads upon his broad forehead. He was breathing deep and evenly, which was good, and his color, though pale, was not cyanotic. Jessica relaxed somewhat. Yes, people did recover from these heart attacks.

Aaron took his father's wrist in his hand. The blue eyes opened. A horizontal line creased Matthew's forehead. "It's about time," he whispered.

"Don't talk, Father."

"I'll talk if I damned well please," he replied slowly. His eyes went to Penelope, to Jessica, to Milicent. "I suppose I messed up your ball?"

"It was nearly over, Matthew," Penelope said and came to stand beside him.

Matthew smiled up at her. "Rolph," he said. "You look just like him at the moment."

"Matthew, I insist that you not talk."

Matthew's eyes came away from Penelope's face and focused on his son's. "Pulse is that irregular is it?" he asked. "Don't you think I can feel it? I can feel that pause, and that heavy beat when the damned heart decides it better not miss a beat after all, much as it wants to." When Matthew saw Aaron's anger at him, he raised one free hand and said, "All right. All right. I'm tired. I'll sleep."

Aaron turned to his mother, who was studying his expression intently. Aaron would know if there was hope. Aaron would know more than Dr. Bryant. What she saw was what Jessica saw. Aaron was deeply troubled. He said nothing until he had taken his mother's elbow and gone out with the women into the entrance hall. "I'll stay the night, Mum. Somebody can relieve me in the morning."

Milicent's brown eyes searched his.

Aaron looked away. "His pulse is irregular, more so than it has been these past few months."

Milicent knew he was not through and waited for his answer.

"I . . . am somewhat disturbed because he is still perspiring, and because he is still experiencing some pain." When he saw his mother pale, he added, "But that doesn't always mean anything, Mum."

To Jessica it meant something. She was remembering old Mr. Dobbs. Mr. Dobbs had continued to perspire for six days after his initial attack, and Aaron had told Jessica, "It bodes ill for a patient to keep having pain and perspiring after his initial attack. I believe that it is a sign that damage to the heart is still continuing. If a patient has an attack of pain and perspiration, the sooner the pain leaves the less damage there seems to be to his heart,

182

and the more likely he'll recover." Mr. Dobbs had died of a second attack within hours.

Oh dear Lord, Jessica prayed. Let his pain stop. Let him recover. Father loves him so. He is loved by so many.

"Let someone else stay, Aaron. You must be exhausted from your journeys," his mother said.

"No, Mum. I must stay tonight. I wouldn't sleep otherwise."

When Aaron had bade them good night, Milicent accompanied Jessica and Penelope upstairs. Jessica was shown Mark Aylesbury's old room and Penelope Aaron's. Jessica was so weary that she barely noticed the old native servant woman helping her off with her frock with its petticoats. She slipped into a cool cotton gown as the woman blew out the lantern and opened the draperies to let in the breezes. She was soon in the bed with its clean linen smelling of fragrant soap and sun. Her heart was heavy. She had a terrible feeling about Matthew. But most of all she grieved because Eric was not here. Eric, who loved him so much. For the first time, Jessica wept for him. She wept for Eric's plight and for his grandfather, and for the hurt she saw on Aaron's face.

Outside the cicadas shrilled and a beetle just outside the house set up his staccato clicking. A cow lowed somewhere near, and the breeze rustled the leaves of the gum trees outside. From the window, where the lace curtains stirred with the breeze, the scent of eucalyptus came with the breeze, along with the faint scent of roses and newly mown hay.

"Eric, please come to us," she whispered into the night. And was answered by the stirring of the trees.

"What do you think, Buck? Is there any way that you

can get word to Eric? Is there any chance that he might hear about Matt?"

Jessica had come down from her room the next morning later than she had wanted to. It was still early; the sun was just coming up in the horizon, but the Crawford men had already arrived and had had breakfast. These were Milicent's brothers, Aaron's uncles, the Crawford men, all four of them standing outside near the veranda. They turned as one body when Jessica came out onto the veranda.

"Morning, Miss Jessica," Owen said.

The others removed their hats and greeted her. It was Owen who said, "We were just discussing the possibility of Eric's hearing about his grandfather."

Jessica nodded and came to stand with the men. Such men. These men had, as boys, come across the ocean from England, along with Milicent and their parents. Upon their coming of age, these men had gone their separate ways—but not far. The Crawfords lived within twenty miles of each other, all staying in the Hawkesbury district.

Jessica shook hands with Thaddeus first, the youngest of the Crawford brothers, a handsome sixty-three-year-old breeder of horses. His handshake was elegantly brief, and his attention left her immediately. Next Buck took her hand. Jessica had to make herself remember that this man was her grandfather, the father of Deen Crawford, her half Aboriginal father. There was no embracing Buck. No one had ever embraced Buck but perhaps Milicent. His handshake was like taking hold of a piece of iron, cold and hard. He nodded, smiling slightly. At sixty-seven, Buck's face was lined, but not with wrinkles. Somehow, Jessica got the impression that those lines had

184

always been there.

"Jessie," he said. Buck was not a man of many words.

"Have you heard from . . . Deen, Buck?" she asked. To address him as Grandfather seemed difficult.

"I believe he's still in Van Dieman's Land. At least he's based there. Likely, though, he's off on one of his own whalers," Buck replied. The answer was a long one for Buck.

Jessica next took Ben Crawford's hand. This was the oldest of the Crawford clan, the big brother of the mob. Ben was white headed and stony faced. Ben, she knew, never smiled. He had never quite forgiven his son, Ben, for choosing to go over the mountains to the Cranston station to work with Aaron, denying any connection with the Crawford dairy. His handshake was firm and warm and damp. "Jessica, my dear," he said. "Is my son well?"

"When we left, sir, Ben had sold two hundred acres of his land to pay his fine."

Ben nodded. It was his son's punishment for not carrying on his father's wishes.

Jessica stood on the veranda and listened as the men's talk turned from her. Buck said, "Eric will hear about his grandfather. There's a thing called the bush telegraph. The bushmen always know."

"What is a telegraph?" asked Thaddeus.

It was Owen, the inventor, who spoke up. "It's that talking wire the Yanks have. They string wire across the country on posts and send signals over it. Certain clicks mean certain letters of the alphabet. We'll have it here soon."

"Sounds like an invention of the devil to me," Ben said.

"Have you any idea where Eric is?" Tad asked Buck.

"No," Buck said.

Owen was whittling on a stick. His curly hair had turned steel gray. Owen was probably the richest of the Crawford clan, with river boats docked at Windsor and smaller craft at his own landing below the Aylesbury place. His furniture warehouse had expanded, and he had a branch manufactury in Sydney.

"Think we ought to contact Deen?" Owen asked.

Buck replied, "I tried."

"Franny?" Ben said.

Jessica noted that the men smiled at him, then, of one accord, and her woman's mind told her that Ben, even at seventy-five, had more than a passing interest in Fran Danbury, Matthew's sister.

"Milly sent word to her. She's to arrive today," Owen replied.

Jessica excused herself and went back into the house where she saw Milicent outside Matthew's door. "Grandmum?"

Milicent put her hand on Jessica's shoulder. "Matthew rested well last night with your father there. I knew he would. He seems better this morning, though he refuses the broth we brought him."

"And Father?"

Milicent's forehead creased. "He won't leave his side."

Jessica took a deep breath. Just like Aaron if he thought a patient was critical. "I'll make him," she said. "May I?"

Milicent smiled and opened the door for her.

Inside, Aaron was sitting beside the bed. His tie had been pulled off, his coat and waistcoat discarded. His shirt was open, and the neck and his sleeves were rolled up. Such a familiar sight to Jessica. He turned to look at

186

her as she entered, his face showing incredible fatigue. His eyes were red.

"Go now, Father. Let me sit with him."

Matthew opened his eyes and he smiled. "There's Jessica." His eyes went then to his son. "Go on and rest, Aaron. Jessica wants to practice being a doctor."

Aaron looked closely at Jessica. "You rested well?"

"Like a baby," she said. "Go. Shoo."

Aaron hesitated. "He seems to be free of pain now," he said, his mouth turning up slightly in a weary smile. He knew she would understand what he was saying.

When he was gone, Matthew looked at her and said, "He's a damned sight better doctor than I ever was. Knows all the latest innovations."

"He's one of the best, Grandfather, but so are you."

The color of his eyes seemed to fade a little as he said, "Jessica, take it from an old physician. This business of being a doctor is too harsh for a woman."

"Grandfather—"

He held up his hand to silence her protest. "Women make the best nurses because of the nurturing, the mothering they do. But . . ." He shook his head. "A lady doesn't have the strength it takes to fix dislocated hips, nor the stamina to operate and suture—" He broke off coughing.

Frightened, Jessica said, "Please rest, Grandfather." She picked up Aaron's book. "I'm going to read this book and I don't want you to disturb me."

Matt smiled, nodded, and Jessica sat down in the hard chair which Aaron had occupied all night and opened the book. It was *Redburn* by Herman Melville, something new, but her eyes were drawn to the window. The early morning sun had painted the white lace curtains orange and was throwing snowflakes of light on the wall above Matthew's bed.

Lack of strength. Very little stamina. The same excuses men had used to keep women from going into professions like medicine since the beginning of time. She looked at Matthew, his eyes closed now. What about knowledge, Grandfather, and ability and ambition? Don't they count for anything in this life?

Life. What was it all about? Here gathered the Crawford clan. Jessica sensed that it was because of the Crawford men's high regard for their sister, Milicent, that they came and they would stay. Milicent had been the one to insist that they stay when their father, Silas Crawford, had died soon after their arrival in New South Wales when the others might have gone back. It had been Milicent who had taken over the running of the farm. She was the strong one. And now that her husband lay at death's door, they came. If he died, they would be here to comfort her. These free settlers from England had never quite approved of Matthew; Matthew who had met Milicent in England before the ships left. Matthew who had delivered the Crawford's mother of a dead child while the ships were stalled at sea. Dr. Matthew Aylesbury, who had given his life to a government hospital in Parramatta treating convicts, when he could have gone into private practice and earned more. Matthew who had become involved in trade and farming and had been a partner to Milicent in making the farms produce. A self-made man. Aaron's father. Eric's grandfather and only her great-granduncle, but he was more grandfather to her than Buck was.

Jessica sat with Matthew until noon. Milicent came often and sat with her, and Jessica was struck by how she

188

sat and looked at her husband, holding his hands. Jessica was struck also by the love that passed between Milicent and Matthew whenever he would open his eyes and smile at her. Cautiously, she began to hope for Matthew's recovery. He remained free of chest pain that day and rested well. Jessica was relieved at noon by Penelope.

Matthew seemed to rest less well with Penelope in the room, and Jessica was reminded that, although Penelope was actually the daughter of Matthew's cousin, she was also the daughter of a woman Matthew had despised, Oliver Cranston's wife, and had been raised by Oliver Cranston himself. Matthew had grown to like and respect Penelope, however. But it was strange, when it came down to it, who sat beside him when he was ill, who he was comfortable with the most, and who made him slightly restless.

The first day of his recovery passed without event. The Crawford men left to tend to their work but were back in the evening, each offering to sit with Matthew. But it was the women who did so. Frances Danbury, Matthew's sister, arrived the morning of the first day from Sydney. Jessica knew Fran well. A tall, rawboned woman, whose dressmaking business had grown from a tiny brick house in Parramatta to two manufactures of women's wear. Fran's gray-brown hair was a mousy gray now and severely pulled back and secured in a round bun at the back of her head. Freckles across her nose had long since faded, but her keen brown eyes still snapped with authority, enough that no one questioned her commands. When Fran entered the household, she took control. Between the four women, Matthew was well cared for, well pampered, and well loved.

Friends came and went, paying their respects, allowed

189

only brief visits to Matt as he lay propped up high in his bed, sometimes grumpy, sometimes friendly.

Glenn Moffett, Jessica's maternal grandfather, came from his farm near the river. She went out into the yard and greeted him. Glenn was getting old, too, seventy-three, but as seedy as ever. His blue eyes were rheumy now, his face still ruddy, and he had grown a beard which he kept close trimmed. And there were more white hairs in it now than brown. He held her at arm's length and said in his deep cockney accent, "Look at ye, Jessie, love. Ain't ye the image of yer mother." Glenn was the only one who saw any of his daughter, Annabelle, in Jessica. "Oh I wish yer grandmum could see ye now." Tears wet his eyes and he had to turn away. "Hello, Aaron, ye son of a gun."

Aaron had been coming from the stable where he had been checking on his horses. "Glenn," he said grinning.

Glenn shook his hand. "Seen any more natives who don't know a man from a woman these days?"

Aaron shook his head. Glenn would never forget that time when they were in the wilderness and Aaron had to be the one to prove to the natives that they were men.

Jessica passed the rest of the third day in helping the other women cook and keep food prepared for visitors and the uncles who came each evening. Jessica marveled that even though she did far less work here than she did at home, she was much more weary at the end of the day. It was the waiting. The watching. The waiting for what?

The cicadas churred softly outside that evening as Jessica pulled the soft white gown over her head, then took down her thick black hair, brushed it, and braided it in one long thick braid. She bathed earlier because of the heat, grateful that Milicent had a bathtub on the upper

190

floor. A copper thing that looked like a conquistador's helmet, but it held several gallons of water and had felt wonderful.

She crawled into bed and lay looking up at the ceiling. The moon was exceptionally bright tonight, and moonlight fell across the linen sheets of her bed. As she listened to the night sounds so familiar to her, she also listened to the sounds of the family getting ready for bed.

She heard Penelope come up to bed, then Franny in the adjoining room, then Milicent. Aaron would stay the night with his father. Soon all sounds within the house ceased. Jessica's eyelids drooped. She heard a sheep's bell tinkle in some distant pasture. A horse snorted somewhere nearby.

Suddenly, she awoke with a start.

"Sh-sh-sh." A hand had clamped over her mouth, and Jessica tried to sit up, already fighting the figure who sought to subdue her. "Sh-sh, Jessie."

Her eyes focused on the face above her. Dark eyes glinted from the light coming from the window. An intense face loomed above her. And then she recognized him. When she relaxed, he took his hand from her mouth. "Oh, Eric," she whispered.

They came together in a violent embrace, and in that frenzied moment, he kissed her bruisingly, her mouth, her face, her eyes, and she held him, grasped him, trying to crush him to her, smelling the scent of him: the travel dirt, sweat, leather, horse. At last he released her and held her from him as he sat on the bed. "Jessie."

"Eric, you heard about your grandfather?"

"Aye."

"But how?"

"I keep my eyes and ears open, Jessie."

"But won't they catch you?"

"I won't be here long enough. They'll play hell trying to follow me over the mountains. I've ridden hard for three days."

"Three days! But I don't think anyone's ever come over the mountains in three days."

"Maybe no one was in as big a hurry as I was."

She smiled and they embraced again. Then she said, "You won't be here long?"

"I had to come. I had to tell grandfather . . . good-bye. If this is good-bye."

"He seems to be recovering. Some people do."

"Thank God." Eric released her and turned to stare out the window.

She touched his arm. "Does anyone else know you're here?"

"No. I left the horse on the ridge in the forest and ran to the house. Climbed up the creeper vine to your window."

"But how did you know . . ."

"I didn't. I just guessed. Mum and Father would have Father's old room. I knew where Grandfather and Grandmother's room was. I knew the room Aunt Fran always stays in when she comes, and I knew she'd be here. And I knew which room you stay in when you visit. So . . ." He grinned, his teeth flashing in his dark face, and spread his arms. "Here I am."

"Here you are," Jessica said, and could not let him go. She held to him. "So you haven't seen Grandfather."

"No, but I must soon. I have to leave here before sunrise."

"Oh God, Eric. Must you go?"

"You know I do."

"Why, Eric? Why are you staying in the Bathurst district?

He smiled. "I'm glad you don't question why I'm running from the police. Jessie, don't ask any questions."

"But . . ."

He turned and took her to him, breathed into her hair, held her close, and made her forget the questions. Made her forget everything but that he was there, and that his hands, moving over her body, made her want him, need him, as their desire built. Their breathing came in deep gasps as he removed her gown, then his own clothes. His lips moved upon hers, and she felt the sweat and dust on his body as he lay half on, half off her. His hand sent trails of hot thrills through her, her skin burning under his touch. He ravished her gently, taking her mouth first, sucking, tasting, then her neck and her breasts which he caressed and tasted. Then he buried his face in her abdomen. His hand cupped her between her thighs, and she grasped his thick dark hair in her hands and pulled his mouth against her abdomen.

With both hands he stroked the insides of her thighs, his eyes shut, his head thrown back, savoring the feel of her, the scent of her. Jessica moaned with love and desire.

Eric could wait no longer. He plunged inside her and gasped with the pleasure. Jessica felt filled, and all her feelings went to the place that enveloped him. "Move."

He began to slide in and out, slowly at first, then the momentum gathered. In a frenzied pumping, he gasped and could feel the throb of him inside her, even as her thighs gripped his hips and her womanhood pulled him, wanting more and more, until she, too, was spent.

He lay down on her then, his breathing coming in rapid raucous gasps, and she hugged his head to her breasts.

He lay for a time, his hands caressing her neck and her breasts. "Jessie, I could go on like this all night, forever, but I must hurry."

Jessica, smiling, opened her eyes. "Yes, yes you must. But we had this moment. And we shall have others again. I know it."

When he did not reply, she looked at him. His eyes had gone again to the window. "I have escaped the troopers thus far because I've never remained anywhere long." He looked back at her and smiled. "So far my fortune has been good. Luck, the Americans call it."

She sat up and ran her hands over his muscular arm. "When you go, Eric, go with my love."

After they had both washed off and dressed, they went downstairs. A candle was sputtering in a sconce outside Matthew's doorway. Slowly, Jessica went into the room first. Aaron looked up from the book lying in his lap, stood up, and smiled. "Anything wrong, Jessie?"

"How is he?"

A line in the middle of Aaron's forehead deepened. "Seems slightly restless."

Jessica looked at Matthew, and although he was sleeping, his hands were moving on the sheet over his abdomen.

"But his pulse is good and so is his breathing," Aaron said.

"I have a surprise for you, Aaron, that can't wait until morning." Jessica stepped inside the room and Eric came in behind her.

For a moment Aaron did not move. Then he came forward slowly, not taking his eyes off his son's face, and gripped his arms. "You're mad, Eric. It's not safe."

"No, but I had to come." Eric's eyes moved to his grandfather. "Can we wake him? I have to be gone before morning."

Aaron nodded, and the two men went to the side of the bed. Aaron lay his hand gently on his father's shoulder, and Matthew's eyes opened. For a moment, he did not seem to know where he was, then his eyes moved to Eric's face. A slow smile crept across his mouth. "Risked your life and limb to see me, eh?" Matthew said.

Gently Eric sat down on the edge of the bed. "I wanted to tell you . . ." He hesitated awkwardly.

"Good-bye?" Matthew smiled. "Well, I'm not dead yet, and I don't think St. Peter's ready for the likes of me yet. Maybe tomorrow," he jested.

Eric grasped his hand. With Matthew, you didn't show any more affection than that.

"Damned if you don't look a lot like Rolph."

Eric smiled, and Jessica knew that he was thinking that, indeed, Rolph was his grandfather rather than Oliver Cranston.

"Did I ever tell you about the time Rolph and me got caught setting fire to Oliver Cranston's corn cribs over in England?"

"You didn't set fire to them, you went to bring Rolph home before there was trouble," Eric corrected him, knowing the story well.

Matthew waved that aside. "Cranston was the J.P. for our shire, you know." He tapped Eric on the arm and said, "That means justice of the peace, if you know your English history as you should. We were arrested along with two other men. Went before the magistrates, in Old Bailey, no less. You know Old Bailey. It's London's most

195

famous court. We even spent several days in Newgate prison." Matthew seemed proud for the first time that he had been connected, however questionably, to something as famous as Newgate and Old Bailey. His eyes went beyond Eric to the ceiling, and beyond, to years past. "Rolph and I were sentenced to hang, but Father's solicitor got the sentence commuted to transportation. Transportation to New South Wales for the rest of our natural lives." Matthew laughed softly. "The prison ship was awful, Eric. Disease, sickness, heat, cold, wet beds, rats, fleas. Terrible food." He tapped Eric's arm again. "Old Hambone was on that ship. And you remember Cranston's old groom, Cricket? He was there, too." Matthew turned his eyes up to Aaron. "Your old teacher Baldwin was on the ship, too." Matthew sighed. "Ah how beautiful the land looked when we arrived in Sydney Cove. The water was the bluest I had ever seen. Then when I heard that your grandmother's ship had arrived safely, too, New South Wales became my home."

"Yes, well you'd best be resting now, Father," Aaron said. "You've talked long enough."

"Don't tell me how much is enough. I was a medical doctor before you were even an egg in your mother's ovaries."

Aaron and Eric glanced at Jessica, who was suppressing a smile.

"It was your grandmother who made a go of it, though. Without her, I don't know where I'd be today. She was my inspiration. Thoughts of her sustained me all across the ocean, and when I was sentenced to Norfolk Island." Matthew grabbed the sleeve of Eric's shirt. "I was falsely accused and finally Governor King himself discovered my innocence and pardoned me. And Rolph at the same

196

time. We were free men. But it was this farm I came home to, and to your grandmother."

Eric nodded and held his hand on Matthew's arm.

Matthew looked up at Aaron. "Remember when Oliver Cranston and I had that duel?"

Aaron nodded.

"Damned son of a bitch."

"Father, Jessica . . ."

"I thought it was his hired man who had my wheat field burned, but now I think it was Lieutenant Kraft. Well, I gave ol' Chance what for anyway. When I got through with him, his face looked like a squashed melon."

"Grandfather," Eric began.

"Father. You've talked long enough."

"Then everybody started leaving. First Rolph. Then ol' Davey O'Shea died. And your great-grandmother. And Aaron went off into the bush like a dingo pup." He glanced up at Aaron. "Got lost out there, too, as I recall. Then my son, my other son, Mark, went off to England. Mark was . . . strange. Scared as hell of me. He died at sea, you know." Matthew shook his head at the tears that threatened his eyes. "But then you remember that, don't you Eric?"

"I remember, Grandfather." Eric looked up at his own father whose face was lined with worry and grief. "And now I must be going, sir."

Matthew gripped his arm. "Go then. Go with God, son. I don't know what you're doing out there in the bush, but I've got this gut feeling that it has a purpose. With you most things do."

Eric nodded and rose. "Good-bye, Grandfather. I'll see you again one of these days."

Matthew nodded. "Go on then, Eric." He nodded. "Aye. You are the very image of Rolph when he was your age."

Eric turned, head down and went out into the entrance hall followed by Aaron and Jessica. Aaron and Eric looked at each other for a moment then Aaron said, "Take care. Your mother worries. You'll see her?"

"Briefly. Then I have to go."

Eric went up the stairs, and ten minutes later was down again. At the door with Aaron still watching, he hugged Jessica to him, then he was gone. But then the moon had set and the night was black as pitch. Jessica stood for a time on the veranda and listened, hoping to hear the hooves of his horse, or see a shadow of him. But there was only quiet; not even the insects made sounds.

Hugging herself, she turned and went back inside. A glimpse inside Matthew's room showed her that Matthew was asleep again, with Aaron sitting beside him.

"Good night, Father," Jessica said.

"'Night, Jessie," Aaron replied looking up at her.

In her bed again, Jessica hugged the linen sheets to her, the sheets that still smelled of him and of their love.

Chapter XI

The end came to Dr. Matthew Aylesbury on the morning of January 30, 1851, four days after his first attack. The roosters were crowing outside and the predawn sounds of spoons on kettles and the chopping of kindling was filtering through the north window along with a cool breeze from the west. Aaron was dozing in a semi-sleep. His book had slid off his lap to the floor. But when his father stirred, he came fully awake.

Matthew did not move but turned his head to see his son. His eyes were bleary as he said, "Son?"

"I'm here, Father."

"Best send for your mother."

A cold hand of fear gripped Aaron's heart. He forgot his doctor's training and everything else. He was a small boy again, and he turned and hurried out into the entrance hall. Penelope was just coming down the stairs and Aaron said, "Call Mum."

Penelope, too, did not question the command but hurried on down the stairs and into the parlor where Milicent was.

Inside Matthew's room Aaron became the doctor again and went to him, taking his pulse. Matthew's breathing was deep and too rapid. Sweat stood in beads on his forehead and ran down the sides of his face. He did not look at Aaron as he said, "Pulse is irregular. Like a galloping horse gone lame."

Aaron was feeling it, missed beats more than ten or twelve a minute. "Don't talk," he choked.

Matthew obeyed and seemed to be concentrating on each breath. When Milicent appeared, she paused in the doorway and saw that the end was near. She came to him and sat down on the edge of the bed, taking his hand in hers. His fingers wrapped around her wrist, and his eyes never left her face. "Milly."

Milicent's mouth worked as she tried to control her emotions. "Yes, Matt, I'm here."

"I did help you with the farm, didn't I?"

Tears ran down Milicent's face as she nodded. "Yes, Matt. You helped."

"And you helped me, Milly. I would never have survived." He took a deep breath. "Survived the ship, or Norfolk . . . without you."

"Don't talk, love," she said and brushed the white hair from his damp forehead.

Matthew looked sad. "Remember how the ships were stalled at sea, when there was no breeze and we sat for days and days on the glassy sea?"

"Yes Matt."

"It was so hot. I feel like that now. Like I'm sitting on the sea, hot, no breezes. I can't move on, Milly."

"Perhaps it isn't time, Matt."

Jessica had been summoned by Penelope and came into the room. Penelope was there and Milicent and

Aaron. Aaron had one of his father's hands, Milicent the other.

"If I could just move on, I could join Mark. Do you think he would still be afraid of me?"

"He loved you, Matt. Mark loved you very much."

"And Rolph. I'll see Rolph. And Mum, and old Davey O'Shea. And Father."

"Sh-sh."

"And your mum." Matthew's eyes widened a little, and one side of his mouth twitched into a smile. "And I'll be damned. There's Elaina Cranston waiting for me."

"Matt, darling . . ."

"There. There, Milly. See? The Penrith. I feel a breeze. The *Penrith*'s sails are filling with the breeze. The water is blue, the sky. The wind. See it, Milly? Beautiful. Beautiful." Matthew's eyes moved from her face to the ceiling. His chest rose one last time and then became still. His eyes fixed on the ceiling, and Milicent lay her head on his chest, pressed his hand to her lips, and wept silently.

Jessica grieved. But she also felt strangely removed from the scene. Another of the old first generation Australians had gone. There were so few of them left anymore.

The funeral was held two days later, and people came from as far away as New Castle, Camden, and Sydney. There would have been friends from the Bathurst district, too, if they had waited longer to bury him. But they could not wait longer than two days because of the heat. In this heat, one had to be buried quickly.

The funeral was held in the house, which was filled to capacity and overflowing onto the veranda and out into the yard. Then Matthew was carried to the Aylesbury's graveyard on the west side of the ridge, and he was laid to rest near Milicent's mother, and Rolph and Davey O'Shea, and little Jessica, and Silas Crawford, Milicent's father. The day was hot, but there was indeed a stiff breeze blowing from the west.

As the mourners left the graveside, Aaron clutched his mother's arm on one side, with Elder Ben Crawford holding the other. Milicent had already done all her weeping, and she was staid and pale, but her back was as straight as ever, and her feet did not falter down the path from the ridge to the waiting carriage.

Jessica followed with Penelope and the other Crawford men, followed by Ben Crawford's nine children, most of whom were grown. At the carriage stood a tall man, his hat in his hand, his hair white with wisps of it blowing in the wind.

Oliver Cranston was handsome, even at seventy-nine. He was slightly bent now, but his only concession to old age was to carry a cane. His eyes were on Milicent as she approached. Jessica heard him speak.

"Milicent. I . . . am sorry."

Milicent nodded. "Thank you."

"I hope you don't hold me accountable."

"I never did, Oliver."

"If you need anything. Ever . . ."

Milicent looked at him long, then replied, "I shan't."

Ben helped her into the carriage as Oliver Cranston stood hat in hand and watched. Aaron rode with his mother away from the site to the house.

As Jessica rode with Penelope and Ben Crawford back to the house—such a short distance any other time, but so long today—she thought about the death of someone you love. She felt grieved and hurt, angry at death, guilt. And yet there was hope and gratitude, too, for Matthew's long life.

Aaron and Penelope and Jessica remained for one more week, and then they said their good-byes. On their way back in their carriage over the mountains, followed by the entourage which had accompanied them to the Hawkesbury district almost two weeks before, Jessica hurt to see Aaron. His face was gaunt, his frame slightly bent, as if he had grown years older in those two weeks. And it was not until the majesty of the Blue Mountains before them, with its deep canyons and chasms so breathtakingly beautiful and where the breezes were stiff and cool, that Aaron seemed to revive.

At an inn on the pass, when the carriage and dray paused for the evening, Aaron stood looking out over a vast, serene depth of blue forests and gray mists, of silences, and sunlit splashes of gold and yellow on the dense forest below.

Aaron drew Penelope to him. "Look at it, Penelope. Father saw the sails of the *Penrith* fill with a sailing breeze when he died. When my time comes, it will be this that I'll see. They call it the Vale of Cwyde."

It was beautiful. Jessica wondered if Eric had come this way, and if he had passed safely.

"'Is tracks plainly came close to 'ere, lass. But the trackers lost 'im two miles from 'ere. You sure you ain't seen 'im?"

Frightened, Carrie shook her head. "I'm sorry, sir, but I have never seen Eric Aylesbury. He was gone before I ever arrived."

Captain Scantlin nodded, grinning. "Aye. That 'e was. Yer new, ain't ye? Came over the mountains with that Chisholm woman, didn't ye?"

Carrie was glancing about, wondering how she had fallen into this situation. The Aylesburys were still gone, having sent word back to the station by one of the hired hands that they were staying in the Hawkesbury district because the doctor's father had died. But they were due home in another day or so. Mrs. Chun had gone to market in Bathurst along with the doorman, Mr. Rogers. She was the only one left in the house. Of course four or five of the ringers were in the yard, but the police were everywhere, going in and out of the stables, the barns, the ringer's huts, the wheat fields, and even the house. Four of them were going through the rooms now, and Carrie didn't like it at all.

She was standing in the kitchen and could hear the policemen rummaging around, picking up the knick-knacks on the tables, fingering the draperies. They had surreptitiously popped some of the tarts Chun had made before she left into their mouths, while this obnoxious captain stood and looked at her boldly. She did not like his pig's eyes. She had seen eyes like his before, on the scum on the London streets, the prisoners in Sydney. Carrie wiped her hands on her apron.

"You'll not find him here. And the Aylesburys will be home any moment," she assured him.

"Will they now?" The sergeant fixed his eyes again on her breasts. "Meantime, all's here is them four ringers out there, ain't that right?"

"Or more," Carrie said.

"Nay. Just four. I checked. I'm always careful about everything."

Carrie's gaze went out the window to where the policemen stood on the veranda, as if on guard. The ringers were free to walk about, so the head stockman, Zachariah Bodine, apparently remembering that she was alone, looked at the house and began to saunter toward it. But the captain saw Carrie's gaze and followed it, went to the door of the house and called. "Sims! Jackson. Keep the men near the stables."

Alarm was growing in Carrie as she watched the officers obey hesitantly. They did not like what they were doing. Dr. Aylesbury was an important man in the district, and they knew their captain.

"They ain't hurtin' nothing, cap'n," one of the men called.

"You keep them there. That's an order. I don't want 'em warnin' Aylesbury if 'es here." Then he turned and looked at Carrie and grinned. "But if 'es 'ere, my men would have found 'im by now."

The men who had been searching the house came stomping down the stairs at that moment. "No one up there, sir. We looked in every nook and cranny," one of them said.

"Then get on out before you break somethin' else."

The two men paused and looked at Carrie and read something in their captain's eyes. "Then hadn't we best be getting on down the track, sir?"

The captain's eyes had not left Carrie for several moments. "In a little while. In a little while. You tell the men to water the horses, eat a bite. I want to question this little lady a moment."

The officer looked from him to Carrie. One of them said, "But sir . . ."

"You heard me, Jones."

The black policeman glanced over his shoulder as he went out the door. You did not argue with a superior officer, and you certainly did not argue with a white man. They left and went on out into the yard with the captain watching. Then Scantlin turned slowly toward Carrie.

"Now," he said and kicked the door shut with his foot. "Suppose you tell ol' Scantlin where you've got young Aylesbury hid."

With a mixture of dread and anger, Carrie said, "I told you. I have never seen Eric Aylesbury in my life."

"No? Well maybe I should look around myself." Scantlin took her by the arm. "Down the 'all, lass. Let's start on the first floor."

He took her down the hall with him until he came to her room. Looking about her room he said, "Now ain't this pretty? So ladylike." He was standing between her and the door of her bedroom now as his eyes slid from the curtained windows to her face. "A fittin' room for a pretty lady."

Carrie did not reply.

"Tell me, pretty lady, 'ave you ever been kissed?"

Carrie knew now for sure what was on the policeman's mind and said, "It's none of your business, sir. Now that you see he's not here, will you please leave?"

"Leave?"

"Please."

He laughed. "I'll wager with a figure like you've got, lass, you've had some before, and I'll wager that you could enjoy kissin'." Scantlin laughed and hitched at his pants. "Suppose you come over to the bed and us try, eh?"

Carrie backed away and said, "One more step toward me and I'll scream."

Scantlin paused but his grin did not cease. "Then I'll just . . ." He made as if to turn away from her. Then in a flash he had her against him, his hand over her mouth. Carrie could feel a hard lump against her hip. "You won't scream, lass. And if you tell, I'll deny it and say you seduced me," he said into her face. "Who's to believe a little chit whore against a captain of the police?"

Carrie brought her knee up but it glanced off the officer's inner thighs.

Laughing, he held both her arms against her sides as he pulled off his stinking neckerchief and stuffed it in her mouth. Then he flung her from him, and she stumbled against her bed. He looked at her a moment, his hands going to his crotch, which he jiggled, grinning. "Afraid, lass? But surely you've seen it before." Slowly he unbuttoned his pants, took out his swollen erection, and shook it. "That's wot I 'ave fer ye, lass. See, it ain't so bad, is it?"

Whimpering with anger and fear now, Carrie made a lunge past him. But Scantlin caught her and flung her onto the bed where she sprawled like a doll made of rags. In an instant he was on her, clawing at the buttons to her bodice. His hand found her breasts, and he moaned as his mouth came down on her throat. His other hand was going up to her thigh under her dress where he fondled her, then pulled down her pantaloons. His hot stinking breath was on her face as he chewed her cheeks and neck and breasts, perspiration dripping off his face and falling onto hers. Carrie shrieked into the kerchief as he spread her legs, grunting foul words all the while.

Somewhere in the distance she heard shouts, but in her panic she could not distinguish what they were. Her world had narrowed to the grunting smell and dampness of the hog on her body.

Scantlin put the head of his erection on her thighs and rubbed it as he laughed, massaging her as she struggled and kicked. Then a grayness came over her, and suddenly Scantlin disappeared.

She heard a thump. She dared not open her eyes. Then she heard a grunt. When her vision cleared, she saw Scantlin struggling with another man. Carrie sat up and yanked her skirts over her knees as she watched Regie Schiller slam the police officer against the wall.

"Don't worry, Miss Carrie," Schiller cried. "I'm here now to rescue you."

But Scantlin yanked his pistol from its scabbard. Reginald's booted foot came up quick and kicked it into the air. Then he drew his own pistol. "Stay there," he said.

Scantlin was leaning against the wall, and his pig's eyes went to the pistol lying on the floor, just within his reach. "You wouldn't shoot, Schiller. You wouldn't dare."

"Would you want to wager on that, Captain?"

Scantlin's pig's eyes studied him. His grin stretched and he chuckled. Then his hand shot out and grabbed the pistol. Regie's finger pulled the trigger of his pistol. It clicked. He pulled it again and it clicked again. His face turned deathly pale. "Damn," he said.

Scantlin, chuckling, brought his pistol up slowly. "Fergit to load it, Schiller? Now ain't that too bad. And now I'll have ta kill you. 'Cause you was molestin' the girl, you see, and I came to rescue 'er and you pulled a gun on me and I 'ad to shoot you."

Carrie had the kerchief out of her mouth by then, and the only thing she knew to do was reach for the heavy porcelain water pitcher on her washstand. Scantlin was so intent on watching Reginald's shattered pride that he did not hear her move. She raised the pitcher high over her head and brought it down with a crash on Scantlin's skull.

The pitcher shattered into a million pieces, and in that awful tense second before Scantlin fell, Carrie watched Reginald's face: a wince, a grimace, then a tentative smile as his gaze followed the slow sinking of the captain's body to the floor.

Carrie stood horrified with the handle of the pitcher still in her hand. Reginald stood with his useless pistol in his hand, and Captain Scantlin lay faceup, unconscious on the floor, with his fly still open and his manhood shrunken.

With a reddening face, Reginald finally moved and carefully spread his neckerchief over the front of Scantlin's trousers. Then with a sigh, he looked up at Carrie. "Blast," he said. "I wanted to be the one to rescue you. Then Jessica would have paid attention to me, once she heard about it."

"Oh but you did rescue me, Reginald," Carrie said trembling, wishing he'd take her into his arms. She needed the comfort so.

Depressed, Reginald picked up the captain's pistol and cocked it to check to see if it was loaded. Then he kicked the man. "I'll deliver him to his own men, and I'm going to make a report of this in Bathurst."

"It will be your word against his, Reginald. But if that's a problem, I'm certainly a witness."

Reginald thought about that.

"But tell me. How did you find me?" she asked.

"I knew the house servants were in Bathurst. And I saw the troopers coming down the track. Me an' Rube didn't like it, so we followed. We watched from the forest north of here. When I saw all the men come out of the house except Scantlin, we knew what he had on his mind. He likes the . . . ladies, and I knew he was no gentleman. So I sent Rube into the bush west of here to set a fire. When the fire started, all the troopers ran for it, and I rode into the yard, told the ringers to let me handle this inside." He ducked his head and blushed. "Well, anyway, you're safe." His eyes slid to her bodice where her fingers were quickly buttoning the remaining buttons. And she could see the memory of what he had seen when he burst into the room. Scantlin on top of her, her dress up to her waist. "Did he hurt you?"

"Another second and he would have," she replied blushing.

Reginald blushed again and turned away. Carrie was still trembling when he hefted Scantlin onto his shoulders and carried him out of her room. She followed him as he took the officer outside the house and dumped him in the yard at the ringers' feet. Reginald was too downcast to tell her good-bye. But the troopers took their sergeant back to Bathurst, and Reginald and Rube turned homeward.

The Aylesburys arrived home that evening. When Aaron heard what had happened to Carrie, he swore that he would leave in the morning to thank Reginald and Reuben and to see that charges were filed against Scantlin.

"I wish we could somehow reward Reginald," Carrie said frowning. "He really did rescue me . . . in his way."

Jessica was studying Carrie and finally said, "Don't worry, Carrie, I've a feeling he'll be rewarded—eventually."

And Carrie was puzzled at the smile that tugged at the corners of Jessica's mouth.

They heard no more from Eric. But during the next two weeks, Aaron pressed charges against Scantlin before the magistrate in Bathurst, and with Carrie and Reginald as witnesses, and the verification of their testimonies by the ringers and policemen, Captain Scantlin was fined and suspended from the police force—but for only three months.

Meantime, the Bathurst newspaper announced that the Port Philip district on the southern Australian coast had received its independence from New South Wales. It was a historic occasion, for now Australia had two colonies: New South Wales and Victoria. Victoria would have its own governor. This meant a victory for the people of Melbourne and the surrounding country, and to the Aylesburys, it meant that Eric could go to Victoria out of the New South Wales jurisdiction and live as a free man.

His clothing was soaked with perspiration, but he dared not move. The hot Australian night had been ear shatteringly noisy that night, but suddenly the din of the insect rhythm band had ceased. Eric had jerked his head up and listened, but heard nothing. He grabbed his pistol and climbed into a fat, stunted gum tree, which was growing near the opening of his cave.

The moon was new, full, and bright. The light glinted off the steel barrel of his Colt as he held it against the fat branch where he crouched. He glanced at Fury grazing at the edge of the brush clearing. The horse lifted his head, swung it around, and pricked his ears forward. Something or somebody was out there.

Eric didn't move for a long moment as he listened. Then weariness overcame him. It had been a long day of hard riding. What he was doing now was harder than mustering and drafting cattle. Victoria was now a separate colony, and it beckoned like a siren song, for now he could go there and be free. And he would go soon, but in Victoria he would have the same job to do as he had in the Bathurst district, therefore he could not be free even there. Not for some time yet.

He jerked his head up to listen. The sound of shod hoof on stone. Or was it? He listened. Heard nothing. Perspiration ran into his eyes. He mopped his forehead on the sleeve of his arm.

A piece of bark fell on his head and he looked up. In the moonlight he could see the bundle of fur in the crotch of the tree above him, a wizened face smiling wisely down. Then the koala reached out and took a handful of leaves and munched them matter-of-factly. Eric smiled.

That sound again. He jerked his face back around. He heard it then, shod hooves. Several. He licked his salty lips. They had found the caves, his hideaway. They were coming. He could see their shadows leading their horses, creeping toward the mouth of the cave. Eric thumbed back the hammer of his pistol.

"Coo-ee. Coo-ee, Eric."

Eric raised his head.

"I say, coo-ee, Eric. Where ya be?"

Eric frowned and smiled at the same time. The voice was Sam's. "Coo-ee yourself."

212

The three men jumped as if they had been shot, and Eric recognized James's station boss, Sam, and two of Ben Crawford's ringers, Coolabah Cecil and the black fellow, Jacky.

Eric swung his leg over the horizontal tree branch, let the hammer down on the pistol, twirled it, and stuck it back into its holster at his hip. Then, as he sat on the branch, he folded his arms across his chest and said, "Now lookee here."

Sam grinned. "We were beginnin' to think you'd humped it on down to Melbourne."

Eric slid off his branch and stood before the men. "What are you doing here?"

Sam glanced at Coolabah. "Tell him."

Coolabah Cecil was a burly middle-aged man with a twitch in his left eye which he claimed he had acquired because people kept making fun of his name.

"Well," Coolabah began, wiping the palms of his hands on his pants. "Now, Ben had to let all his ringers go, Eric. Including me and Jacky."

Jacky nodded. The whites of his eyes flashed in the moonlight.

"We can't find work anymore. Not in Bathurst district. We thought about waltzin' matilda down the track to Melbourne, now that the Port Philip district has become a state. Melbourne's a small town and squatters are gettin' rich and need station hands. Mought as well turn to bein' rouseabouts on a sheep station and musterin' jumbucks, we thought. But . . ." Coolabah paused.

"Go on," Eric prompted.

"Well, folks around Bathurst are beginning to think

213

you're the new bushranger. The one who's got a vendetta against Judge Livingston, on account of Ben being your relative."

"We decided to join ya, boss," Jacky put in, grinning.

Eric frowned. "Join me? Become an outlaw?"

The two men looked at Sam.

Sam licked his lips and said, "Bein' James Cranston's station boss, I've seen some funny goin's on lately. And I been puttin' two and two together." Sam indicated the nearest cave where a fire was still glowing within. "We been on the bloody track all day. Could ye spare a bit of tucker and a cuppa while I tell ye what I figured out?"

Eric glanced at the cave. "I don't need mates in my business."

Sam nodded. "I figure you do."

Eric studied him a moment, then nodded. "Hobble your mounts then, mates, and I'll hear what you have to say."

"It's like this, Reginald," Mr. Hargraves said as he stood with one foot propped on a boulder. "I'm not the first man to find gold in New South Wales. A convict or two found a few nuggets when they were buildin' the road over the mountains back in 1813, and there were other men, too, who found a few grains or nuggets. But there's a thing called the Royal Mines law which says that all gold and silver found in an English colony belongs to the crown. Now I needn't tell you that this discourages men from huntin' for it. But a governor can dismiss that law if he's a mind to. Our governors in the past haven't been of a mind to because they didn't want gold rushes started in a convict colony. It would cause convicts to bolt for the gold fields."

Reginald and Reuben had heard Hargraves themselves in the tavern in Bathurst claim that he had discovered gold on the Turon River north of the town. Hargraves was a tall man with a long black beard and a steely glint in his eye that discouraged a man from refuting his word to his face.

"So I aim to force the governor's hand, to recognize my discovery, my find, lads, by training some of you fellows to find gold yourselves. Enough of you blokes find it and he'll have to recognize it. Now here's how you go about panning for gold in a creek."

The Schiller brothers were standing on the bank of the Turon, a tributary of the Macquarie River. It was a wide stream running low because of the drought, and therefore perfect for panning gold.

Reginald was trembling. He believed Hargraves. He'd seen the nuggets with his own eyes. Besides, he believed Hargraves because he wanted to. *Gold.* If he and Rube found enough of it, why, they could buy their stepfather a new farm and Mum and the kids some clothes. And maybe, just maybe, he'd find enough to be rich enough to ask Jessica Aylesbury to marry him.

Hargraves waded into the creek ankle deep, and with a small shovel dug some of the silt at the bottom and dumped it into the shallow tin pan. "Here's how you do it, boys," he said.

Reginald and Rube had their own pans and they shoveled and washed, letting the silt and sand float out of the pan and leaving pebbles to settle in the bottom.

There was a bit of fall in the air that day in March. The air blowing from the south was cool and stirred the curls on the Schiller twins' golden hair where it stuck out under the brim of their hats. They panned and washed and found nothing.

In mid-afternoon, Reginald hobbled to the tent which he and Rube had set up and sat down. He looked at the countryside, rock-covered hills and yellow-brown soil. Gum trees and wattle thick and wild on the hills. Somebody owned this rocky, rugged country, but he didn't envy them much. He scanned the terrain. Three other tents had been set up along the creek by men from Bathurst who believed Hargraves's story. Some were digging on the riverbank, dumping shovels of wet sand into gold cradles and rocking them, washing all the sand out and hoping to catch grains of gold on the little ledges of the cradle. Others were panning the creek.

Reginald snorted. He was discouraged. Hargraves had gone to California where there was a gold rush going on there, and when he had seen the area where the gold seekers were finding gold, he had realized that it looked a lot like the area around Bathurst. Hargraves claimed that he had immediately gotten on a ship for Australia and headed straight for the Turon. He hadn't kept his movements much of a secret either. He'd told a few blokes about finding nuggets, but nobody was too excited.

"Regie! Hargraves!"

It was Rube, still panning the creek. Reginald's scalp crawled, and he jumped up and went bounding down to Rube, who was bent over the pan he held in his hand.

Hargraves had run ankle deep into the creek to him, and the other gold seekers were converging on him. Regie clamped a hand on his brother's shoulder and looked down at the pan he held in his hand.

There, gleaming almost pure of quartz, was a large

216

nugget as gold as Rube's hair. And there were other smaller ones, too.

Hargraves picked the nugget out of the pan and held it up. "By Jove! It's big as a hen's egg, lads," he exclaimed.

Reginald took off his hat and threw it in the creek. "Yeehi!" he cried. "Gold, by damn!"

Hargraves's eyes twinkled. "Now all we have to do, gentlemen, is convince Governor Fitzroy."

No one had to convince Reginald. He had caught gold fever the instant he saw the nugget gleaming in Rube's pan, and within seconds he was on his knees in the creek, clawing handsful of sand and gravel from its alluvial bottom.

Autumn came, and on a cool day in May, Reginald and Rube rode into the Aylesburys' yard whooping, slinging their hats over their heads. "Gold, gold," Reginald shouted. "The surveyor general confirmed it himself. There's gold on the Turon!" And in one motion, he tossed a nugget as big as a hen egg at Jessica's feet.

She bent down, picked it up off the veranda step and looked at it. Tidbits of gossip had been trickling back to the Aylesbury station ever since a man named Hargraves had begun to show several Bathurst men where his gold discovery was. But Jessica hadn't really expected anything to come of it. But now, suddenly, she sensed a great change coming to the Bathurst district, to the people, to Australia, to the Aylesburys themselves. Absentmindedly, she handed the gold nugget to Carrie, who stood beside her.

Aaron looked at Penelope. "If they've discovered gold, men will go crazy. There'll be a rush to the district like nothing we've ever seen before."

"Let them rush," Penelope said, her eyes going beyond the yard to the hills.

Jessica agreed, thinking that perhaps gold fever would take the police's mind off of Eric. Eric, wherever he might be.

Part II

August, 1851

Chapter XII

Even though Jessica had been fully warned what to expect, she was deeply appalled at the squalid living conditions she had discovered at the massive gold diggings centered in and around Sofala. For the last three or four months, men had flocked to the Bathurst district in droves, passing over the rutted land trails in drays, on horseback, or by foot, pushing wheelbarrows or pulling small carts behind them. Many had footed the long distances from the various settlements of Australia with nothing more than a swag over their shoulders and a dream in their hearts. Hundreds of men desperately sought their fortunes throughout the Macquarie Valley. Sofala merely represented one of the many gold sites along the Turon River and was really no more than a huge camp of battered tents and *gunyahs*, the throw-together shelters made out of large strips of bark propped up by long sticks, structures that closely resembled the tiny card houses she and Eric used to build as children. There was only a small cluster of actual wooden buildings in Sofala and even those looked as if they might tumble with the next hard wind.

When Jessica and her father had pulled up to the commissioner's tent that first day, she had been aware of the peculiar undercurrent of animal excitement as the men went about the back-breaking business of searching for gold. Never before had she seen so many men so hard at work. The area, treeless except for the broad mimosa and cascading river gums that lined the curving riverbed, was literally honeycombed with narrow shafts and sinkings, dry diggings they were called.

As she had gazed across the scene that surrounded them while her father had sought the commissioner's help in getting a central location to set up his tent, she noticed the place bustled with constant activity. The men diligently worked their claims either along the trickling river or inside their narrow mining shafts. Ochre-colored dust rose over the diggings like an early morning haze, which made breathing difficult and coated everyone and everything around; but no one else seemed aware of the problem. The diggers' minds were too keenly focused on the tasks at hand.

Jessica had now been at the gold fields near Sofala for over a week and had grown accustomed to the manner in which men were willing to live in order to have a chance at instant wealth. Few men had more than a tent with a minimum of bedding to go to at the end of a very strenuous day. They fought sand flies by day and mosquitoes at night, and unless they were fortunate enough to have set their camp near an ant bed, they fought fleas constantly, but then they had to contend with the ants themselves.

The sun bore down mercilessly, the temperatures unseasonably high for August; in fact they had been unseasonably high all winter. Rain had been scarce, and as a whole, the men suffered from sunburn, blisters, and fatigue. They looked pale and haggard. Most were unwashed. Many fell prey to cramps, infected blisters, colds, rheumatism, eye burns, diarrhea and dysentery; a few had come down with attacks of high fear and ague, dying horrendous deaths in a very short time. That was why Aaron had felt so compelled to erect a medical tent at Sofala in the first place.

Jessica wrapped her arms tightly around her shoulders in an effort to stave off the evening chill and thought back several weeks to when Regie Schiller had ridden into their yard begging Aaron to go with him immediately to the crowded little mining town. His friend, Howey Nichols, had come down with an extremely high fever which had rendered him unconscious for several hours, then suddenly he had come down with a bad case of the shakes.

Having just witnessed another man die of a similar fever, Regie had been frantic for his friend, and Aaron had wasted no time in having his gig made ready while personally getting together the instruments and medications he felt he would need in his medical valise.

Having seen how badly medical attention was needed at the fields, Aaron decided to set up this medical tent right away. He'd returned to his cattle station just long enough to pack what he thought he would need and explain to Penelope his plans. Although she had been reluctant to see him leave, knowing he might be away for months, she had agreed he should go where he was needed. She would handle any problems that might arise at their station while he was gone.

Originally, Jessica had had a hard time convincing

Aaron she should go with him. He had seen the cramped and dirty conditions in the gold fields and did not want her subjected to it, but in the end she had worn down his resistance and had been allowed to accompany him in order to work as his assistant. And work she did, from sunup till sundown, aiding Aaron in any way she could. Rare had been the moments when she was able to leave the tent during the day, even for a leisurely walk or to visit with the few other women who were there.

Wearily, she leaned against one of the poles that braced the tent and watched while men all over camp hurriedly but orderly put away their tools and headed for their tents. As nightfall quickly descended, Jessica reflected that it was a good thing Aaron had allowed her to come with him for there were far too many injuries and ailments for him to handle alone. Being the only doctor in the area, patients were brought to him from camps all over. At times, whenever there was an unusual rash of injuries or an outbreak of collapse from sheer fatigue, she had fervently wished Aaron had agreed to let Carrie come along with them, too. They could have used her help in preparing bandages ahead of time and in keeping the bedclothes and instruments cleaned; but then it was good to keep busy, and if Carrie had been there, Jessica would have more time to worry about Eric.

"Tired?" she heard Aaron's voice as he stepped out of the large tent that housed only six patients at the moment. Four had been seriously hurt in accidents, and the other two had taken ill and were running extremely high fevers. Because of the nature of the fevers, Jessica knew Aaron would sleep in the main tent again that night.

"Yes, very," she responded with a slow smile as she

brushed several dark curls away from her face.

"Glad tomorrow's Sunday," he muttered as he sat down beside her on the low overturned crate that served as a bench. A grateful sigh escaped his weary body as he stretched his legs before him. "There will be very few men working their claims tomorrow."

"Which means fewer accidents." Jessica nodded, her face showing the relief she felt. She was truly grateful that most of the diggers respected Sunday and allowed themselves a day of rest, a day in which they took the time to relax and prepare themselves a decent meal, because what little they took time to eat during the week was sorely lacking in true nourishment.

Glancing out at the campfires that were slowly coming to life across the darkened camp, Jessica realized it was time to worry about their own nutrition. Slowly she rose to her feet and started toward the smaller tent that lay just behind the medical tent. It was their personal lodgings, only a third as large as the medical tent, but still she realized it was quite a bit larger than most of the other tents crowding Sofala.

Inside, she and Aaron had done what they could to make their tent as pleasant as possible. Rather than set their bedding down on bare earth as so many men did, they had taken the time to lay thick strips of bark down for flooring, and she had chosen to hang empty flour sacks between the sleeping areas near the back of the tent to enable them privacy and had laid more of the sacks as they came to be empty on the floor to be utilized as carpets. Near the center of the tent, Jessica had used her practical sense and made a small dining and cooking area, using a tall overturned wooden crate for the table and two short, fat logs set up on end for stools. The only chairs

Aaron had thought to bring were being put to use in the medical tent as was the tiny table he used for his instruments.

Quickly, Jessica went to the back of the tent and brought out the last of the mutton stew from the tiny wooden safe. Gazing into the large pot, she felt there would be just enough to feed them and the six patients, especially since the two patients with fever would barely be able to tolerate a watered-down version of the broth alone. Tomorrow she would have to spend some time preparing another hardy stew, and maybe she could borrow a bit of sugar from Mrs. Clacy and make a little duff. Yes, a nice plum pudding would be just the thing. She had already been given everything else she would need. Since money was scarce at the diggings, most having spent all they had on what supplies they could manage at the outrageous prices being asked, a good number of the men and women Aaron had cared for over the past week insisted on repaying his favors with either foodstuffs or firewood. They had been so generous, in fact, that this was the first time Jessica had found herself out of sugar.

Shortly after she and Aaron saw to the needs of the remaining six patients, spoon feeding the two men too weak to feed themselves, Jessica insisted Aaron join her in their private tent for their own meal. They had hardly spent any time alone together since they first arrived, and she was eager for a little conversation that didn't deal with either injury or illness.

Because the evening chill had already set in, the temperature quickly dropped from the middle sixties fahrenheit to the lower fifties and was still dropping. Aware of the change, Jessica donned her heavy woolen

226

shawl and placed a large piece of firewood into the small fireplace Aaron had fashioned out of green wood and rock near the far end of the tent. Quickly the embers came back to life, and in moments she had the last of the stew simmering again.

"That was delicious," Aaron told her when he scraped the last bite of stew out of his tin plate and then wiped the smooth surface clean with a small piece of johnny cake. "Who would have ever guessed you could cook." His brown eyes twinkled with amusement.

"I may never have had the inclination to do much cooking at home, but I am not entirely incompetent when it comes to domestic activities," she responded lightly.

Never would she admit that, although she had watched Mrs. Chun prepare the family meals before and understood basically what went into a stew, she had not been exactly sure what to do or when. She had eventually gone to Mrs. Clacy several tents down for complete instructions on how to prepare a simple mutton stew and had since been told in minute detail how to make plum duff, johnny cakes, damper, lamb chops, boiled turnips, oatmeal, and green tea. She had yet to try to make coffee, a brew more to the Americans' liking anyway, but Mrs. Clacy had already told her exactly what should be done, and she was ready to give it a try should the need ever present itself.

"I guess you heard the latest on the escapades of the Flash Brigand," Aaron said, keeping a keen eye on her as he picked up his cup and sipped lightly at his still warm tea.

Jessica's blue eyes never failed to light whenever the notorious bushranger, who had recently been dubbed the Flash Brigand of Bathurst, was mentioned, nor did Aaron's.

"No, what has he done now?" she asked eagerly, ready to hear of his latest exploits. Her heart leapt in anticipation.

"Stole Judge Livingston's supper right off his table," Aaron said and shook his head in disbelief. There was a hint of amusement twinkling in his eyes, though clouded with the deep concern he felt for his son.

Jessica's smiled faded. Eric was starting to take needless chances and not only did it worry her, it angered her that he could have so little regard for himself. "Why did he do that?"

"Was probably hungry." Aaron shrugged. "Who knows? But he took the judge's piping hot beefsteak and vegetables right from his table, plate and all. Even took the bottle of chilled wine the man had just started to open. Seems a small fire broke out in the paddock just behind the judge's shearing shed, and while he and his men were busy stamping out the flames, someone scrambled through a few of his personal papers, then made off with his meal. No one actually saw him this time, but everyone, including the judge, knows it was either the Flash Brigand or one of his new gang harassing him again. I hear it is driving the good judge into a fine state of madness not knowing who is after him or why. I hear he has offered some sort of reward for the man's capture. Fifty pounds I believe."

"And that doesn't worry you?" Jessica asked, staring at her hands.

"No more than before." Aaron shrugged. "He seems to know what he is doing well enough and now that he is no longer working alone, I feel much better about his welfare. At least, now if he gets hurt while eluding the police, he will have someone to help him."

"I just wish he would leave New South Wales entirely. There are too many men looking for him here, especially in the Bathurst district. The odds are less and less in his favor every day."

Aaron grew solemn for a moment as he thought about that. "He'll be careful. There's too much at stake for him not to be."

"The judge will see him hung if he is brought into Bathurst for trial. Though no one can actually prove it, we both know Judge Livingston has full control of what goes on in the courts around here."

"That's a fact. If the Flash Brigand is brought in to Bathurst, there won't be much hope. He will be hastily tried and sentenced to his death," Aaron agreed glumly. "That is if he is still alive when he is brought in. With the laws being what they are now, it's no crime to shoot a bushranger on sight if there is any indication or even a slight suspicion that he is armed."

They both sat in silence a long moment before Jessica rose and, biting back her burning tears, she asked if it would be all right for her to leave the dishes for awhile and take a walk.

"Certainly, go ahead. The fresh air will do you good. I can handle any problems that arise here. I'll be in the ward if you want me when you get back. I need to keep an eye on those two men with the fevers."

Hurrying out into the brisk night air, Jessica pulled her shawl closer around her shoulders and skirted through several dimly lit tents on her way to the outer boundaries of the camp. How she hated tears. She hated for anyone to see her cry. Blinking furiously, she fought to control the emotions that had been building inside of her for so long, until she was well away from any of the tents. Then, once alone and unable to hold back her bottled emotions any longer, she broke out in quiet, rasping sobs and felt the tears stream endlessly down her cheeks, hot trails of misery that quickly turned to cold, wet streaks of anguish.

There really was no hope for Eric as long as he insisted on staying in the Bathurst area. He tempted fate far too much by continuing this brash vendetta against Judge Livingston. Did he think he was invincible? Eventually he would slip; his luck would run out, and he would be caught, or worse, he could be killed. Either way, Eric was acting as his own hangman by continuing to plague the judge. Why couldn't he give up his quest for vengeance and go away to either Port Philip or Western Australia where he could once again live as a free man? Why did he feel so compelled to tempt fate so? Hadn't he done enough to rectify the terrible wrong done to Ben? After all, Ben was back on his feet now, having received that mysterious shipment of supplies and equipment last month, including the horse and dray that had brought it to him. No one had seen it arrive. It was just there one morning when Ben woke up with a note attached wishing him well.

If Eric loved her, if he truly loved her, he would go to another colony, go to the Port Philip district, to the recently formed colony of Victoria, like he had once promised, and start anew. He would be out of the jurisdiction of the New South Wales police and out of the immediate danger of arrest. Then he could send for her like he had claimed he would that morning just outside the caves. A cold shiver darted down her spine as she remembered how her beloved had been openly betrayed by his own uncle, James Cranston. Wiping the tears from her eyes, she wondered what sort of evil had hidden itself away inside that man, possessing him, causing him to do such a wicked thing. True, he had nobly claimed he had done it for Eric's own good, but his words had been so laced with lies that even Penelope had recognized them.

"Isn't it a might chilly for an evenin' stroll?" The words came from behind her and slowly broke into her haze of misery. Quickly Jessica dabbed away her tears with the corner of her shawl and took a long steadying breath before she turned around. She hoped the night shadows would conceal the fact that she had been crying.

"Yes, it is much colder than I had realized," she said and attempted a smile. "It's so cold that the air is starting to sting my eyes and make them watery. Looks like we may be in for a little winter weather after all. I was just about to turn back."

Regie stood and looked at her for a long moment before speaking again. "Mind if I walk with ya?"

Although she would much rather be alone at the moment, she could think of no polite way to refuse him. As he fell into step beside her, she turned her thoughts from Eric's hopeless plight and asked, "What brings you away from your campfire on such a chilly night?"

"You," he said bluntly. Nervously, he drew his arms behind his back and interlocked his hands together, absently letting his thumbs spar with one another. "Pa and Rube are at a neighbor's tent playing poker. So's Howey. I was feeling a might lonely sittin' in our tent all by myself so I was on my way to your tent to see if I could talk ya out of a cup of hot tea when I noticed ya leave and come out here. I was sort of hoping we could visit for awhile. I just want someone to talk to." Then, upon seeing her doubt, he promptly broke his hands apart and held them up as if in surrender and added, "That's all— just talk."

Although Regie Schiller would not ordinarily be her choice of a companion for the evening, she realized his company would help her keep her mind off of her worries, if only for a little while. Glancing over at him, expecting to see that half leer of his lurking on his lips, she realized he was sincere this time, and even if he wasn't and had hopes of a little sporting pleasure at her expense, her father would be in the next tent, in easy earshot of any cries she might make for help.

"I think there should be enough tea left in the billy can to fill a couple of cups," she finally said and smiled, remembering that Regie was the one who had come to Carrie's aid when Captain Scantlin had set about to have his way with her. Therefore, Regie was not all bad, at least not to the bone like she suspected Rube might be. Quiet Rube, always watching, always waiting, lurking in the shadows and speaking only when it served his purpose. Rube reminded her of a wild dingo on the prowl, creeping through the shadows while Regie was more like a curious but bumbling koala, eager to explore.

"I think this is the first time I've ever seen you smile close up," Regie commented awkwardly as they continued toward her tent.

Jessica thought for a moment and let her smile broaden. "This is the first time you have ever given me reason to smile. You do have an exasperating way of annoying me, you know."

Regie laughed and glanced at her briefly. "That's true, and to be honest, I do it so that you'll pay me some attention."

Not liking the direction in which this conversation was headed, Jessica abruptly changed the subject.

"I hear Captain Scantlin has been restored to the police force," she said with a scowl, knowing how hard Regie and her father had fought to have the wicked man permanently removed from duty.

"I know. Rube told me about it last week after he had a little run-in with him when he'd gone to Bathurst for supplies. Seems the old captain is fully restored of his authority and now lists me among his personal enemies. Your father's now on his list, too. I'm afraid Old Scant Face will be keeping a close eye on us for awhile." Regie frowned at the thought of having an enemy so high up in the police force.

"Do you regret having interfered when you did?"

"Naw, not in the least. I'd do it again. I only regret he wasn't punished for his behavior more than he was. Three months' suspension! Now he's back in a position to continue his underhanded deeds with the force of the law to back him. And there's nothin' we can do about it."

Jessica paused just outside the tent to look at Regie in the soft glow of the oil lamp as it filtered through the canvas walls of the tent. His anger was clearly evident on his handsome young face, and for a moment, she felt her heart go out to him. She'd never suspected either of the twins to possess a shred of decency, yet here Regie was raging over the obvious miscarriages of justice from which they all suffered these days.

"I'd like to give that man a matched set of ears." He grinned and politely pulled the flap of the tent back to allow them to enter. "Too bad Eric's aim couldn't have been a little off that day."

Jessica laughed. "Carrie said just about that same

233

thing to me."

"Did she now?" Regie asked with raised brows. "A girl after my own heart."

As Jessica put the billy can back over the fire to reheat, she wondered if Regie realized just how true his last statement really was. All Carrie could talk about these days was Regie's attempt to rescue her. The poor lass had stars in her eyes when it came to Regie Schiller and, looking at him now in the soft lamplight, Jessica could almost understand it. Regie was indeed handsome, in a roguish sort of way. And when he made the effort, he could be very charming. She just wished Regie felt the same way about Carrie, but that was not very likely. Regie seemed to go for women with a little flash and daring. Carrie could not make the score on either count, though she was very pretty and had a heart of pure gold. But alas, Carrie's was not the sort of gold Regie Schiller longed for.

"Speaking of Eric," Regie continued as he eased himself onto one of the upended logs, "do you hear anything from him?"

Jessica paused with a brightly colored potholder in her hand, her gaze suddenly solemn. "No, nothing lately."

"Then you have heard from him?"

"When his grandfather was dying," she said sadly. "He took the chance of paying a brief visit. But then he took immediately to the bush again."

"And you don't know where he's gone off to?"

"No one does," she responded. Finding his curiosity unnerving, she added innocently, "I do know that he was headed south the first time he escaped."

"South? Then I'll wager he's somewhere in Victoria, probably working as a stockman somewhere. That will

234

put him safe from the likes of Captain Scantlin. I know for a fact that Old Scant Face would love to get his sights on Eric once more. Your father and I are high on his black list, but Eric heads it. Scant has sworn that one day he will get even . . . an ear for an ear. Only I don't suppose Scant will stop at just an ear. If you do hear from your brother, you might ought to warn him of that. It would really be best if he never sets foot again inside the boundaries of New South Wales. It just could mean his very death."

Chapter XIII

"Do you really want to learn how?" Regie asked with a tilt of his head, laughing at the absurdity of the idea as he gazed up at her standing on the shallow rise above him.

"Yes, I do. And why do you find it so amusing?" Jessica asked, putting her hands on her hips and grinning down at him, despite her best efforts to scowl with indignation.

"I don't know. It's just not the sort of thing I reckoned you'd want to do."

"Why not?"

"For one thing it's hard work. It might not look like it takes much effort, but it does."

"And do you think that everything I've been doing to help my father hasn't been hard work?" she asked with a raise of her brows. "I'll have you know I work very hard and without rest for as long as I'm needed. As it so happens, this is the first time in all the weeks we've been here that I've had any time whatsoever during a day, besides Sunday, to get away from that medical tent and all the work."

236

He would not argue that point. She was loyal to her father's needs. "What about a license? You know you are supposed to have a license before you go lookin' for gold."

"I'll take my chances," she retorted smoothly. "Just like most of these men around here are doing."

That was true enough. Most men could not afford the thirty shillings it cost to get a gold license but took the risk of searching for gold anyway. "Uh—what about those skirts?" he asked, letting his gaze drift down her slender form to the volumes of material that surrounded her.

"What about them?"

"I don't think skirts are the right kind of clothes for panning gold, but if you really want to bad enough, I'll show you what to do. Come on down here," he said and waved her toward the edge of the Turon River where his and his brother's claims lay side by side. His father's claim was a little further up the river near a slight bend, which made it a good spot for gold sediment, but there had not been room for all three of them there. By the time they had decided to give the gold a try, most of the prime locations had already been claimed. He was glad they were able to secure places by the river at all. Those men further away from the river had to resort to sinking shafts, and that was far more work than he could ever tolerate.

"That's better," Jessica said triumphantly and quickly did as he bade and joined him at the river's edge.

"You're really one to have your way." Regie laughed good-naturedly as he bent over and picked up a strange-looking metal pan. In the last few weeks, he and Jessica had finally started to become friends, though the going had been far slower than he would have liked. For the past three Sundays he had managed to capture several hours of her time, joining her in leisurely strolls or listening to her read from the book of poetry she had brought along, but she had always cut their afternoon short in order to cook for her father and whatever patients they had. And on an occasional Saturday night, he had managed a few extra hours of her company, though they were always confined to the tent. Once he'd even come close to holding her hand.

He gladly would have found time on any of the other nights during the week to visit with her, but she was usually too busy helping Dr. Aylesbury or far too tired for company. She was right; she did work hard and it caused him to admire her even more. Smiling inwardly, Regie realized that the past few weeks were a dream come true for him, and he felt that if he continued to be very careful and take things nice and easy, keeping to his best behavior when he was around her, he might somehow be able to work his way into her heart.

"I warn you, though. You just might go and get your shoes wet and probably your skirt, too," he said as he pushed his cabbage tree hat back from his forehead and smiled down into her impatient blue eyes.

"My slippers will dry, I assure you," she informed him, glancing down at the curious-looking tin pan he now held. "Let's get started already. How does one find gold?"

"Panning is the simplest way to separate the heavy metal from the sand and rocks that line the bottom or along the sides of the river," he started to explain while demonstrating his words with action. "First, you will take the pan in both hands like this here. Then you'll have to bend over at the very edge of the water and scoop up either the mud from the bottom or dirt from the drift at the sides of the river. Only fill the pan about an inch deep. Then you bend way over and place the pan underwater like this, keepin' the back a little higher than the front. Then, while holding the pan real good with one hand, you begin to stir the mud with the other. Slowly you start to wash the lighter dirt and rocks away like this here, keepin' your eye on the part that's left in the pan. Look over all tiny rocks for insets of gold before tossing 'em out." As he said that he examined several rounded stones, then tossed them into the center of the river.

"When you get down to just a spoonful of sediment, you scatter it in the bottom of the pan and look for color." He frowned, then dumped the entire contents into the river. "If you were lucky enough to find bits of gold, you would pick them out with your fingers and put them in a bottle or somethin' and at the end of the day, you would set the gold out to dry."

Jessica listened intently, then accepted the pan offered and knelt at the side of the river. As Regie had predicted, her skirts fell into the water, wetting the hem. Frowning, she gathered up the material and tucked it between her knees where she was able to secure it out of her way. Regie's eyes lit at the sight of her slender ankles and for the life of him, he could not keep from staring.

"Let's see, I scoop up an inch of mud," she said more to herself than to Regie, unaware of the distraction she was providing not only for Regie but for several other men who had been busy panning for gold nearby. "Then you stir the mud with your hand . . ."

By now even Rube had stopped his work at the cradle, a larger device for washing dirt and mud away, and stood motionlessly watching her. There were no fewer than two dozen pairs of eyes trained on her slim white ankles and at the way her blouse pulled against her breasts when she stretched far enough to be able to keep the pan in the water without getting her slippers wet.

"There's no gold on either of these rocks, so I toss them away . . ." she went on, concentrating fully on her own actions.

"I've got it down to a spoonful," she said over her shoulder. "What do I do now?"

Regie quickly knelt at her side and put his hand beside hers on the pan. His thumb brushed the side of her hand and caused his heartbeat to race in his chest. Taking full advantage of the situation, he placed an arm around her in order to place his other hand on the pan and showed her how to swirl the sand around in order to inspect it for particles of gold. He breathed deeply the floral scent of her long, dark hair, glad she had chosen to wear it loose instead of tied back in that peculiar little knot she seemed so partial to. Letting his thoughts drift to the warm feel of her in his arms, he wondered what sort of soap she used that smelled so sweet.

"Look, Regie, look," she said excitedly, turning just enough in his arms to be able to look into his eyes. When she did and realized the passion she saw in their dark-blue depths, she instantly tried to wrench herself from his grasp, causing them both to lose their balance and topple face forward into the cold water with a loud splash.

Rube came instantly to her aide, sloshing out into the water and offering her a helping hand before Regie was able to rise up out of the water and do the same.

"This water is freezing," she gasped as she accepted Rube's hand and let him pull her out of its shallow depths. Realizing she still held the pan in her hands, she looked quickly down at it and frowned. "I lost them.

240

There were several tiny pieces of gold in the bottom of that pan, and I lost them all."

In a fit of frustration she flung the pan aside and stood ankle deep in the water with her hands on her hips, unaware at first that her clothes now clung to her curves like a second skin. The white blouse and chemise she had on were wet to the shoulders and had become almost transparent to the eye. When she realized just what it was all the men were standing around gaping at, she quickly drew her arms across her chest and felt her embarrassment creep up her neck and enflame her cheeks.

Regie had gotten to his feet by now and, immediately realizing her predicament, reached for the lapels of his jacket, but because his coat was just as soaked as the rest of him, he had a hard time getting it off. When he finally had tugged himself out of it, he felt awkward handing over such a wet garment for her use, but she snatched it to her like her life depended on having it.

"Here, take mine instead," Rube said gallantly and ignored the brooding look in his brother's eyes as he quickly peeled out of his own jacket and offered it to her. "We'd better get you back to your tent right away before you catch your death. It wouldn't do for the doctor's own daughter to become ill, now, would it?"

Regie stood shin deep in the cold water, the only dry clothing on his entire body being a now lopsided hat, and he watched helplessly as Rube slipped his jacket over Jessica's trembling shoulders and assisted her out of the water by her elbow. As the two stepped onto dry land, he saw his brother take the wet jacket away from her and drop it casually in the dirt.

Regie was too embarrassed to follow them. Frustrated that his growing passion has been brutally doused and that his brother had so competently come to Jessica's aide, he reached up and jerked his hat off, then as he watched his brother turn back and offer the men still staring after them a rakish grin, Regie flung the crumpled hat down into the water and kicked at it, missing the hat entirely and almost falling again in the process.

Looking around at the leering expressions on the men's faces, he realized glumly as he stomped out of the water that the two brothels that lay on the outskirts of Sofala were sure to do a brisk business that night.

Jessica's teeth chattered by the time she reached the tent. Words she had spoken that very morning in praise of the cooler weather of the past week came back to haunt her. When dry, the temperatures were quite pleasant, but when wet—she could not remember ever having felt so cold, so completely miserable in her entire life.

"Thank you for the use of your jacket," she said to Rube as she pulled away from him and hurried to jerk back the canvas flap at the front of her tent. "I'll have it for you in a minute."

She went straight to the back of the tent to stand in front of the tiny fireplace, pulling off Rube's jacket and tossing it aside as she went. Her fingers went immediately to her wet, clinging blouse, and she had three buttons undone before she realized Rube had followed her inside.

"Rube," she said in exasperation. "I'm getting undressed." When he neither said anything nor moved toward the door flap, she added. "Please, step outside so that I can get out of these wet things. I'm freezing." She felt a chill from more than the wet clothing grasp her body when she realized he was taking in the view her wet clothing provided. Panic gripped her at the smoldering emotion she saw in his dark-blue eyes. Crossing her arms in front of her, she took in a slow, deep breath, ready to call out for her father's assistance, when suddenly he turned to leave.

Just before he reached his hand out to push away the flap, he turned back to face her and tugged briefly at the broad brim of his hat. "I'll be happy to wait outside. Pardon the intrusion."

Not quite trusting Rube not to peek, Jessica stepped away from the fire's warmth and did her undressing behind the flour sack walls that surrounded her bedding. Once she had replaced her wet clothes for dry, she picked up Rube's jacket and carried it out to him.

"Thank you again for lending me your jacket. I was in quite a predicament, to say the least," she said and offered him a sincere smile of appreciation, but when he did not return her smile, she felt her own fade from her face.

"I didn't like the way all those men were starin' at you," he stated simply. "I didn't feel they should have the privilege of viewing your fine body, and I'm afraid that with your blouse wet the way it was, it didn't leave much to the imagination."

Jessica felt herself blushing, unable to believe he had the gall to mention such a thing to her. When his gaze dipped and lighted once more on the curves of her blouse, she realized he well remembered what he had taken the liberty to view earlier. She wanted to run from his penetrating gaze, but proudly stood her ground as she held out his jacket to him. When he did not immediately take it from her hand, she stammered. "I guess I really shouldn't offer it back to you while it is still wet. If you'd like, I can hang it near the fire for awhile and return it later when it is dry."

What she intended to do was give it to Regie the moment it was dry and let him be the one to return it to Rube. She would prefer to stay as far away from Rube as possible until his memory had had a little time to fade.

"Should I return for it tonight?" he asked. "Will it be dry by then?"

"It should be."

"Good, then I'll come back by for it then, right after tucker time." He nodded politely, then turned and strolled back toward the river.

Jessica hurried back inside and stirred the fire to a bright blaze, adding several small dry logs, which would burn quickly. She intended to have the jacket dry in plenty of time to return it before dark. Just the thought of Rube's having a reason to come over made her skin crawl. There was just something about him that caused her to feel vulnerable, and it worried her.

To her relief, the jacket dried quickly, and she hurried to the Schiller's tent, hoping she would find either Regie or Karl, their father, and not have to even set eyes on Rube again, much less allow him to set eyes on her.

"Is anybody home?" she called from just outside the tent. Self-consciously, she held the neatly folded jacket close, as if deriving protection from it.

"Jessica!" she heard from within and was relieved to recognize Regie's voice.

Pulling back the door flap and poking her head inside, she asked, "May I come in?"

"Oh, aye," he responded eagerly, reaching for a shirt and slipping it over his shoulders in a gentlemanly gesture that she certainly appreciated.

"I came by to return Rube's jacket. Would you see that he gets it? I didn't feel it would be right for him to have to make a trip by our tent tonight just to retrieve his jacket." Her gaze quickly swept the scant furnishings of the Schiller tent as she handed Regie his brother's jacket. Other than their bedding which was spread out on the bare earth, there were only a few crates of supplies and a small three-legged stool, which probably served as a table, for there was a deck of playing cards and a small, half-filled tin cup resting on top of it.

"I'll take it to him right away," Regie promised as he stared down at the folded garment that had been fortunate enough to caress her lovely shoulders.

"I've already thanked him for lending it to me, but you might thank him again for me." She turned to leave. "I guess I'd better get back there and start supper. It'll be dark soon."

"Jessica?" he called after her. "I am sorry for what happened. I know it was all my fault."

"How can you be to blame for my clumsiness?" she said offhandedly, feeling a twinge of guilt at the expression that was so deeply embedded in his face. Suddenly it was apparent to her that Regie's feelings for her had surpassed a simple friendship. Why had she not seen that coming?

"Jessica," he said with such hesitation that she was afraid of what he was about to say to her.

"Regie, I think we need to understand each other," she said softly. She did not want to hurt his feelings, but she also did not want him to hope for affection that would never come.

Regie's shoulders dropped slightly. "You don't need to say it. I think I know what you are about to say. You don't want me comin' round no more."

"No, it's not that. Ever since you stopped trying to be such an obstinate show-off all the time, I've come to enjoy your company. It's just that I think I need to make it clear that what we share is a friendship. Nothing more."

Regie stood staring down at his muddy boots for a long moment, then looked up into her searching eyes, smiled, and for the first time she was reminded of his Aylesbury ancestry. At that moment he looked a lot like she remembered Eric's Uncle Mark.

"Too bad about losing the gold you found," he told her. "Maybe next time you'll do better."

"It's his leg," Regie said to Aaron as he helped his brother into the tent. "He hurt it somehow while working the cradle. I think he may have broke it. It hurts him bad to even try to stand on it."

"Help him to that chair and I'll have a look at it just as soon as I finish wrapping Andy's shoulder," Aaron told him, indicating one of the two chairs near the front of the tent. "Jessica, bring a wet towel to wrap around Rube's leg to help keep any swelling down until I can get over there."

Rube grimaced with pain when Regie helped him ease down into the chair, but his eyes were on Jessica as she dipped a towel into a pail of cold water and brought it to him.

"Where's the injury? Which leg?" she asked in a cool, professional voice as she knelt before him. She could feel his gaze bear right through her.

"It's my ankle. My left ankle," he told her as he

worked his trouser leg up.

If the ankle had not been red and slightly swollen, Jessica would have believed he had conjured up an injury just to be able to come inside and torment her. Ever since she had thwarted his attempt to come around that night with the pretense of getting his jacket back, he had been openly watching her every move. In the evenings, she could not step outside her tent without finding him nearby, staring at her. He had made her so ill at ease that she was extremely careful never to be alone at night.

"Keep that towel wrapped tightly around your ankle until Father gets over here," she ordered him, then stood and hurried away to the far side of the tent in order to escape his close scrutiny.

The examination took far longer than she would have liked, but soon she heard her father say, "Looks like you just sprained it. Keep a cool towel wrapped around it for awhile and stay off that foot for a few days."

"Maybe I should stay here tonight. It's quite a far piece back to our tent," Rube suggested. "I might do that ankle further harm if I was to try to walk all that way."

Jessica did not look up from the bandages she was folding.

"I really don't have room for you," Aaron explained and gestured to the already crowded tent.

"I'll help him get back without hurtin' his ankle any," Regie said, his expression tight. "He can use me as a crutch. And me and Pa will see to it he don't use that ankle for several days. Thanks, doctor. What do we owe you?"

"Nothing," Aaron said in his usual response.

"No, we owe you something," Rube put in quickly. "And we Schillers always pay our debts. I'll see to it.

Somehow, someway."

As Regie helped Rube out of the tent, Jessica dared to glance up, and to her dismay she found Rube's eyes still on her, even as he was being led away.

Over the next several weeks, many of the diggers and panners who had swarmed to the Sofala area grew discouraged. The gold had started to run out. Word of better finds further inland reached them and, one by one, the tents came down. As the population dwindled, Aaron decided there was no longer a pressing need for him to stay any longer.

"I think I'll start taking down the medical tent tomorrow morning," he finally told Jessica one afternoon as they sat watching the men who had stayed to work their claims. Except for one man who had gotten a sharp piece of rock in his eye, they didn't have a patient all afternoon. "There hasn't been a serious injury in days, and now that everyone's not living cheek and jowl, sickness is not as likely to be a problem. At least no more than anywhere else."

Jessica nodded in agreement. "I'll help you. I'm more than ready to go back home."

"As I. I miss Penelope. And I want to see how the station has fared these past two months. With the coming of spring, there will be lots to do. Zachariah and Hiram will already be arguing about whose needs are the most pressing: the cattle's or the sheep's. I can't expect Penelope to handle it all, though I'm sure she would and without complaint. Well, without too much complaint."

Jessica laughed. "I miss her, too. Maybe if we get started this afternoon, we could be ready to leave sometime tomorrow."

"Let's give it a go," he said as he jumped up and hurried inside the tent. "I'll gather up the bedding and you start packing away the medications and instruments. We'll be home by tomorrow night."

Aaron and Jessica worked well into the night, folding and packing by lamplight. Regie and Karl came over to help when the time came to load the heavy canvas and some of the bulkier crates onto the dray. For once, Rube was no where to be seen.

When they finally went to bed that night, everything was packed away except for the smaller tent and their personal bedding. By mid-morning, they had all their belongings securely loaded and were on their way home. Several hours later, they finally pulled into the yard only a few feet from the front door. Their mounting excitement quickly gave way to concern when no one hurried outside to greet them.

"Where is everybody?" Aaron called out as he climbed down from the driver's seat.

Jessica looked around. Everything looked as it should. There were sheep grazing in the distance and beyond them, the cattle were in such number she concluded that Penelope had already had them mustered and counted. Sliding to the ground, she followed Aaron through the front veranda and inside.

"Is anyone at home?" he called out. His concern was evident on his face when he looked back to Jessica. "Where can they all be?"

At that moment, Mrs. Chun stepped through the back door and smiled. "I thought that was your voice I heard over my cooking. It's nice to have you two back."

"Where is everyone?" Aaron asked, his frustration

growing. "Where's my wife?"

"She's gone to town after a few things. Took Carrie with her." Misreading his frown, she added, "Sig went with them. They'll be safe."

Aaron's shoulders slumped noticeably. He had so anticipated Penelope being home and rushing into his arms. Heaving a sigh, he said, "Well, I guess I'll go out to the barn and see how Zachariah and Hiram are doing."

"Hiram's away on some sort of business, but you'll find Zachariah around here somewhere," Mrs. Chun put in. "Jessica, you look exhausted. Why don't I go back out to the summer kitchen and heat up some water for you and let you have a long soaking bath before supper."

Jessica moaned with pleasure. A smile curved her lips as she started up the stairs to get undressed, and before long she was shoulder deep in a tub filled with warm, scented water. Such utter ecstasy. She was on the verge of drifting off into sweet oblivion, and probably would have, if she hadn't heard Penelope's high shriek followed by Aaron's deep, golden laughter. Next she heard a set of heavy footsteps bounding up the stairs, but it wasn't until she heard more laughter coming from just down the hallway, followed by a door's prompt closing, that Jessica realized tonight's supper would undoubtedly be served a little later than usual.

Jessica gently leaned her head back against the high edge of the tub and closed her eyes, knowing she still had plenty of time to enjoy her bath. Slowly, her pleasurable thoughts turned to Eric as she gently swirled the warm water around her sensitive skin.

Chapter XIV

It was one of the things Jessica had missed most during the two months they had been in the mining camp. While they were at the diggings, there had been very few of the many bird sounds so common to Australia. She supposed all the digging noise and continuous activity the men created had scared the birdlife away. Or maybe the heavy dust had discouraged them; or it could be that too many trees had been felled in order to provide enough firewood. But whatever the reason, there had been no early morning ruckus from the lively kookaburra, no distance calls of the magpies or crows. No exquisite little finches whirred and wheeled in the treetops of the few remaining trees along the river's edge. No tiny starlings, no budgerigars had flitted from branch to branch.

As she urged Chelsea forward into the sparsely wooded area of the small rise where she loved to sit and think, and enjoy what nature had to offer, she listened intently to the lively screaming, the brash laughter, the incessant chattering and whistles of the different birds trying to imitate anything that had ever produced a sound. When she rode beneath a large pepper tree with its dense pale green fronds, she was able to look up and catch sight of a pair of scarlet and blue parrots; and further up there was a pure white, yellow-crested cockatoo. She smiled to them, for they were sitting among the upper branches with their heads cocked, watching her, too.

"Good afternoon," she said with a polite nod. The two parrots looked to one another, then back at her as if trying to decide if they should bother with a response. She laughed when they chose to ignore her, and they hopped over to a branch that was further away instead.

For someone who had cried herself to sleep that night before for sheer want of Eric, she was in very high spirits. Maybe it was the bright and beautiful spring day they had been blessed with, or more than likely it was the fact that Penelope had started to discuss the Christmas holiday meal with Mrs. Chun, though Christmas was still over a month away.

Christmas was not just a religious holiday, it was a family holiday, and the Aylesburys had always held it dear. Excitement welled up inside of Jessica when she considered that maybe, just maybe, Eric would find a way to be with them over the holidays, however briefly. Maybe he could steal into their house under the cloak of darkness and spend a few hours on Christmas Eve with them. Just the thought of it made her heart soar to the lofts of her soul. How she longed to be held in his arms again, to be reminded of his love for her.

Leading Chelsea toward a tree, Jessica started to laugh again for absolutely no reason other than she was full of hope. She hummed a tune she wished she knew the words to as she looped the reins around one of the low branches of the tree.

Once she felt certain the horse was securely tethered, she walked over to a small boulder and looked around at the lavish surroundings while contemplating what she might make Eric for Christmas. Whatever her gift was, it had to be special. While she considered the many possibilities, her eyes were drawn southward to gaze across the rolling plains and the bush-covered hills. She wondered if Eric was out there somewhere; or had he finally moved on, realizing how dangerous New South Wales had become for him?

It had been over two weeks since Jessica had heard any news about Eric's daring exploits, and she hoped that maybe he had finally decided to leave the Bathurst district and go on to Victoria where he would be safe at last. It was a hope she held dear to her heart. And the moment he sent word to her of his whereabouts, she would go to him gladly. In Victoria, they could be married and lead a normal life, as normal as being with Eric could provide.

She smiled at that thought, for Eric would always be an adventurous sort and would not be willing to bow passively to traditional ways. But whatever sort of livelihood he chose to pursue, she would stand proudly by his side as his wife and helpmate. She loved him. What else could she do?

A warm west wind played with wisps of her hair while she stared up into the clear blue sky and smiled at the heavens. Slipping to the grassy ground, she leaned back against the small boulder and closed her eyes against the sun's gentle warmth, allowing the familiar image of Eric's smiling face to form beneath her lids. Absently, she listened to the intermittent chirping of a pair of crickets, wondering what it was they were saying to each other. Was it a message of love? Or was it a challenge between two unhappy males, fighting to win the attention of the one they both found themselves attracted to?

Then suddenly the sounds stopped. Next she heard a faint crackling sound in the near distance, as if someone or something had stepped on a twig and snapped it in two. Knowing there had been recent reports of wild pigs sighted in the area, she turned toward the sound and stared across the high grass for sight of movement. When she heard nothing more, she decided it must have been Chelsea moving around in an attempt to reach sweeter grass, and she leaned back against the large rock, closing her eyes again, though her ears were now finely tuned for any further sounds.

This time it was a thud, and it came from the opposite direction. She brought herself to her knees and searched again for a movement, but again saw nothing more threatening than a huge dragonfly lying idly on the current of the warm breeze. As long as it was not one of those savage, flesh-eating wild hogs or a scavenging dingo, she would not worry, but just the thought that it could be either one crouched out there made her edgy. Slowly she rose to her feet, her eyes focused on the area the last noise had come from. Rather than take any chances of what the tall grass might be hiding, she decided to leave. Turning abruptly, she bumped right into something solid and was so startled by its presence that she screamed before the hand could come up to cover her mouth.

Instantly she was aware that what she had bumped into was a man. She panicked, but it took her only a second more to realize that the man was Eric. Despite the dark golden color of his skin and the fact that he had grown a thick, but well-kept beard, she recognized him, and as his hand released her and his arms came up to surround her, she threw herself against him.

"Eric, it's really you!" she sobbed, her eyes filling with instant tears of joy. "It's really you!"

"Far as I can tell, it is," he laughed and drew her tighter against him, briefly lighting his lips on hers for a sweet taste. "Ah, Jessie, how I have missed you."

"Eric, how I have missed you, too," she sobbed and met his lips once more for a longer, more demanding kiss. So many questions presented themselves to her, but she did not break away to ask them. They could wait. For now, she needed to have the passions, the overpowering desires that had been building within her for over eleven months finally quelled, her hunger sated. She had to have Eric; she had to once again know the pleasure of his lovemaking.

"Jessie, my Jessie," he breathed softly into the sweet depths of her mouth. "I couldn't go another day without seeing you. I'm so glad I discovered you out here."

Jessie could not respond with words. Her emotions had swollen in her throat, making it impossible to do more than sob aloud her rapturous joy. With trembling hands she felt every inch of his strong, muscular back. Even through the soft material of his dark-blue serge shirt, her fingertips could sense the feel of his warm, taut flesh. But it was not enough; she had to touch the skin itself. She had to explore every inch of him, prove to herself that this was real. Prove it was not just another dream.

Eagerly, she pressed her hand between them and sought the small wooden buttons that held the garment closed. She was so intent on her task at hand that she was

255

barely aware he was doing likewise with the tiny pearl buttons along the back of her riding shirt. Soon they were both exquisitely naked, and their bodies melded one to the other. Jessica's smoldering desire had ignited into a wild fury of passion as she felt the evidence of his own desire pressed against her.

Slowly, they knelt to the warm, grassy earth. Jessica lay back in the seclusion of soft green and drew him to her, the only man she could ever love. In a frantic exploration, their hands roamed over each others bodies as they reacquainted themselves with the curves and flat planes, which they had not touched in so terribly long. Willingly, her mind sank into the swirling sea of sensations he always aroused in her. The sweet taste and familiar scent of him only served to intoxicate her further. Her heart raced, her pulse pounded vividly in her throat as her eager body yielded to his masterful touch.

Their parting had been too long, their needs had become too great, and their desires too long denied. With their passions ready to explode, they met in a perfect union of ecstasy. The pinnacle so tremendous, so overwhelming, that Jessica cried out in sheer wonder. Only after their passions had been met, their love fully satisfied, did she take time for questions.

"What are you doing here?" she finally asked while she lay cuddled next to him, her gaze drifting over him, recalling every detail of the man she loved so dearly.

"I'm going to be leaving the Bathurst district, and I had to try to see you one more time before I left," he said simply. His own eyes took in every detail of her creamy-mocha body that spoke of her Aboriginal ancestry and the perfectly shaped face that made his heart quicken.

"You're leaving?" she asked eagerly, her excitement evident.

"I'm glad to know how sorry you are to see me go," he responded sarcastically, though a smile betrayed that sarcasm. "Don't care to have me around? Is that it?"

"What good does it do to have you nearby? I never see you," she retorted quickly.

"But at least I was able to see you on occasion. I've suffered the torment of watching from afar while you traveled down the track into town or whenever you took it upon yourself to pay one of the neighbor's a visit while I was about. I even got a glimpse of you at Sofala." Suddenly his smile faded, and his brown eyes turned as black as midnight. "Since when have you and the Schiller twins become such friends?"

"Do I hear a hint of jealousy?" she asked and couldn't help but grin at the misery she saw in his dark expression. "Oh, Eric. Regie and I became friends out of sheer boredom. He's changed a lot lately. He's finally started to grow up, late though his maturity is in coming. And it's only Regie that I have become friends with. Rube will never change. What did that active imagination of yours have you believing? That I had chosen Regie Schiller over you? How absurd! You should have more faith in me than that!"

Eric drew his gaze away from hers and stared up into the bright blue sky overhead for a moment. "You're right. I should have, and I'm sorry I suspected anything more than friendship might be growing between the two of you. It's just that I . . ." Rising up on one elbow, he explained with a deep felt emotion. "It's just that I love you so damn much! I wish things could be different for us. I wish we could go right now and announce to the

257

world that we are in love and plan to be married. I want you to be my wife so badly that I ache."

"In my heart I'm already your wife. And once you get established elsewhere, just send word to me and I'll come running. Then we can be properly married." Lying back and staring up into the same blue sky he had been studying so intently, she sighed out her joy. "Just think. It won't be long now. As soon as you have found us a place to live, send word. I'll leave that very day."

Eric lay back in silence a long moment. "I don't know that it's going to be all that simple. It may be quite awhile yet before we can be together."

"Why?" she asked as alarm gripped her. "Why could it be awhile? How long can it take to get settled somewhere else? If it's money you're worried about, you still have that money Aaron put aside for your education, and I even have a little stored away."

"There's more to it than money, I'm afraid."

"What more?"

"I can't talk about it. I'm not sure you would understand anyway," he responded broodingly, then closed his eyes to the anguish he felt.

"Have you so little faith in me?" she asked, feeling an anger swell up inside of her. "Haven't I been understanding so far? Have I questioned you about why you allowed yourself to become a bushranger? Have I lectured you on any of your little pranks thus far?"

Eric's eyes flew open. "How did you . . . what do you mean, I allowed myself to become a bushranger?"

"Eric, I know you as well as I know myself," she said, realizing his alarm. "Although no one else has said anything to the effect, I know in my heart that you are the Bathurst bushranger, the one they have started to

258

call the Flash Brigand. I don't know who else is working with you, but I know you have been terrorizing Rodney Livingston and those associated with him ever since you escaped from the Bathurst jail. It is just like you to harass him after what he's done to Ben and some of the others around here. And you are so selective in who feels the brunt of your anger. Deny it if you feel you must, but I know it's you. And I think Father suspects, too."

"What has he said?"

"Nothing as to the bushranger's identity, but he does love to talk of your exploits. I think that deep inside he is proud of you for what you are doing. I know I am, or I was at first, but lately you and your gang have been taking unnecessary chances, and some of the stunts you've pulled have been senselessly dangerous. Like starting a little fire so that you could slip in and steal the man's supper off his table. What did that prove? Within the hour he had another meal laid before him."

"I'm not saying I'm the bushranger, but did it ever occur to you that the man's supper is not all that was taken?"

"You mean the wine? Well, I'm sure that made it worth the effort," she retorted. She hoped to lead him to tell her more with a challenging banter.

"No missing papers were mentioned?" he asked and eyed her suspiciously.

"No. What sort of papers?"

"How would I know? I hear the talk that's going around, too. Such gossip reaches the bush."

Jessica stared at him a long moment, then decided to let him keep his secrets. "Are you going to chance seeing Father and Mother before you leave?"

"No, I don't dare risk it. That house is being watched

constantly. Captain Scantlin seems to be taking the fact that I nipped off the lobe of his ear a bit personally. Seems he has set plans for my own ears." Eric's brown eyes sparkled with some hidden amusement.

"What if I went down and told Father and Mother where they could find you?"

"No, I've got to be going. I had no idea that I would find you out here alone. I had hoped merely to catch one last glimpse of you. I told my mates that I'd be back within the hour, and I'm sure they are getting to be more than a little concerned that I didn't return on time." He grinned, his beard stretching with the smooth spread of his lips. "They worry about me."

"I'm glad they do." She smiled back. "Do I know any of them?"

"You certainly do ask a lot of questions." He laughed as he reached for his clothing. "I wish I had time to stay here and satisfy your insatiable curiosity, but I don't." His eyes twinkled. "I wish I had time enough to satisfy more of your other insatiable needs as well, but I *must* leave now." As his wistful gaze swept her naked body, he reluctantly began to pull his buff trousers back over his stockinged feet. "If you would kindly cover that magnificent body of yours, it would certainly make my leaving a little easier."

"I don't want to make it easy for you to leave me. I don't want you to go," she stated simply then stretched out leisurely before him, allowing him easy view of her entire body.

"Vixen! If I didn't know for certain that my mates would be out searching for me, I'd risk taking more advantage of your charms."

Jessica gasped and grabbed for her riding skirt as her

260

eyes scanned the area for evidence of riders. "You think they would come searching for you? Here?"

"If here is where I've gone to. Aye, they are a loyal lot," he said and stood straight before bothering to rebutton his shirt. "Don't worry. They are not around here yet. I've not heard a kelpie's bark, the signal that tells we are about."

"You know, you certainly have picked up a bit of a brogue there," she commented while carefully fastening the waistband of her dark brown riding skirt while trying to keep hidden within the tall grass. "It's a lot like Coolabah Cecil's used to be. Hmm, and him up and missing and all."

"Don't start trying to solve the mysteries of the world. It'll just make you lose sleep and will put dark circles under those pretty eyes of yours." Having finished redressing, Eric knelt and helped Jessica with her high-topped riding boots. Then when they both were fully dressed, he stood again and offered her his hand.

Jessica's face grew pensive as he pulled her to her feet, the muscles in her jaw taut. "How long until I see you again? Another eleven months?"

"I hope not," he replied.

"Why is it you are willing to try such daring feats as bailing up the judge's gig in broad daylight, almost within sight of town, but you can't seem to find a way to see me?"

"You are still assuming I'm the Bathurst bushranger. But the reason I don't try to see you is that I don't want to put your life in danger. When and if Captain Scantlin ever finds me, he would not stop short of killing a woman in order to get his quarry. He's an unscrupulous man, far more than anyone realizes."

"I know. He tried to rape Carrie right in her own bedroom," she said bluntly.

"He *tried?* Who stopped him? Father?"

"No, Regie Schiller."

"Regie?"

"Regie has changed over the past few months. You might even say he's almost likable."

"Just don't you go liking him too much," he warned with a raised brow.

"There's only one man for me," she assured him as she stepped forward for a good-bye kiss.

Waves of sadness overtook her as he slipped his arms around her one last time and drank lingeringly from her lips. By the time he had stepped away from her and was running toward the cluster of trees where Chelsea was still bound, huge tears had formed in her eyes.

"Send word, Eric. Send word to me and I'll come," she called out as he ducked into the trees and beyond, quickly disappearing from her sight.

"I ran into Betty Schiller today when I was in town checking on the mail," Jessica said as she handed the bowl of corn into Aaron's waiting hand.

"Oh, and how is she doing?" Penelope asked as she took a steamed potato off of the small platter and passed the rest to Jessica.

"She misses Karl and the twins," Jessica replied. "You remember—a few weeks ago they passed by here on their way to Ballarat?"

Penelope nodded. It had been a terribly hot day early in December, and the three of them had stopped for a quick dipperful of cool water, them and hundreds of others on their way to the newly discovered gold fields in southern Victoria. The Victorian government had gotten their wish; they had offered a reward to the first man who could make a major find in Victoria and thus bring their population back from the New South Wales gold mines, but Penelope did not believe they had fully thought out the consequences. Victoria had just now earned self-government and was still testing out this newly acquired freedom. The last thing the new government needed was a huge mass of gold-hungry men moving in and disrupting things.

"Well, they've reached the place and have staked their claims. She had just gotten a letter from Regie, which told her all about their arrival and how awful the conditions are there."

Aaron pointed his fork at her, letting her know that he had something to say as soon as he had cleared his mouth. "What are the conditions? Did she say?"

"According to Regie's letter, Ballarat is nothing like the mining towns around here. He said that the place was chaotic and wild. No one looks out for anyone else. It's every man for himself. Seems Karl was hit over the head and robbed of what little gold he had taken down there to buy their licenses with before they even reached Melbourne. They are now short of supplies, and only Karl has a license to legally allow him to dig for gold in Victoria. Mrs. Schiller is worried that the twins will be caught digging without one and be carried off to jail or worse. In Victoria, the punishment for not having a license is severe. Mrs. Schiller was going around town trying to find someone who might be headed that way. Someone she could trust to take a little of the money Karl had left with her on down to him so that the twins could purchase their licenses and also so they could have food enough to last them until they strike it rich."

Aaron shook his head. "I've been hearing stories about how bad the conditions are down there. It's a shame that man can't be more charitable to his own kind."

"Mrs. Schiller also mentioned how Karl's head wound has not healed properly but that Regie explained how there is no doctor to take him to," Jessica continued. She watched closely to see what his reaction would be to that.

Penelope sighed and laid down her fork. "No doctor?"

Aaron's gaze came up to meet his wife's. "Now don't start worrying just yet. I haven't made up my mind on this."

Just then Carrie came in with a fresh pitcher of water and began to fill the half-empty glasses.

"If you do decide to go to Ballarat and set up your tent again, you must realize that I intend to go with you," Jessica stated firmly.

"Not this time. Ballarat is far too rowdy for a woman's presence."

"You'll need an assistant. If it is as rowdy and crowded as they say, there will be far more accidents and sicknesses than you will ever be able to contend with. You will need my help. Remember, you admitted to me on several occasions that you never would have been able to make it at the camp near Sofala without me. You will need me even more at Ballarat."

"I'll try to find some man down there to help me," he insisted. "I can't be responsible for taking you into that hellhole." Widening his eyes, he glanced at Penelope and got the reprimanding look he had expected.

Carrie stopped pouring to stare at Aaron and Jessica.

Her lower lip was drawn anxiously between her teeth.

"She's right, Dr. Aylesbury," she finally had the courage to say. "You'll be needin' her. Those men down there aren't goin' to want to be workin' as a doctor's assistant for you when there's gold to be found. Besides she's already got the know-how of what to do."

"Thank you, Carrie." Jessica responded with a triumphant smile for she had already glimpsed her father's weakening.

"And Dr. Aylesbury, you might be needin' more than just her help. I'd be glad to go along and do what I can. By washing the bedclothes and instruments for you and doing the cooking and other chores, I'd be freeing up more of Miss Jessica's time to help you do the important things."

Aaron opened his mouth to voice his objection but Carrie continued: "Please, Dr. Aylesbury. You know I'd work hard. I really do want to go and help." What she didn't say was that more than anything she wanted to go and be near Regie, but already Jessica had guessed and smiled knowingly at her.

"Yes, Father, she would be a lot of help and with the two of us sticking together, we would be in less danger."

Aaron looked to Penelope, who smiled and shook her head, knowing they were already defeated.

"I do think they need to have a doctor there," he said lamely.

Penelope let her smile grow into one that bespoke the admiration she felt for her husband. "I'll see to the station while you are away. When do you think you will be leaving?"

"Not until after Christmas," he said. His voice

265

sounded apologetic.

"That gives you a full week to get your supplies together."

"Yes, that gives us a full week," Carrie said with a firm nod as she resumed filling the water glasses.

Aaron's eyes continued to look into Penelope's, and Jessica readily understood the meaning that lay beneath their locked gazes. It left them *only* a week.

Chapter XV

"Father, I found out where the Schiller's setup is located," Jessica said as she entered the medical tent. She found Aaron busy sorting through his instruments, putting them into the proper drawers of the instrument hutch he had decided to bring along with him this time, knowing it would be best to keep his things under lock while in Ballarat. Carrie followed in right behind her.

"How far from here?"

"Not very far. It's on the other side of Bakery Hill, down in the ravine."

"You mean they are right here at the Eureka fields? How'd you find this out?" He looked up from his work and wiped his brow with a folded cloth that was lying nearby. It was eighty degrees outside, and practically no breeze filtered in through the open tent, for the usual light southwest wind did not seem to make its way down this side of the hill.

"While we were resting in front of the other tent, Howey Nichols passed by. His claim is right next to theirs."

"Good. I can finally give them that money Betty Schiller asked me to deliver. I'll rest a lot easier once it is safely in their possession. As soon as I'm finished locking these away, I'll see if I can locate their tent and get this money off my hands."

"Carrie and I have finished putting our things away in the other tent. Why don't you let us take it to them? Then you won't have to stop your work in order to do it."

Carrie's green eyes lit with anticipation, and she quickly added, "Yes, Jessica and I have worked hard, Dr. Aylesbury. We could use a break."

"I don't know. It might be too dangerous to have you carry such a large sum of money on you. There are far more ruffians here than in Sofala."

"You don't have to keep reminding me." Jessica smiled at his open protectiveness then assured him, "No one will know we even have money with us. I can bandage it to my arm and even hide the bandage with my sleeve. No one will be any the wiser. Even should they see the bandage, they would be inclined to believe I simply injured myself somehow."

"Pretty crafty," Aaron agreed and returned her smile. "I *would* like to get finished here as soon as I can. Word is getting out that a doctor's in the camp. I've already had two men brought in here for treatment. That's why I'm so far behind in getting these instruments put away. Both were cut up pretty badly."

"Mining accidents?" Carrie asked.

"No, brawling over a boundary dispute," Aaron explained with a solemn shake of his head. "This is nothing like Sofala. There may have been lots of accidents and some sickness, but at least everyone tried to get along, and people did not go around fighting or stealing from his neighbor."

"I don't think the bad is in everybody," Carrie commented philosophically. "But it is in enough of these men that it makes it seem like the whole place is full of vile and ruthless men. Most claim it is those pardoned prisoners from Van Diemen's Land and the Californians causing the trouble. The Vandiemonians don't care about anyone's rights, and the Californians are trying to take too many rights. Have you heard about the Geelong gang?"

Carrie paused, and when Aaron shook his head, she went on: "Now there's a group of truly evil men. The man who has that strange-looking mud hut next to our tent told me how the Geelong gang shot and killed a mail coach driver the other day for no reason other than the lust for blood. They had already taken the man's rifle away from him, and he could've done them no harm. And then they made one of the young women who was ridin' as a passenger take off all her clothes and dance for them. They might have done worse to her if a group of other riders hadn't been heard approachin' right then."

Carrie's eyes were wide with horror as images of Captain Scantlin and what he had almost done to her flashed before her mind. She fought tears of shame but knew that it would never happen to her again, not now that she had a small derringer tucked away into the side of her boot. She had secretly sold the bracelet Miss Penelope had given her for Christmas in order to buy a gun before they left for this godforsaken place. No man would *ever* take her favors from her without her full permission.

"No, I hadn't heard any of that. I haven't had a chance to get out and really talk with anyone since we got here,"

Aaron said and frowned. "As soon as I get everything squared away, I think I'll try to find out if anyone around here sells a newspaper. I'd like to know what all is happening around this place, so I'll know what to watch out for."

"I'll ask the Schillers if anyone around here sells newspapers when we take the money to them," Jessica offered. "If it isn't too far out of the way, I'll stop off and buy one on the way back. I'd like to catch up on all the news around here, too. Maybe I can also find out where we can pick up the mails."

"Why? Are you expecting a letter?" he asked curiously.

"Not really," she responded quickly, though she was hoping. If Eric managed to get settled earlier than he expected, he might try to write her and tell her where to meet him. Just before they left, she had thought to ask Penelope to forward any important mail to them. "But I might want to send one. I'd like to let Mother know we have arrived safely, and exactly where we are so that she can get in touch with us if she needs to."

Aaron nodded. "We can write her tonight, but for now, I've got work to do."

Less than an hour later, while Jessica and Carrie searched for the Schiller's tent, they noticed that these gold fields were more crowded than the ones near Sofala had been, and as a result there was more activity. The river and small stream that snaked through the area were lined with men either panning for gold or working their cradles. The reddish-brown land surrounding the river was pockmarked with hundreds of shallow sinkings. Further away from the river along the grayish-brown sloping hillsides and curving plains, deep mine shafts, digger huts, tents, horse-driven whips, and Chilean mills cluttered the landscape. There was something everywhere.

As they made their way through the all confusion and disorder, Carrie spotted Regie Schiller first, and since Jessica had agreed to let her be the one to carry the money strapped to her arm, Carrie hurried over to him to tell him of their arrival and all about the money they had brought to them. Watching Carrie, Jessica followed at a leisurely pace.

"Regie. Regie Schiller," Carrie called out to the tall, lean blonde who busily worked the wooden crank handle on a rickety-looking windlass, a device used to draw the dirt and gravel up from the shaft, much like the one used to draw water out of a well. Regie's blue flannel shirt was soaked with sweat and sticking to the firm contour of his back, proof of his hard labor.

Carrie's soft voice was almost lost to the din of noise that surrounded them, but Regie must have heard her for he looked up in surprise just before she reached him. "Carrie? What are you doing here?"

"I came to help Dr. Aylesbury and Jessica," she started to explain between her excited breaths.

"Jessica? Jessica's here?" he asked eagerly, paying no attention to Carrie's disappointment as he looked around to see if he could possibly locate Jessica in all the chaos that surrounded him. When his gaze lighted on her only a few yards away, a huge, delighted smile stretched across his dirt-smudged face, and he hurriedly wound the crank until a dust-trailing bucket, overfilled with dirt and rocks, was drawn up out of the ground and within his grasp. As he laid the bucket aside, he shouted down into the deep hole, "Hey Rube, we've got company up here."

"Who is it?" came an irritated voice from the ground.

"Jessica and Carrie," Regie told him, still amazed.

"Jessica? Jessica Aylesbury? What's she doing here?"

Regie grinned and relayed the question, making it his own. "What are you doing here?"

"Father felt he was needed," Jessica answered briefly. Well aware of the hurt on Carrie's pensive face, she tried to include her in the conversation. "Carrie and I came along to help. And Carrie has brought you money from your mother."

Regie's eyes finally turned back to Carrie. "Money? From Mum?"

"She was afraid you might be arrested mining without a license," Carrie explained softly, her enthusiasm gone. "She sent enough for you and Rube to get your licenses and some more for food and supplies."

"I hope she sent a lot," they heard Rube say as he pulled himself out of the hole and sat at the edge. His booted feet dangled while he took the scarf that had been tied around his face and wiped the grit from the back of his neck. Though he had responded to Carrie's words, his gaze was trained on Jessica. "The prices here are outrageous."

"I'm not sure how much there is. It's in a sealed envelope. Should I give it to you here? Out in the open?" Carrie asked. Her eyes swept the hundreds of men who were working around them, any one of whom might catch sight of what they were doing and decide to pay the Schillers an unexpected visit later.

"No," Rube responded quickly as he rose to his feet and dusted off his clothing. "Regie, go with Carrie into the tent so she can give it to you without anyone watching and becoming suspicious. I'll stay out here and keep Jessica company."

Jessica felt her stomach tighten and had an immediate urge to follow Carrie and Regie inside the tent, but for Carrie's sake, she fought the desire to flee Rube's penetrating gaze and stayed where she was, boldly facing his wicked smile.

"It's a pleasure to see you here," Rube told her. His gaze dipped down to take in the curves of her snugly fitted bodice showed so well. "I've been needing something to break the boredom of this place. Life can't be all work."

"Are you finding much gold?" she asked, choosing to simply ignore his brash comments.

"Nothing yet," came the reply from behind her, startling her. It was Karl Schiller. "But a man jus' two holes over done hit it big, real big. It's just a matter of digging down to dat same level of pipe clay, I t'ink."

Jessica was relieved to be able to turn her back to Rube in order to talk with his father. "Hello, Mr. Schiller. What do you have there?"

"Hello, lassie, it's a pleasure to see such a pretty face for a change." He smiled warmly, displaying a missing tooth which, she supposed, was the result of the brutal attack he had suffered. Nodding at the huge barrel he carried as he bent over to gently set it down, he answered her question. "Had to go buy some drinking vater. De men hafe dat river so stirred up it ain't fit to drink." He shook his head glumly. "It cost nearly as much as a key of stringybark or a small jug of rum."

"But I thought spirits were forbidden in the goldfields."

"Dere are still vays to purchase a little sly-grog," Karl replied with a twinkle of mischief in his eyes. "So, tell me, vat brings you to dis awful place? Is your father plannin' on putting up his medicine tent here, too? I must say his skills are sure needed around here." Never giving her the opportunity to respond to any of his questions, he reached up and touched the swollen, red wound at the side of his forehead and continued. "Vhere's he puttin' up his tent at? I need him to take a look at dis. Ve vas bailed up even before ve could get into Melbourne to secure our licenses. Wretched men—took all de money dey could find on us. All ve vas left vith vas a small bag of gold dust I had hidden avay inside my flour sack." He shook his head sadly. "Dey even took de fancy pocket vatch my Bet gave me right after ve got married."

"Pa, Mum has sent us more money," Rube said as he stepped closer so he could speak more confidentially. "Jessica's little housekeeper, Carrie, is in the tent handing it over to Regie right now."

"Praise be," Karl said with a heavy sigh. "Ve sure can use it. Rube, your mum is a saint, a true saint." Absently, he reached up and probed the unhealed wound at the side of his forehead again.

"Let me have a look at that," Jessica said and tiptoed so that she could peer closely at the jagged tear bulging with infection. "Yes, Mr. Schiller, you do need to let father have a look at that. I think he will want to lance it and let all the infection drain out. Then it'll need a clean bandage."

"Lance it?" Karl's eyes grew wide with horror. "No, on second t'ought, I t'ink it vill be just fine given a little more time to heal."

Regie and Carrie rejoined them, catching the last of the conversation. Regie stared intently at his father. "Jessica? When will Dr. Aylesbury be ready to start seein' patients?"

"By tomorrow."

"Then Pa will be there first thing in the morning to have his forehead looked after," he said firmly. "Or I'll never tell him where I hid the money Mum just sent us or let him read the letter that was with it."

Karl Schiller frowned at Regie and started to offer a comment but was interrupted by Jessica.

"Good. An infection that close to the brain can become very serious," she cautioned then winked. "And who knows, maybe Father will see fit to administer a large dose of whiskey beforehand."

Karl smiled again. "Say he's got viskey?"

"Real Irish whiskey. For purely medicinal reasons."

"Hmm, den maybe I should go see him in de mornin'," he mused, then bent over and picked up the barrel of water and carried it on into the tent.

"I suppose we've kept you from your work long enough," Jessica said, still eager to get away from Rube's unrelenting gaze. "Regie? Is there someplace around here where I can buy a newspaper and some tooth powder. I forgot to pack any. And there are a few other things I find I need."

"There's no real center of things here, although I hear they are surveying some land west of here to mark off a place for a real town. But you can pick up some of your stores at Fanny Taylor's hut. Her sons bring in a wagon load a day from Melbourne. And if she don't got what you need, you can order it from her and she'll have it here in a about a week, that is if it's to be had in Melbourne."

"And she'll have a newspaper?"

"It might be several days old, but she usually has some."

After receiving directions to Fanny Taylor's hut, Carrie and Jessica left the twins to their work. As they walked, Jessica noticed that Carrie was strangely quiet and knew the reason had to be the way Regie had practically ignored her. She wished she could offer her a few encouraging words, but she felt that would not be fair of her. He would never notice anyone as plain and simple hearted as Carrie. Regie was attracted to outward beauty. That brought an idea to Jessica. Carrie did not always have to be so plain. A pretty dress and a fancy hairstyle might do the trick.

"There's the hut," Carrie pointed out, interrupting Jessica's thoughts as she pointed to the small cob structure nearby.

Realizing she only had a few shillings with her, Jessica knew she would not be able to purchase Carrie anything pretty to wear today, but maybe later, a special dress or even pretty green ribbon might be just the thing. It would help bring out the emerald highlights of her eyes.

"G'day, lassies," a gruff voice sounded as they stepped inside the small mud and post hut. A stout woman about the same height as Carrie, just a few inches shorter than Jessica, pushed herself out of a creaky wooden chair and came toward them with a broad smile on her rounded face. As she came closer, Jessica noticed the large pistol strapped around her thick waist and for the life of her, she could not help but stare at it as the woman spoke to them. "How kin I help you two?"

After a moment, Jessica managed to pull her gaze away to the crowded contents of the room. "We need tooth powder and a newspaper, if you have them."

"Got 'em both," she said and stepped backward to the overloaded shelves near the back of the hut. She never turned her back on either of them as she scrounged through the merchandise piled haphazardly on the rough boards that were spaced apart by whatever she could find to hold them up. Finally, her hand brought out a small box of tooth powder.

"Is there anything else?" she asked as she snatched up a copy of the *Melbourne Argus* and folded it around the box.

Seeing that Carrie's thoughts were elsewhere, Jessica asked in a hushed voice, "Would you have a pretty green hair ribbon?"

"Nay, can't say that I have. But I can get one. Have it here next week," she replied in a coarse whisper when she realized that the conversation was not for the other girl's ears, then in her usual voice, she said, "That'll be two shillings."

Jessica started to protest the price but realized it would do her no good. Carefully, she reached into the deep folds of her skirt and came out with the amount. "I'll be back for the ribbon."

"Pleased to do business with ya," the woman called out with a deep chuckle as they left the hut.

When they reached the tent, Carrie went straight to the camp stove Aaron had bought and started to prepare supper. Jessica decided not to interfere with Carrie's mood and stepped outside to look over the newspaper. When she unfolded it, she noticed the date as Thursday, 15 January, 1852. Good, it was only six days old. The news would still be fairly current.

Quickly, she scanned the front page and her eyes were drawn to one particular headline near the bottom of the page. Her heart froze when she read the words written there in bold, black print: The Flash Brigand Strikes Again.

No. It could not be true. It just couldn't be. Eric would

not continue his exploits down here. He would have no reason to. Victoria was to be his haven, and Rodney Livingston was hundreds of miles away.

Trying to control her shaking hands enough to be able to read the fine print below the headline, she read the story with heartbreaking concentration.

Tuesday, 13 January, the notorious Flash Brigand recently from the Bathurst District, bailed up a dray owned by William MacKenzie on the road from the Ballarat diggings near Golden Point. As is reportedly his custom, the flash bushranger quickly relieved the driver of his boots while his masked cohorts made off with a most peculiar item. His three mates loaded a coffin the man was carrying into their own wagon and took off. The Flash stayed behind long enough to secure his gang's getaway, then nodded politely to the man and wished him a good day.

Jessica blinked in astonishment. What would Eric want with a coffin? For the first time she began to seriously doubt that the Flash Brigand was Eric, for the bushranger was now involved with incidents that obviously had nothing to do with Judge Livingston and did not fit Eric's character one bit. A coffin? Drawing her lower lip between her teeth, she read on.

William MacKenzie felt fortunate that all they took from him was his boots, because he had several valuable coins on him. The coffin he freighted belonged to one of Melbourne's local undertakers, Gilbert Livingston. When contacted about why the

278

Flash and his men might be interested in one of his coffins, Mr. Livingston hadn't a clue.

Gilbert Livingston? Jessica's heart felt as if it had twisted into a tight knot. Gilbert was Rodney Livingston's son. The Flash Brigand had struck again, only this time he managed to take a coffin from the judge's only son. But why? Did he hope the news of this deed would reach the judge and perhaps bring him tearing down here in a fit of anger? That surely must be his reason, but why?

Jessica fought the anger and confusion long enough to remain rational. It had to be just a coincidence that the Flash had decided to come to Victoria around the same time Eric had. The Flash Brigand could not possibly be Eric. Eric would not jeopardize their chance at happiness for something so foolish! No, the Flash Brigand had to be someone else, but who?

Jessica made regular trips to Fanny Taylor's hut to buy newspapers and to the commissioner's tent where the mail was delivered almost daily. Although she strongly suspected now the Flash Brigand was not Eric, Jessica still liked to keep up with the daring exploits of the bushranger who had turned his attention to the judge's son and anyone the young man did business with. More than a few enterprises felt the brunt of the Flash's attacks, and Jessica could only assume those enterprises were somehow connected to Gilbert or his father.

Although Jessica felt a little sorry for Gilbert, who had always impressed her as being extremely shy and completely manipulated by his father the few times she'd had occasion to meet him, she was amused at some of the things the Flash did to him in order to attract the attention of Gilbert's father. It made much better reading than the ruthless deeds of many of the other bushrangers. The Geelong gang seemed to be the worst of the lot.

For the first time since Jessica had started making her daily pilgrimage to the commissioner's tent, there was a letter for her, but to her initial dismay, it was also addressed to her father and was written in Penelope's neat script. Nothing from Eric. Wistfully, she wondered where he was at that very moment and how close he might be to getting settled. She longed to be with him, to be his wife, to once again be held in his strong, loving arms. She was not sure how much longer she could tolerate this infernal waiting.

At least she no longer had to worry about his fate. Now that she had come to realize he was not the Flash, she knew his only danger lay back in New South Wales in the forms of Captain Scantlin and Judge Livingston. She wondered if the foolish captain was still busy keeping a keen eye on their house, waiting for Eric to show himself, when, in fact, Eric was safely tucked away in Victoria somewhere with no plans of ever returning. She smiled with wicked delight at the thought of the fat old crow sitting out in the hot sun, sweating profusely and plucking uncomfortably at his genitals. For she knew that as long as Eric remained safely down here in Victoria and the captain stayed put up there, Eric's precious earlobes would be forever safe from any harm.

Chapter XVI

"Ready to break camp?" Eric asked when he tossed the last of the coffee out of the billy can and into the fire. Carefully, he tucked the smoke-blackened billy can inside his blanket roll, then proceeded to cover the sputtering fire with loose dirt.

"Ready and willin'," Coolabah said as he tossed his swag over his shoulder and bent down to pick up his rifle.

"How much longer before we can slip on over to Portland and have a few nights in a hotel?" Sam scratched at the sparse blond beard covering his young face a moment, then added, "I'd sure like me a shave, a tall mug of sangaree, and a pretty woman."

"In that order?" Jacky asked, a wide, youthful smile stretched across his black face.

"I'll take it whatever order I can get it," Sam shot back with a grin. "I'm not a hard man to please."

"Well, if all goes right, we may be heading to either Portland or Warrnambool to lay low for the next few days. After this heist, he'll have every man on his pay docket after us," Eric told them. Lifting his chin high, he finished fastening the buttons on his black serge shirt, then wrapped his black neckcloth around his throat and tied it loosely to the side.

"Say, boss, are you going to get yourself a shave and a pretty young lass to warm your bed?" Jacky asked Eric.

Eric frowned. "I'm not shaving this thing off again till I'm through with it. It itches too bad when it starts to grow back. I think I'd better leave well enough alone and just let it grow long like Coolabah's."

"What about the pretty young lass?" Coolabah asked with a raise of his heavy brow.

"I've got my eye on a pretty young lass all right, but I don't think I'll be seeing her any time soon," Eric responded with a distant smile, his mind's eye going far beyond the tall gum and pepper trees that secluded them.

The other three exchanged glances. It was the first he had spoken of such. They had started to worry about their leader for he never seemed to have much of an eye for the ladies.

"And do we know this young lass?" Coolabah asked.

"I would think you might. You three seem to have made it your life's work to keep up with everything about me," he bantered good-naturedly. "Especially you, Coolabah. You're worse than my own mum."

Coolabah scowled. "Someone'as to be lookin' after ya. You would be dead twice over if we didn't keep a good watch. And I'll be holding a good eye on you today, too. There's too big a price on your head not to."

"You know, Coolabah?" Jacky said with a slow rub of his grizzled chin. "We could easily collect that two hundred pounds reward for the Flash Brigand for ourselves and not have to work so hard for quite some time."

" 'Tis true," Coolabah said, drawing his face up to what he felt appeared serious. "Two hundred pounds sure would make life easy for a year or two. Especially when you consider I was just making three pounds a month working as a ringer for Ben. Aye, we could live right high for awhile, we could."

"Oh, quit you're yabbering. We've got work to do," Sam said as he slowly mounted his gray and white horse. "I'm ready to get this thing done so we can head for Portland." It was becoming quite clear that Portland had become Sam's preferred destination.

"Would it be that you long to see that pretty little Jeanne Holt again?" Coolabah teased. "Well, let's do hurry men. Sam's got places to go, people to see."

With a quick exchange of smiles, the four of them rode off in the direction of the main track that wove through the Black Forest on its way northeast from Melbourne to the Bendigo diggings. They remained seated on their horses as they waited patiently in the bush for the Roddon Gold Escort to pass by.

"I brought you the latest newspaper," Regie said as he handed the folded paper to Jessica and turned to give Carrie a cordial nod as soon as he had entered their tent. He smiled briefly at Carrie and commented on the lovely green ribbon she had on before he sat down beside Jessica. "The newspaper came while I was at Fanny's, and I knew you'd want to see one." Actually he had made it a point to keep an eye out for the Taylor wagons so he would know when they arrived and have an excuse to visit Jessica during the week. "I already glanced over it. I'm afraid it's got some bad news."

Before Jessica could open the paper and read for herself, he went on: "You know how Governor LaTrobe has been tryin' to recruit some of the policemen from Sydney and other places in New South Wales in order to replace those he lost to the goldfields?"

Jessica nodded. Within the first month after gold was discovered near Ballarat, the police force in Victoria had reportedly dropped to only forty men and that included all areas of policing from the mounted troopers patrolling the bush to the city footmen. All were resigning to go off to the goldfields to try their luck at the diggings.

"Well, guess who joined up with the goldfield police force."

"Who?" Carrie asked impatiently.

Regie's eyes grew wide when he suddenly realized how this might affect Carrie. He had not thought about that when he started all this, for Carrie had more right than any one of them to hate the man. Standing, he stepped over to take her hand in a friendly gesture. "I'm 'fraid it's Captain Scantlin. I guess the lure of higher wages was more than he could stand. He was sworn in with half a dozen others that came down from Bathurst last week. He started patrolling the bush the very next day."

Carrie's eyes narrowed with a deep loathing. "Will 'e be comin' here then?"

"Not right away. According to the story in the paper, he and his group have been dispatched to the Bendigo area. But those goldfield troopers go everywhere. He just might show up here one day, but don't worry. He wouldn't dare try to come near you. Not with me and Aaron around," he said but did not know how much reassurance that might be, for he had done little good against the man during that last encounter. When he did not see the strangled look of fear leave her lovely face, he

284

added with a boyish grin, "Besides, I plan to buy ya a new water pitcher to protect yourself with. You're right deadly with a fine piece of porcelain."

She finally looked up into his eyes, and the smile he had hoped for came to her face, and they stood looking at each other for a long moment. Jessica, too, was smiling, for she had seen the deep breath Regie had taken in just after Carrie's smile had touched her face. Looking back down at her newspaper to give them a feeling of privacy, she realized there just might be hope for Carrie Crocker yet.

"'Ere they come, mates," Coolabah said in an almost soundless whisper and glanced around to be sure everyone else had heard the coach and horses approaching. From where they were hidden in a dense thicket of wattle and pea vines on a slight rise just above a short span of straightaway, they would be able to see the gold escort as soon as it rounded the bend.

Jacky already had his bright red neckcloth in place over his lower face. Bright colors were his trademark as black was Eric's. Jacky's voice was almost inaudible, too. "This is it."

Eric nodded and adjusted his own neckcloth to mask most of his lower face. His brown eyes were trained on the rutted track where the gold escorts should be seen at any moment. He expected at least two mounted escorts to precede the coach and as many as four to follow it. Usually there was one guard on board the coach itself along with the driver; occasionally there might be two guards or even three. As the first mounted escort came into sight, Eric pulled down the wide brim of his black felt hat and prepared for what was to come.

Drawing a deep, steadying breath, he finally glanced over to Sam, the fashionable one of their group. Sam always dressed for the occasion in a fine cutaway frock coat, with his cravat knotted in a wide bow, and both his neckcloth and his top hat made of the finest silk. Sam enjoyed impressing the ladies, though there would be no ladies involved in this heist.

Eric waited for Sam's eyes to meet his. The rush would come at their mutual consent. When Sam's eyes came around to meet Eric's, they both nodded their agreement, and the four of them tore out of the thicket and down the sloping embankment toward the gold coach, which was now about halfway between the last bend and the next, only a few dozen yards below them.

Coolabah fired the first warning shot into the air, as they rapidly pounced on their prey. The startled troopers made no move for their weapons, but the guard sitting on the gold coach next to the driver had held his carbine rifle poised in his lap, ready to shoot. Hastily he raised the weapon and fired, missing his target in his excitement. With no time to break open the breech and reload, he dropped the now empty rifle to the deck and made a reach for the pepperbox revolver on the seat beside him, but it was too late. The Flash Brigand and his gang were already upon them with their weapons drawn and aimed at their hearts.

"Hands up, mates," Coolabah called out as he dropped his reins from his teeth. In both his huge hands, he held Colt revolvers, and each was aimed at a different man. "You are 'bout to be bailed up by the notorious Flash Brigand and his most astute gang of bushrangers." As he threw his long leg over his horse's back and prepared to drop to the ground, he sang out the rest of his speech. "Don't do nothin' foolish and no one will get hurt, will they, Flash?"

When Eric did not respond, the other three looked at him curiously.

"Flash?" Jacky prompted as he dropped lithely to the ground, careful not to use real names.

"Something's wrong here," Eric said, his black horse dancing nervously under him, ready to be given his head and allowed to run. Eric trained his eyes on the lead escort who should have at least *tried* to fire on them. "Something's mighty wrong."

When the tall escort he studied nervously cut his eyes back down the track, Eric shouted, "Remount! Get the hell out of here!"

Jacky did not ask questions. He reached up for the brass saddlehorn of his fancy American-made saddle and swung himself up and back into place. Coolabah and Sam were already backing their horses away, their weapons still holding aim.

At that moment a shout was heard in the distance, followed instantly by the thunder of horses as dozens of hooves hit the soft earth. Just before the first shots were fired, Eric buried his heels deep into Fury's side. "Get back up the slope. It's the traps. We've been had."

Given the freedom he wanted, Fury loped up the side of the hill with agile ease, sending gravel and rocks spraying behind. Coolabah and Sam were ahead of him, and Eric could hear Jacky's horse clammering close behind his. Branches tore at his clothing and lashed his right eye, causing an instant whelp to rise and force his eye closed. Tears streamed from the injured eye, but Eric did not take the time to wipe them away.

"Jacky? You behind me?" he called out over his shoulder.

"Right behind you," Jacky shouted back in a high voice

in order to be heard. The noise they made crashing through the thick brush was tremendous. After another shot rang out, shattering a limb just over his head, he added, "But, my friend, I'd much rather I was ahead of you at this moment."

Eric smiled grimly. As they reached the top of the hill, he pulled hard on Fury's reins and jerked the horse around so that he could take a quick look at how many troopers were following them. His quick count let him know that there were at least eight troopers tearing their way through the bush, four of them far too close for comfort.

Jacky passed him just before he reined Fury back around and prodded the animal into another run. The horse lunged forward with such a force that it jerked Eric's hat off his head and sent it sailing behind him.

"We're going to have to split up," he called out to Jacky. There was another blast from a rifle, and a large plug was torn out of a tree trunk just a few feet from Jacky's shoulder. "It's every man for himself."

Eric bore Fury to the right, away from Jacky's trail, through a mass of twisted bush and into the darkness of a thicket of pea and blackberry vines. He would head for the densest growth, make a stand against the ones who followed him if he had to, then try to make his way to the Red Rover Hotel near Eaglehawk, where he would find refuge until he could discover where the others had gone. There was always sympathy to be had at the Red Rover.

Eric did not take the time to look back and see exactly how many of the troopers had decided to follow him, though he knew many of them would. He was the leader. He would be the one they wanted the most. It was another reason he had chosen to break away from the others. Branches continued to take angry swipes at his face and arms, shredding his clothes and yanking out pieces of his hair.

More shots were fired, and he realized their aim was getting better. A tree limb splintered in front of him. He felt the tiny pieces of wood pierce his face. He closed his good eye and offered a quick prayer, for all he had protecting him from certain death at that moment was his own Maker. Another shot rang out. Eric felt the bullet tear deep into his left shoulder. He heard another shot and again he was struck. This time his neck. Biting his lower lip against the pain of that last bullet, he bent over in his saddle, hoping to make himself less of a target. He felt himself weakening as his horse valiantly fought his way forward through the thick tangle of vines, wattle, and gum trees. Carefully, Eric tucked the fingers of his left hand under the front of the saddle to help him grip the edge better, and he tried his best to hold onto the reins with the other as the darkness of the forest slowly folded over him.

"Where is 'e, Corporal?" Captain Scantlin asked as his horse plodded along behind two others while he worked his way through the dense brush to where six more of his men sat on their horses, waiting for him to catch up. Though his men's uniforms were tattered from the assault of the thick brush they had ridden through, Captain Scantlin's uniform had somehow remained perfectly neat, though straining noticeably across his wide girth. His fine gold braid and silver buttons were all still intact and his clothing unrumpled, proof that he had not followed with quite the determination as his men.

When all the captain was offered in the way of a reply

to his question was a shrug of the young man's shoulders, he shouted angrily, "I was told 'e was wounded. I was told 'is blood was leaving us a clear trail. You should have 'im by now."

"He was wounded," Anthony Alson, one of the young troopers, responded. "And it was his trail of blood that brought us as far as this creek. But here's where the blood stops." Seeing the growing anger in the captain's face, the young man quickly added, "He can't have gone far, sir. He's lost too much blood. He's fallen from the saddle by now. It's just a matter of finding him."

"Then find him, by damn," Captain Scantlin blustered. "I want that man and I want 'im now." One of the main reasons he had been sent to Victoria to join the goldfield police was to bring down the Flash Brigand. But although those were his orders and he would be rewarded well, he had his own personal reasons for wanting to get the Flash Brigand, for he had long suspected the notorious bushranger was none other than Eric Aylesbury.

"Divide up into two groups and follow the creek bed both ways until ya pick up 'is trail again. When you do, fire a shot and wait for the rest of us to join ya," he told the men as he pulled out a handkerchief and mopped the heavy coating of sweat from his brow. Damn all this heat. "And be quick about it!"

As the men divided and went their different directions, the captain watched, absently letting a stubby white finger run along the scarred edge of his ear, where his lobe had once been. His eyes narrowed with growing impatience as he scanned the ground on the far side of the creek for traces of blood that these incompetents might have missed. He had his own debt to settle, and he wanted to find Aylesbury before the young bastard managed to bleed to death. Eric Aylesbury must know

290

exactly who the man was that had outsmarted him. He wanted his own face to be the very last thing the friggin' rotter ever saw.

"Jessica, I thought you were goin' to go to the anniversary picnic with me," Regie said, concerned to find Jessica still dressed in the gray duffle dress and white-linen apron, which she always wore when she worked in the medical tent. "The games'll start in less than an hour. We won't get a good place if we don't leave now."

"I'm sorry, Regie," she said as she glanced around at all the patients in the tent. "But as you can see, we are very busy here. I can't leave my father to take care of all these men by himself. I wouldn't be able to enjoy myself if I did that."

"But I have all this food I paid so dearly for." He frowned and raised the large wicker basket for her to see. "I've been lookin' forward to this day all week. And besides, I have us entered in the wheelbarrow race."

"I'm sorry, I just can't go." She shrugged, then, without any indication that this was all planned, she added, "But as far as I know, Carrie can still go. You'll find her in the other tent."

Regie's frown deepened. "But I wanted you *both* to go."

"I can't," she said, then turned her back on him and returned to her father's side. "I wish I could but I can't."

"But, Jessica . . ."

"Give it up, lad," said an elderly man who was lying in a nearby cot with a bandage wrapped from his ankle to his mid-thigh and had listened to the entire conversation. "She's needed 'ere. Go get the other young lassie and be off with you."

Regie stood staring helplessly as Jessica knelt at her

291

father's side and started to help him bandage a young man's knee. Noticing the admiring look the scamp was giving her, Regie scowled, then turned so abruptly on his booted heel that he left a mark on the planked floor.

Jessica looked up from her work in time to see Regie and Carrie pass by on their way to the picnic. Carrie looked beautiful in the pale green silk dress with its dark satin trim. Jessica had thought to pack the one party dress just in case there was just such an occasion, and now she was glad she had. And the only altering they had been forced to do was shorten the hem a few inches. Otherwise it fit Carrie perfectly. Jessica smiled to herself when she noticed Carrie's arm tucked neatly beneath Regie's. Jessica could not remember ever having seen Carrie look so happy.

Jacky cautiously drew his horse to a halt and listened. Not only had he not caught sight of any troopers behind him, he did not hear any horses plowing through the bush anywhere nearby. Just as he had suspected. He was not being followed, not by even one of the troopers. The sound of a distant shot caught his attention, followed by another, and another. Evidently they had all taken off after Eric. Jacky was seized by sudden panic as the faraway sounds of rifle shots continued one right after the other. Immediately, he turned his horse in the direction of the rumpus and urged his horse into a dead run.

Bending low to avoid as many of the limbs and branches as he could, he rode toward the noise. Suddenly the shooting stopped, but Jacky continued to ride, hoping against hope that he would find Eric still alive when he got there. If he was still alive, but had somehow been captured, Jacky planned to do what he could to free him, even to the point of risking his own life. Eric had to remain free.

After a few minutes, Jacky slowed down to decide which direction he should ride toward. He was close enough to catch the faint scent of burnt gunpowder but still heard no further gunshots. Then he noticed the steady sound of a horse crashing through the bush up ahead to his right and, judging by the intensity and the speed, he realized the horse was about to cross his path just a few hundred feet ahead. His heart leapt to his throat when he considered it might be one of the troopers. Quickly he drew his revolver from its holster and prepared to shoot if necessary, but when the horse came into sight, he realized that the black shadow darting through the dense bush was Fury.

Every muscle in Jacky's body tensed when he got his first good glimpse and saw that Eric was no longer astride the spirited animal. The horse was riderless. Eric was either captured or dead. Then when the animal came closer, Jacky felt a great surge of relief. He realized Eric was still on the horse, draped over the saddle and leaning heavily to the far side so that he was barely visible to him.

"Eric, over here," he called out. When there was no response, Jacky realized Eric was unconscious. He must have been wounded. If he leaned any more to the right, he would fall out of the saddle and injure himself further.

"He's been shot. Go, boy! Git!" Jacky called out as he turned his horse to the left to run at an angle. He hoped to cross in front of Eric's horse in time to cut him off. Urgently, Jacky drove his heels into his own horse and prayed the animal would somehow be able to outrun Fury

293

for once. Oblivious to stinging slashes of the brush against his bloody skin, Jacky rode with sheer determination. He must not fail. Eric needed him.

"Go, boy, faster," Jacky urged in desperation. Overwhelmed by fear, his blood pounded furiously in his ears, drowning out the clamor of the horses' hooves as they struck the earth again and again. The wild panic that filled him was deafening. Although the animals galloped at breakneck speed, it seemed to Jacky that they barely moved at all.

Still unable to head Fury off, Jacky drove his heels into his horse again and again, trying to force the animal to give more. Gradually his horse began to overtake Fury, and Jacky was able to lean over in his saddle far enough to catch hold of one of the reins. Finally he pulled the two animals to a stop and continued to hold onto the captured rein while he leapt from his horse and rounded in front of Fury, trying to hold him still.

"Whoa, boy." He soothed the skittish animal in a low voice. When he reached to pat the horse's neck, he noticed the animal was soaking wet, as if he had been running through the water so he could avoid the heavy brush that grew on the dry land and tore at his black hide. Fury nipped at his shoulder, but Jacky managed to dodge in time. "Calm down, Fury. Calm down, boy."

The horse rebelled a moment longer, prancing and pawing at the ground, before finally relenting. At last the animal stood motionless, though still protesting with loud snorts and wild jerks of his head. With the end of the rein still in his hand, Jacky was finally able to step back and examine Eric. He could tell by the blood soaking his friend's entire left side that Eric had been shot somewhere high near his shoulder, and when he tore the shirt away, he discovered a large bullet wound just inches above his left shoulder blade.

"Eric?" he asked in a rough voice, his throat tight with emotion. He pressed his ear to Eric's back but heard no heartbeat, though his body was still warm and his blood still flowed from the wound. "Eric?"

With trembling hands, Jacky hefted his friend back into the saddle, then reached up to untie the black neckerchief so that he could search for a pulse. He realized that the only reason Eric was still in the saddle at all was because his left hand had somehow gotten caught between the saddle and the horse's back, and it was Eric's own weight that had held the hand in place. Jacky noticed the other rein was still in Eric's right hand but only because it had become tangled in his loose grip.

"Please be alive," Jacky pleaded softly while he removed the ragged, blood-soaked cloth that clung to his friend's neck. Jacky's stomach wretched at the sight of the gaping wound he found there. It looked as if half the muscle had been torn away, leaving a bloody mass of flesh on the whole left side of his neck.

"Eric, no," Jacky cried with a strangled sob and could not prevent the tears that suddenly blurred his vision. He knew he had to get Eric out of there in a hurry. The troopers would try to follow his trail, and when Jacky had looked down, he had seen what a fine trail of blood Eric was leaving for them. Jacky rushed back to his horse and yanked his rifle out of the scabbard. He also took time to grab his swag and toss it over his shoulder.

Quickly, he tied his swag onto the back of Eric's saddle and climbed onto the very back of the seat, behind Eric's slumped form. Wasting no further time, he took the reins and gently urged Fury forward, leaving his own horse behind to fend for himself. He hated the thought of having to give up his own horse, but dragging it along would only slow him down, and he needed to get Eric to help as quickly as possible. He also hated the thought of leaving his fancy new American saddle behind, but that could not be helped, either. Maybe someday he could save enough money to get himself another one just like it. Right now, his only concern was his friend.

"Hang in there, boss. I'll get you out of here. You'll be safe. You just hang in there."

Chapter XVII

There was no time to glance back and try to see who or what was behind them. Every second was precious, and Coolabah and Sam both pushed their horses to their physical limits until they finally reached a large cluster of gray boulders they had used for protection once before. Having had a better headstart than either Eric or Jacky, they quickly hid their horses behind the boulders and climbed up into the narrow crevices to prepare to make a stand. As soon as Eric and Jacky were safely past, they would open fire on the troopers. They hated to have to wound innocent men, but it was the only way they knew to save the lives of their mates. If it came down to either kill or be killed, they would choose to kill. They had known of the severe risks involved with this way of life from the very first.

"I don't like this," Coolabah finally said in a low voice after having waited several minutes with his gray-green eyes keenly trained on the area they had just traveled. "Eric and Jacky should have been here by now."

"We'll have to backtrack," Sam said. His brows drew

inward when his eyes slowly met Coolabah's. Neither spoke his fears aloud. Neither had to for they both knew that when Eric and Jacky failed to follow them, the two had met with trouble, maybe even death. As Sam and Coolabah both slid back into their saddles and quickly took up their reins, the sound of several shots echoed in the far distance. Coolabah motioned for Sam to hold still.

"It's comin' from that direction," he stated and nodded toward the northeast. "Must mean they are still alive if the troopers are still shootin' at them."

"And in bad need of our help," Sam agreed with a flick of his reins. "I just hope we can get there in time to do them some good."

Nothing else was said as once again Sam and Coolabah drove their horses to their limits. The sounds of the gunfire grew louder while they plowed their way through the tangled forest, praying all the while that they would be able to get there in time to help. As they rode, Sam quickly pulled off his now tattered frock coat and his black silk neckerchief, the last remnants of evidence that could link him to the Flash Brigand's gang, and tossed them away just in case they should happen onto any of the troopers. Coolabah did the same with the huge blue and white neckerchief he had used for a mask. Though they knew they would still be subject to suspicion, they had no intention of providing the police with actual proof.

The moment the two of them had crossed over a small creek, which flowed in the same direction from which the noise came, Coolabah turned his horse to run along the far edge. The trees grew thicker along both sides of the tiny river, and taller, but the undergrowth was much thinner due to the lack of sunlight, enabling the horses to make better time in the flat shallows of the water's edge. Sam followed only a few yards behind Coolabah, not caring that he was getting drenched.

Both were aware of the exact moment the shooting stopped, and they pressed their horses harder. Coolabah did not dare allow himself to think about what they might find when they got there, should they even be able to locate the place. It was hard to find anything in the thick-forested area below Bendigo, as familiar as they had become with the area over the past two months. It was the main advantage the bushrangers had over the traps: their knowledge of the bush and their ability to get around in it safely.

After having ridden much further than he had judged necessary, Coolabah reined in his horse and waited for Sam to pull up beside him and stop. His heavy brows were pulled down into a grim scowl, and his lips pressed hard together, causing his mouth to completely disappear in his thick reddish-brown beard.

Both sat perfectly still with their heads cocked, listening for a sound that might offer a clue as to the right direction. They both heard the steady splashing of a horse's quick steps in the water up ahead. Coolabah silently motioned for Sam to slip into the brush to their right while he slowly directed his horse to the opposite side of the creek and into a small patch of wattle that grew beneath the towering gums. Slowly, he eased his rifle up and out of its scabbard in preparation for an ambush. He could see that Sam had done the same. Moments later, the tall gray and white horse came into view.

Coolabah's startled gaze met Sam's as his hand came up to cover the gasp that wanted to burst from his burly lips. It was Jacky's horse—and the saddle was empty.

Sam spurred his horse out of the bush while Coolabah stayed back to see if anyone might be following the horse. When no one appeared along the creek and no other set of hooves could be heard, he sent his horse to catch up with Sam. By the time he reached him, Sam had already dismounted and was carefully looking over Jacky's horse.

"There's blood here on the scabbard," Sam said quietly, unable to lift his gaze to meet Coolabah's for fear the older man would catch sight of the sudden moisture in his eyes. "And some more on both the saddle horn and stirrup."

"I wonder if they got Eric, too." Coolabah voiced his worst fears. His gaze wandered to the direction from which the horse had come, his anguish clear on his weatherworn face.

"The shooting has stopped," Sam pointed out, finding it suddenly hard to talk and even harder to try to swallow. "They are either captured or . . ." He let his sentence trail off unfinished.

Coolabah stared at Sam without really seeing him for a long moment before he drew in a long, steadying breath through tight lips. "Or they are out there making their way to the Red Rover," he said. "Jacky may be wounded, but I refuse to believe either one of them is dead. Even if they were captured somehow, they will attempt to escape, and we already know how good Eric can be at escapin'."

"Aye, and if Jacky is injured, they will need to get to a place where they know they can get lots of help without worrying about bein' turned over to the stinkin' traps. You're right. They are probably headed for the Red Rover right now."

"Even if it turns out they've been captured and not

able to escape, we will need to get up some reinforcements 'fore trying to rescue them. It would be foolish for the two of us to go trapsin' in there alone. We'd just end up gettin' ourselves caught, too. It would be better if we went on to the Red Rover and waited. If they don't show up within two days, we can try to find out where they've been taken to and plan some way of springin' 'em out."

Sam nodded his agreement, ready to latch on to any hope, however vague. "I'll bet Eric's with Jacky right now, and they are both already on their way. The blokes will probably get there before we do."

"Hand me the reins to Jacky's horse so I can tie him to my saddle. Jacky'll be wanting the animal back. He may even offer me a big reward for bringin' him back that fancy saddle he spent so much money on. Let's go. Time's wastin'."

Eric never made a sound while he hung limply in the saddle in front of Jacky. The wounds in his shoulder and neck continued to seep blood, though Jacky had slowed the flow by tying the neckerchief back around Eric's neck just tight enough to help hold back the blood, but loose enough to still allow him to breath. Since he could not find anything that could work as a bandage for his boss's shoulder, Jacky held pressure directly against the open wound with the palm of his hand, aware that his friend could not have much more blood to loose.

Just as night descended, they came across a small station house with a clump of buildings centered in a tiny clearing near the edge of the heaviest part of the forest. Not sure if he would find friend or foe, Jacky rode into the yard but did not approach the house when he called out for help. He dismounted, but kept a hand on Eric to prevent him from slipping out of the saddle.

"Hello? Is anybody at home? I need some help here," he shouted. Although there was no response, he had seen a slight movement in one of the windows. Someone had peeked through the brightly colored calico curtains, but had not bothered to respond to his cries for help.

"My mate's been injured. I need a bucket of water, a washcloth, and a couple of bandages if you can spare them." His eyes went first to the window where he had seen the curtains move, then to the door of the small house built of split slab and rounded posts, very common to the area. The roof was just as typical, made with sapling rafters, crisscrossed at angles to support the overlapping bark that covered it. Still other saplings had been laid across the top and tied down to hold the bark in place, helping to make the house covering watertight. As Jacky's gaze went from window to window along the narrow veranda formed by the overlapping roof, he saw no further movement. The only response to his presence came from the noisy kookaburra in one of the nearby pepper trees as it heralded the coming of night.

"Please, have a heart. I promise we will be on our way just as soon as I've taken care of my friend. At least you could spare us a drink of cool water."

Finally the narrow door opened, and the heavy end of a two barreled shotgun eased out of the shadows from the doorway to greet him.

"How'd he get injured?" a craggy voice called out.

"He was shot," Jacky answered honestly, not sure if that voice had come from a man or a woman. "And he's lost an awful lot of blood. All I want is a bucket of water and a cloth so I can wash him up some and maybe a

302

couple of bandages if you can spare them. I don't mean you no harm. Here, I'll lay my weapons on the ground where you can keep an eye on them, and I'll leave them there until I'm ready to leave."

"You do that," the voice shouted, still from just inside the darkened doorway.

Slowly, so that he would not alarm whoever was behind that gun, Jacky took both his and Eric's rifles and gently laid them on the ground several yards away from where he had been standing. Then he eased his revolver from his holster and placed it beside the rifles.

"There, see? I'n now unarmed," he said as he backed away from the guns and returned to Eric's side. Eric had started to sag to the right again, and Jacky got there just in time to catch him as he slid completely out of the saddle.

"What about the other man's gun?"

"All he has is the holster. He lost his revolver earlier."

"Bring him in here," the voice commanded as the barrel of the shotgun disappeared. "Then you go hide that horse in the barn. I don't want no trouble with the traps."

Shifting Eric's weight evenly in his arms, Jacky did as told and carried his friend directly into the house. When he stepped inside the roughly furnished living room of what was mostly homemade pieces, he saw that a small elderly woman, barely five feet in height, had laid her huge weapon down and was holding another door open for him. Jacky found it hard to visualize the tiny woman, already bent and gray with age, even lifting the cumbersome weapon that now leaned against the wall, much less having aimed it as level as she had. That was a lot of iron for those two thin arms to have raised and held.

"In here. Lay him on that bed there. I'll have Toona get some water to heatin' while you go put that horse of yours away."

"Yes ma'am," Jacky said with a grateful smile. He wondered who Toona was but didn't ask. Knowing it was an Aboriginal word for a tree, he figured Toona was her black housekeeper. "I hate to put you out like this, but he needed a rest from the saddle, and I have been wanting to get a closer look at those wounds of his. He's been shot up pretty bad."

"I'll see to his injuries. You see to the horse. And as soon as I've tended him, I'll take a look at some of those cuts on your own face. Then I'll see to Toona getting some supper served. We're havin' wallaby stew and, if we can wake this fellow up, we need to try to get some of the broth down him."

"Yes ma'am," Jacky said again and quickly turned to go do exactly what he had been ordered to do.

"And you better give that horse of yours some of that grain that's in the bin. With him havin' to tote the two of you, he's bound to be half starved. And there should be some water already in the trough."

"Aye."

It took almost ten minutes to see that Eric's horse was properly rubbed, fed, and watered; and by the time he had returned to the house, Jacky found the woman had already washed off the fresh blood from around the wounds and had placed clean pads of folded cloth over them. She was now busily scrubbing away the dried blood that had caked to his skin elsewhere.

"There isn't enough of this shirt left to do this young man any good," she said and finished tearing it off.

"Reach inside that top drawer there and get one of my husband's shirts. He sure won't be needing it for awhile. He's still got nearly half a year of jail to go."

Jacky wondered what a man as old as this woman's husband probably was had done to be put in jail, but again did not ask. He knew it really was none of his business. Pulling out the top drawer of the only piece of furniture in the room other than the huge bed Eric lay in, Jacky came out with a blue flannel shirt that looked as if it was going to be a little small across Eric's broad shoulders, but at this point, he was not about to complain over the size. The shirt would cover him and help protect that wound from the elements.

"I'll put that shirt on him as soon as I've finished washing him up," she said, never looking up from her task. "Get yourself one, too. Your shirt isn't much better off than his. You two bushrangers? No need in answering. Of course you are." After a lengthy pause she asked, "He sure does have on a lot of black. Tell me, is he the Flash Brigand I've been reading so much about lately?"

"Aye, ma'am, he is," Jacky said, not seeing any reason to lie.

"What do you know about that," she chuckled, clearly amused by the fact that she had the Flash Brigand in her very own house, in her very own bed; then her smile faded. "He's pretty weak. I wish I could offer you a place to stay, but I don't dare."

"I understand. And I didn't expect you to," he told her as he slipped into a red and white flannel shirt and started to button it from the waist up.

"If I get caught offering any kind of aid to a bushranger, I can be jailed."

"I know and I do understand."

"That's why my husband is in jail right now. He helped a poor young lad who had ridden up with a bullet lodged in his hip. Robert took him in and removed the bullet. Then just a few hours later, just after dark, the traps rode up and, upon searching the place, found the boy and carried Robert away right then. Didn't even give him time enough to put on his boots." She fell silent a long moment before saying, "Besides, you need to try to get this man to a real doctor if you can."

"I intend to. It's not too much farther to a place where I can get plenty of help, and the traps will be none the wiser."

"I hope you don't mean the Red Rover," she said and stopped what she was doing to look at Jacky. "The man who owns it was hauled off to jail two weeks ago for suspicion in aiding bushrangers. And the way the magistrate feels toward anyone who helps a bushranger, that man has probably already been tried, found guilty, and is serving a long sentence in one of the Melbourne jails by now. You'll have to find somewhere else to go. He got any family?"

"Aye, but it's too far, and the traps would be sure to be watchin' his family," Jacky said and wondered what he was going to do.

"What about you? You got any family?"

Of course! Mundora. She would help. She would understand. The rest of his people might not understand his bringing Eric there, for they had not understood why he had decided to work in the white man's world in the first place, but Mundora would understand. And she would help him.

"Why yes, ma'am, yes ma'am, I do. I should have

thought of that. My sister would know what to do for him. And she's not that far from here."

"Then you best be getting him to her," the old woman said with a grim shake of her head. "He needs to get somewhere where he can be watched after proper, and he needs to get there quick. He won't last much longer without some good help. You'd better be on your way just as soon as you've had something to eat."

"You bloody fools have done such a slapdash job of findin' the man's body, that I've already sent Corporal Kilburn back to Melbourne to get me some black trackers. Maybe they will be able to figure out 'ow you managed to lose track of a dying man. How incompetent can you be? The man was bleeding, for God's sake," Captain Scantlin complained, his rounded face blustery red. When no one dared a response, he grumbled: "The trackers won't be 'ere until sometime tomorrow afternoon, so I want you fops back out there searching at the first break of light, for wot little good it will do. The man's sure to be dead by now, but you men could at least provide me with the body."

"We'll find him, sir," one young trooper promised. "It just got dark too quick, and you can't find signs of blood or hoofprints in the dark. As soon as it gets light, we'll find the trail and get you that body."

"You'd sure as hell better," the captain snapped. He had never felt so frustrated. He had so wanted to be able to tell that young cur, Aylesbury, just who had been responsible for bringing on his doom. He had wanted to see a glimpse of realization in the bastard's dying eyes. Now that had been denied him, for the young wretch was

307

sure to be dead by now. Damn fate for refusing him that one little pleasure.

"And hurry with that tent. I'm tired of waitin'," he grumbled and yanked at the tight crotch of his britches.

To the captain's further dismay, it was well into the following afternoon before the black trackers arrived, leaving them barely two hours of daylight to search, but he was pleased with the way they managed to pick up a trail that lay right in the water itself. He followed closely behind as the three black men pointed out overturned stones and broken branches that had lain waterlogged on the creek bottom. Their adeptness at tracking amazed him, and he felt certain they would find the body before nightfall, but then, suddenly, the creek deepened into a small pool and the trackers lost all trace. He had the trackers and his men continue along the water's edge on both sides of the creek for several more miles, and although they came upon a place where three riders had come through the creek recently, they never found the trail of the Flash again; not even a trace of dried blood or a track that belonged to a lone rider.

As darkness descended once again, Captain Scantlin decided he would leave a group of men behind to continue the search, but he would have the rest of the men fan out and check any dwellings they could find in the area. It could be Aylesbury managed to find help with one of these local bleeding hearts. If that did not net them physical evidence of the Flash Brigand, then he would send for more troopers and comb the entire Black Forest. He bloody well was going to have that body with him when he returned to Melbourne.

*   *   *

308

"Is he any better?" Jacky asked when he entered the small hut of his half sister.

Mundora glanced up briefly and shook her head before returning her attention to the young white man who lay facedown on a bed of tender young gum leaves in a dark corner of the room. "Two days and he still sleeps."

"Did you remove the bullet?"

"Though Grandfather would have scorned me for doing such a thing, yes I did. I cut into the wound in his shoulder and finally found the bullet deep in his chest. I could see the movement of his heart nearby. He is a very fortunate man. Much lower and that bullet would have pierced his heart."

"What's that you have lying over his wounds?" Jacky asked as he knelt beside his sister and let his gaze rest on his friend.

"I made a special syrup from the resin of the gum tree and bottle brush and covered the wounds with it. Then I covered the syrup with clean mud. It will help stop the bleeding and numb the pain a little. It is the best I can do until he wakes up and can swallow."

"I want to thank you for helping my friend the way you have and also for not asking any questions."

"I have no need of answers," she said and smiled warmly at him. "I just wish it did not take things like this to bring you to my hut. I miss my little brother."

"I've been busy," he answered.

"Working the white man's cattle must be hard work then," she said. "Does the man Crawford work you too hard?"

"I don't work for Ben Crawford anymore. It's a long story, but I now work for this man."

"He is your boss as well as your friend?" she asked,

then smiled down at the man lying unconscious before her. "This is good."

"He is the best friend I ever had," Jacky admitted. "He has risked his life to save mine more than once."

"Is that how he came to be shot?"

"In a way, yes. He tried to draw some of the danger away from me and two other of our friends, and ended up with all the danger on himself."

"He is a brave man," she noted and bent over to run a damp gum leaf over his brow. "You are lucky to have such a friend."

Jacky watched as his sister tenderly stroked Eric's pale brow with the wet leaf that was supposed to have strong medicinal powers. He remembered how his own grandfather had used the resin of the tree as well as the younger leaves in many ways, though he had never fully understood it as Mundora did.

Mundora. To Jacky she was beautiful. Her skin was lighter than most of the tribe, but that was because she had been born from a ruthless assault on their mother by a white man. She was the child of a vicious rape.

To have been born of a rape was bad enough, but to have been born from the rape of a white man had caused Mundora to be treated differently all her life. She was unsuitable for marriage by any of the Aboriginal men, for she would surely bring the curse that had run in that white man's blood into her own children. And she was just as unsuitable for marriage to a white man, for her skin bore the color of sun-bleached almonds; her eyes were dark, her lips full. The Aboriginal blood had predominated in Mundora. Poor Mundora. Though beautiful, she was doomed never to marry, never to bear children. She was nearly thirty years old now. Other women of the tribe that age had children nearing adulthood.

She was the only one Jacky had regretted leaving behind when he decided to strike out on his own. He had seen that the future of the land belonged to the white man, and if he wanted a place in that future, he needed to learn to work with them. Although their grandfather had been heartbroken over the decision, hoping Jacky would have been the one to follow his ways as medicine man, Mundora had understood. She had sensed his need for adventure, his desire to succeed, and had wished him well.

"His eyes move," he heard her say, her words penetrating his thoughts.

"Is that a good sign?"

"Yes. His eyes now see whatever images are in his brain. He dreams."

Jacky stared at Eric's closed lids and could detect the movement. "I wonder what he dreams of?"

At that moment, Eric's mouth came open and he mouthed a word, but no sound came forth.

"Eric? Eric are you awake?" Jacky asked, his chest suddenly filled with hope. "Eric? Can you hear me?"

"Jessie," the word finally sounded. "Jess . . . ie." Then he was still again.

"Who is this Jessie?" Mundora asked as she leaned over Eric and studied his eyelids closely.

"His sister. His half sister."

"He must be very close to his half sister. Not like some brothers I know." There was a light of amusement shimmering in Mundora's dark eyes.

"They are very close. I've met her. She is very nice. She is a lot like you."

311

"Then she must be nice." Mundora laughed and reached up to adjust the lovely red neckerchief that Jacky had given her. "How old is she?"

Jacky thought about that. "I guess she's about the same age as Eric. I really don't know which of them is older. She's a medicine woman, too. Their father is a doctor, and she helps him much like you used to help Grandfather."

"I like her." Mundora's smile widened.

"You would," he muttered, then stood to leave. "I think I'll go out into the bush and find you something to cook besides emu. Although I like emu, I'm getting awfully tired of it."

"I take what I can get, and emu is what they bring me."

"Well, I'll bring you something better. You just take good care of my friend while I'm gone."

Chapter XVIII

"Would it be much out of our way to walk down by Regie's claim and say goodday to him?" Carrie asked shyly. Her shining green eyes only reached high enough to stare at Jessica's slender throat.

"I don't see how it would be that much out of our way, and there are very few patients to tend to today. Besides, it is such a beautiful day; I think I would enjoy the extra walk," Jessica told her as she tucked the folded newspaper under her arm. She had expected the request, for although she had not bothered to change out of her gray duffle working dress, Carrie had taken the time to put on a pretty yellow cotton dress with a billowing overskirt edged in satin ribbon and white lace and had rearranged her long brown hair to include a bright yellow satin ribbon as well. Carrie was becoming quite accustomed to wearing pretty things, and Jessica enjoyed having been the one who introduced her to them.

While Carrie carefully scanned the area where she knew she would catch sight of Regie, Jessica let her eyes turn heavenward. There was hardly a cloud in the pale blue sky overhead, but that was common for early February. These long hot days with little rain were expected to last for at least another month, then in March, the first signs of autumn should finally present themselves. There would be several months of bluer skies before the gray of winter set in. Jessica loved autumn and looked forward to the changing of the seasons when the air would become cooler, crisper, and certain trees and hundreds of different wildflowers would bloom vivid colors while Mother Nature allowed summer to go out in its usual blaze of glory.

At Carrie's startled gasp, Jessica snapped her sights and thoughts back to the ground, and she immediately saw the source of Carrie's concern. The small troop of goldfield police were riding into Eureka, followed by more than a dozen foot soldiers, all in search of gold licenses. Although Regie had shown the good sense to buy his with the money his mother had sent, Rube had viewed it as a waste and had refused to pay his thirty shillings for a ridiculous piece of paper. If Rube was caught digging without one, he would be handcuffed and marched to the Melbourne jail. His fine would be so high he would not be able to pay it, and he would end up in one of the already crowded jails, maybe even on one of those horrible prison hulks. Since so many ships had been deserted due to the gold rush, the Melbourne government had turned several of them into floating prisons, and the life on these prison hulks was rumored nearly unendurable.

The moment the police had been spotted riding into camp, several young men tore off running in different directions, and it was these men whom the troopers went after first. Through the dust that stirred around all the action, Jessica saw that Rube was one of the runners. She held her breath as she waited to see what was to become of Regie's twin brother.

Rube ran with agile speed, cutting and darting in and out of the many tents, huts, and windlasses, making it difficult for the trooper to maneuver his horse in pursuit. Rube ran hard and continuously turned in different directions, but when he finally ran out of breath and could run no further, he was not very far from where Jessica and Carrie stood watching with mouths agape. Suddenly Jessica realized it was not Rube at all, but Regie who had run.

"Present a license or prepare for arrest," the trooper commanded haughtily from astride his horse. He already had his hand on his revolver so that he would be ready to enforce his command.

Regie looked up as if he were seeing the trooper for the first time. Between desperate gulps for air, he asked, "Are you . . . talkin' . . . to me, sir?"

"You know I am. Show me your license."

Regie heaved in several more much needed breaths before he moved to comply. Slowly he reached into the small leather pouch attached to the side of his belt and pulled out a folded piece of paper. Wetting his dry lips with the tip of his tongue, he smiled, his chest still heaving, and presented the paper to the trooper with a courtly bow. "Here you are, sir. Sorry for any inconvenience I may have caused you."

The trooper snatched the paper from his hand and glanced over the writing, then tossed it into the dirt at Regie's feet. "I don't like games. Do that again and I'll arrest you anyway."

"Sorry sir," Regie said again. By now he had noticed

Jessica and Carrie standing with wide-eyed concern. He grinned sheepishly.

The trooper glanced back to see who the digger was smiling at and noticed the two women standing nearby with their smiles barely hidden behind their raised hands. Angrily, he jerked his horse around and headed back to where the chase had originated, but by that time Rube had taken full advantage of his brother's diversion and was safely hidden.

Watching the trooper, Regie bent over, picked up his license and returned it to his pouch before coming to talk with them.

"G'day Carrie, Jessica," he said with a cordial nod as he came to stand before them. Both women noticed with delight that he had mentioned Carrie's name first. "Had a little run-in with the traps," he explained.

"More like a runaway than a run-in," Jessica commented. "I suppose that little episode was for Rube's benefit. Wouldn't it be easier for all concerned if he just bought himself a license?"

"Rube doesn't like the idea of having to pay a fee just to be able to look for gold. He thinks it would make better sense to have a fee or tax of some sort set up for the men who actually find gold. Then a man could afford it. But not just for looking. He doesn't believe the license law is right, and he'll never pay for a license. Besides, we don't have enough money to buy him one even if he was to change his mind."

"Do you think they'll find him?" Jessica asked and glanced passed him to where a few of the troopers had already handcuffed several of the unlicensed diggers to their saddles and continued to search for more.

"Not if he is where he's supposed to be, balled up at the

bottom of one of our trunks and covered with a blanket," he answered, though his eyes lingered on Carrie. "Seems contradictory to me. He's too proud to buy a license, but not so proud that he won't hide like the criminal the law makes him out to be."

Jessica watched the way Regie kept looking at Carrie with keen interest. She was inwardly amused at how they allowed their eyes to meet, dart away, only to be drawn back and meet again. A smile tugged at her lips, but she managed to keep it controlled for fear they might feel she was making fun of them. It did her heart good to know that not only had Regie finally noticed Carrie, he obviously liked what he saw.

"Well, well, wot 'ave we 'ere?" The gruff voice was familiar to all three of them. "It's so nice to run across old friends in a place like this."

Jessica felt her stomach recoil as she turned her cold gaze up to Captain Scantlin as he leaned forward in his saddle and peered down at them. Her eyes went immediately to the mangled edge of the ear missing a lobe when she responded in a stiff but polite tone: "I can't recall that we were ever friends, Captain Scantlin."

Aware of where her gaze had lighted, Captain Scantlin absently reached up and gave his ear a self-conscious tug. "I agree we could 'ave been closer friends had I been allowed to have more of my own way," he said, purposefully letting his eyes drift down her slender form, then over to Carrie's. "Maybe I should rephrase that to old acquaintances, then."

"Maybe you should," Regie said coolly, his nostrils flaring at the edges with the contempt he felt for this man. "I certainly don't want to be referred to as your friend."

The captain raised his eyebrows and stared down at the insolent youth before him. "You would do well to keep a civil tongue in yer head," he warned. His mouth grew taut and the muscles along his jowls flexed with the anger that consumed him. "You may wish someday you 'ad chosen to be my friend instead of insisting on becomin' my enemy."

"Your enemy? Is that what I am?" Regie asked, his brow drawn. Suddenly, his face relaxed and he nodded with a wide smile. "Good. I like that. I'll do my best to try to live up to it."

The captain's beady eyes narrowed, and he stared down at Regie for a long time. Boiling with anger, he made a mental note of how he would see to it that one day very soon this young man would be made to fully regret his arrogance. Then he let his attention be drawn to the little lass at the young man's side, half hidden by his shoulder. At first he had not recognized her, for she had changed a great deal over the last few months. She had matured, grown more lovely, more desirable than ever. He felt a sudden prickling in his loins that let him know how much he still wanted to take her, feel her struggle against him. A ghost of a smile lifted his lips as he made his decision to catch that young bitch off alone somewhere and soon. He was eager to finish what he had started, and might have finished if this meddling buffoon hadn't interrupted him. He felt his loins grow tighter at the thought of what lay beneath that lovely yellow dress and remembered with vivid clarity what a fine fight the lass had put up. Aye, he would do what he could to find her off somewhere alone. He would definitely finish what he had begun.

Regie, realizing where the captain's gaze had gone,

stepped fully in front of Carrie and asked, "Is there something we can do for you?"

"No, but there's something I can do for you."

"And what could that possibly be," Jessica asked.

"I can let you in on some of the latest news," he said with extreme satisfaction, for he was certain they had not yet learned of their dear Flash's fate.

"I have a newspaper right here. I'll get all the news I care to know from it," Jessica said and indicated the paper still tucked neatly below her left arm.

"I hope it is a current paper. Current enough to tell all about how I finally ridded Victoria of that insipid lowlife, the Flash Brigand." He watched closely for a reaction.

"You arrested the Flash Brigand?" she asked, clearly disappointed, but not as devastated as he had expected her to be.

"Not arrested. Killed. Up around Bendigo. He tried to bail up a Roddon gold coach, but we outsmarted him. It was a setup. There wasn't even any gold on board the coach. The Flash, in all his greed, was drawn into our clutches like a moth to a flame. Now the poor bloke's dead. And I'm two 'undred pounds richer."

Jessica had had enough of Captain Scantlin's company. Turning to Regie and Carrie, she ignored the captain's presence and told Regie, "Father is expected back from Melbourne sometime today. He should have that medicine for your father's cough. Be sure to stop by later to see. We don't want his cough getting any worse than it already is."

"I'll do that," Regie responded, turning his shoulder to the captain as well. "I may have to tie him up and hold him down to get him to take it, but I'll see that he does."

Carrie was the only one left facing the captain, and when she glanced up to find him staring at her loosely fitted bodice, a cold shiver ran down her spine. She gave him a defiant look, letting him know that she dared him to try anything with her again—especially now that she had a derringer tucked away in her boot and had learned how to use it.

"Don't you realize who the Flash Brigand was?" he asked loudly, eager to strike out at these impudent youths.

Jessica turned around and stared up at him, hating the wry smirk on the captain's fat lips.

"Don't you know that the Flash Brigand was really Eric? Don't you realize I'm trying to tell you your brother's dead?"

His words lashed her like a whip. "Liar," she called out accusingly. It couldn't be. Eric wouldn't have jeopardized their chance for happiness here in Victoria just to continue plaguing Livingston. But the gleam in the captain's eyes told her it was true.

"I was sure you would know about Eric being the Flash. I thought you two was supposed to be real close. I thought your whole family was supposed to be real close."

Tears stung her eyes, but she held them in as she proudly turned to stare into Carrie's horrified face. "Come, we need to be getting back. With Father away, we need to stay as close to the tent as possible."

Though her insides were a twisting, crumbling mass of pain, she managed to calmly say good-bye to Regie, and she walked away, never looking back and not daring to give into the waves of dizziness that pulled at her brain. Eric was dead. Her dear precious Eric was dead. Killed by the likes of Captain Scantlin. Eric. How could she go on living without him?

It was not until they were safely inside their tent and Carrie had silently gone to her and enveloped her in her arms that Jessica finally gave in to her tears. The pain was so severe, she was not sure she could bear it. Slowly her legs collapsed, and she sank to her knees. Carrie went with her to the floor, never lessening her embrace. Jessica was barely aware of her friend's comforting efforts. How was she going to tell Aaron? How could she explain to him that his only son was dead? It was going to break his heart, crush his very soul as it already had hers. Somewhere deep inside, she hoped her stepfather would never learn of Eric's death, but she knew that was impossible. It would be in the papers. It would become the main talk of Eureka, for the Flash had become a symbol of freedom, of justified rebellion to them all. Many men would mourn his passing, but none with quite the depth she would. Never had she felt such a sense of loss, such emptiness. Eric was gone and a major part of her was gone, too. All the future held for her now were her tender memories.

"Tell me, Jacky. How did you come by such a beautiful and saintly sister," Eric asked and held the two pieces of wood in place with his right hand so Jacky could tie them together with heavy bullock straps. The two of them had grown tired of always having to sit on the dirt floor and had decided to build themselves a couple of chairs.

"Saintly?" Jacky questioned in disbelief. "Mundora? Many things she is, but saintly isn't one of them."

Mundora glanced up from the oily mixture she was

making out of crushed gum leaves, powdered bird excrement, and animal fat. Neither Eric or Jacky knew the exact benefits she would derive from the mixture, but they both knew it was for the injured boy who had been brought to her the day before. Although she had allowed his parents to take him with them that same afternoon, she had visited the boy several times since to keep up with his condition. "I like this word saintly. I like the way it sounded on your friend's tongue. Why am I not this?"

"Because it refers to goodness, and there is far too much meanness in you." He grinned when his remark got its intended response.

With a playful scowl, she warned, "The day will come when you will need your sister's help again. Hope that she does not instead sit with her arms folded and remind you of your words." Then turning to Eric, she asked, "Would you speak to your sister Jessie in such a way?"

Eric had been smiling at the easy banter between the two but that smile quickly faded. Jacky noticed this sudden change.

"Jacky has told you about my sister," he said. "No, I would never speak to Jessie like that. I wouldn't dare. She would chase me down and slap me silly."

"Ah, a good idea. Such spirit she must have. I like this sister of yours more and more with every new thing I learn."

"Er-ric!" Jacky pleaded. "Don't be putting such ideas into her head. She's hard enough to get along with."

Eric attempted a smile and tried to listen to the banter that continued between Mundora and Jacky, but his thoughts had been torn back in time to a beautiful spring day in the month of November high on a grassy knoll. A very special day, in New South Wales. Once again he was secure in Jessica's arms, tasting the sweetness of her lips, feeling the warmth of her embrace. Oh, how he missed her, how he would love to have her right there with him. But that was impossible. Even though he had learned she was no further away than Ballarat, he knew it would be impossible for him to see her. Ballarat was too closely guarded. All he could do was hope that the future would somehow find them together again.

"Eric, where are you?" Jacky asked, then when he was certain he finally had his friend's attention again, he told him, "I said I was planning to ride into town tomorrow and get you a decent shirt, one that fits, and a few supplies. It won't be long now before you will be strong enough to ride again. You'll also need a revolver and I need a good horse. Is there anything else you can think of for me to get while I'm there?"

"Aye, get a newspaper. And ask around and see if you can find out what happened to Coolabah and Sam."

"Anything else?"

"Aye, one more thing. See if the mercantile there has a music box."

"A music box?" Jacky asked, surprised at such a request.

"Aye, a music box. I happen to know someone who is very partial to them, someone who has a birthday coming up in early June. I want to start looking for one to send her." Then glancing over at Mundora who had done so much for him, he added, "Get two."

"I'll do what I can," Jacky said with an approving smile.

"You can't be serious," Captain Scantlin said as he eased his heavy bulk into the small wooden chair beside his friend and leaned his elbows on the table in front of them. He had just returned from a lengthy trip to New South Wales in order to pick up his reward in person and had not heard the latest news.

"Aye, I'm very serious. It seems the Flash Brigand is still very much alive and as busy as ever. Either that or someone else has decided to take his place. The leader of the gang that held up that gold coach last week was dressed all in black and rode a spirited black stallion. And he was with a black fellow who wore a bright red and orange neckerchief and a fancy young lad in an English frock coat. They also had the big, burly man with the lilting brogue doing their talking, and he kept referring to the man in black as Flash. The driver said he seemed to be making a point of it."

"How could 'e have escaped us? It can't be true. No man could have survived after 'aving lost that much blood."

"But you never did find a body," his friend reminded him. "It seems to me you still have work to do. You haven't really earned that two hundred pounds you so eagerly collected."

"I'll get right on it," the captain said with a scowl. "If it is Eric Aylesbury, 'e shan't escape me a second time. This time I'll fix it so that I can personally watch 'im die. I'll pluck out his heart with me own hands and deliver it to him in person."

"Aylesbury isn't going to fall prey to a trap quite as easily as before," the young man cautioned him.

"He will if the bait is just right," the captain said, his eyes lighting with a sudden plan. "And I know just the bait to lure 'im right into our waiting arms."

*   *   *

"Father, Father!" Jessica called out, trembling with excitement as she ran toward the medical tent, stumbling over loose rocks in her haste. Never had she felt such pure elation as she did at that very moment. "Father, he's alive. Eric is alive!"

Aaron rushed out of the tent to meet her, hope pulling his brows together. The lack of sleep and his deep grief over the loss of his son had taken their toll on him over the past two months. Deep, dark semicircles constantly framed the lower side of his eyes, and his skin had lost all its color. But he had continued his work, pressing himself beyond the normal point of endurance, hoping to lose his thoughts and his pain in his everyday tasks. Now his heart leapt to his throat.

Realizing that several pairs of eyes were on her when she came to stand in front of her father and also realizing she had used Eric's name, she hurried him inside their private tent. She didn't want these men to realize the link between Aaron's son, Eric, and the Flash Brigand.

"Here, read this," she said, waving the paper in front of him, still unable to contain her excitement. "Read this."

"I would if you would hold it still long enough," he told her and finally snatched it out of her hands. Quickly shaking out as many of the wrinkles as he could, he scanned the paper for sight of something that could have caused such a reaction in Jessica, his heart anxious to find whatever it was. Then he read the uppermost headline: The Flash Brigand Returns From The Dead. His mouth slowly fell open, for here, at last, was proof. Blinking back the tears of joy that filled him, he read on:

In a daring bail up on the track to Geelong, the

Flash Brigand has shown the goldfield police that the recent report of his death by Captain Theodore Scantlin is very much exaggerated. Without so much as firing a shot, the Flash and his men managed to get away with a shipment in gold valued at over three thousand pounds and eight pairs of boots which were only valuable to the escort men whom he left stocking footed. Gilbert Livingston, who is part owner of the Rodden Gold Escort Service, is furious that he has been singled out once again. He announced yesterday that the reward for the Flash's capture has been raised a full fifty pounds as a result of his latest escapades. Notices of the new reward have been posted all over Melbourne and in many of the neighboring towns and mining camps. The Flash can be proud of the fact that this is now the largest reward ever offered in Victoria for the arrest or proven death of a bushranger.

Aaron's eyes rose to meet Jessica's and she went to him, hugging him close, trembling with him. "He's alive," she sobbed with joy. "That's why there never was a body for us to claim. He is still alive."

"We must write Penelope right away. She may miss this in the papers," Aaron said eagerly. "And Mum. She needs to be told, too. They can stop their grieving. Just like I tried to tell everyone all along, Eric is alive."

Jessica hurried to do just that, and within the hour she had several letters ready to post, letting Penelope, Grandmum Millie, and Eric's Grandfather Oliver know that Eric was indeed alive. She hurried to the commissioner's tent to be sure the letters left on the very next mail coach.

"A man was just in here asking directions to your place," the man told her as he accepted the letters. "I gave him directions on how to get over there. You probably passed him."

She had passed hundreds of men and had been in too much of a hurry to notice any of them anyway. "Was he in need of a doctor?"

"No. Said something about being a cousin of some sort to the doctor. But he seemed most interested in knowing if you were here, too."

Jessica felt her eyes grow wide. "Was he a tall man? With curly black hair and big black eyes?"

"Aye, that's him. Though his black hair had started to turn a little gray in places. A seaman as far as I could tell. He carried a duffel bag with him like the ones you see most of the sailors bring with them. He smiled mighty big when I told him you were here, too, and that he would find you and the doctor just over the next rise."

Jessica bit her lower lip in nervous excitement. It was Deenyi, her father. Her real father. It had to be. What other cousin of Aaron's would be so interested in her? Buck might be, but Buck wasn't his cousin; Buck was his uncle. It had to be her father. Jessica stared unseeing at the man for a long moment, then she caught herself and explained that the man was a part of the family they hadn't seen in years. Jessica had never seen her father. Oh, but the stories she had heard about him, of his adventures at sea, of how dearly he had loved her mother, Annabelle, but could not marry her because he was half Aborigine and she was white. To have married his beloved Annabelle would have evoked a riot among the white men that would have resulted in his own death and

Annabelle's becoming an outcast.

Poor Deen had been forced to stand aside and watch his cousin marry her in order to assure his child a name. He had stayed nearby long enough to learn that his child had been born and was a beautiful, curly-headed girl, a girl named Jessia—Jessica Aylesbury. It was shortly after he had seen his daughter and was assured she and Annabelle were being taken care of that he left for the sea. He started out working on a small whaling vessel in the South Pacific, and now he owned his own fleet of whaling ships based in Van Dieman's Land just off the coast of Victoria.

Jessica was aware of only one time that Deen had returned to Hawkesbury in New South Wales. Shortly after her mother died, he had gone to visit the grave in Windsor and had come back to visit first with Glenn and Sally Moffett, Annabelle's parents, and then with Milicent and Matthew Aylesbury, his aunt and uncle. He had not even stayed the night. Jessica had wished then that he had made the trip inland to visit with Aaron so that she could have met him. She had always wondered about him.

Here she was almost twenty-seven years old and about to really meet her father for the first time. Suddenly, she was afraid. Jessica's blood felt as if it had turned to water, leaving her weak and causing her heart to work ever harder. She retraced her steps with far less enthusiasm than she had when she first left the tent. It was very difficult for her to swallow; every muscle in her throat had been drawn tight. What if he didn't like her? Would he be disappointed when he saw that she did not possess many of her mother's traits? Would he think her ugly because of that? What should she do when she finally came face to face with him? Should she offer her hand? Or should she place a light kiss on his cheek? Her insides were in utter turmoil, spinning and wheeling in all directions, as she grew closer to the medical tent.

That's when she saw him. She knew him from the descriptions everyone had given of him. He was indeed tall, though broader across the shoulders than she had expected. She watched him from a distance. He was standing motionless outside the opened end of the tent, looking in as if hesitant to enter, maybe trying to decide whether or not his coming had been such a good idea.

Without taking the time to worry if she was doing the right thing, she lifted her skirts and broke into a very unladylike run. The closer she got to her father, the wilder her heartbeat. Then when she came within a few yards of him, he turned and knew her immediately. Now that his shining eyes were upon her, her courage to rush and embrace him left her and she stopped short, staring up at him in open-eyed amazement. For there before her, looking back at her, were eyes shaped identical to her own, only black in color.

"Do I call you Father?" she asked, feeling more timid than she could ever remember having felt in her entire life.

"Or Deen, whichever you feel most comfortable with," he replied. His expression was blank, but his eyes eagerly ran across her face, searching for familiarities, memorizing every detail. "Do I call you Jessica?"

"Or Jessie. Eric and Father have always called me Jessie," she told him, then worried that she had referred to Aaron as her father in front of him. Would that hurt him somehow?

"Jessie," he said, trying it out, his eyes still drinking in every detail of his daughter, all grown up. "You are beautiful. You have your mother's bearing and her sky-blue eyes."

"They may be blue like Mother's were, but they are shaped like yours," she said as she, too, studied every detail of her father. A smile touched her face when she added, "And now I know who I can blame my hair on."

"But you have beautiful hair," he protested.

"Unruly around the hairline," she complained and reached up to pull at one of the tiny loose curls at her temple. "See? It does what it pleases."

Deen grinned. "Should I apologize?"

Jessica saw her own smile in this man's face even to the curving dimples at the outer edges. It was a strange feeling to find so much of herself in someone else. He had the same mocha-colored skin, only faintly darker than her own, like creamed coffee. "No, I guess not, for I do like the nose you gave me."

"Aye, definitely a Crawford nose." He nodded and his smile broadened.

"Father? I mean Deen? No, Father. Oh, I don't know what to call you!" she said in exasperation.

"Call me whatever you want. I've probably been called worse."

"I've referred to you all these years as Deen. Would it hurt your feelings if I continued to call you that?"

"Not at all. It would be easier for me. I'm not sure I could adjust to a grown woman such as yourself calling me Father anyway. It makes me feel old. I've got enough things reminding me of my age as it is," he said and gestured to the gray pepperings in his hair.

"What brings you here?"

"I no longer have enough crew to man my whalers. I

came to Melbourne to see if I could muster up enough disillusioned gold diggers to reman my ships. While I was in port, I ran into Weldon Braxton, and he told me about Aaron having set up a medical tent here in Ballarat. Being this close . . ." He shrugged as he searched for the words he wanted. "I just decided to come on up here and visit."

"Father will be delighted to see you. He loves to talk of the childhood pranks you two used to pull. Come on, let me be the one to tell him you're here." She stepped toward the tent, but when she looked back, she noticed that he had not thought to follow. He was still looking at her as if he could not quite believe what he saw. Suddenly the urge came to her, and she did nothing to stop herself. Taking several quick steps in his direction, she found herself in his arms, pulled hard against his chest. She did not dare look up for tears had once again invaded her eyes, and she did not want Deen to think his daughter was weak. She had no way of knowing that similar tears had also worked their way into his dark eyes, forcing him to close them or be found out.

Aaron was just as surprised to see Deen as Jessica had been, and as soon as he finished checking on the last of his patients, he invited Deen back to their private tent and demanded he share supper with them. Then, after supper and hours of reminiscing their childhoods, catching up on all the years missed, Aaron ordered Carrie to go into the medical tent to gather bedding, for Deen was to stay right there with them. Even after the bed had been made in the front corner of the tent, Aaron, Jessica, and Deen stayed awake until nearly sunrise, talking about anything and everything that came to mind.

All the following day, Jessica and Deen shared each other's company. He explained to her why he had stayed away all these years. He had been afraid of placing the stigma of being part Aboriginal on her should anyone realize he was her father. She understood and was grateful that he had felt the need to explain. She had wanted to ask but had been afraid to, yet he evidently had sensed her reluctance and her need. He showed an uncanny way of knowing what she was thinking and when. He was no longer a stranger, yet he was not exactly like a father, either. He was more like a close friend. So close and so understanding that by the end of the day she found herself telling him how she felt about Eric. Instead of shunning her for having fallen in love with a man she had grown up believing was her brother, he understood her feelings and accepted them.

"Will you be getting married whenever he finally gives up these bushranging pursuits?" he asked.

"We've talked of it. But I'm not sure where we can go to get away from the threat of his being arrested. You see, the police have learned he is the Flash Brigand, and now it's not safe for him to stay here as Flash or Eric Aylesbury. Same goes for New South Wales. I guess we will end up in western Australia somewhere."

"You could come to Van Dieman's Land, though I don't recommend the island as a place to raise children; too ruthless. You do intend to have lots of children don't you?"

Jessica smiled at the thought. "Aye, I hope to give Eric many children."

"I'll be a grandfather then," Deen said with a quick draw of his sea-worn brow. "Of course, I'll be a very *young* grandfather."

Jessica laughed for she realized that although he was only forty-six, he had become quite age conscious.

"Grandpa Crawford," she teased. "You should start trying to get used to it because it is inevitable."

By dark, their staying up most of the previous night and working hard all day took its toll on all three of them, and they retired early by mutual agreement. When Jessica rose to prepare for bed, she bent first over Aaron and placed a perfunctory kiss on his cheek, then turned to do likewise with Deen.

Chapter XIX

It was the firm pressure across her mouth that roused Jessica from a deep, dream-filled sleep. In her sleep-muddled state of mind, she reached up, with her eyes still closed, to brush away whatever it was, but when her hand came into contact with the solid warmth of first a wrist and then the broad hand that was pressed firmly yet unpainfully against her mouth, her eyes flew open and she saw the tall figure looming over her. Her first instinct was to scream for help, but her efforts came out muffled.

"Şhh, Jessica. Don't. Eric sent me," a whisper told her. "I have a message for you. You are Jessica, aren't you?"

Jessica stopped her struggle, nodded that she was, then lay still and stared at him. Her eyes tried to focus on the features of the man's face, but she was unable to determine anything about him. He was a mere shadow against the dim glow the moonlight had cast over the canvas tent above them.

"Do I have your word you won't scream if I let go of you?" the whispered voice asked. When she nodded her agreement, he gently eased his grip on her mouth and held it inches away until he was confident she would keep her unspoken promise.

Jessica's tongue went to her lips as she stretched them wide, trying to bring blood back to where his hand had pressed firmly. She could taste the musty sweat the man's hand had left on the outer edges of her mouth.

"It's not safe for me here," the man went on to explain. Something about his manner made him seem young to her, but she still could not see his face well enough to verify his age. "But Eric wants to see you. He asks that you be on the next coach out of here to Bendigo."

"Am I to meet him there?" she asked, breathless. Her entire body filled with anticipation. Her heart leapt with sudden hope.

"He didn't say. All he said was for me to tell you to be on that next coach. That's all. Do I tell him you plan to do what he asks?"

"Yes! Yes, of course. I'll be on the coach, the very next one to Bendigo. He can count on it," she answered eagerly. Her voice rose slightly in her excitement. Eric had finally sent for her. Their moment had come. "I've already told him I'd gladly go anywhere he wanted. I'll do whatever it takes to be with him."

"Shh, I can't chance being found out," he warned again. "I'll tell him you will be on the coach so he'll know to watch for you."

Before she could question him further, the dark form turned and knelt at the edge of the tent wall. Lifting the side only a couple of feet, he ducked outside and was gone like a black spectre in the night.

Jessica blinked with muddled confusion. She tried to

decide if any of that had really happened or if the man had been some sort of apparition, a figment of her imagination. It had occurred quickly. Had she simply wished so hard Eric would finally send for her that she dreamed the whole thing? It was the lingering taste of the man's sweat mixed with old leather still on her mouth that let her know her night visitor had, indeed, been real. Her pulse raged wildly through her body, and her heart quivered with such vibrance in her chest that she felt certain she would actually burst with her joy.

At last she was going to see Eric again. After four long months, she was finally going to see him, touch him, be with him. She could hardly wait to hold him in her arms again, to devour his kisses with her own. She hoped the next coach to Bendigo would be soon, very soon. There was no regular schedule of coaches going on up to Bendigo yet.

With little chance of her falling back to sleep now, Jessica slipped out of her bedding and lit the oil lamp that she kept nearby, unperturbed by the slight chill in the air. Keeping the glow of the lamp dim, she began to search her trunks for the things she felt she might need. She would limit herself to one bag until she knew more about Eric's intentions. If he was finally ready to give up the bush and leave Victoria, go somewhere where they could marry and settle down, then she would send for the rest of her things; but if all they were going to have were a few precious days, she would not need much.

As she folded her things and placed them into the bag, she decided to carry enough clothing to last three or four days, but no more. She wished Eric had told the man more about what his plans were, but then it could be that Eric did not truly trust him, what with two hundred and fifty pounds' reward on his head these days. That much money could prove quite a temptation, even for a friend.

When daylight brought the distant laughter of the kookaburra, rousing the rest of the tent, Jessica was packed and ready to leave. What she planned not to take with her, she had already locked away in her two trunks. If by luck the next coach for Bendigo was this morning, she wanted to be ready to leave.

"What are you doing up so early?" Aaron asked when he stepped through the opening in the flour sack wall and sat down on an upended log to slip on his boots. "And why are you dressed in your finest?"

"I may be leaving," she told him cautiously, about to burst with her secret joy. "And it could be that I have to leave this very morning."

"If you wanted my attention, that sure got it," he told her as he bent over and laced up his boots. "Just where is it you plan to go? Back to the station?"

"To Bendigo." Then, knowing her plans would be safe with Aaron of all people, she quickly told him all about her visitor in the night and how Eric wanted her to be on the very next coach out.

"And you plan to go alone?"

"Aye, I do."

"It might be wiser if you asked Carrie to go with you."

"Go where?" Carrie mumbled as she entered the area, rubbing the last muddlings of sleep from her eyes.

"To Bendigo," Jessica said, then quickly added, "but I don't want anyone to go with me. I might not be coming back." In answer to their questioning expressions, she explained, "You see, Eric and I have plans to be married, and I honestly suspect that our marriage is the reason he has finally sent word for me to come to him."

"Marry?" Aaron stopped bothering with his laces and stared into Jessica's beaming face, his brown eyes wide.

"Aye, marry. You know, make our vows before both a minister and God, and then live and love with each other until death us do part," she teased playfully.

Aaron sat studying her face, then slowly raked his hand through his tousled hair. "I guess I should have seen this coming, but I honestly didn't. I knew you two were close, but I had no idea there was that sort of love between you."

"You don't disapprove do you?" She suddenly frowned.

"No, not at all. Why should I? I love you both, and if that's what you want, then it's what I want. I just hope this is the right time for you two to get married. He is still wanted by the police, and there is that reward for his capture, which makes almost anyone a potential threat to his freedom, and his life."

"I'm aware of all that, and I don't intend to let him stay around here and risk capture or death. After we are married, I plan to convince him to go somewhere else to live, probably out in western Australia. He'll be safe from the Victorian police's jurisdiction there, and that of New South Wales. It's further away than I want to be from you and Penelope, but it's Eric's freedom that I must be concerned with the most. At least we won't have to worry about what the neighbors think of our getting married. Out there, they won't have any idea that we once considered ourselves half brother and sister."

Aaron's face grew pensive, his expression distant. "I wish there was some way Penelope and I could be there for the ceremony. I would love to see you two wed. So would Penelope and both his grandparents."

"I'd really like for you all to be there, too. I'll see what we can arrange," she promised. "I'm not even sure that's what this trip is all about. But I'm almost positive it is. We've discussed getting married more than once. He promised to make it happen as soon as he possibly could. And he told me he would send for me as soon as he could arrange definite plans."

Carrie's eyes were wide with her romantic notions. "Just think, running off to be with the man you love."

"Aye." Jessica felt herself blush. "And I do love him."

"Then nothing should keep you from going to him." It was Deen's voice this time.

Jessica turned to see Deen standing just a few feet away, holding his folded blanket. His eyes glistened with emotions. She felt her heart go out to him for she knew he had never had that opportunity. Instead he had been forced to leave behind the only woman he loved—in the arms of another man, in the arms of his own cousin. "Nothing will keep me from him. I promise you that." It was a promise she intended to keep.

Jessica went right away to find out when the next coach to Bendigo would be and never felt more frustrated than when she learned there would be no coach headed north that day, but there was to be a coach due in the afternoon from Melbourne that would leave for Bendigo the following day.

The next morning, she was saying her tearful goodbyes to Deen, Aaron, Carrie, and Regie. She would miss them all dreadfully, but she promised to write as soon as she knew more about Eric's plans.

"I feel a little guilty leaving like this during your first visit," Jessica told Deen just before boarding the coach. "I hope that you will come and visit Eric and me once we

339

get settled in somewhere. I know you will like Eric."

"Don't feel guilty," Deen told her while he studied her face one last time through the narrow opening that served as a window in the coach. "I plan to visit with my favorite cousin here a few more days. It may be hard to believe but there are still subjects we haven't even touched on yet. After all, we have over twenty years to catch up on. Then I'll have to be getting back to Melbourne and find me that crew. I can't make money with my ships bobbing anchor in port."

"Will you come visit us?"

Deen smiled and nodded. "Aye, I'll come. Especially if there is a grandchild to visit and tell my stories to."

Jessica blinked back the mist of tears caused from leaving the friend and father she had just come to know. "I consider that a promise." Then to Aaron, Carrie, and Regie standing just behind him, she said, "And I'll want you to come visit us, too." Glancing beyond them, she noticed Rube standing in the distance, watching her with a smoldering expression, but she chose to simply pretend she had not spotted him. Ignore him completely. After all, in a very few minutes, she would be leaving her watchful shadow far behind.

"Just let us know where," Aaron assured her while Carrie choked back a strangled sob and allowed Regie to comfort her.

"Send him his mother's love." Aaron avoided Eric's name when he called his message out just as the coach pulled away with a heavy lurch. "And tell him how proud I am of him."

"I will," she called back to him. Fresh tears filled her blue eyes. "I will."

Soon the many gold fields of Ballarat were gone from

her sight, and Jessica finally dropped the canvas dust curtain she had been holding. Leaning back in the upholstered seat with her lower lip absently drawn between her teeth, she tapped her fingertips nervously against one another, barely aware of the other two passengers in the coach. Her anticipation was too great to allow her to listen to the conversation between the two gentlemen she faced. Her thoughts were solely on Eric as she wondered what lay ahead for them.

Only hours into the day-long trip, Jessica was unaware she had nodded off. The rocking motion of the new-styled coach, suspended from flexible leather straps rather than supported by stiff iron springs, had lulled her into a peaceful dream state. It was not until the Concord coach jerked to a stop that she realized she had actually fallen asleep. Coming awake with a start, she had no way of knowing how long she had dozed, but was certain it had not been long enough for them to reach their scheduled midday stop just yet.

"Wot's 'appening?" she heard the two fellow travelers ask after one had checked his pocket watch. The other traveler, the younger of the two, reached for the canvas curtain and curled the edge back about the time they heard the first voices from outside.

"Bushrangers!" the younger man said with a gasp. "We are being bailed up!"

Bushrangers? Jessica's heart pounded in her chest as she tried to remember if she had brought anything they might find valuable enough to steal. She had a broach they might want to take, but it was packed away in her bag, and unless they took the time to search the lining of her carpetbag, they would never find it. She had purposely not worn any jewelry for fear of theft. The

341

most she would lose was the handful of shillings she had in her handbag at the moment.

Feeling less terrified, knowing she had little for these men to steal, her attention was drawn to the two men's quick movements as they hurriedly detached their watches, pulled out their wallets, and searched the inside of the coach for a place to hide them. Finally they decided to tuck everything into the crevice between the seat and the side of the coach. She guessed by the way the oldest man trembled that he had a lot to loose in that wallet.

With the canvas curtains securely drawn over all the windows, except the one the younger man had looked out of a moment ago, they all turned to stare at it.

"Can you see any of 'em?" the older man asked and stretched his neck to try to see through the tiny space where the one canvas still gapped open.

"I see two of them," the other man answered. "One's a black man with a red scarf over his face and the other is a white man dressed all in black."

"The Flash Brigand's gang," the older man said in awe. His fear slipped from his face. "We are being bailed up by the Flash Brigand's gang."

Jessica's eyes grew wide as she felt her elation surge through her like a bushfire gone wild. So this was why Eric had wanted her on this coach. How clever he was and how delighted she felt to know she would not have to wait until the coach reached Bendigo to see Eric. Eagerly she gathered up her handbag and waited, wondering if he would take over the coach or if he would simply have an extra horse for her to ride.

"Better be gettin' your boots off," the older man told the younger. "That's about all he will be wanting from us. He don't hanker to rob the workin' man; just big companies with lots of ill-gotten money."

"But I just bought these boots," the other man complained, then frowned down at them. "I haven't even got them broke in good yet."

Jessica felt sorry for him and decided she would make a special plea for these men. She would see to it that their boots were left where they could get to them soon enough. She did not feel either of them would offer much threat to Eric, anyway. Barely able to contain her excitement much longer, she leaned forward and peered through the gap in the curtain. She wanted to catch sight of her love, but all she could see at that moment was the black fellow with the red scarf get down off a gray horse.

"Out," they heard as the door on the side of the boxlike coach swung open. "Ladies and children first!"

The other two passengers seemed more than willing to oblige the request and remained seated until Jessica was completely out of the coach.

"I guess you two don't really 'ave to get out. Just toss me your boots and your valuables."

"Our valuables?" Jessica heard the older man ask, clearly confused.

"Aye, your valuables. You know, watches, wallets, rings, whatever you got that you think might interest us."

Jessica frowned. Something wasn't right. Eric was well known for not taking anything from the passengers, only from the coach itself. Quickly, her eyes sought for the man in black but he and the other two had ridden to the other side of the coach. She could hear the sounds of the horse's hooves and the scrambling noise of someone on top of the coach going through the baggage.

"They don't have any valuables," Jessica told the

343

black bushranger. "They told me they never travel with anything of value anymore due to all the bail ups. Nobody does."

The black man looked at her with cold, black eyes, and she felt an icy shiver travel through her. She had an urge to call out for Eric to come around but did not want to alert the passengers inside to the Flash's real name. Surely Eric was not aware that this man actually intended to rob the people inside.

"Then off with your boots. And your britches. We don't want any of you trying to take in after us."

"Our britches?" There was so much indignation in the older man's voice that Jessica again felt sorry for him.

"Leave them their britches. Take the horses and they will have no way to follow you anyway."

At that moment the man in black rounded the back of the coach astride a tall black horse, and she quickly searched his eyes for familiarity and recognition. That's when she became fully aware that these men were not the Flash Brigand's gang at all, and the man in black was definitely not Eric. Fear swept through her like an icy wind when she realized this was a real robbery. Terrified, she took a tiny step toward the coach and hoped they would allow her to climb back inside still unharmed.

"Where do you think you are going?" the man in black asked from astride his dark horse.

"I have nothing of value either," she told him. "I was just going to get back inside so that I could take off my shoes for the man."

"I think you do have something of value. A lot more than your shoes," the man in black told her with a decisive nod. His eyes sparkled with his own amusement. The black neckerchief that masked his broad face puffed and pulled where his mouth was as he shouted out to the others. "Hurry with the search. We've got to get out of here."

Jessica made another tentative step toward the coach, wishing the black fellow who still blocked the doorway would move away so she could climb back inside. She hated facing these men alone.

"No, lassie, you are going with us," the man dressed in black told her.

"No," she cried out in horror.

"Aye, lassie, and you can either climb up on this horse with me right now on your own accord and ride out of here without a struggle or I can have Lightnin' there to tie you up and drape you across this horse where you will be forced to ride like a sack of potatoes. It's your choice."

Jessica's blood turned painfully cold, and it felt as if her heart had suddenly refused to force it on through her veins. The man fully meant what he said. Her stomach twisted into a tight knot as she tried to think of a way out of this, but she had no other choice but to do as he said. She knew it would be better to have her hands remain untied if she wanted to take advantage of any opportunity for escape. Although she was so terrified, her legs feeling as if they might buckle at any moment, she slowly walked toward the horse and stared up at the man. She wondered how she was going to climb up when he had his feet lodged in the stirrups.

Suddenly she felt huge hands clamp around her waist, and she was lifted up and unceremoniously seated sideways across the narrow space of the saddle, in front of the man dressed in black. Seated sideways the way she was, she wondered what she was supposed to hold onto in order to keep her balance. This saddle had no handle nor did it have a saddle horn. But when the man spurred the horse into motion, she discovered she did not have to find anything to hold onto, for the man in black had definite plans of holding onto her instead.

Jessica was too afraid and too angry to cry. The whole time, the man took full advantage of her precarious position in front of him and reached into her clothing to fondle her often. She fought her disgust and tried to think of some way to free herself. Surrounded by his arms, she knew any escape attempt would have to come after they reached their destination, wherever that might be.

To her growing concern, they rode on and on, going deeper and deeper into the bush. The further they rode, the more worried Jessica became, coming to realize her fate. Even if she should escape now, she knew she would never be able to find her way back out to safety and would probably be recaptured in a matter of hours. They obviously knew the area well, and she did not know it at all. And she had seen no signs of a house nor even a track that might lead to a house.

Dismally, she realized there was nowhere for her to run, and the man in black made no secret of his desire for her. After having dipped his hand into her blouse again and again to fondle and grasp, he had shouted back to the others that she was to warm his bed that night. Only after he had had his fill of her would he allow the others to take their pleasure. Jessica felt her stomach recoil and become hard as stone at the thought of this man atop her, taking that which should only be Eric's. It was almost more than she could stand to even have his hands fondle her breasts.

Jessica continued to study the direction they headed,

as well as the way they had just come, trying to memorize the unworn trail they took. Despite the hopelessness, she would attempt escape. If she died trying, so be it. She would rather be dead than be forced to succumb to the lust of these men. Her thoughts turned to Eric waiting for her in Bendigo. Would he think she had ignored his message to come to him? Or would he hear of the bail up and try to find her? Would he want her if, when he did find her, he learned she had been raped?

Suddenly, her thoughts were interrupted. Out of the shadows, a band of four other masked men charged them, firearms blazing. One of the men wailed out a loud "coo-ee" as they charged.

"Wot the hell?" she heard the man behind her gasp. "Lightnin', take off with that gold. The rest of you spread out. Different directions."

The men took off in all different directions, but she was aware that rather than dividing up and chasing them down, a man for a man, all four had decided to pursue the one she rode with. Though she couldn't be sure her fate would be any better off with these other bushrangers, she felt a sudden wave of relief and started to struggle with the man who still held on to her by her waist. She tried her best to keep him from grasping his sidearm.

Several shots were fired in their direction, but the aim was poor, for the man she struggled against never fell nor did any bullets come close enough to hit her. In a way, she wished their aim would prove truer because she would rather die from a bullet wound than be raped by any man.

Finally, despite her efforts, the man she rode with managed to wrench free of her grasp and pulled his pistol from its holster. With only a glance over his shoulder, he fired back at the men closing in on them. Jessica made another lunge at his arm, causing him to lose his grip on the weapon, and watched with a sense of accomplishment as it fell to the ground.

"You damned whore," the man shouted in a rage just before she felt the crushing blow of his hand across her cheek. With dizzying pain, she felt herself fall backward. The side of her head smashed against the trunk of a gum tree with a deafening thud before she was hurled to the hard ground. The horse's hooves barely missed her when she rolled and tumbled to a stop against the side of a small boulder. The blue sky became a gray haze of fog before her eyes, but she struggled to keep her eyes open.

The men who gave chase were a blur of movement, but she could tell that one of them had stopped to check on her while the other three continued on.

"Are you all right?" he asked, his face a mere streak of color in front of her. Through her dim vision she could tell that the man bending over her was dressed all in black, and at first her heart cringed with fear, but then she realized his voice was different; it was not the same man who had just struck her. But this voice was familiar to her somehow.

"Eric?" she asked and reached out to try to touch the face but was unable to. She felt herself being lifted and pressed against a strong chest. There she found a familiar warmth and knew that the man was, indeed, Eric.

"Eric, you saved me," she said just before she slipped into a peaceful realm of darkness.

Eric could not respond with words. His throat was too tight with the emotions that choked him. All he could do was hold her close and wait for the others to return.

*   *   *

When Eric finally heard the approach of horses, he drew his revolver from his holster and waited to see if it was his men coming back to help him or if it was some of the Geelong gang returning, hoping to retaliate. To his relief, it was Sam and Coolabah. The sound of a third horse let him know Jacky was not far behind. With their help, he would get Jessica on his horse, and they could finally get her out of there. Having seen the gaping wound on the side of her head, he had decided not to try to take her far, probably only as far as the tiny cob hut they sometimes used as a hideout. Then he would send Jacky for his sister. Or else he would have to send for Aaron. He knew that sending for Aaron would be a risk to everyone's safety, but if that's what it took to save Jessica, he would risk it. His mission be damned.

"How is she?" Sam asked as he swung his leg over his saddle and dropped to the ground where Eric sat holding Jessica close, her blood soaking into his black shirt.

"I don't know," Eric told them, then pressed his cheek against the top of her head while he tried to hold back his fear. "I don't know how she is."

Jessica's head rolled away from Eric's chest and leaned heavily against his arm, letting them all see the horrible wound along the side of her face where a large gash of flesh had been taken by the huge tree she had fallen against.

"I've felt better," she muttered weakly, then slowly smiled, though the effort proved painful.

"Jessica?" Eric cried out. "You're awake?"

Her eyes finally opened and she tried to smile again. "Who could possibly sleep with all the rumpus you keep making?"

Sam and Coolabah laughed while Eric hugged her to him. His arms trembled with an overwhelming relief.

When Jacky rode up and slid off his horse beside Sam, he too, learned what she had said and, shaking his head, laughed along with them. Jessica glanced up at them, and now that they had pulled their masks down around their necks and her vision had started to clear, she recognized them all. Two of them had worked as ringers for Ben Crawford and the other one had been a stockman for James Cranston for awhile. So these were the three that made up the Flash Brigand's loyal gang. As soon as she felt a little better, she would try to get to know all three of them. These were Eric's most trusted friends. They had helped him save her virtue if not her very life. She not only wanted to thank each and every one of them personally, she wanted to make them her friends, too.

Chapter XX

The pain shot up the side of Jessica's head and grew worse with each jolt of the horse's loping gate until she felt as if her entire head might explode. Her eyes were pressed shut. Never had she endured such a strong, physical pain. It was so severe that she had a hard time concentrating on the sound of Eric's voice behind her. His words reassured her that they did not have far to go. How she prayed it was the truth.

"There it is, just up ahead there," he finally said, to her overwhelming relief, but when she opened her eyes and looked for a house or a barn, or any form of shelter, she did not find anything. Just a dense growth of trees, wattle, vines, and bushes for as far as her eye could see.

"Where?"

"You'll see it better when we get closer," he promised, and the arm that held her securely against his chest pressed her closer, giving her a feeling of more than security.

She was back in Eric's arms, and as soon as they got somewhere where she could lie down for a little while and

351

rest her aching head, she would be as good as new and eager to be alone with him. Just as soon as this heavy throbbing subsided.

"There, see? In that big clump of wattle over there," he told her. Two fingers of the hand that gripped the reins in front of her stretched out to indicate just where to look, for there were thick clumps of the tiny trees everywhere.

Jessica looked in the direction he indicated. There, just off to their right, almost completely hidden by wattle and pea vines, was a tiny cob hut with a canvas and gum sapling roof and no windows. The narrow door was made of wattle poles jammed together and tied into a solid piece, which blended perfectly into the surroundings. The entire structure did.

"Cleverly hidden." She nodded with admiration, then gasped from the pain that resulted from the thoughtless movement.

Coolabah rode ahead of them and dismounted. He stood and waited with his arms held out until they finally reached the hut. There was no yard, for the wattle grew thick and wild right up to the hut itself. Tall gum trees with their long, dripping leaves surrounded it, further masking it from the attention of most. While Sam rode up and took the reins of Coolabah's horse, Coolabah shouted for Jacky to open the door for them.

"Careful as you go," Coolabah warned when Eric gently loosened his grip on Jessica's waist and allowed her to slip down into his strong arms. Smiling broadly to lessen any concern she might have about being handled by a complete stranger, Coolabah set her gently on the ground and asked, "Can ya stand?"

"I think so," she replied, but clutched his shoulder for

support when he slowly released her. Coolabah let out a slow sigh of relief when she did not topple immediately to the ground, but the moment she tried to take a step toward the door on her own power, her knees buckled and Coolabah brought his arms immediately to capture her.

"But then again, I've been wrong before," she agreed with a sheepish grin and Coolabah laughed.

"I wish I could have that in writing," Eric teased good-naturedly when he came around to walk just in front of Coolabah. "She'll never admit to that again."

Laughing with Coolabah, he pushed the wattle and undergrowth aside, clearing a path, until they finally reached the hut. Then he stood to the side and let Coolabah and Jessica enter ahead of him, giving a quick look in Sam's direction to make sure he was taking care of all four of the horses.

Because the only light inside the tiny hut came from the open doorway, Jessica could not tell very much about the one little room other than there was a small, homemade bed against the far wall. Off to one side stood a rickety-looking table made of several wooden slabs butted together, tied in place with a rough, horsehair rope. On the table sat an oil lamp and a tin cup filled with matches. Just before the door closed and left them in almost total darkness, she noticed the black fellow, whom Eric kept calling Jacky, had also come inside and was busily trying to light the lamp for them.

"Pull one of those plugs. I can't see to light this thing," Jacky muttered.

A peculiar stream of light pierced the darkness like a fine white saber, giving off just enough glow to satisfy Jacky's needs. Coolabah waited until Jacky had the lamp

353

burning brightly and had moved back out of the way before stepping over to the bed and setting Jessica on the surprisingly soft mattress with a gentle ease.

"Jacky, we need someone to take a look at that injury on her head," Eric said matter-of-factly as he pushed a small piece of wood back into the hole, about the size of a man's fist, which had been carved at eye level in the dried clay wall. "I don't want her to have to ride any further. I doubt she could stand it. Do you think Mundora would come here?"

"I'm positive she would," Jacky told him and smiled encouragingly as he reached for the door latch that was crafted out of gumwood. "Do what you can for her. I should be back with Mundora by dark."

"Who is Mundora?" Jessica asked as soon as Jacky had left. Although she found she could not raise her head without pain, she discovered she could lie on her side, with her head resting on her folded arm in relative comfort. Gently she probed the injured area with her other hand, flinching when her fingertips came to the deep gash, which now protruded along the crest of a huge swollen mass that had grown at the side of her forehead.

"Mundora is Jacky's half sister. She's an Aboriginal medicine woman," he explained. He stood beside the bed and watched her explore her injury, his stomach twisting into a tight coil. Unaware of his reaction, his hands curled into fists so tight his knuckles turned white.

"Aboriginal?"

"Didn't you notice? Jacky's a black fellow," he teased. He looked away briefly in order to settle his churning stomach. "Don't worry. She's good at what she does. She saved my life."

"Then you *were* shot?"

"Very much so, and it was Mundora's care that saved me. I would have bled to death if she hadn't known what to do. Her ways are different, but she's good and she will come with Jacky. I'm sure of it. But for now, I want you to lie still and rest. Sam and I will have to leave for a few hours, but Coolabah will be here. He's better than any nursemaid."

Coolabah raised a heavy eyebrow but said nothing as he unbuckled his gunbelt and laid it across the table with a loud clunk.

"Where are you going? When will you be back?" she asked fearfully and tried to sit up, only to be met once again with a severe pain along the entire right side of her head. The pain frustrated her. She wanted to get out of that bed and stop Eric from going. After four long months, they were finally together. She did not like the idea of his leaving her again for even a few hours.

"I'll be back late this afternoon. I'll probably be here before Jacky returns with Mundora," he assured her, then knelt at the side of the bed so he could kiss her goodbye. "You must rest while I'm gone. Don't get out of that bed. In fact, I'm leaving Coolabah with strict orders to make sure you stay put until I get back. He's to tie you down if it becomes necessary."

Jessica wanted to protest further but found herself smiling up into Eric's concerned face instead. It had been too long since she had been able to gaze into those handsome brown eyes of his. "It sounds as if you don't fully trust me to follow your orders while you are gone."

"Never have trusted you." He laughed softly and brought his hand to caress her cheek. He tried not to look at the grotesque injury on the right side of her forehead, for the sight of her blood made his stomach crawl with

355

sympathetic pain. "And with good reason."

She found she could not offer a suitable retort, for all she wanted to do at that moment was look at him, memorize every detail about him. Slowly she smiled.

Gently, Eric traced the outer edge of her mouth with his fingertip, then bent forward and kissed her lightly on her waiting lips. His own smile faded and his eyes grew smoldering dark when he lifted his head and again stared down at her, so beautiful. He realized how close he had come to losing her. The Geelong gang was notorious for their ruthless treatment to their captors, especially the females. Though two women had somehow lived to tell their grim tales, one woman was not so fortunate—if being left with the nightmares of the other two had to suffer could be considered fortunate. Gently, he lowered his lips to hers again and took a longer kiss, and when her arms came up to grasp his neck, he moaned aloud and pulled away before his passions got the better of his common sense.

He ignored the curious look Coolabah gave them when he rose and turned to leave. Then, pausing in the doorway, he looked back and asked, "What were you doing on that coach anyway? Where were you headed? Home?"

"Don't you know?" she asked and tried again to lift her head but found the effort too painful. "Didn't you send word for me to be on the next coach from Ballarat to Bendigo?"

Eric's eyes met Coolabah's. "No, I didn't send word for you to be on any coach to Bendigo."

"But a man slipped into my tent the night before last and told me you had sent him to ask me to try to catch the very next coach north."

"What man? What did he look like?" Eric asked and returned to her side. His dark brow was drawn and his eyes flashed an emotion Jessica had never seen in him before. It was more than concern or anger, but she was not quite sure what. Whatever the emotion, his expression sent a chill shivering through her body.

"I don't know what he looked like. It was dark. He seemed young and was slender in build, but I never could make out his face. What's the matter? Who was he?"

"What did his voice sound like?"

"I don't know. Like a man's voice. He sounded Australian, I guess."

Eric's jaw worked furiously as he stood again and turned to Coolabah. "Keep that door shut and don't open it for anyone. We'll try to get back just as quick as we can."

"Sounds as if your sister was set up for a kidnapping, don't it?" Coolabah surmised thoughtfully. "Suppose they intended an even trade? Her life for yours?"

"I wouldn't be too surprised," Eric muttered, his voice hardened with the fury that raged inside of him. "If that's so, it means they have figured out just who I am and don't care who they have to use in order to get me."

"Better let 'em all know that," Coolabah said and frowned. "I wonder what else they've got figured out."

The more Jessica listened to their exchange the more confused she became. Who was out to get Eric? The police? No, that was definitely not the police who had tried to kidnap her. Nor could they have been a special detachment of one of the many detective forces serving the government these days. Then who could they have been? Other bushrangers? But why? Had he somehow intruded on another gang's territory? So many questions. "But Eric, if you didn't even know I was supposed to be on that coach, how did you—"

"You need your rest," he interrupted her harshly, then softened his voice before he continued. "Get some sleep. I'll be back in a little while."

"But . . ." It was no use. They no longer paid any attention to anything she might have to say. Coolabah followed Eric outside, and Jessica was left all alone in the small room to try to sort through her questioning thoughts. She lay there, unable to get out of bed, held captive by her own pain, staring at the door, and she wondered exactly what was going on. She hoped Eric would realize her deep concern and come back inside to try to explain some of it to her, but when she heard the sounds of horses leaving, she knew he and Sam had gone, and finally she allowed herself to fall asleep, knowing that when he returned she was going to demand a few answers.

"Jessica?"

Though Mundora had spoken the name softly, Jessica awoke with a start. She blinked up at the sagging canvas and gumwood ceiling in confusion.

"Jessica, I am Mundora. I am here to help you," she told her in an almost musical voice as she knelt beside the bed and began to feel of the wound with gentle fingers. "Jacky, bring the light closer."

Jessica's eyes left the mocha-skinned, smiling face of Mundora, drawn to the movement across the room. Jacky did what he had been told and brought the lamp closer. Jessica watched as he knelt beside his sister and held the lamp level at the side of her head. She squinted from the initial impact of the bright light on her pupils.

"How's it look?" Jacky asked.

"She will mend," Mundora told him simply, then reached inside the bundle she had brought with her and pulled out what she thought she might need.

Jessica's eyes were still trained on Jacky when he turned and asked over his shoulder, "When did the boss leave out of here?"

"Right after ya left to go get your sister," Coolabah replied.

Jessica let her gaze drift until she caught sight of Coolabah standing just inside the closed door. She could tell by the way his huge hands played nervously with the stock of the carbine rifle he held in his folded arms that he was worried. For some reason her eyes were soon drawn from Coolabah to one of the small holes in the wall. The wooden plug had been removed again and, by the blackness that filled it, Jessica knew that it was night.

"Eric is not back?" she asked, her voice raspy at first. "Where did he go?"

"You must lie still," Mundora told her, then brought out a handful of fresh green gum leaves and laid them on the bed beside Jessica. Turning to look at Coolabah, she asked, "Can you bring me water?"

"Aye, 'ow much you need?"

"Enough to clean the wound and make my poultice," Mundora told him, not knowing just how to describe the amount. Then with her hands held out, cupped together to form a bowl, she said, "This much."

"I'll 'ave ya some in a flash," he said, opened the door, and was gone.

"I'll help him," Jacky put in a little too eagerly, then pulled the table closer, letting the legs scrape the earthen floor, and set the lamp on the closest edge so that the light would still fall on Jessica's face.

Mundora glanced at her brother as he hurried out the door, but if she found his behavior peculiar, it did not show in her features.

"I am told you are a medicine woman, too," she said as she sat back on her heels and waited for them to bring her the water.

"In a way. I assist my father, who is a doctor, but because I'm a woman and white men do not feel women are as competent as men, I'll never be a true doctor. I hope someday to become a midwife. Women have no qualms about letting other women assist them in having their babies."

"The ways are the same with my people. I am called upon to help with the sick and the injured but do not get the respect of a medicine man." She smiled, revealing lovely white teeth. "We are much alike, you and I. Your brother has talked much about his beautiful sister."

Jessica frowned. Brother? Sister? Hadn't Eric told them? Just then Coolabah and Jacky returned with a billy can sloshing with water and handed it to Mundora.

"Eric is not really my brother," Jessica told her. She wanted to clear that misunderstanding right away. "I am the child of his father's first wife, sired, though, by another man."

A huge grin spread through Coolabah's reddish-brown beard, and he nodded as if he had suspected as much.

"Eric is Aaron's son by his second wife. Aaron's true son. So, you see, although we were raised in the same house, we are not truly brother and sister."

Jacky leaned back against the hard clay wall and rubbed his grizzled chin with his long brown fingers, as if trying to fully absorb what she had just revealed to them. "So Eric is not your half brother."

"No, actually we are distant cousins. My grandfather and his grandmother were brother and sister. But that's the only relation we have to each other."

"That sure explains that kiss you two gave each other," Coolabah chuckled. He winked at Jacky and told him. "It was not exactly a brotherly kiss. Suppose this might be the lass Eric told us 'e already 'ad his eye on? Suppose she's why 'e has never shown an interest in the ladies."

Jacky smiled and nodded.

"What do you know about that, Jacky, me boy? He said we probably knew 'er. He was right about that, but 'e didn't bother to mention we knew 'er as his sister. He's a clever one, that Eric Aylesbury." Suddenly Coolabah's smile faded and he drew a hand up as if to silence everyone. "Riders," he warned in a harsh whisper, then quickly turned and fitted the barrel of his rifle into the wide hole in the wall behind him. Jacky reached for his rifle and headed for another hole in a different wall.

"Mundora, turn down the light," Jacky ordered, almost breathless. His eyes were wide with concern.

Terrified by their reaction to the fact riders might be headed their way, Jessica felt the thud of her heart pounding blood against her injured forehead. Then, when Mundora reached over and extinguished the light completely, it took all the willpower inside of her to lie still. It was several moments before she heard the horses Coolabah had warned them about. Nobody moved inside the hut. Nobody spoke. Nothing could be heard but the steady sound of horses' hooves, then the loud shrill of a distant nightjar.

"It's Eric," Coolabah sighed with relief. "Light the lamp back. It's only Eric and Sam."

After a few moments, Coolabah said again, "Come on, mate, light the lamp back so we can see in 'ere."

"I'm trying. I'm trying," Jacky muttered. "But I can't find the blasted table. Ouch!"

"I think you just found it," Coolabah chuckled, then broke into deep laughter when a match light flared and he saw that it was Mundora who had found the table. Jacky was not even close.

"Damned wall," Jacky grumbled, then scowled as he turned to glare at Coolabah, as if blaming him for moving the table.

"I thought you Aborigines were supposed to be good at finding your way around in the dark," he prodded, still laughing, but before Jacky could respond, there were three short raps on the wall, then the door slowly swung open.

By the time Eric and Sam were safely inside with the door shut behind them, Mundora had the lamp glowing brightly and was again at Jessica's side, dabbing the wound with a wet cloth.

"What took you so long?" Coolabah demanded to know while he leaned over and carefully propped his rifle in the corner.

Eric's eyes first met Coolabah's in a meaningful gesture, then swept across the small room to Jessica.

"Coolabah? How about helping me outside a moment," Sam said as if he had been given a special cue to speak.

"Sure," Coolabah responded quickly, no questions asked.

"You too, Jacky," Sam said over his shoulder before

he reached for the door.

"Right behind you," Jacky replied and followed them out with his rifle still in hand.

"What's going on?" Jessica wanted to know, her eyes narrowed, revealing her suspicion.

Eric studied her face a long moment before he answered. "Sam, Jacky, and I have to leave again, but Coolabah will be here to keep an eye on you and Mundora."

"Leave? Again? Tonight? But you just got back," she protested and tried to sit up, only to find Mundora's hand restraining her. She squinted from the resulting pain but tried to push Mundora's hand aside so that she could sit up and face Eric.

"Jessica, don't," he said sternly, then knelt beside Mundora and forced Jessica back down against the mattress with both his hands. "Something has come up. We have a little business that has to be taken care of tonight. I don't want to have to leave you again, but it simply can't be helped."

"But why? What sort of business?"

"I'll be back as soon as I can," he promised and ignored her questions entirely. "You let Mundora take care of you." Then to Mundora, he said, "I'm afraid you'll have to stay here until we get back."

"I'll be fine here," she told him, never looking up from the strange mixture she was making out of gum leaves, fresh clay, and ash. "I need a fire. Will Coolabah build me a fire?"

"A fire?" Eric frowned as he considered her request. A fire could give away their location.

"Yes, I need a fire to heat this," she said, indicating the contents in her shallow clay bowl. Then, as if she instinctively understood his hesitation, she added, "It does not need to be much of a fire and can be put out just as soon as my medicine is ready. The night is dark, the smoke will not be seen, and the blaze can be hidden inside a pit."

"All right, I'll have Coolabah build you a small fire," Eric conceded, then leaned forward to kiss Jessica's questioning brow lightly. "Jessie, I want you all better when I return," he said, his brown eyes twinkling, then he rose and headed for the door.

Just as he placed his hand on the latch, the door swung open and Coolabah and Jacky entered.

"Ready?" Jacky asked, his gaze set on Eric's face in solemn question.

"Ready." Eric nodded to Coolabah and smiled reassuringly. "Take care of things here. Oh, and Mundora needs a fire. Make it small. Conceal the flames as best you can. Mundora suggests a pit. Then put it out immediately after she is finished with it."

"Aye," Coolabah agreed, trying to sound unconcerned but failing miserably. "Don't worry about us. Just you be careful."

"I will," Eric assured him and patted his friend firmly on the shoulder. Nodding that he should follow him outside, Eric waited until he was certain they were out of Jessica's earshot before adding, "And if we aren't back by tomorrow night, you will have to assume the worst has happened. Take the two horses we have left penned up for you in the gully and get both of the women to Ballarat immediately."

Coolabah drew in a long, slow breath and nodded grimly. "Aye, boss. You know you can count on me."

*　　*　　*

The three of them rode through the night in silence. All Coolabah had told the women when he had brought the horses around was that he was following Eric's orders and planned to take them to Ballarat. He had ignored Jessica's endless stream of questions and sat in mute silence as they made their way along a narrow track that wove its way south through the dense bush toward Ballarat.

"We are nearly there," he finally spoke after several hours of refusing a word, surprising Jessica from her troubled thoughts.

"To Ballarat?"

"Aye, it's just over that furtherest rise," he explained. "We can move out onto the main track once we see the camps."

Jessica looked over at the dark form of the tall man astride the shorter of the two horses. Although she could not see his face for the darkness, she knew what expression she would find there. She had seen the apprehension settle onto his heavy features early that afternoon and by nightfall, his worry was clearly evident, his brow furrowed with deep lines. Something had gone wrong with Eric. She just wished she knew what. Her insides were a twisting, coiling mass of confusion and fear. If only she had some idea of what was going on.

"How's your head?" Coolabah wanted to know.

"Better. The poultice Mundora made has not only helped ease the pain, it has caused the swelling to go down considerably."

"I know what I do," Mundora put in proudly.

It was the first Jessica had heard from her since they had left the hut. If it had not been for both of Mundora's arms wrapped around her middle, Jessica might have forgotten she was even there.

"Well, I had my doubts when I saw you take those spiderwebs off the ceiling and mix 'em with the rest of that concoction," Coolabah said, and for the first time, his voice lifted and he sounded less worried, more like he had earlier that morning. Jessica wondered if that was because they had taken his mind off of Eric or because Ballarat's close proximity would somehow solve some of his worry.

"Slows the blood flow," is all Mundora had to say in defense of the spiderwebs.

"Just don't go puttin' no spiderwebs on me," he said firmly and shuddered at the thought of it.

"Coolabah?" Jessica asked softly.

There was a long pause before he responded, "Ma'am?"

"I know you are not going to tell me where Eric went or why he didn't return or even why we could not wait for him at the hut, but can you at least tell me why we are avoiding the main track the way we are?"

There was another long pause before he finally answered. "It might not be safe."

Annoyed by his continuous lack of information, Jessica's shoulders sagged. She had guessed that much. "But why?"

"Don't you read the newspapers? No one's safe on the main tracks these days."

"Coolabah, there's a special reason why it is not safe for us out on the main track, and I wish you would tell me exactly what it is. If there's danger out there for us, don't you think we should be made aware of it?"

There was another long pause before Coolabah spoke again. "It will be a few days before I can take Mundora back to her village," he said. Again he completely ignored her questions. "I sure hope you can put her up for a few days. I don't got no money for a roomin' house."

Jessica exhaled sharply, exasperated. "We will find room for her in our tent. That won't be a problem. She'll be more than welcome. But before you go trying to change the subject again, I want you to know I am going with you when you leave to take her back."

"No, I can't allow you to do that," Coolabah said quickly. "Can't allow that at all."

"Allow it or not, I'm going . . . even if I have to follow you from a distance. I'm going. That's all there is to it."

Coolabah's groan was just loud enough to be heard over the gentle hammering of the horses' hooves as they continued to make their way across the rugged Australian countryside in the very wee hours of morning.

Chapter XXI

Jessica used her head injury as an excuse not to help Aaron for a few days, which enabled her to keep a constant eye on Coolabah. She was not about to give him the opportunity to leave Ballarat without her. If and when he went to the livery for his horse, whether or not he had Mundora with him, Jessica intended to be right behind him to fetch Summerfield. She had meant what she said about going with him when he left, and all the arguments he had given her since had not lessened her determination.

So far her task had not been very hard. Although Coolabah had been extremely restless over the past two days, he rarely strayed very far from the Aylesburys' two tents. It was as if he impatiently waited for something, some word of what to do or where to go. It seemed to frustrate him to no end that the papers he bought continued to be at least two or three days old, despite the many improvements that had been made along the track between Melbourne and Ballarat, but still he made a daily trek to Fanny Taylor's tent to get the latest issue of the

Melbourne Argus, and he always scanned all the headlines before he headed back to the tents.

Jessica felt a little guilty at having to lie about her injury the way she had, for in all honesty the wound was healing nicely. Whatever Mundora had placed over the injury had worked wonders, because now the bandage annoyed her far more than the injury itself. She had to pretend it had left her weak and queasy so that she would not be asked to help in the medical tent. Besides, Mundora had been very eager to do what she could to help, and Aaron had been just as eager to let her. They were pleased to be able to teach each other their different methods of treatment. Already Aaron experimented with tonics and salves of his own, using the same indigenous plants Mundora used. He seemed especially curious about the gum or eucalyptus leaves that had been used to ease the pain and help heal Jessica's deep head wound.

Deen voluntarily postponed his departure in order to help Aaron and Mundora for a few days. The reason he gave was the recent outbreak of dysentery that had brought more men to Aaron's tent than usual, but Jessica had come to suspect the real reason he stayed on had to do with the fact that Mundora was so beautiful. Deen seemed far more interested in helping her than in helping his own cousin, and he had gone from wearing his typical moleskin trousers to ones of white duck, and he suddenly found reason to change his shirts every day. The shirt he had chosen to wear that morning looked suspiciously new. What else but a woman could cause a man to take such care in his appearance and give him such a keen willingness to help! When Mundora had asked for freshly cut wattle, Deen wasted no time. He headed right out of the tent to fetch his ax, more than eager to meet her approval.

From the resin of the wattle Deen had brought back and the bruised leaves of the century plant she had in her own bundle, Mundora made a tonic and offered it to Aaron to use on the men with dysentery. Though he had a tonic of his own he used, he was curious to see if the mixture made from local plants and thus more readily accessible would work as well. To his delight it worked just as effectively, and he spent over an hour taking careful notes when she made her next batch. Mundora was proving to be such a help, Jessica was barely missed, which suited her purpose perfectly.

Coolabah was not interested in helping in the medical tent at all. Although he split their firewood into more manageable pieces and had mended a broken chair, he mostly continued to pace the area just outside the two tents, and Jessica was careful never to let him out of her sight. Even at night, though Coolabah insisted on sleeping outside in front of their tent, Jessica slept just inside the front opening where she could keep an eye on him. She had insisted Mundora have her bedding behind the flour sack walls that separated it from the rest of the tent in order to provide her new friend a little privacy. She had explained that because Deen was actually her father, it would be far more appropriate for her to sleep out in the living area with him than it would be for Mundora to. And from where she placed her bedding each night, Jessica could watch the area Coolabah slept through the front flap, which was always left opened a little to allow in the fresh air Aaron was so fond of, cool though it was. Even now, as she sat inside the tent, mending one of Aaron's shirts, she could watch Coolabah through the thrown-back opening as he paced the tiny yard, restlessly waiting.

"How're you feeling?" Carrie asked when she stepped inside the tent. It was only a few hours before sundown, and she had come in to start the evening meal.

"Still a little weak, I'm afraid, but I'm in no real pain," she responded with a smile, glad for company at last. Although Coolabah had come in a few times and chatted for awhile, he could not seem to stay put and would be off again, wearing deep paths around the two tents.

"It still amazes me that you are doing as good as you are," Carrie said with a slow shake of her head. She walked to the back of the tent and lifted her apron from the nail on the rear post, placing it over her pretty green muslin dress. Carrie had bought two new dresses from Fanny the day Jessica left, and the amount she claimed she had paid for them made Jessica furious. Carrie should have been able to buy four ready-made dresses for such a price, but to a girl hoping to impress a certain young man, the price had seemed well worth it.

"Imagine being kidnapped by the Geelong gang and managing to get away," Carrie went on to say, her voice filled with awe.

"I didn't manage it, Eric did," Jessica reminded her. "Thank goodness I didn't know at the time it was the Geelong gang that had me. I might have fainted dead away had I realized just who had me. They are well-known murderers and don't care if it is a man or a woman they kill when they are lusting for blood."

"I know I would have fainted," Carrie admitted, her eyes wide at the thought of it, then fell silent as she started her work.

Jessica tried *not* to think about what might have become of her if Eric had not come to her rescue like he had. But what she did dwell on and often was the curious fact he had even been there at all. She wondered about that and had asked Coolabah about it more than once, but Coolabah chose to tell her very little. He had marked it up to fate, pure and simple, but Jessica knew it was more than that. Coolabah was definitely keeping his secrets—secrets she intended to find out for herself.

That night, after everyone had finally talked out and retired to their beds, Jessica again positioned her own bedding so that she could watch Coolabah while he slept. If he got up in the middle of the night for any reason other than nature's call, she wanted to know about it. For once, she was glad that sleep mostly eluded her, and although she dozed on and off through the night, she awoke with a start each time Coolabah or Deen as much as turned over in their sleep.

Several hours into the night, a tiny noise woke her, and her eyes went immediately to Coolabah to make sure he was still just where he was supposed to be. That was when she noticed a movement, a shadow in the darkness, just beyond the medical tent. She rolled over on her stomach and watched carefully through the narrow opening, when she realized the shadow was coming closer to Coolabah. Her first thought was to call out to Coolabah and warn him of the intruder, but before she could put that into action, she realized the intruder meant him no harm. There was just enough moonlight for her to make out the slender shape as it knelt beside Coolabah and gently shook him awake. Soundlessly, the two of them rose to their feet and crept away.

Jessica flung her covers back and took just enough time to grab her shawl and throw it around the shoulders of her nightdress before she followed behind at a safe distance. Keeping as much to the shadows as possible, she rarely let them slip from her sight. It was easy for her to distinguish which of the two figures was Coolabah, for he was taller and broader than the other man, and when they approached a tent at the outskirts of the camp and one of them ducked inside, she realized it had been Coolabah. But because the other man hung back to guard the tent, leaving her unable to move any closer, she had to be content with a distance of a few dozen yards.

Hiding behind a wheelbarrow someone had conveniently left on its side in front of a nearby tent, she was able to watch the man unnoticed as he knelt beside a low-burning fire and poked at it with a stick. A blaze flickered to life just long enough to let her see that she did not know the young man. His face was unfamiliar.

Huddled and shivering, more from anticipation than the autumn night air, Jessica waited for Coolabah or someone else to come out of that tent. As she kept her vigil, a light came on in the tent. Dim though it was, she was able to make out the shapes of two men leaning over a table, as if studying something. A map perhaps? She wet her lips with the tip of her tongue and debated whether or not she should try to storm the tent and see who the other man was or continue to hide and wait. Could it be Eric? She studied the silhouettes. No, it did not appear that the man on the right had a beard, although he was tall enough. Besides he was too thin to be Eric. But who could it be? Would whoever it was have any information concerning Eric? Why such a clandestine meeting anyway?

As she considered all the questions spinning around inside her head, the light went back out and Coolabah's dark form appeared through the opening. He stopped only briefly to speak to the man who still knelt beside the smoldering fire before he turned back in the direction he had come.

Jessica did not know what to do. He was sure to pass right beside her. What if he noticed her? He would know she had spied on him. She froze and waited for the worst to happen, but he was too intent on getting back to his bedroll before he could be missed, for he walked within feet of her and never looked down. She waited until he passed her before she dared to move. Slowly she raised her head high enough to peer over the wheelbarrow again and saw that the young man was gone. She hoped he had decided to go inside and was not roaming around where he might see her when she decided to make a run for the tent.

"Oh, no!" She gasped a silent breath when she realized she would not be able to get back inside the tent without first passing Coolabah. Even if she skirted her way around to the far side of the tent, he would still get there first. She would have to pull up several tent stakes before she could slip in under one of the canvas walls, and that would surely make enough noise for him to notice, especially awake like he was. What was she going to do now? Finally she decided to wait right where she was for awhile and see if the man inside the tent would come out so she could get a look at him. Even if he didn't come out, she needed to give Coolabah enough time to fall back asleep before attempting a return to her bed.

The light came back on inside the tent while Jessica sat deliberating her fate, and Jessica was immediately able to detect two forms moving around inside. The other man had, indeed, gone back into the tent. That gave her the courage to try to get a little closer. She noticed a small wood heap near the front of the tent that appeared to be positioned just about right for her to get a look inside. Crouched low, she slowly and steadily made her way to the wood heap, relieved when she managed to do so without making any noise.

Once she was settled in behind the small pile of firewood, she carefully eased her head up so that she could peek over it. She noticed a horse tethered at the rear of the tent and realized the rider had either come in too late to make use of the livery or planned to leave too early. Through the narrow slit at the opening of the tent, she could see the movement of colors inside, but from that distance, she could not tell whether or not it was the men she saw. Bravely, she decided to edge her way closer, despite the fact that there was very little to use in the way of cover between her present location and the tent.

Soundlessly, she maneuvered her way to within only a few feet of the opening, stepping barefooted on a sharp rock as she made her way, but somehow she managed not to cry out and alert those inside to her presence. When she was finally close enough to the opening to see the interior, she pooled her courage and peered inside. She was so startled by what she saw that her anger overwhelmed her, and she barged right in, giving her present state of dress little thought.

"What the . . ." the two men said in unison when the apparition dressed all in white appeared just inside their tent.

"James Cranston, I want to know what's going on, and I want to know right now!" she said, her indigo eyes flashing with determination.

"Jessica, what are you doing here?" he asked, still too

startled to get up from the corner of the table where he sat beside a pile of maps, dumbfounded.

"That's my question. What are *you* doing here?"

"I-I . . ." His eyes searched the room as if hoping to find an answer in his surroundings.

"And I want the truth this time," she added, letting him know she had never fully believed him before.

"Does your father know you are out at this late hour traipsing around in your nightgown?" he asked, indignant.

Jessica's eyes dipped to take in the fact that he was right; she was in her nightgown; a fact she could hardly conceal. She pulled her shawl closer around her, though, when she noticed the wide eyes bulging from the young man across the room as he stared at her bare feet, but she decided not to let her present state of dress distract her. "No, nor does he know that I'm here confronting you at last, but I doubt he would disapprove."

"You'd better get on back to your tent," he said as he finally rose from the edge of the table and came toward her. His eyes drank in the beauty before him, for her hair, which was usually confined to a tight knot at the back of her neck, spilled wildly about her face, hiding her bandage and adorning her face. Her blue eyes were wide and glittering with deep, fiery emotion.

"No. I want to know what's going on, and I'm not leaving until I do. Why did Coolabah come here?"

"You followed him?"

"Yes, I did. He's refused to answer my questions, so I decided to see if I couldn't get a few of the answers myself."

"I suspect the biggest question in your mind right now concerns Eric," he said, his expression grim.

"You got that right." She nodded impatiently. "What do you know about him?"

"He's safe."

Tears sprang to her eyes. How she had worried.

"That's all you really need to know," he went on to say and placed his arm around her shoulder in a comforting gesture, fighting the urge to pull her to him. How he longed to embrace her.

"But I also want to know where he is."

"That I can't tell you."

"Can't or won't?"

He paused a long moment, searching her eyes, then looked away. The deep concern he saw in her eyes for Eric was almost too much for him to bear. His heart ached with longing. "Won't."

"But why? You of all people should know how much I love him. Or maybe that's the reason you won't tell me. You are jealous of our love, and it's made you bitter."

Her sharp words struck their mark, for James flinched and turned away. His hands drew up into fists before he found the words to speak again. "Get out of here, Jessica."

Jessica realized she had hurt him deeply but did not care. He was hurting her by not telling her where Eric was. Did he truly think he could keep them apart so easily? "I'll find out, you know. I don't know how, but I'll find out where Eric is and I'll go to him."

When James did not bother to respond to her words again, she left in a rage. She was more determined than ever not to let Coolabah out of her sight. She was certain now that he would eventually lead her to Eric. And when she did find Eric, she had a few things she wanted to say to him. How dare he put her through all this emotional torment without offering as much as an explanation. He would rue the day he had ever decided to keep secrets from her.

The next morning, Coolabah was up early, and Jessica almost did not have time to get dressed in the pale gray cotton and wool dress he had laid over a chair before he headed off for Fanny's hut. She hurried to catch up with him and walked the last part of the way at his side.

"Did you sleep well?" she asked in a casual tone, though her eyes watched carefully for his reaction.

"Like a babe," he responded brightly. It was easy to see his spirits had been lifted by whatever he had learned from James Cranston.

"Me too," she lied. She had not been able to go back to sleep at all.

"No offense intended, Miss Jessica, but you don't appear to be very rested. Are you sure you are well enough to be up and about this mornin'?"

"I'm much better," she said assuredly as she followed him inside Fanny's crowded hut. She watched from just inside the doorway as he purchased a paper and a small package of tobacco, appalled by the price he had to pay for the two. Realizing Fanny loved a good argument over what she charged, Jessica kept quiet. She decided to wait until they were well on their way back before she spoke again, planning to casually work James Cranston's name into the conversation.

As they walked away from the hut, Coolabah took a quick glance at the front page, as if searching for one specific item, and when his gaze fell on it, Jessica watched his face lift into a broad smile. He nodded to himself, for whatever he read had just verified something he must already have suspected.

"What is it? Good news?"

"Aye, according to this headline, the Geelong gang has been captured," he told her, then handed the paper to her. His gray-green eyes literally sparkled with delight. "They won't be out there hurting the likes of you anymore."

She stopped walking long enough to read the newspaper account, aware that Coolabah had stepped behind her and was reading it over her shoulder. There under the simple headline, Geelong Gang Captured, was a brief account of how a secret detective force working for the governments of both New South Wales and Victoria had captured the entire Geelong gang during the night while they lay camped along Forest Creek. No names were given of either the detectives or their nine prisoners, but they would be published just as soon as that information was made available.

"Good," Jessica said with a satisfied nod. Her nostrils flared in remembered disgust. "I hope they rot in jail."

Coolabah reached for the paper, but just before she handed it back to him, she happened to catch sight of the date. April eighth. That was just three days ago. But that couldn't be. That meant this paper was printed the day after she, herself, was attacked by the Geelong gang. Or was it really the Geelong gang who kidnapped her? Why would Coolabah have lied about something like that? Or maybe he didn't. Maybe that night the Geelong gang did ride on to Forest Creek and made camp there, and maybe the secret detectives were already waiting for them. She could have been caught in the middle of the whole confrontation. Her face drew into a frown as she tried to sort it out in her mind.

"Eric," she gasped, her eyes wide with sudden realization.

"Where?" Coolabah asked and looked around for him.

She turned her accusing expression on Coolabah and nodded defiantly. "Eric. Eric had something to do with this, didn't he?"

Coolabah's mouth moved, but words did not immediately come to him.

"He did," she said, throwing her hands up and grasping the sides of her face as it become more and more evident to her. "I know he did. And that's why he had to . . ." Seeing the truth in Coolabah's eyes but knowing he was not about to admit anything to her, she spun on her heel and hurried toward the tent where she had last seen James Cranston. She could sense that Coolabah was right behind her, but she never turned around to be sure. She kept her eyes trained on Cranston's tent at the very outskirts of the camp.

To her relief the horse was still tethered at the back of the tent. He must still be there. Without a moment's hesitation, she marched right inside the tent and did not falter in her determination when she found James standing in front of a mirror, carefully shaving the underside of his chin, clad in nothing more than his flannel undergarments.

"Jessica!" he exclaimed and squatted down behind the table to hide from her. "When in the blazes are you going to learn to announce yourself?"

"I'm sorry, but I have just figured it all out," she said, turning so that he could reach for his britches and pull them on without her audience. When she looked up, she saw that Coolabah had, indeed, followed her and now stood just inside the tent's entrance, staring wide eyed at them both. His mouth hung limp as if his bushy beard had suddenly become extremely heavy and his jaw muscle very weak.

"And just what is it you have figured out?" James asked when he finally had his britches on and had them securely fastened.

"Eric. I know now that Eric is somehow involved with one of the governor's secret detective forces," she said and turned back around in time to see the accusation in James's face when he looked at Coolabah.

"I didn't tell her nothin'," Coolabah stated quickly, his hands raised as if to show they were clean as the blue flannel shirt he had put on that morning.

"That's true. He didn't have to. I concluded this all on my own. Eric is working with the secret police. He helped capture the Geelong gang, didn't he?"

James quickly shrugged into the beige shirt that hung on a nail beside his tiny shaving mirror and slowly began to button it while he studied how much he should tell her.

"Yes," he finally admitted and lifted his gaze from his buttons to Coolabah's concerned expression. "She knows enough to jeopardize the entire project unwittingly." He looked back at Jessica. "Who have you discussed this with?"

"No one. I just now figured it out when I read the newspaper story about it."

Coolabah groaned, for he was the one who had brought her attention to the story in the first place.

"You haven't told your father or perhaps your young friend, Carrie, about your suspicions?"

Jessica was not sure which father he was talking about, but she answered, "No, I've had no chance to tell anyone."

"Aye, Captain, that's true enough. She came right here the minute she finished readin' the newspaper,"

Coolabah put in quickly.

"Captain?" Jessica questioned, her brow drawn, for her brain was already working with that new bit of information.

James ran his hand heavily over his face, then said, "This can go no farther. You must promise me you won't tell anyone any of what I'm about to tell you until this is all over."

"I promise, but what . . ."

"I am a captain—in a special undercover police force that was formed by the governor of New South Wales a little over a year and a half ago, but has since grown to include Victoria, too. Stuart Mays recruited me only days after he had been asked to head up this particular force. Eric became a necessary part of our plans, though quite by accident."

"Eric?"

"Aye, we needed a group of men who could penetrate the bush, learn the goings-on of the different bushrangers and their sympathizers, especially those we felt somehow had governmental connections. Our strongest suspicion was that Judge Rodney Livingston, among others, was using his position as magistrate to offer certain bushrangers a sure verdict of not guilty, and in return, he asked that they work for him, killing those he needed killed and stealing what he could not obtain through his power at the court. The Geelong gang was a band of just such men. They all had been prisoners brought before Livingston's court, and all had been relieved, nice and proper, mind you, of whatever charges held against them."

"Eric knew that man was rotten to the core," Jessica

said, though she never would have believed him to be this rotten.

"In some cases evidence conveniently disappeared," James went on to explain. "The grateful wretches then did whatever the good judge asked of them, knowing he could just as easily see that the evidence resurfaced and that charges were brought back against them. Besides, he made their cooperation well worth their while."

"How'd you find this out?"

"We were aware something crooked was going on, so we planted a man inside the jail, a vagrant. He kept his ears open. Although he was never personally approached, he heard tales of others who were, others who were willing to work for the judge, though no one ever actually named which judge. That's why we needed Eric."

"I don't understand. Surely Judge Livingston did not approach Eric. He hates the Aylesburys with a passion."

"No, and we didn't expect him to. That's why I planned his escape."

"You did?"

"Aye, but before we could plan his escape, we had to have him recaptured. Served two purposes, actually. It made me seem like an ally to Livingston, which makes me privy to information that might not otherwise be available, and it gave me the opportunity I needed to convince Eric to join us. We needed him out there and in the bush, plaguing Livingston at every turn until the good judge felt inclined to use his powers against him. And what better way than to let him appear to be a typical bushranger? As one of them, Eric was able to infiltrate the bush without arousing suspicion. And by gaining the other bushranger's confidences, he was able to learn quite a lot about Livingston's many shady dealings, more than we had ever suspected. We have nearly enough evidence right now to put the judge away for a good long time, not to mention several members of the Bathurst police and even a few men down here on the new goldfield patrols."

"Captain Scantlin?"

"Aye, he's definitely on Livingston's payroll. Always been handy whenever Livingston needed someone accused of a crime and arrested."

"Like Ben was."

"Aye, exactly."

"Then Eric's not really a bushranger?" Her heart swelled full with joy and hope. If Eric was not really a criminal, not only could they be married in a proper wedding, they could eventually live wherever they wanted.

"No, he's not a bushranger. He's one of us. And when this is over, if he decides he no longer wants to be a part of us, he can resign, no questions asked, though he will be required to serve two years in reserve. That was the deal from the start."

"You said you nearly had enough information already. How much longer until you have all the information you need?" she asked excitedly, eager to be able to make definite plans.

"Hard to say. But I personally think we are closing in on him pretty fast now. I honestly think we'll have all the goods we need in a couple of months, maybe sooner. Until that time, I have to ask that you not tell a living soul about any of this. Until then, Eric is simply the Flash Brigand, out seeking vengeance against the man he believes stole his best friend's land."

"I understand. I won't tell anyone. But I must warn you: When Father reads the newspaper and finds out which night the Geelong gang was captured, he might figure it out all on his own just like I did."

"Then see that he doesn't read it. Maybe when he hears about it from the talk that's sure to go around, he won't learn exactly which night it was. Even so, he might not piece it together as well as you did."

"But what do I tell him about Eric? He needs to know his son is safe."

"You can tell him nothing. Coolabah is to join Eric tonight with the latest plans to bail up Livingston again. This time they will hit one of his son's ships moored at his private docks in the bay at Melbourne. We have every reason to believe the ship is carrying a lot of the gold the judge's bushrangers have stolen for him. It was carried on board in coffins, of all things. Once the news of that robbery hits the papers, Aaron will know Eric is safe."

"But will he be safe? Won't the ship be guarded?" Her joy quickly gave way to deep concern, and she felt her stomach curl into a tight knot as she more fully realized the danger that must be involved in such an act.

James's expression hardened, revealing none of the conflictng emotions he felt at that moment. Though he knew it could mean Eric would be out of the way forever, leaving the path open to Jessica's heart at last, he could never wish harm to his nephew, for he loved Eric, too. "He'll be as safe as we can make him. Go on, now. And I'm trusting you to keep our secret at all costs. For Eric's sake as much as our own."

Chapter XXII

"The bumblin' buffoons," Captain Scantlin muttered as he slung the newspaper across the room in a fit of frustration. "Then it's true? It's all true?"

"Aye, I'm afraid it is," the young man told him, his pale brown eyes meeting the captain's head on. "I don't know how the girl escaped them, but evidently she did, and must have before they ever reached Forest Creek, because she is not mentioned in any of the accounts I've read concerning the gang's capture. But I know for a fact she was successfully kidnapped from the coach. The driver verified that when he returned."

"Does anybody 'ave any idea where she is now?" the captain asked and leaned heavily on the wobbling surface of the small gumwood table he was forced to use as a desk. His hardwood chair creaked from the abrupt shift in weight.

"Aye, back at her father's tent in Eureka."

"How'd she get back to Ballarat?"

"Some man known around the area as Coolabah Cecil and some half-native woman brought her into camp a couple of days later. I suspect they found her roaming the bush and offered her a ride on the woman's horse. When they rode in, they only had two horses. Jessica must have escaped our men on foot."

"Coolabah?" the captain repeated and tapped his fingers impatiently against the surface of the table as he played with that name in his mind. His face twisted into a frown, which caused his heavy jowls to puff out, giving him a bullfrog appearance. That name was very familiar to him for some reason. Where had he heard it before?

"That's the name I was given. He's described as a tall, burly-looking fellow with a bushy red beard."

"Coolabah! Of course, 'e was one of the men who worked for that Ben Crawford fella your father 'ad us frame up last year for aiding escaped convicts. You remember, so 'e could buy up all that land with water on it—over where 'e set up the Stone Sheep Station. Coolabah was one of Crawford's ringers, a big, stupid lookin' man. I wonder what 'e's doing down 'ere?"

"Looking for gold, I suppose. After he found himself without a job, he probably decided to go for some easy money like all these other blokes around here. He must not have figured out that there are even easier ways to get rich than breaking one's bloody back trying to dig up gold." A wide smile stretched across the young man's thin, aristocratic lips.

"Aye, Gordon, much easier ways indeed." The captain chuckled and leaned back in his chair to look up at the young man. Although Gordon had not inherited the striking good looks of his father, Judge Livingston, the young man dressed impeccably in the latest styles of Europe and kept his hair cropped to match whatever was popular at the time. Even now, the lad's brown hair was cut short with a part at the side, and he wore a handsome brown frock coat and matching trousers with a cream-colored waistcoat over a loosely fitted ruffled white shirt—very stylish indeed. His tall brown boots were also of the latest fashion and gleamed from the constant attention given them, as did the tiny brass buttons at his sleeve hems.

"And it would be even easier for Father to amass his fortune if we could finally get Eric Aylesbury off our backs and either in jail or at the end of a rope, where he belongs," Gordon reminded him. "What are we going to do about that?"

"Has your father given you any more ideas?"

"I haven't spoken with him since we first set up that kidnapping. He's already gone back to Bathurst and is waiting for Eric to be brought to him. He may not even know about the interference of those bloody detectives yet. What rotten timing that was!"

"Do you figure any of them men will tell the Melbourne police what all they know about the judge's operations? They just might be eager to bargain for their freedom."

"No, not if they value their lives. They know better. They have been clearly warned that the judge has friends everywhere, and if they ever betrayed him he would surely find out, and he'd see to it they never lived long enough to reap the rewards."

"That's a relief. But for our present problem, we can either wait until the judge has time to recruit new men into our little family to take right up where the Geelong gang left off, or we can take care of this matter ourselves," the captain told him. His eyes narrowed in thought as he considered just how he should go about it.

"What can we do?" Gordon asked when he sat down in the hardwood chair beside the captain. Suddenly he had grown very interested in the conversation. "How can we take care of this without having to bother Father again?"

"Just like we originally planned. We kidnap his sister and offer to trade 'er for Eric."

"But how? How can we kidnap her now? She's back in camp, surrounded by her family and all those other people."

"Not always. As you recall, your father had me keepin' a close watch on 'er whenever I was over there 'round Eureka way. While doin' just that, I noticed that almost every Sunday afternoon, unless it rained, she let that Regie Schiller pay a call on her. They usually took a little stroll away from camp to a peaceful little clearing where they could have their privacy." The captain's eyes sparkled with the plan already formulating in his head.

"Jessica Aylesbury and Reginald Schiller?" Gordon questioned and tilted his head to stare at the captain in disbelief. "Alone? In the bush?"

"Not exactly alone. Her pretty little 'ousekeeper always goes along as sort of an escort. They 'ave to keep it nice and proper, you know. The three of them go up there together, and Jessica usually reads to them from some book." The captain paused as he further thought over the situation. A wicked smile lifted the corners of his lips as he considered how he might also manage to get even with Regie Schiller for all the trouble he'd caused back in Bathurst, all at the same time. He could handcuff the lad to something so that the bloke could do no harm. Then he could take his pleasure with Jessica Aylesbury right in front of young Schiller's very eyes. Then, when he was through with Miss Aylesbury, if he still had it in him, he

389

might even finish what he'd started with that pretty little housekeeper, too. Yes, this was going to be quite a pleasure. A very profitable pleasure, for, no doubt, the judge would reward him well when he finally brought Eric Aylesbury to his very door and no one would be the wiser.

Jessica had never felt so restless in all her life. For days now she had waited for word of Eric and had grown extremely impatient. She kept a constant watch in the newspaper for any mention of one of Gordon Livingston's ships being bailed up, but to her mounting frustration, she found nothing. She only hoped the long delay was due to careful precaution and not because something terrible had happened. What if Eric had been found out? Some of Livingston's men very well may have caught up with him and had him killed. Jessica's heart ached at the very thought of it. In a way, she wished she had never found out all she had from James Cranston.

"Are you ready?" Regie asked when he came to stand in front of her.

Although she had realized Regie was in the tent, for some reason his voice startled her, and she threw her hand to her breast, her eyes wide in reaction.

Regie looked curiously to Carrie, who shrugged.

"Jessica, are you ready to go?" he tried again. "There can't be too many more afternoons good as this left before winter sets in. Let's make the most of it."

"Just a minute and I will be ready. Let me get my book and my shawl."

"You won't need your shawl," Carrie told her. "It's a beautiful day outside."

"Then let me get my book and tell Father we're leaving." Quickly she went to her trunk and picked up the small volume of poetry that lay on top of it before heading out of the tent in search of her father. Ever since Deen had left the morning before to escort Mundora back to her people's village, her father had slipped into another one of his quiet, introspective moods. When he was not working in the medical tent, he simply sat alone and stared off into the distance, lost to his thoughts for hours at a time. Jessica knew it was because he finally had time to worry about Eric. How she wished she could tell him what she knew. But then he might end up just as worried about the upcoming attempt to rob Livingston's ship.

"Father, we're leaving now. Is there anything you want us to do for you before we go?"

"No, not much happening around here. You three go on and enjoy yourselves." He smiled and turned his cheek to her for her customary good-bye kiss.

"We won't stay long. Send word if you need us. You know where we'll be." Feeling a little guilty that she was keeping important information from Aaron, which concerned his own son, she turned away from him and found that Carrie and Regie had followed her outside. Pointing the way with a wave of the small, cloth-bound book in her hand, she motioned for them to go.

Carrie had been right about not needing a shawl. The day was perfect. Although the temperature was probably only in the middle sixties, the bright autumn sun shown down and warmed them comfortably. As they left the camp and made their way along the little worn path that led into the bush at the northern end of camp and on toward their own private little haven, they could hear the lively chatter of the birds in the trees overhead. The sounds delighted Jessica, and as she spotted the red-tailed cockatoos and the emerald green lorikeets perched in the spindly gums up ahead and a rose-breasted galah in a poinciana tree right above her, she could not help but smile. The native birds of Australia were so beautiful.

Though nature surrounded the goldfields on all sides with dense bush and plush forests, most of the birds avoided the more populated areas, and even the ones that did brave the goldfields could barely be heard over the constant noise the diggers made while hunting their gold. It had become a special treat for Jessica to be out among the wildlife at least once in the week. It made her chaperoning duty that much more a pleasure.

"Jessica, do you mind if I hold Carrie's hand?" Regie asked, temporarily bringing her thoughts down out of the trees and to the couple walking beside her.

"I think you should ask Carrie if *she* minds," Jessica teased. "After all, it's her hand you'll be holding."

Carrie smiled and blushed but held out her hand to Regie rather than make him have to gather the courage to ask again, and he accepted it eagerly. Jessica kept her eyes on the pathway ahead rather than embarrass the two by looking at them, but she could not keep from smiling at how awkward the two seemed when they were around each other. It was the same awkward feeling she had experienced when Eric had first taken her aside and kissed her.

When the three of them finally reached their favorite spot, a small grassy clearing where the sun shone brightly through the break in the trees, Jessica crawled up on a small, flat boulder and made herself comfortable, knowing that Regie and Carrie would choose to sit together on the side of the fallen tree that lay only a few feet away.

"What shall I read?" Jessica asked as soon as she had her skirts arranged just so. She had read the book through for them once and now only read whatever they wanted to hear a second time. For Carrie, there were certain poems dealing with the prospects of new love that she liked to hear again and again, so Jessica was not too surprised when she was asked to reread "Into your eyes" by an American poet named Thames.

Captain Scantlin watched them leave with extreme satisfaction, and since he was almost certain of their destination, he did not bother to tail them. Instead, he waited until they had completely disappeared from his sight before he mounted his horse and headed into the bush. Although eager to confront them, having fully planned the attack in his mind for days now, he knew he must not let himself grow too eager. He could not afford to be careless. The outcome of this was far too important. That's why he had decided to work alone. He wanted full credit for capturing the girl. Besides, he did not need an audience for what he planned to do before he was finished with those three.

Slowly he made his way through the dense growth of trees. Having chosen plain clothes over his uniform, he patted the deep pocket of his coat again to be absolutely sure he had the handcuffs. They were there, all three sets, unlocked and ready for use. He had already checked his revolver. It was fully loaded and so was his carbine rifle. And, purely as a safety measure, he had thought to strap a small dagger to his calf, though he was certain he would never need it. No, he would have the element of surprise on his side. They would not even realize what was happening to them until it was too late. It was all he could do to keep from chortling out loud. He was looking forward to this.

When he finally neared the spot where he expected to find his three unsuspecting victims, the captain dismounted and eased his carbine from its leather scabbard. He led his horse by the reins, then slowly and carefully made his way closer to the clearing and was delighted to find the three of them so lost in conversation that they had not heard what little noise his horse had made. His blood began to race through his body with uncontrolled excitement as he raised his rifle and aimed for the ground just below where the royal Miss Jessica Aylesbury sat perched on her huge, gray-rock throne. His heart thudded in his chest as he anticipated their reaction. The women would probably faint dead away, and Regie Schiller would probably become a stuttering fool.

Ping! The bullet just grazed the side of the boulder, causing a puff of gray-white dust to billow out only inches from the ground.

Jessica and Carrie both screamed. Regie rolled instantly to his feet and looked around in confusion, trying to figure out where the shot had come from. Although Regie did not have a gun with him, his hand went immediately to the leather thong that looped around and held the handle of his knife in place just above the narrow sheath.

"I wouldn't do that if I were you," the captain called to them just before he stepped out from a clump of fallen gum limbs, still leading his horse behind him.

"Captain Scantlin! What are you trying to do, kill us?"

Jessica demanded angrily. She had not yet realized the full danger.

"No," the captain answered quickly. He smiled at the wit he was about to bestow on them while he dropped his now empty rifle from his hand into the dirt and quickly replaced it with his revolver. "At least not yet."

Laughing, he took great pleasure at the sight of the three of them huddled together, looking startled and confused, the women more behind Regie than beside him. "Like I said once already, I wouldn't do that if I was you," he told Regie, indicating the knife Regie had just slipped into his hand. "Pitch that knife over 'ere nice and easy like, or I'll fire the very next bullet into your pretty Miss Aylesbury there."

He pointed the pistol directly at Jessica's heart to indicate to them that he meant business and was pleased to find Regie so cooperative. Carefully, the captain stepped over to where the weapon landed, only a few inches from where he had dropped his rifle a few moments ago. Slowly he knelt down, picked the knife up, and held it comfortably in his left hand, all the while keeping his revolver trained on Jessica with his right. Grunting as he forced himself back to his feet, he tossed the knife into the bush behind him where it would be of no use to anyone and took several more steps toward his victims, delighted at the deep fear and hate he saw in their eyes, especially in that little housekeeper's eyes. She looked as if she would dearly love to rip his heart out.

"What do you want?" Jessica demanded to know and showed more courage than she felt by taking a step forward.

"You," he answered simply enough.

"Me?" she responded, perplexed.

"What do you want with Jessica?" Regie asked as he stepped around to stand protectively in front of her again.

"To put it simply, I'm here to kidnap her. And it doesn't really matter to me if I take 'er dead, alive or badly injured, although I must admit she'll probably do me more good alive and healthy. But that's up to you."

Regie looked questioningly back at Jessica, then at Carrie. When he returned his gaze to Captain Scantlin, so much raw hate glowered from his blue eyes that it caused the captain to take a step back. He wanted to keep at least twenty feet between him and them until they were safely handcuffed to something.

"Behave yourselves and do just what I tell you, and Jessica won't 'ave to get shot at all. None of you will," he told them, then reached into his coat pocket and pulled out the handcuffs. After singling out two pairs, he tossed them to the ground just in front of Regie's feet and quickly put the other pair back in his pocket. "Those are for you and the little 'ousekeeper there. First, snap one cuff on the 'ousekeeper's right wrist . . . what's her name?"

Regie stared in silent defiance. He had no intention of giving the captain her name.

"Carrie, Carrie Crocker," Carrie told him, afraid for Regie. This man was truly mad, and might decide to actually shoot Regie for refusing to answer so simple a question.

"Carrie it is then. You, Schiller, take one of those sets there and put one end on her right wrist like I told you, then . . ." He paused as he looked for something to anchor them to. Seeing that there was nothing really secure available to him, he started his horse in their direction. "Then snap the other end to one of those brass rings made into my saddle, but do it where I can see what you're doin'."

Regie stared down at the handcuffs and then brought his eyes back up to the captain's as if he honestly contemplated defying the man. It was Carrie who bent over and picked up both sets and handed them to him. "Do what he says or he might kill us all."

With the muscles in his jaws working furiously, Regie turned and snapped one metal cuff around Carrie's extended wrist, then when the horse came close enough to be able to capture his reins, he handed them to Jessica to hold while he snapped the other end of Carrie's cuffs to one of the six brass rings made into the side of the captain's saddle. He had seen such rings as these used by the goldfield troopers and knew that they were practically impossible to break loose.

"Now, I want you to tie that horse to that tree there," he told him. He watched carefully to be sure Regie tied the reins in a secure knot. "Tug on them so I'll know you did it right."

Regie tugged on them sharply, then went to stand beside Carrie. Jessica stayed where she was. She did not want to put the other two in danger when it appeared she was the captain's main target.

"Now take that other set of cuffs there and put one end around your own right wrist and close the other end around another one of those brass rings until it clicks. I want to hear that click." The captain studied the handcuffs as best he could from where he stood. "Now tug on them so I can be sure you did it right."

"I wouldn't chance you hurtin' Jessica," Regie told him as he and Carrie jiggled their cuffs back and forth to demonstrate they were securely handcuffed to the horse's saddle.

The captain smiled, contented that they had, indeed, done exactly what they had been told to do, and started toward Jessica. Just before he reached her a noise, like a twig snapping, brought him whirling around with his revolver ready. Regie tried to take advantage of the distraction and attempted to jerk his hand free of the cuff but found he was unable to.

"What did you do, toss a rock?" the captain asked, grinning at how ridiculous that had been, then his smile dropped and his eyes grew cold. "Try that again and I'll kill you."

Carrie reached for Regie's arm and pleaded with her eyes for him to behave himself.

"How touchin'," the captain said and placed his hand over his heart in a melodramatic gesture. "Seems the little whore 'as taken a likin' to ya, lad." When Regie took an angry step in his direction, only to be reminded of the handcuff, the captain laughed aloud then, knowing Regie Schiller could do him no harm. He returned his attention to Jessica.

"Don't want you to feel left out, darlin', so I brought a third set of 'andcuffs just for you," he told her and reached into his pocket to get that last set. The sound of his horse's snorting brought his attention back to Regie and Carrie. The animal pranced about nervously, drawing the captain's suspicion. "What ever you two are up to, you'd better think twice about it. That is, if you care anything at all for Miss Aylesbury here."

Regie's eyes met Carrie's, then nervously flitted to the captain.

"Did you 'ear me?"

"Aye, we heard you," Carrie responded quickly. "But what could we do handcuffed to your horse the way we are?"

Nodding at the truth in that statement, he turned back around to Jessica and found her eyeing his revolver. "Don't try it. Don't even think about it. Now, turn around with your 'ands stuck behind you."

Though Jessica wanted to put on a brave front, she could not keep her hands from trembling when she turned away from the captain and placed them behind her. She shut her eyes when she felt the cold metal surround her wrists one at a time and snap shut. She felt like crying out when he jerked on them and forced her to spin back around to face him.

"Now I've got a little surprise for ya," he said and smiled as he moved closer to her. When he took her in his arms, she could smell his foul, fish-smelling breath even before he pulled her against him. It was all she could do to keep from retching.

"Or maybe I should say I have a big surprise for you," he chuckled as he pressed the evidence of his intentions against her thigh.

A sob stuck in her throat when he reached for her skirt and slowly started to inch it upward. That's when it occurred to her that she would rather risk getting shot in the back than tolerate what the captain had in mind. Without taking the time to think it through, she jerked herself free of his grasp and started to run.

"Do that and I'll not only put a bullet in you, but I'll shoot your friends, too," he warned.

She took several more faltering steps before coming to a complete halt and turning to look at Regie and Carrie. Carrie motioned with her head for her to go on and try for an escape, but Jessica could not do that to her friends. She could never risk their lives. Trembling out of control, she started back toward the captain. She would have to endure whatever he had planned for her.

"That's a good girl," the captain purred and came to meet her halfway. He bent his head and watched with growing interest as he slowly inched her skirts back up, exposing first her ankles, then her calves, then her lily-white knees. Running his tongue over his lips in anticipation, he chortled. "Oh, how I'm going to enjoy this." Then, looking over at Regie, he asked, "She's got pretty legs, don't ya think? Want me to bring 'er closer over there so you can get yourself a better look?"

He did not wait for Regie's response. He turned back to look at Jessica's legs again and resumed inching the skirt up, eager to see the rest of her but wanting to make the moment last. He was totally unaware that anyone else was present until he heard the footsteps of someone running in his direction, but by then it was too late. The man who had charged out of the bush was already upon him. The very knife he had just tossed into the bush flew through the air and caught him in the left shoulder.

Jessica watched in horror, unable to scream, unable to move, as Rube dove headfirst into the captain's side, plunging them both to the ground to scuffle in the dirt and grass. As the two men struggled for possession of the captain's gun, Jessica stood by and watched helplessly. The weapon remained hidden between them where Jessica could not see it. Her heart pounded furiously against her chest, for she could not tell who had the advantage in the struggle. Then, realizing she could be the one to help make the difference, she dropped to her knees and, unable to free her hands, began to pound on the side of the captain's head with her knee.

It was an endless moment later that the gunshot was heard and another endless moment before Rube rolled off the captain, his face contorted with pain and his hands clutching his gut.

"Rube!" she cried out and reached for him.

"Don't touch the bastard!" the captain ordered her in a cold, quaking voice.

Jessica's eyes went to where Regie was writhing in his effort to free himself from the cuffs. His eyes were dark with hatred and fury. Beside him, Carrie had collapsed to her knees, dangling by her right arm, her green eyes wide with the horror of what had just happened.

Captain Scantlin was in such a rage, he shook as he rose to his knees and pointed the gun at Rube's head. The knife still protruded from his shoulder. A dark circle of blood surrounded it. More blood was splattered over his white shirt front, and Jessica realized that blood had come from Rube. Waves of nausea flowed through her when she looked from the captain to where Rube lay clutching his abdomen, blood oozing through his fingers. It was her intense fear that kept her from giving in to the nausea.

"Don't shoot him again. Do what you want with me, but don't shoot him again," she pleaded and started to move toward Rube despite the captain's order against it. She wanted to see how bad the wound was, but by the putrid odor the blood was giving off, she already knew it was bad.

"I said don't touch him," the captain repeated, his voice seething as he got to his feet and stood over Rube, his gun still pointed directly at Rube's head. "Look at me, you sorry son of a bitch. I want your eyes on me when I pull the bloody trigger."

Rube forced his eyes open, and he stared up first at the gun barrel pointed into his face, then at the man holding it. His only movement was the heavy rise and fall of his chest as he struggled for each breath.

"You deserve this, you bastard," the captain told him, his nostrils flared and his eyes so full of rage they had gone black.

Jessica could not stand to watch and turned away wishing she could cover her ears. Tears streamed down her face as she waited for the gun blast that would end Rube's life. When it finally came, she cried out with horror. Forcing several hard breaths into her lungs, she found the strength to turn around.

It took a moment for what had happened to register in her brain. The captain staggered around to face Carrie and Regie, then slowly raised his gun, aimed, and to Jessica's confusion, collapsed to his knees. Before he could get off another shot, he fell face forward in the dirt and grass.

Jessica's eyes quickly darted to Rube, who still lay with his eyes open, watching. Then she looked over at Carrie and Regie. That's when she noticed Carrie standing there with her arm still raised, a smoking derringer in her hand. Regie continued to struggle against his handcuff, blood drenching his wrist from his vain effort.

"Bring me the gun," Rube said in a raspy voice. His eyes were now on Jessica.

Jessica looked at him a moment, then looked at the captain. His face was pressed against the earth, and she was only able to see one glassy eye but knew he was dead.

"There's no point in it. He's dead. He can't hurt us anymore."

"No, bring me Carrie's gun. Put it in my hand." When Jessica did not respond, he explained. "If you don't bring me that gun, Carrie's going to end up on trial for murder, and the way the courts are around here, she could be found guilty. She'd hang. That's why you have to bring me the gun. Make it look like I killed him."

Jessica grazed her cheeks one at a time with her shoulders in an effort to wipe away enough of her tears to allow her to see what she was doing. Slowly, she began to scoot across the ground toward the captain.

"What are you doing?"

"I'm going to get the keys to these handcuffs so I can set us all free."

"No, don't. If you three are still handcuffed when they find you, no one will ever suspect Carrie, or any of you. Someone's bound to have heard the shots. It will take them a little while to get here, but they will come running."

"But how can I examine your wound?" Jessica argued and continued to scoot across the ground toward the captain's body.

"No need," Rube told her weakly. After a long pause he added, "Jessica, the gun."

Biting back the sobs that racked her throat, Jessica managed to get to her feet, and she walked over to where Carrie stood with the derringer hanging limply in her left hand. No words were spoken. When Jessica turned her back to Carrie, Carrie placed the tiny pistol in her hands. Regie watched, his face twisted with the sheer agony that overwhelmed him. Tears ran down his cheeks from his red, swollen eyes in wide, steady streams, for it was his brother, his twin, who lay dying several feet away, and he could not go to him.

When Jessica finally felt the gun's weight in her hands, she closed her fingers around the now cold metal and hesitated only a moment before she returned to Rube's side. Kneeling with her back to him, she bent far enough over to be able to put the pistol right into his hand. She turned and saw that he barely had the strength to grip it.

"When you give me credit for this, try to make me sound like a real hero," he said. His lips twitched as if he wanted to smile for her but couldn't.

"You are a real hero," she sobbed uncontrollably. Never had she felt so helpless.

Rube fell silent and stared up at her for a moment. She felt as if he wanted to say something more, but he never got the chance, for seconds later, he was dead. Unable to bear the pain that consumed her, Jessica leaned forward and pressed her cheek against his. How terribly she had misjudged Rube.

At first her tears came with huge, rasping sobs. But eventually the sobs gave way to an introspective silence, for there was so much to sort out in her mind. Why had this happened? What had Rube been doing out in the bush? Had he simply been following her like he had so many times before, or had he seen the captain and become suspicious? Had he known he was headed for trouble when he came?

Quietly she grieved the loss, his cheek still warm against hers, for there was a part of Rube she had never realized existed—a part of him she had gotten only a glimpse of at the end, a part of him she truly would have liked to know better.

Chapter XXIII

"Regie!" Jessica called out when she looked up from her mug of hot tea and saw him standing just inside the tent. Rising quickly from the table, she hurried to him.

"I've come to let your father look at my wrist," Regie said. His red-rimmed eyes searched the tent for sight of Aaron. It was obvious that Regie had done a lot of crying since he'd left them. "He wasn't in the other tent, so I figured he must be in here."

"No, he's gone to the commissioner's tent," she explained, then motioned to the chair she had just occupied. "Come sit down. He should be back very shortly. All he has to do is verify that Captain Scantlin did, indeed, die from the bullet wound in the side of his chest. After he is finished with that, he should be right on back here. I imagine you've told your father about what happened by now."

Regie nodded that he had. "The same version we told the police. I figured he'd like that story better, and if for some reason he got questioned, he wouldn't have to know he was lying."

"How's he taking it?"

"Pretty bad. Just as soon as the police release the body, he plans to carry Rube on back to Bathurst for a proper burial. He's out seeing if he can trade anyone our claim and most of what equipment we got on it for a decent wagon right now. Soon as he's got one, he plans to get Rube and go home. And when we leave here, we aren't comin' back. He's disgusted with the goldfields now. Hates 'em. Besides it would be too hard for just two men to try and work that hole alone. We're givin' it up," Regie said, then shrugged while he held his injured wrist lightly in his left hand. A deep, gaping wound encircled his entire wrist. Normally such an injury would be extremely painful, but Regie was still too much in shock to truly realize the pain. "Where's Carrie? I need to talk to her."

"She went to find you. When you didn't come over to have that wrist looked at, she got worried."

"Pa and Howey wanted to hear the whole story about what happened before he even went down to see about the body, and even though they wouldn't give us Rube's body yet, Pa and me still had a lot of other decisions to make, and I wanted to change clothes before I came," Regie explained, then fell silent for a long moment while he studied his injured wrist. "Do you suppose the dead have a way of lookin' back on the living?"

Jessica gave that question serious thought, but before she could decide just what she believed, Regie went on: "I hope Rube did. I hope he was able to see the tears Pa cried when he learned about his bein' dead. Rube always had the notion that because we were never Karl Schiller's real blood kin, we didn't matter much to him; we never truly fit in somehow. But you should have seen the way Pa cried. Like a babe he did." Regie looked at Jessica.

406

Tears had filled his own eyes again, and his voice started to tremble. "I never saw him cry like that before. Not even back when he learned of his own mum's death. He shed tears then, but he didn't break down and weep like he did when I told him about Rube. He said losing Rube was like losing a part of himself. I sure hope Rube got to hear some of that. It would have made him right proud."

Jessica felt a warm rush of compassion for the man she had so misjudged while he lived and an odd need to comfort Rube, though she knew she could not—no mortal could offer Rube compassion now. She looked away from Regie and did her best not to cry.

"He loved you," Regie said quietly. "I hope you realize just how much he loved you. You always fascinated both of us, but for Rube it was something deeper. He didn't talk about it; he wasn't much on talking about what was in his heart, but he didn't have to—at least ways not with me. I could see it easily enough. He was always following you just to be able to get a look at you. That's probably what he was doing at the clearing this afternoon. He just wanted to be able to watch you, be near you. He knew you could never love him. We both knew you would never love anyone like us. We both always realized you were something extra special, but still he liked to pretend."

"I never knew." Jessica felt her throat tighten and knew she could say no more than that. Never had she felt such a deep, painful guilt. How could she have read something so terribly sinister into the reasons why Rube was always following her, watching her; but then, again, how could she have known? She pressed her lips together and held back the woeful cry of shame that welled deep within her, and she knew that if they did not change the subject immediately she was going to start crying all over

407

again. It was getting harder for her to bring herself back under control each time she did. Her head already throbbed from all the crying she had done so far. "So when do you and your father expect to leave?"

"Just as soon as he can get us that wagon and the police give up Rube's body. They told Pa that would be after all the reports had been filled out and signed by all the right people. They already took down my statement and I signed it. I stuck to our story all the way."

"So did I. They should never suspect Carrie of being the one who fired the gun. As far as anyone else is concerned, Rube did it while defending my honor." Jessica spoke very softly so that no one could possibly hear her. "I was glad all the major asked Carrie was a couple of questions that simply verified what I'd already told them. The way she trembled, I was afraid she might break down and confess the real story. That would put us all in a lot of trouble."

"I think Carrie's stronger than you give her credit for. She'll hold through this just fine. And I am hoping she won't be here to have to answer any more questions anyway. I've come to ask her to be my wife and go back to Bathurst with me."

Jessica's mouth fell open and hung limp until his words had fully soaked in, then slowly the corners drew up and she smiled. "Your wife?"

"Aye, if she'll have me. I don't much like the thought of going back home without her. Dr. Aylesbury might be down here for another year yet before some other doctor decides Ballarat will make a stable enough town to set up a real practice."

Jessica's hands folded over her mouth in an attempt to hold in the squeal of delight that swelled inside her throat. It took her a minute to decide what she should do to help this situation along. "I'll go see if I can find her. You wait here for Father. I'll bring Carrie to you."

Blushing at the way Jessica carried on, Regie lowered his gaze and agreed not to leave until she came back with Carrie.

Jessica was so excited and eager to locate Carrie that she found she could not be content to simply walk. Hiking up her skirts a few inches, she ignored the raised eyebrows and took off running in the direction of the Schiller's claim. That would be the most likely place to find her.

Sure enough, when she reached the Schiller's tent—so badly out of breath that at first she could not talk enough to call out Carrie's name—she found her sitting on a small three-legged stool with her chin planted firmly in her hands and her elbows propped against her knees. But as soon as she glanced up and noticed Jessica, she was up on her feet and asking what was wrong.

"Nothing's wrong," Jessica assured her between her heavy gasps for air, wincing from the burning sensation in her lungs that each breath of cool air caused. When she finally managed to get her breathing better under control, she started to explain. "Regie . . ." She paused and tried to think of a way to state it so she would not give everything away. She wanted it to be a complete surprise for her friend. "Regie is already at the tent. You two must have taken different routes. You just barely missed each other."

"And you ran all that way to tell me that?" she questioned suspiciously as she reached up to catch hold of the loose strands of hair the brisk autumn wind kept blowing across her face. Appropriately, within an hour of

Rube's death, a wall of dark clouds had moved in, and the temperatures had taken a quick plunge.

"I didn't want you to worry about him. He's there having his wrist tended just like he promised. I thought you would want to be there with him." Carrie had already started walking toward the medical tent, and Jessica fell quickly into step with her. "He seemed a little disappointed that you weren't there when he arrived. He asked where you were."

"How'd he look?"

"Sad," Jessica said, summing up his pale, drawn appearance into one word.

"Has he told his father?"

"Yes, that's why Mr. Schiller isn't at their tent. He's off trying to get a wagon so they can take Rube's body back to Bathurst for burial. They'll have to leave just as soon as they can so they can get there before the body . . ." She broke off the sentence and left it unfinished, for she did not even want to think about such a thing.

"I figured they would try to take Rube back home for burial, especially with the weather turning cool. I wonder how long they will be gone."

"They are not coming back. Regie says Mr. Schiller is too disillusioned now to want to come back. He just wants to go home."

Carrie stumbled, sending a hand out to grasp Jessica's shoulder to steady herself, then stopped to look at Jessica. "Regie isn't coming back either?"

"No," Jessica said and tried her best to sound somber when her insides were about to burst with giddy excitement. Carrie's fondest dream was about to come true. A moment's heartache would not do her much harm.

410

Carrie blinked several times in an effort to hold back her tears, then started walking again. No further words were exchanged while they continued on toward the medical tent. When they pulled back the flap and entered, they found Regie sitting in a chair beside Aaron with his eyes closed tight while Aaron gently scrubbed the injured area that completely encircled his wrist with a small piece of cloth.

"There now, that ought to do it," Aaron said as he tossed the soiled cloth into a small bucket. "All I have to do now is bandage it and I'll be finished."

Regie opened one eye and examined the swollen area that now oozed fresh blood. Then, when he decided that he, indeed, was going to live, he opened the other eye and relaxed his shoulders.

"Now when it comes time to change the bandage, you might want to soak it in clean water for a few minutes. The bandage will come off easier and not stick to the wound as bad," Aaron went on to tell him. When he noticed Carrie and Jessica standing nearby waiting, he nodded and smiled, though his smile did not reach into his dark eyes. Jessica knew then that his mind was on something other than the task he was performing.

Regie turned to see who Aaron had smiled at and found Carrie's sad eyes staring directly into his. The smile he gave her was warm. When she did not respond with a smile, he quickly frowned and looked to Jessica questioningly.

"I haven't said a word," Jessica assured him. He nodded that he understood, and the smile returned to his face.

"Haven't said a word about what?" Carrie asked. Her eyes went from one to the other and back.

"We'll talk about it in a minute," Regie told her. "Just

as soon as the doctor here gets finished with me."

"All done," Aaron told him and stood up. "You're ready to go. Just remember what I told you about keeping that wrist as clean as you can and keep it bandaged pretty tight so that you aren't so inclined to bend it. I don't want you reopening that wound."

"Aye, doctor, what do I owe you?" Regie asked Aaron.

"You can take a letter to my wife for me when you leave," Aaron told him. "Come back by in a little while. I'll have it written and ready to go." Then he left the medical tent to search for his pen in the other tent.

"I'd better go help him. He can never find anything. You know how men are," Jessica said quickly as she began to step backward, toward the front opening. "Carrie, you and Regie can have your talk here if you like."

Jessica hurried outside and waited between the tents. Unable to stand still, she paced the small area, wringing her hands impatiently, until she heard Carrie's loud cry of joy. She turned and faced the medical tent and waited for Carrie to come bursting out with her news and grew disappointed when she did not. Her curiosity drove her to leave her spot, and she slowly circled around the medical tent until she could peer inside. Her smile stretched as far as it could when she saw Carrie and Regie locked in a passionate embrace, kissing each other hungrily. Tiptoeing lightly away, she returned to the other tent to wait until Carrie was ready to come tell her the good news.

Weeks passed and still no word concerning Eric. Nor had James Cranston returned to his tent, and the man who stayed there refused to admit that he even knew a

James Cranston. All Jessica could do was wait. Wait until either the newspapers revealed something or Eric sent word to her. How she loathed waiting. Even the surprising news of Deen and Mundora's upcoming marriage did not alleviate the frustration. Everyone's future seemed to be working out except her own.

The ceremony was planned for this coming Sunday, and although it was to be nearly as simple as the one Regie and Carrie had hurried through, at least it was something to take her mind away from her worries while she altered a beige and white lawn dress Aaron had purchased for a wedding present. She was trying to size it down to fit Mundora's slender figure. The dress was all Fanny had had that was even remotely suitable for a wedding, but it was a good two sizes too large. As inept as Jessica was at sewing, it was taking her a lot longer to complete the job than she had anticipated. Why sewing this flimsy material was so much harder for her than suturing human skin she had no idea, but the more she worked at it, the more frustrated she became and the more she missed Carrie, for she knew Carrie would have had the dress completely finished by now.

Thinking of Carrie reminded Jessica of the letter she had received the same day Deen had come by to announce his wedding plans. Although Carrie and Regie lived with the Schillers for now, Regie had already started to clear a patch of land on his own ten acres for their house. It would be spring before he could really get to work on it, but for now they were content to take long walks in the evening over to his land and stare at the empty spot where their house would one day stand. Just remembering how happy Carrie had sounded in her letter made Jessica smile. One day she, too, would have such happiness, such wonderful dreams to share and her own special future to plan for—with Eric.

"Push off, Jacky," Eric commanded, his voice hushed yet just loud enough for them all to hear. Even though they were casting off well over a mile from their eventual destination, he did not want to take unnecessary chances.

"Done, boss," came Jacky's reply from the rear of the small scull boat as he shoved the muddy bank with the sole of his boot. Because they had waited for this night with no moon and Jacky had dressed all in black except for his red neckerchief, which he finally had agreed to tuck inside his collar, Eric could not see Jacky at all. Jacky had simply vanished with the darkness, an advantage the rest of them did not have, for although they, too, were dressed all in black, their skins reflected just enough light from the distant docks to let Eric know where they were, even though they had rubbed charcoal on their skin.

"Coolabah, you and Sam put some muscle into that rowing," he said. He chuckled at the way Coolabah first muttered to himself, then retorted, "Aye, aye, captain!" He was clearly not pleased that he and Sam had drawn the shorter straws and had to man the oars. Coolabah never liked it when Jacky got to hold the straws, and he had voiced his protest openly, claiming it always warranted him bad luck for Jacky to be the one allowed to hold the straws.

"Be a good sport about it, mate," Sam said in a strained voice as he pulled on his own oar. "Somebody has to row this bloody thing."

There was a moment of silence. The only noises came from Coolabah and Sam who grunted slightly when they rowed and splashed the water gently with the oars each time they lifted them or plunged them back into the water as they made their way across the bay near where the Yarra River emptied into it. Finally Coolabah spoke again. "Eric, I know this is not the best time to be bringin' this up, mate . . ." He paused, hesitant to reveal his secret to everyone aboard, especially Jacky.

"What is it?" Eric asked Coolabah, though he faced the front of the little dinghy while he spoke. He squinted in the darkness and tried to make out the shape of the *Lady Fortune* in the far distance. There were too many ships at harbor though, and he knew he would have to wait until they were closer, much closer.

"Well, the thing is . . . what I thought you really ought to know is . . . well . . . damn. I can't swim."

There was total silence before Jacky's voice shattered it with his high-pitched laughter. Eric and Sam followed with outbursts of their own. Sam laughed so hard that he lost his grip on his oar, and the boat started to turn in a circle as Coolabah continued to row his side with a vengeance.

"Proud to know you all find my predicament so amusin'," Coolabah grumbled and continued to heave his oar with all his might, unaware as of yet that his efforts were for naught.

"Coolabah," Eric said when finally he could. "You are not alone. Neither can Sam or me."

"Oh, *wonderful*. You mean 'ere we are out in this rickety little boat, preparing to sneak aboard a well-guarded ship while it sits moored in the bay, and Jacky's the only one among us that can swim?" Coolabah quit

415

rowing now, and the boat stopped making its wide circle and glided to a stop.

"That sums it up rather nicely," Eric said and grinned at the disgruntled sound in Coolabah's voice. "And since none of us three can swim a stroke, my advice is to stay out of the water."

Coolabah did not appreciate Eric's humor. "Well, that man Captain Cranston promised us had just better be aboard that friggin' ship. And that rope had better already be lowered by the time we get there. I'm not about to try to swim around to the docks in order to try to storm the gangplank."

"The rope will be there. The man signed on to Livingston's ship over a week ago," Eric assured him. "He's been on that ship ever since. It'll be in place. There should be no reason for any of us to even get wet. All we have to do is climb up that rope."

"I just 'ope my arms aren't too worn out from all this bloody rowing. What about the distraction? That all set?"

"Yes, the fire has been set for one o'clock. That'll give us plenty of time to get over there and in position."

"Fire? I thought the captain planned on having two of Belle's bawdiest ladies flounce around on the docks to distract them."

"Well, Coolabah, I'll be honest with you. James gave it serious consideration but decided on a fire instead. I think he was worried that the ladies might prove to be too much of a distraction . . . on you. He thought we would have better luck with a fire on the docks."

When all Coolabah could do was splutter at such a remark, Sam snickered and Jacky broke out in deep laughter that took several minutes to get back under control.

Eric went on to explain: "We've bought an empty warehouse that sits right next to Livingston's with the sole intention of setting fire to it. That should worry the sailors on board Livingston's ship, because if no one puts it out in time, that fire could very well burn on over into one of Livingston's warehouses."

"That would be too bad," Sam commented, still fighting his laughter.

"Say Jacky," Coolabah called out after a few minutes of thoughtful silence. "You sure you can swim?"

"Yes, I learned how when I was a boy," Jacky confirmed.

"You pretty good at it?"

"I guess so. Why?"

"Let me ask you a question. If something was to go wrong and one of us was to fall into the water by accident, would you be able to save him?"

"Probably."

"What if two of us were to fall into the water? Could you save two of us?"

"I'd try."

"What if all three of us were to fall into the water?"

"Coolabah. I don't think you have much to worry about. Even if you do fall into the water, you're not going to drown."

"How can you be so sure?"

Jacky started to chuckle even before he could answer. "Because lard always floats."

"Be damn with ya then! Even if I do fall in the water, don't you go makin' no effort to save me. And if I do drown, I hope it weighs heavy on your conscience, Jacky, my friend, for the rest of your bloody life. Sam! Pay attention. You got this damn boat goin' in circles again!"

The last half of the trip across the bay was made in silence. The closer they got to their destination, the more careful they had to be in order not to alert the sailors who stood guard on board the *Lady Fortune*. When they knew they were less than a few hundred yards away, Sam and Coolabah began to take special care not to let their oars slap the water and continued to glide their small craft slowly in and out of the ships moored along the waterfront.

Just enough light glowed around the dock area to allow them to see each other plainly. Words became unnecessary. Hand signals were used to communicate any messages they needed to relay to one another, and sometimes a simple look or a nod was enough. When they had the small boat in position where they could watch the entire length of the *Lady Fortune*'s starboard side without being spotted from the deck, they pulled their neckerchiefs up to cover their faces and waited.

Though the tension was taut, Eric could not help but grin when Coolabah turned sideways and nodded toward the ship with his bushy eyebrows raised accusingly, for no rope dangled over the side. Nothing to help them climb aboard. Eric pulled out his pocket watch and held it up so that he could see what time it was. In an effort to reassure Coolabah, he pointed to the watch, then raised one finger to indicate they still had almost a full hour before the fire would be started. There was still time.

After what seemed an eternity to the men, a dark form

appeared at the railing. A huge rope was gently let down to where its knotted end dangled only a few feet above the water. Then the form disappeared. Eric turned to be sure Coolabah had taken note of that and found that his friend had become too interested in poking his finger into the cold water to notice anything. Tapping Coolabah's knee with the toe of his boot, he got his attention and pointed toward the rope. Though Coolabah's mask was in place, Eric could tell his friend had responded with a reassured smile. Now all they needed was that little fire off the other side to distract the sailors who were guarding the ship and they could finally do what they had come to do.

"Fire! Hey, that warehouse is on fire!" The shout finally came. Eric could see an amber glow flickering across the sails of the large schooner they used for cover and knew that the fire was already well established.

"Some of us had better get down there and help," came another shout, and Eric knew that had come from their own man aboard, for the man had been instructed to encourage everyone to leave the ship. "That's one of the boss's warehouses right there next to it."

"Aye, grab a bucket, men, and come on," someone else cried out frantically.

"I'll stay here and guard the gangplank. The rest of you go help put that fire out! Don't let it spread over into any of Livingston's warehouses." Again from their own man. Eric listened in earnest for the reply to that but did not quite make it out. He hoped it had been an agreement of some sort. Heavy footsteps were soon heard on the wooden docks as someone took charge and began to give the commands that would set up a bucket brigade.

Eric waited a full two minutes before he turned to give the others the signal to move. Slowly, and quietly,

Coolabah and Sam took up the oars again and eased them forward across the smooth black surface of the water until they were directly below the rope. Eric and Jacky both lifted their anchors and slipped them quietly into the water, while Sam held them apart from the side of the ship with both arms. As soon as the boat was stable and Eric was assured they would not bang into the ship's side, alerting anyone to their presence, he nodded, and the four of them tugged out of their boots. Then all but Coolabah, who had neglected to put any on, stripped their feet of their stockings. Only Eric noticed that Jacky's stockings were as bright a red as his neckerchief, and at any other time he would have brought everyone's attention to that fact. As he stuffed his own stockings into his boots, he made a mental note to be sure and question Jacky later about those red stockings. He would give Coolabah a fair chance to get back at him for all the ribbing he had taken tonight.

As soon as his boots were aside, Eric stood and took hold of the wide rope with both hands. Slowly, he pulled himself up by his powerful arms, catching the bottom of the rope with his bare feet in order to secure himself until he could reach higher and pull himself up further. As soon as he was halfway up the rope, Sam started up the rope, followed by Coolabah, who used the rope to pull himself up while his bare feet walked up the side of the boat. Jacky tied the large leather pouch to the bottom of the rope and made sure it was secure before he shimmied up the rope after them.

When Eric was finally high enough to peer over the top rail, he carefully searched the weather deck, then the quarter deck for any sailors who might have remained on the ship. The amber reflection of the fire flickered across he area and made it hard for him to detect movement, but he soon was satisfied that the only man who had stayed aboard was the man guarding the gangplank with one rifle in hand and several abandoned rifles leaning against the railing beside him. Eric hoped the man was their own and quickly pulled himself over the railing and onto the deck.

It was not until Coolabah was on board that the man became aware of their presence, and for one tense moment, the man turned and looked in their direction. But when he merely offered them a quick nod and returned his attention to the dock below, Eric knew for certain the man was their own and signaled for the others to follow him below.

It was not hard to locate the gold, for it was right where they had been told it would be. Though there were several coffins in the hold for them to choose from, it was easy enough to pick the one which held the gold. It was the only coffin someone had bothered to nail shut. Even so, Coolabah had refused to look on as Eric began to pry the lid. Within minutes they had the coffin opened and emptied. Eric took just enough time to place the lid back on top of the coffin before he gathered up his share of the load and led them away.

Weighted down with heavy canvas sacks that bulged with their precious content, the four of them headed back up to the main deck. Being the strongest, Coolabah was so loaded down with his cargo that he had to trot sideways behind Sam in order to see where he was going.

When they reached the rope, Eric laid his heavy sacks on the deck beside his feet and quickly hauled up the rope. He loaded two of the large bags of gold into the leather pouch and, even though the men on the docks were shouting and making an awful racket with their bucket brigade, he took his time in lowering the pouch so that it would not bang against the side of the ship and draw unwanted attention.

As soon as the gold reached the bottom and the rope was drawn taut, Eric helped Sam set his load down and watched while Sam lithely climbed back down the rope and emptied the pouch. Meanwhile Coolabah and Jacky set down their loads and kept a watch on the gangplank and the decks of the surrounding ships. As soon as Sam tugged the rope to indicate he was ready for it to be hauled up again, Eric pulled it, hand over hand, until the pouch was once again in his hands.

Load after load of gold was lowered and emptied into the tiny scull boat until it was all down below. Jacky was next to slide down the rope while Sam held it secure from below. Then, just when Coolabah slung his leg over the railing to follow, they heard voices that seemed louder than the rest. Someone was coming up the gangplank. Coolabah hurried.

"What's wrong? Why are you two coming back aboard when there's still fire to be put out?" asked the man guarding the gangplank as a way of warning Eric that the men were close and on their way.

"Need more buckets," one of the men called out, and while Eric waited for Coolabah to climb down far enough to allow him to follow, he could see the heads of both men as they walked further up the gangplank. Quickly he straddled the railing and glanced from Coolabah to the men and back. Finally Coolabah was low enough to allow him to start down and, just before his head slipped out of sight, he was sure one of the men had spotted him.

"Hurry," he whispered, breaking their code of silence

or the first time in over an hour.

Coolabah worked his way down as quickly as he could without chancing a fall. But because he was not as agile as Sam or Jacky, it took him longer. Eric kept his eyes trained on the railing above, fearing what would happen if the man had actually spotted him. Able to hear the sound of footsteps running along the wooden deck toward them, he realized he had, indeed, been spotted. He prayed they could somehow get into the boat and around to the other side of the neighboring ship before either of the men were able to fire a good shot. It terrified him that they were not in familiar surroundings like they always had been whenever they struck from the bush. It also terrified him that three of them could not even swim.

Chapter XXIV

"Would you like a room, ma'am?" the desk clerk asked politely when he looked up from the docket he had just totaled and found Jessica standing there watching him.

"Yes, sir, I would," she responded with a smile, glad he finally noticed her. "By any chance would room six be available?"

"Room six?" The clerk turned around to see which room keys were missing.

"Yes, sir. The two times I've stayed here before I was given room six and found the room to be quite pleasant," she lied, glad to have learned from the groomsman outside that the desk clerk was new, for until a very few minutes ago, she had never even laid eyes on the captain's quarters and had to stop twice to get directions before she found the place. If the truth were to be known, she had never as much as heard the name before yesterday afternoon.

"I'm sorry, ma'am. Room six is already taken. But I can let you have room five. It's right next to room six, and I assure you it is just as comfortable in every way and has the same lovely view of the harbor."

Jessica's smile broadened. Her plot had worked perfectly. "Room five will be fine."

"How many nights do you plan to stay with us," the clerk asked as he turned the registration book around and handed her a freshly dipped pen.

"I'm not sure. It will depend on how long it takes me to conclude my business here in Melbourne," she told him while she bent over and scribbled a name onto the tiny line the clerk indicated.

"Business? What business could a pretty lady like you have in Melbourne," he asked with a too-friendly smile.

"Family business," she told him with a cool nod.

"I see," he said, his smile fading. He looked down at her signature. "Well, Miss Penn," he paused then asked, "it is 'Miss' Penn isn't it? Or will you have a husband joining you?"

"It's Miss Penn," she responded. It had been the first name that had come to her mind when the time came to sign the register. She had not wanted to draw attention to who she really was.

"Very well, Miss Penn, I'll have Jason bring your luggage right away," he told her, then reached for a small brass bell and jingled it lightly. An older man appeared almost immediately at Jessica's side. "Jason, please see to Miss Penn's luggage."

"Where is it, ma'am?" the old gent asked as his eyes left the one bag at her side to search the room for more.

"I'm afraid all I have is this one bag," she said curtly.

"Travel light, do ya?" the man responded cheerfully, then bent to pick up her one bag. Having underestimated its weight, the man stumbled and let it fall back to the ground with a loud thud. "I take back what I said about

425

traveling light. What's in this thing?"

"Books," she lied. She wasn't about to tell him that the bag was packed nearly full with medications and doctor's instruments.

"Are you a school teacher, ma'am?"

"Why, yes, how'd you guess?" she said brightly.

"You sound kinda like a schoolteacher. You talk so proper and all," he explained and made a second effort to pick up the heavy bag.

"How very astute of you, sir," she said with a regal nod of her head, practicing her new identity.

"Thankee, ma'am," he said, blushing. Then he looked at the desk clerk and asked, "Where to?"

"Room five," the clerk told him and held out the key. "And be sure the lady has fresh water and a clean towel. She's a regular guest."

Jessica would never have believed she could be such a talented liar, but she had both these men believing she was Miss Catherine Penn, a teacher visiting Melbourne on family business. Now if she could only remember who she was supposed to be whenever she was addressed in public.

"Here ya go, ma'am, I hope you enjoy your stay," Jason told her when he held the key out for her. As soon as he had set down her bag inside the room, he quickly checked her water pitcher and sniffed at her towel, then went to the window and pulled back the heavy velvet drapes so that she could see what a lovely view of the harbor she had.

Jessica was very impressed with the room. It was a spacious room, furnished with a beautiful, ornately carved rococo bed plumped high with thick blue and white comforter quilts and oversized pillows. Near the huge window, where the guests could sit and stare out at the crowded bay, was a lovely pale blue, tufted sofa and a matching chair with a richly carved marble-topped table between them. The floors were carpeted in dark blue and the walls covered with a fancy white, textured wallpaper. A mural of the seashore done in pastel blues and grays embellished the entire far wall. Quite an elaborate place for a hideout.

"Thank you very much," Jessica said as she pressed a coin into the old man's weathered hand.

"Will you be wantin' a bath?" he asked, eager to please now that he knew she was so generous with her rewards.

"Oh, yes, I would dearly love one," she responded quickly, her eyes wide at the thought of such a luxury.

"Then I'll have a tub brought right in, and the girls will have you warm water within the hour," he told her.

"No, I have business to tend to first. What about later this evening, around seven?" she asked, certain she would be through with Jacky by then.

"Aye, seven it is," he told her and, lacking a hat, he tugged on the front lock of his hair as a courtesy to her and left.

Jessica wasted no time. She opened her bag and slipped out her personal belongings, tossing them haphazardly across the sofa. Then, with only the medications and instruments left in the bag, she carried it over to the door and set it on the floor where she would be able to get to it easily when the time came.

Because she expected to return immediately for the bag, she did not bother to lock her door. She simply closed it behind her as she stepped out into the hall. First though, she had to make sure James had given her the right room number.

After a quick glance in both directions to be sure she was alone, Jessica moved to the door with a huge brass six centered on it and knocked lightly on the hard wooden surface. She continued to glance up and down the hallway while she waited for someone to answer. Her heart thudded in nervous anticipation when she heard someone stir within. It very well could be Eric who answered the door.

"Mundora!" she exclaimed softly when the door finally swung open. She stepped inside the room and shut the door, instantly aware of the faint scent of steamed gum leaves. "What are you doing here?"

"Jacky has been shot," Mundora told her simply and turned to look at her brother who was quietly watching them from the bed.

"I know. That's why I'm here," Jessica explained, then noticed Deen sitting in a nearby chair also watching them, and she nodded to him in greeting before going on. "When James Cranston came by our tent looking for you yesterday and I told him you and Deen had come to Melbourne for a few days, I made him explain why he was looking for you. He told me how Jacky had been shot and had refused to let a stranger treat his leg. When no one could convince Jacky otherwise, James had set out within the hour for your village but when he got there, he was told you had gone to Ballarat, so he had come to our tent in hopes of finding you there. Not certain he would be able to find you in Melbourne the way things are around here these days, I volunteered to come here and see to Jacky's leg myself. After all, I'm not exactly a stranger to Jacky anymore. But since you are here, I guess I am not really needed."

"Stay. Eric will want to see you," Mundora said, and a

warm smile stretched across her face.

Jessica's heart sent her blood coursing tingly trails through her at the mere mention of his name. Just the thought of finally being able to see Eric again made her all giddy inside, like a child awaiting Christmas, but she tried not to show her excitement. "How did Uncle James find you so quickly? He couldn't have gotten here more than a couple of hours ago," Jessica said, still amazed, for she had struck out for Melbourne almost immediately. As crowded as Melbourne had become since the discovery of gold in Victoria, it could almost be classified as a miracle.

"Eric found her," Deen put in. "Quite by accident. He was coming out of a gunsmith down by the docks just as we were passing in front of it, and he grabbed hold of Mundora and started to drag her along the street even before he could fully explain why."

Jessica walked over to Jacky. "How's the leg?"

"Better." He smiled though it clearly took a lot of effort for him to do so. His usually glowing brown skin had a washed-out appearance, and his eyes looked sunken and dark.

"He lost a lot of blood," Mundora went on to explain.

"He was lucky. The bullet went clean on through his leg," Deen commented, then joined Jessica and Mundora at Jacky's bedside. "Mundora didn't have to cut into him to search for a bullet. I don't think he could have stood any more blood loss."

"Not only did it go clean through my leg, it went clean on through the boat." Jacky chuckled and, as if he had found a new burst of inner strength, he went on to tell them more. "You should have seen Coolabah's eyes when he realized that I'd been shot. Without thinking, he jumped up to come help me. When his weight joined mine at the back of the small boat we were in, he almost sank us instead. And when he saw the bullet hole near the bottom of the boat and that water was bubbling through it like a small fountain, he nearly went berserk. But eventually Eric got him calmed down enough to start rowing again while I stuck my thumb into the hole and kept the water from flowing in quite so fast. I passed out before we ever reached the bank where we'd left our horses, but somehow they got me here. When I came to, they had some man I had never seen before wanting to probe my bullet wound. That's when I demanded someone get Mundora. I wasn't about to have a stranger poking around on me."

"Stubborn," Mundora commented with a pleased smile.

"No, he just knows who can give him the best care," Deen said affectionately and bent to place a gentle kiss on Mundora's cheek. Jessica watched with true amazement, for it was not customary for a man to show such open affection toward his woman, especially in front of others, but then Deen had never been one to defer to custom.

"He took a big risk," Mundora admonished, staring down at Jacky with a sisterly raise of her brow. "If that leg had continued to bleed until I got here, Jacky would already be dead. All the care I could give him would do him no good."

Jacky turned his head to study the ornately carved plaster ceiling, as if he was suddenly more interested in the elaborate design than this particular conversation.

"Like I said, he is stubborn," Mundora commented and laughed lightly at her brother's disinterest.

The metallic sound of someone slipping a key into the

door lock drew everyone's attention. Jessica looked questioningly first to Deen then to Mundora. Mundora nodded with a growing smile. "Yes, that should be Eric. Only he and Coolabah have keys."

Jessica watched the door latch as it slowly turned. Her heart seemed to stop beating even while her hand went to the throbbing pulse of her throat. The moment his handsome face came into view, her feet took flight, her arms flung wide.

"Eric," she called out, already blinking back tears of joy as she hurried to him.

A smile burst across his face at the unexpected sight of her. He took her into his arms and swung her around and around. "Jessie!"

"Now that we've established that you two remember each other by name," Deen said with a pleased smile of his own, "would one of you reach back and close the door before some curious soul comes by and sees too much?"

Without bothering to put Jessica down, Eric kicked the door shut. His eyes never left hers. His arms never lessened their embrace. "What are you doing here?"

"When Uncle James came by and told me about Jacky, I volunteered to come here and help," she explained.

"Why did he come to you with that? He was supposed to be going after Mundora."

"He was trying to locate Mundora. Someone at her village told him he would find her in Bathurst, but because Mundora had gone with Deen to Melbourne for a few days and because I was afraid Uncle James would never be able to find her in time, I volunteered to come and see what I could do for Jacky myself. A leg wound can be a very serious thing. I had to do something."

"You are a kind and generous woman," he said, his

eyes taking in every lovely detail of her face as he spoke. "To think, you'd come all this way to treat a man you barely know."

"Maybe not as kind and generous as you think. I had another reason for wanting to come. I knew there was a good chance I'd get to see you while I was here, and I couldn't pass up an opportunity like that."

"I'll correct that then. You are a kind, generous, and wanton woman, Jessica Aylesbury," he said laughing.

"And don't you forget it," she said with a meaningful raise of her eyebrow, then, suddenly realizing there were three curious sets of eyes staring at them, she pushed on his shoulders and made him set her down. "I came as quickly as I could, but it seems I'm not needed here after all. Mundora has been found and she has things well in hand. All Jacky needs now is a little rest, and I'll do my part toward that by going back to my room now."

"I'll walk you," Eric volunteered quickly. "Can't have a beautiful woman like you roaming around the halls alone, can we? No telling what evil might befall you before you finally reach your room."

"That would be nice," she said and smiled up at him, not about to mention that her room was right next to this one. She purposely avoided the knowing looks the others in the room gave each other when she accepted Eric's proffered arm. Another charge of excitement swept through her from the mere touch of their arms. She could hardly wait for those arms to sweep back around her and hold her close, this time in private.

"How far to your room?" he asked as soon as he had closed the door behind them.

"Not far," she replied, then fell quiet long enough for them to take six more steps. "We're there."

432

"Room five?"

She nodded and bit her lower lip with nervous expectation as he reached for the door handle and turned it. In a very few moments they would finally be alone. They both checked the hallway to make absolutely sure it was empty before slipping into the room unnoticed. Instantly the door was closed and Jessica turned to face him.

"Ah, Jessie," he said with a soft sigh as he pulled her instantly into his arms. "I have missed you so."

"And I've missed you," she told him. "I can hardly wait for all this to be over so you can give up the detective force and we can finally be married."

He remembered what Coolabah had told him about what she had learned about their operations, and he pulled her closer. "My dear sweet Jessica, sometimes you are too nosy for your own good." When he saw that her pout had turned into a frown, he bent low and kissed her nose gently. "But I guess if I had a nose as lovely as yours, I'd put it to good use, too."

"Is that all I get?" she said teasingly. "I haven't seen you in over a month, then only briefly, and after all that time of having to be without you, all I get is a tiny peck on my nose? I thought you said you missed me! Eric Aylesbury! Either you fully apologize for your thoughtless neglect or kiss me right now!"

"In that case, you'll get no apology from me," he said with amusement and grinned briefly just before he brought his lips down to meet hers in a deep and hungry kiss.

When he took his lips away from hers in order to stare back down into the shining blue depths of her eyes, a languorous smile spread slowly across her face and she murmured, "No apology necessary."

He laughed but his eyes glittered with much more than simple amusement. His breathing had become ragged and she could feel his warm, moist breath fall lightly across her face when his lips once again dipped down to close over hers, far more gently this time.

This kiss was warm, tender, yet extremely persuasive as it quickly worked its intended magic on Jessica, and she felt her legs weakening, causing her to lean heavily against his strong body. His lips parted and, in a natural response, she slipped her tongue into his mouth and tasted the sweet, familiar taste that was so uniquely Eric.

Eric responded with a groan from the inner depths of his throat. One hand moved to caress the curve of her cheek and felt the exquisite softness of her tawny skin, while the other slipped to her waist and pulled her closer against him, melding her body to his.

Jessica's desire flared. It burned deep with sensations that had lain smoldering inside of her for far too long. Her hands slid upward along his back, and she fleetingly marveled in the firm contour of his strong muscles before allowing her sensitive fingers to inch ever higher until they were finally entangled in the soft thickness of his dark hair. With a growing sense of urgency, she pressed firmly against the back of his head, unable to bring him close enough. With the furor of a starved animal, she crushed him to her and buried her lips into his, as if in doing so she could somehow make him a part of her, so much a part of her that he could never leave her again.

Eric's hand left her waist and slowly slid upward to caress the under curve of her breast as he remembered well the womanly perfection that lay beneath the smooth fabric of her dress and the pleasures it could bring him, pleasures his body now craved with total abandon.

Their passions mounted further and the kisses became more and more demanding, their needs more pressing. Soon they were pulling at each other's clothing, eager to share what they had denied themselves for so long. Eric's hands moved quickly to the tiny ivory buttons at the back of her dress, working frantically with them, until Jessica could finally feel the material slacken around her. His fingers left tantalizing trails of warmth along the sensitive skin of her back as they brushed against her again and again. Eagerly, he continued with his task of undoing the rest of the buttons while their mouths continued to hungrily devour each other.

The moment he had the final button undone, he slid his hands beneath the fabric, against the warmth of her skin, and slipped the dress from her shoulders. It fell lightly down around her waist. It took him only a few seconds more to untie the tiny silken straps that held her lacy camisole in place, and it, too, fell to her waist, exposing her extreme beauty. Unable to resist such a strong temptation, he sent his hand to cup one of her breasts, and he lightly caressed the tip with his thumb until it strained against his hand with intense desire.

Jessica quivered with anticipation as his lips slowly left hers and made their way down her throat then across her collarbone. She arched her back eagerly when his lips neared her breasts, and the moment the warmth of his mouth finally surrounded the straining bud, she pressed him into her softness, urging him on. She was on fire and wanted to draw him into her flames.

Unable to bear much more of this sweet torment, she clutched at his shoulders and prayed that he take her soon. With every stroke of his skillful hand and with each caress of his hungry tongue, she wanted to give him more, so much more.

"Take what you want, it's yours," she muttered in a deep, passion-filled voice.

Having heard that, he brought his arms around her and lifted her high into his arms. In three long strides, he had carried her the short distance to the bed and lowered her into its softness. He watched her breasts heave with mounting desire as he gently slipped her dress down over her hips, then to the floor. Her heavy underskirts and flimsy undergarments soon followed, and he was finally allowed a full view of her beauty. Hurriedly, he removed his own clothing, then joined her on the bed, gently lowering himself on top of her.

Her breasts flattened against his chest, and it seemed so natural, so right, for her to have him there. She ran her palms across his naked back, again marveling at the feel of his strong, taut muscles. For a moment the two simply reveled in the glorious feeling of lying naked together. But, unable to resist her passion-swollen lips further, his mouth dipped down to reclaim hers in another powerful kiss while his hand moved to continue caressing her breast.

Reaching down to press her hands into his lower back, she knew she wanted him more than she ever had. She could feel the evidence of his own desire against her and knew his needs were just as intense, just as demanding as her own. It was more than she could stand. She had to have him now.

But Eric was not yet ready. He wanted to make the moment last forever. His kisses retraced a fiery path down her neck while his hands slowly slid up her shoulders to become entangled in her thick riot of hair.

He wanted to leave no part of her unexplored, no part of her untouched. Burying his face between her breasts, he breathed deeply the scent that was Jessica, sweet Jessica, while against his abdomen, he could feel the heat of her womanhood.

Finally, he trailed his moist tongue over the sensitive skin that covered her breast until it once again found and reclaimed the still hardened nipple. Drawing on it hungrily, he brought his hand out of her thick mane of hair and let it stroke first her arm, then her rib cage, then the other breast. Sparks of searing heat shot along her every nerve, setting fire to every last inch of her body. Moaning aloud, she was not sure how much more of this sweet, deliberate torture she could stand. How much farther would he want to take it before bringing them to their ultimate climax? She bit her lip to restrain the cry of sheer pleasure when his hand left her other breast and gently stroked ever lower, until it finally found the center of her femininity.

Her body could no longer be denied, and she pressed herself up against his hand as he continued his explorations. She had to have Eric now. Pulling at his arms, then at his hips, she finally drew him away from her breast. His lips came once again to reclaim her mouth, but that was not what she wanted. She tugged again at his sides, then his hips, and he finally rose above her, then down. She responded with the wild fury of her unleashed passions. Eric had finally become a part of her. Her breaths came in shallow, halting gasps until the pinnacle of her needs built higher, ever higher, and in that wondrous moment of ultimate ecstasy, she cried out his name. Eric responded with deep, shuddering groans that racked his entire body again and again. Once fulfilled, they both fell back into the softness of the pillows, their energy spent, languid in the aftermath of their love.

Eric made no effort to leave, and the reunited lovers remained in each other's arms. Jessica pressed her cheek against the strength of his warm, muscular chest and lay quietly, unmoving, listening contentedly to the steady pounding of his heart. Soon she was aware of his heavy, rhythmic breathing and knew he was asleep. She thought of wakening him so that he could get back to Jacky's room before anyone became suspicious, but she decided she would rather keep him beside her for as long as she possibly could. Wistfully, she closed her own eyes and dreamed of the day when they would finally be married and Eric would be safely and completely hers.

Chapter XXV

Eric leaped from his chair, unable to believe James could even suggest such a thing. "I won't let her do it. I won't even give her that choice. I'm not having her involved!"

"And I'm not saying it's the only way, but it would definitely hurry things along. Just consider the lives it could save," James said in ready defense of his idea.

"I'm thinking more of the lives it could risk."

"But if Livingston was to learn about your upcoming marriage and if he heard that the marriage was to be soon, I honestly think he would step up his action in order to do something about you before the blessed event could take place. He would not be able to stand the thought of you having even a moment of happiness. You have always been our bait to draw him out, and now that he has more reason than ever to avenge his hatred of you and the Aylesbury clan, why not? Why not go ahead and lure that sly fox into our trap now? Why wait for him to fall in it of his own accord."

"Because it puts Jessica in danger! It puts my whole

family in danger!"

"They could be warned of the danger. Besides, I feel almost certain Livingston would make his move before the wedding even has a chance to take place. Why not put the pressure on him to do something before he's really ready to? Force him to become reckless in his decisions. Don't give him time to regroup. He'll give it a go. I just know he will."

"No! We'll continue the way we have," Eric said, his eyes narrowed and his bearded jaw granite hard. "Eventually he'll make the mistake we've been waiting for."

"Don't I have a say in this?" Jessica asked as she came from the dressing room, her hairbrush still in hand. Her dark hair fell softly past her shoulders and down her back in a shining cascade of color.

"How long have you been standing there?" they both asked at the same time.

"Long enough," she told them and offered no apology for having eavesdropped on their argument. "I came in because I want to hear more about Uncle James's plan."

"It has to do with you two going ahead with your plans to get married," James stated, defying Eric's angry glare.

"I like this plan already," she said whimsically, then turned to Eric. "Is that what you have against it? It'll mean we'll have to get married sooner than you planned?"

"No, of course not. I don't like it because it will put you in needless danger," Eric responded. His jaw flexed with a barely controlled rage. "What James has suggested could put the entire family in danger."

"But it could force Livingston to make his move prematurely," James quickly put in. "If driven by his deep hatred of the Aylesburys, especially his hatred for Eric here, Livingston just could get careless in who he goes to for help. After all, he doesn't have the Geelong gang to rely on anymore. Nor does he have Scantlin. My guess is he'll recruit new help and in a hurry, and there's every chance it will be one of our men. Then we'd have him, dead to right!"

"You are giving me guesses and chances," Eric shouted and brought his hand down on the hard surface of the marbled table. "I won't let Jessica's life be put in danger over your ridiculous guesses and your damned hopeful chances! I won't have it!"

Jessica watched as the two of them stared defiantly into each other's eyes, then calmly she stepped over and took Eric's hand in hers, gently running her finger along the reddened area along the outer edge. "And how long will it take for you to get Livingston if you continue along the way you are going?"

"Maybe only a few months, a year at the most," Eric told her.

Jessica's eyes went immediately to his, then out to the gray early morning mist that hung over the wide harbor. "This is nearly the end of June, middle of winter," she spoke quietly, sorting through her own thoughts. "And I so hoped for a spring wedding. October would be nice. But that's less than three months away."

"Jessica," Eric said in a warning for her to stay out of this matter.

"Do you have something against October?" she asked, her jaw jutting out as she returned her gaze to meet his.

"No, not against the month, but against us getting married in that month," he stated bluntly.

"I agree. September would be better. September it is,"

she said and smiled when she turned to James. "Would you be able to make it to our wedding in September? We'd love to have you."

James smiled at Jessica's cool courage. "In all fairness to you, I want to be sure you understand that if I have misjudged the situation, though I doubt I have, this could mean real danger to you."

"I've already been in real danger," she pointed out. "I've been kidnapped once by a gang of the most malicious bushrangers Victoria has ever known, and then almost kidnapped again, and I came very near being raped that second time. Too many people have already been hurt or killed at the hand of Livingston, either directly or indirectly. I'm ready to do something to help bring an end to all this."

"Even if it means endangering the entire family?" Eric asked as he plopped down on the sofa and folded his arms across his chest.

"How?"

"It could be that Livingston waits until the wedding itself to do whatever he intends to do to me. That could put everyone who attends that ceremony in danger!"

Jessica thought about that. Although she was more than willing to put herself in more danger, she did not want to risk the lives of anyone else not already involved.

"Then if Livingston hasn't made his move by our wedding day, we simply call it off . . . or rather postpone it. I like the sound of that better."

"And what excuse do we give for that?" Eric said, still argumentative.

Jessica sighed at his reluctance to accept the idea. "People do get sick, you know."

"And keep in mind, there's a good chance Livingston

will try to get his hands on you well before then," James pointed out. "He will probably strike at the first available moment, and my guess is it will be at a time when there won't be so many witnesses as there would be at the wedding itself." James walked over to stare out of the window. "Hmm, if rumor should reach Livingston that you are sneaking home early, maybe to be sure all the arrangements have been made . . . I know! We can let it get out that you are, indeed, coming in early and plan to hide out at Ben's for a few days before the ceremony. He'll probably choose to strike there."

"I don't like all these probabilities you keep giving me," Eric told him, but Jessica could tell he was weakening. The thought of their being able to get married as early as September made her insides churn with excitement. She would soon be Mrs. Eric Aylesbury. Her heart soared with utter delight at the mere thought of it, causing her to feel giddy and light-headed, until James's next words sent it suddenly plunging to the very depths of her soul.

"And we will give you and Ben the best protection we can, considering the circumstances," James said. His tone was encouraging, but his words pierced Jessica like a knife.

"I know you will. It's not my own danger that worries me. I've always known the risks. I just didn't want to have to get Jessica any more involved than she already is."

"But you do see how this could help speed things along, don't you?"

"Sure I do. He'll have to make hasty decisions, and hopefully he'll be careless in making them. With what we have on him now, we can't be sure he'll be convicted of his crimes, but if he should make the wrong move now . . ."

"Or the right one, depending on how you look at it," James put in with a wry smile.

"We could have him behind bars for a good long time!"

"Aye, maybe even a lifetime."

Aaron pushed his hair back out of his face with the side of his hand when he entered the tent and made straight for his bedding. He knew he should take the time to eat something, but he was too tired. Ever since Jessica left to go to Melbourne to help Eric's injured friend, he had been swamped with patients needing his attention. The medical tent was full, so full that there was no longer room for his own bedding. And what time he had not spent tending directly to the injured or the sick, he boiled bandages for reuse, cooked stew to serve them all, and made the necessary tonics to administer to his different patients. He was exhausted. Even the news that another doctor had set up a tent over near the new Ballarat township and was preparing to move into a permanent structure had not done much to ease his workload, though now at least he could refer the excess of men to the new doctor and no longer worry that they would have to go untreated.

If he ever managed to get the energy and enough time, he planned to pay the new doctor a friendly visit. He'd heard the man's name was Green, Dr. Kevin E. Green, and that he was fresh from the mother country. Chances were he would be in need of certain medications and instruments. Aaron would be more than willing to share his if the young man would only take a fair share of the patients.

Sighing aloud, Aaron settled into his bedding and had barely closed his eyes when he heard horses clammering outside. Every muscle in him tensed as he waited to see if anyone was coming to his tent. He was in no mood for visitors and was not sure he had the strength to treat even one more patient. All he wanted was to sleep for a few uninterrupted hours.

"Aaron," the familiar voice called from just outside the tent.

"Jessica?" Enough of his strength returned for him to roll himself out of bed and head for the front of the tent to greet her. Before he could cross the room, Jessica rushed in and caught him in a light embrace.

"You look terrible," she admonished as soon as she had released him. She raised her brow accusingly as she took in his unkempt hair, the five days' growth of beard, and the deep shadows under his eyes.

"Thank you," he responded with a smile and rubbed his whiskered chin as if showing off the stubbled growth. "It's nice of you to notice."

"I shouldn't have stayed gone so long," she said and winced from a sharp pang of guilt. He looked as if he had not slept in days. "I'm sorry. It's just that Eric and I had a lot to talk about."

"Eric? Then you did get to see Eric? How is he?"

"As good as can be expected for a man about to be married."

"Married? It's all set?"

"Yes, that's what we're here to talk to you about," she explained and turned toward the door expectantly.

"We? Is Eric with you?" Aaron's face lit with hopeful

anticipation as he, too, turned to stare at the door.

"No, not Eric," she started to explain but before she could say more, James walked in.

"Aaron," he said in greeting and extended his hand. Then with a concerned frown, he looked Aaron over and stated bluntly, "You look awful."

Aaron frowned. "So I've been told. What are you doing here?"

"Can't I come visit my favorite brother-in-law without a special reason?"

"I'm your only brother-in-law," Aaron pointed out. "And I doubt you are here just for a friendly little family visit. What's up?"

"Let's sit down first," James said and gestured to the two chairs in the room. "This will take awhile. I'm here to ask for your help, but before you say anything I want you to hear me out."

Aaron listened carefully while James explained about his and Eric's involvement in the detective force and how instrumental Eric had been in capturing the Riley gang in the Bathurst district and the Geelong gang down in Victoria, and in obtaining evidence against Judge Livingston. At first, Aaron was furious for having been left out of everything for so long, but eventually, James was able to make him understand the great need for secrecy, even from him. As he further considered everything James had told him, Aaron felt a deep surge of pride mixed with a father's natural concern when he heard how Eric had risked his life time and time again in order to see true justice finally done.

"So just what is it you have come to me for?" Aaron asked, ready to know more about what he could do to help.

"I know it is asking a lot, and you may as well know that Eric was initially opposed to it, but if it works, we will have the judge right where we want him and a lot sooner than we would otherwise."

"What? If what works?" Aaron asked, his voice showing its first signs of aggravation. "What is it you want me to do?"

James explained about the trap they planned to set for the judge and that it meant bringing the trouble back to Bathurst and possibly involving some of the rest of the family. "But keep in mind there's only a small chance that Livingston will do anything to any of the rest of you. He mainly wants Eric and if things go according to plan, he will make some attempt on his life, or have someone else make that attempt, and we expect it to happen days before the wedding, at some time when there will be very few witnesses around him. Although we haven't actually verified all this with Ben yet, I know he will go along with everything. When it gets out that Eric will be using Ben's place to hide out until the wedding, old Livingston is not going to be able to resist a chance at him. Especially with Eric being practically at his own back door."

"You are leaving something out," Aaron said and frowned as he sorted through all he had been told so far. "How is this attempt on Eric's life going to help?"

"With the entire Geelong gang still in the Melbourne jail and with Scantlin dead and Lieutenant Fagan, another of his favorite lackeys, being held in Melbourne for questioning, Judge Livingston is going to be hard pressed to find someone to do his dirty work for him. It is my strong belief that he will have to recruit someone entirely new, especially with such short notice."

"And how's that help you?"

"We've got men planted in both the Bathurst and Sydney jails right now whose sole purpose is to attract the judge's attention and try to bargain for their freedom. Then we'll not only have an eyewitness to the judge's actions, we'll carry it as far as we can in order to incriminate as many as we can. We hope not only to get Livingston but also as much of the sorry riffraff who work for him as we can."

"But what if he doesn't approach one of your men? What if he goes to someone else? What if there's still someone he can turn to and still not have to recruit someone new?"

"That's where the danger comes in. Our men will try to find out who the judge does decide to deal with, and we will try to keep an eye on whoever it is, but there's a chance he will manage to employ someone without our even knowing it. I'll do what I can to use my own influence with Livingston in order to find out what he's up to, but he might not confide even in me. In that case, we can only hope that the men we send with Eric will be able to protect him."

"And what about Penelope and the people who come for the wedding? Will you have men at my place, too?"

"Yes, of course. In fact, I'll be one of them. After all, I'm family. It won't draw any suspicion to have me there. And Stuart Mays has even mentioned an interest in being there, and since he was such a good friend of your father, no one's going to question his presence. And Tony Allon and Walt Jamison, the two men who will travel with him, happen to be two of the best detectives we have stationed in New South Wales. The four of us ought to be able to provide you and your family with adequate protection."

"Sounds as if you have thought this out pretty well," Aaron said, nodding.

"I have tried to foresee all the possibilities. Your family should be safe enough. Besides, I don't think old Rodney Livingston would want to do anything that might hurt Penelope in any way. I think he still carries a torch for her and always will. The real danger lies with Eric. He's the bait. He'll be the target."

"And all you want from me is my approval?" Aaron looked across the room to Jessica who stood near the doorway staring at him, her expression noncommittal. Evidently, she did not want to influence his decision in any way. She wanted it to be entirely his own.

"And I want your oath of silence," James added.

"You have them both. Except I will have to tell Penelope. I won't have her in the dark on something like this."

James stared at him a long moment then nodded. "If you think that's best. At least she will finally know I'm not the traitorous brother she thinks I am. She never has forgiven me for leading Captain Scantlin to Eric the day after he first escaped. Maybe now she will see that I had to do it. It not only made Livingston think of me as an ally, it gave me the opportunity I needed to talk to Eric. Whether or not he had agreed to join us, I intended to see that he escaped again, only the second time with better provisions. He wouldn't have been any worse off even if he had declined to help. After all, I love him, too."

Aaron thought about what James said then asked, "Who knows about Eric's involvement with this detective force of yours? I gather Ben does."

"No, not yet, but he will have to be told. Other than

449

you and Jessica, the only other ones who know right a
this moment work for us. Or so we hope."

It was the middle of July before Jessica and Aaron were
able to finally leave Ballarat and return home. Though
the new doctor had greatly reduced Aaron's workload
almost as soon as he was in his office, Aaron had waited
until the young doctor was completely settled in and fully
understood the workings of the area before he left. But
when the time finally came for them to go, it had only
taken them a day and part of the next morning to pack up
their belongings and be on their way. It had been six and a
half months since they had seen Penelope and everyone
at their station. They were very eager to be home again.

While they traveled northward, the weather took a
turn for the worse. The temperatures dropped into the
lower forties with a nasty wind that whipped at their
backs as they rode along the rough and rutted track,
which eventually would lead them back into New South
Wales and on to Bathurst. Dressed in a doubled layer of
underskirts and wrapped in two woolen capes, Jessica
tried to keep her thoughts on the upcoming wedding and
off her chattering teeth and numb toes. In only two
months, she would become Mrs. Eric Aylesbury. Her
most secret and treasured of dreams would finally come
true.

She wondered how the neighbors were going to react
when they learned of the wedding. Most of them still
thought Eric was Jessica's half brother. It was going to
come as quite a shock for them to learn that Jessica was
not Aaron's daughter. She wondered how long it would
take the gossips to start speculating on the past. They

would want to know just who her father really was, and Jessica had already decided not to hide Deen's identity from anyone. If they asked and she felt they had a reason to know, she would tell them. She liked Deen and was proud that he was her real father. Of course, she would always consider Aaron her father, too. After all, he had raised her. He had been there for her skinned elbows, bruised knees, and had helped see her through all her childhood crises.

Taking a long side look at Aaron as they rode, she could not help but smile. Yes, he was just as much her father, if not more. His blood did not flow through her veins, but his teachings were in her brain and his love had nurtured her growth. When it came time for her to walk down the aisle, she already knew that she wanted Aaron to be the one at her side. Deen would understand. She was sure of it.

Aaron flicked the reins one more time. Able to see the station house clearly now, he felt as if he were going to burst with his eagerness to see Penelope again, at last. If those lazy horses did not hurry up and get him there, he felt as if he might be tempted to get out and push them along. And if that did not help, he would abandon them completely and make the last of his long journey on foot.

Sighing aloud with frustration, he looked at Jessica and frowned. He saw by the smile curling on her lips that she was openly amused by his futile efforts to get the stubborn animals to move any faster.

"I've never seen them be so slow," he muttered and returned his gaze to the track ahead then to the house in the distance. "You'd think they had lead in their legs."

"It's been a long trip. I imagine they are tired," she said in defense of the poor animals. "But as soon as Summerfield catches the scent of home, I expect you will find a little life left in him yet."

Only seconds later, Summerfield's ears pricked forward, and he began to make a more visible effort to move forward. The horse at his side sensed his eagerness and obliged by stepping up her pace to keep up with his.

"That's better," Aaron said and flicked the reins again. This time both horses responded by trotting a little faster. "Yeeahh, come on Summerfield. We are almost home. Your old stall's waiting for you."

When they finally turned off the track and into the yard, Aaron could sit still no longer. Handing the reins over to Jessica, he tossed a leg over the side, hesitated only a moment longer, then jumped to the ground and took off running for the house.

"Penelope," he called out when he crossed the well-swept yard and headed for the front door. "Penelope, please be home this time." He did not think he could bear it if she was in town. The last few hours had been hell enough.

At that moment, the front door opened and out stepped Penelope, wiping her hands on the lower corner of her apron. Her green eyes were wide with questioning hope as they searched for sight of Aaron and when she spotted him already on his way to her, she threw her arms wide and ran to meet him. The squeal of delight came out as she found herself being swept into his arms and spun around and around.

Slowly, he brought her down against his hard, muscular frame and kissed her long and hard. Never had she tasted so sweet to him. Never had she looked so beautiful as she did at that moment, with her brown and silver hair piled high up on her regal head and a rosy winter's glow on her fair cheeks.

"I've missed you so much," he growled just before his lips descended on hers for yet another kiss. This time the kiss was less demanding and more exploring, allowing him to deeply savor the taste, gentle textures, and warmth that was Penelope.

"And I've missed you." She sniffed, unable to hold back the emotions that had so quickly consumed her. "It's been so lonely without you."

By now Jessica had pulled the wagon to a stop but made no effort to climb down and join them on the veranda until Penelope called to her. While Jessica made her way to Penelope's waiting arms, Gomer came striding out of the stable and headed for the horses. He had grown another foot, and his scuffed brown boots protruded half a foot beneath his outgrown pants.

"Gomer, find Hiram and Zachariah. See that the wagon is unloaded and the horses tended," Penelope called out automatically, forgetting that her husband was back now and could take charge.

"Aye, Mrs. Aylesbury," Gomer said with a sharp nod and spun on his heel to go do as he had been told.

"Let's go on in and get out of the cold," Jessica said and indicated the opened door. "I'm eager to get out of these cloaks and stand by a warm fire."

"Better yet, I'll have Mrs. Chun prepare you a hot bath," Penelope told her as she walked inside with Aaron's arms still around her. "And then I'll have her prepare you both something hot to eat."

"Food can wait," Aaron told her, and when she looked up questioningly into his eyes, his smoldering gaze spoke clearly his reasons. "Jessica, you go on out and tell Mrs. Chun we are home and have her prepare you your bath or whatever you want. Penelope and I have important things to talk about first. Upstairs."

Chapter XXVI

"If he doesn't make some sort of move by morning, I want you to instruct Jessica to postpone the wedding just like we planned. And I want you to see that she does, after all, she can't very well have a wedding without a groom, and I won't be there if Judge Livingston hasn't shown his hand by then," Eric told James in a hushed voice as they both sat side by side on a small, flat boulder, their keen eyes trained on the thick bush that surrounded them. They both searched the early morning shadows for any unnatural movement, even though Sam and Jacky were well hidden in the dense foliage of nearby trees, acting as their lookouts.

"I can't imagine why he hasn't done something by now," James replied. "I know the word's out that you are already at Ben's. The rumors have gotten back to our men on several occasions. Your wedding is all Bathurst is talking about, behind raised hands, of course."

"So I've heard," Eric muttered with a deep scowl. "Seems a few of our neighbors don't think so highly of the idea of me and Jessica getting married at all."

"It'll take them all awhile to adjust to the fact that you two are not truly brother and sister," James put in encouragingly. "Besides, what do you care what a few closed-minded old fools have to say? You'll have Jessica. That should make it all worth while."

Eric fell silent for a moment while he thought about that. Soon Jessica really would be his wife. Soon he would be able to leave the detective force behind, his name cleared, and he'd finally be able to provide a home for her. They would never again have to be apart. It brought a contented smile to his lips. But then, when he remembered that if Livingston or one of his men did not try something before morning, their wedding would have to be postponed, and there would be no way to know for how long. Frustrated, he scanned the bush again in a hopeful search for movement. He wished he could catch sight of someone lurking in the shadows, though he knew that he would have heard Jacky's or Sam's warning if even one of Livingston's men was close by. Jacky especially never missed anything.

"Has any of our men in either jail heard anything at all about what Livingston might be up to? After all, tomorrow is supposed to be the big day," Eric said. He took off his broad-rimmed hat and ran his fingers through his thick, unruly hair in a disgruntled gesture.

"As far as our men know, he hasn't approached anyone in either jail," James replied, watching as Eric got up from the boulder and started to pace the small clearing. Gray dust clung to his dark brown moleskin trousers, but James made no mention of it. "But that's not to say he hasn't approached someone who already works for him. There are bound to be possibilities we haven't covered. Men we have no way of knowing about.

But I honestly don't think he will be able to let this opportunity pass him by."

"Unless he smells a trap," Eric pointed out. "What if one of Ben's ringers mentioned something to one of Livingston's men about how two of Ben's old ringers are suddenly back and brought two friends with them and were all four instantly hired. Ben's place isn't that big, and he did not really need four new ringers."

"Two ringers and two stockmen," James corrected him. "Don't you think that the fact we increased Ben's herd right after our men got hired helped him account for the extra help?"

"I don't know. His place really isn't large enough to accommodate all that cattle," Eric said and continued to walk restlessly around the small area in no set pattern until the grass was pressed flat from his weight. "Maybe someone has realized that and thought it suspicious for Ben to overwork his land. Maybe not. Oh, I don't know. I'm just trying to figure out why our trap isn't working. Why hasn't Livingston recruited someone from either of the jails? That's what we expected him to do."

"But then again, he may have talked some of his regular station hands into doing this particular job for him. You were the one who realized that was a strong possibility. And it still is a strong possibility. At this point, we just don't know."

"Haven't you heard anything from Coolabah?"

James frowned and looked down at his interlaced hands. "Not a word."

"And that doesn't worry you?"

James stared down at his hands a moment longer, then looked Eric directly in the eye. "Yes, it does a little. He was supposed to meet me here last night, but he never came. He didn't come the night before, either. I've sent Carlotta over there to act like she was trying to sell fresh baked bread to Livingston's cook, but Coolabah never showed himself the entire time she was there."

"Why didn't you tell me about this earlier?" Eric shouted, forgetting the need to be quiet. "What if they've somehow found out who he really is!"

"I don't see how they could know who he is. As far as Livingston or any of his men should know, Coolabah's just a drifter passing through. Even if someone should happen to remember him from when he worked for Ben, how could that link him to you? Besides, Coolabah knows to pretend he resents you for having helped lose him that job at Ben's."

"I don't know if that con would work. Livingston's a crafty one. I'm worried. When is your next scheduled meeting with Coolabah?"

"Tonight. Same time, right here," James told him.

"What time is that?"

"Nine o'clock."

"I intend to be here, and if he doesn't show tonight, I'm going over there and see if I can find out what's gone wrong." Eric slammed the side of his fist against a small gum tree so hard that the entire tree shook and several leaves dislodged and drifted to the ground.

"It might be that he simply couldn't get away," James said, hoping to calm Eric down. "I told him not to take any risks in reporting to me, unless it was an emergency."

"You may be right, but I'm not taking chances where Coolabah's concerned. If he does not show up here by ten o'clock tonight, I'm sneaking over there and finding him myself." Eric finally brought a halt to his nervous pacing

458

and stood rubbing the reddened side of his hand. "And I imagine Jacky and Sam are going to want to go with me."

"Let them go instead of you." James stood and faced Eric. "It is far too dangerous for you to go over there yourself. Let Sam and Jacky slip in and see if they can find out if anything has happened to Coolabah. If they are caught, we'd still have our bait. We'd still have you."

"I don't know. I just don't know. I don't think I could simply sit back and not do anything to help. What if Sam and Jacky do get caught snooping around and then can't get away?"

"Tell you what. We will all meet here tonight and if Coolabah doesn't show, I'll go with Sam and Jacky and wait on the ridge between his place and your father's while they go in. I'll be able to see the house from there and if I think Sam and Jacky have fallen into trouble, I'll go back to your father's place and get Tony and Walt, then we'll go in there and—"

"Why not have Tony and Walt already with you? Then you could send one of them back here for the five of us, and we all could go in there together. Keep in mind, Livingston's got at least twenty men working for him on that place."

James fell silent and studied the bright yellow blooms of a nearby wattle. "Everyone but you. I can't risk you being there. If he caught you, you'd be a dead man. The rest of us would still have a chance, but not you."

"And I can't sit back and not be a part of it. I can't do it."

"You'll have to. That's an order," James said sternly. "I'll agree to sending Sam and Jacky in, and I'll agree to backing them up with the rest of our men, but not you. If Coolabah doesn't show tonight, you are to go back to

Ben's and wait. We can handle it."

"Ah, but I won't be protected there," Eric said and his face lifted with a cagey smile. That should change his mind. "Ben can't be expected to try to protect me all by himself, and his men don't even know what's going on."

"Then I'll have to leave a couple of our men with you. You are not going to be a part of this." James could see the anger and frustration in Eric's eyes, and although he understood how his young nephew felt, he could not give in. "Look, there's every chance Livingston could have something planned for tonight. If that's so, you should be right where you are supposed to be. Besides, all this could be for nothing. Coolabah probably just got caught up in a poker game or something else he could not get out of for these last couple of nights. He'll probably be here right at nine o'clock with a simple explanation, and he might even have a clue about what Livingston is up to or why he hasn't done anything yet."

"I hope so. I really hope so," Eric muttered and raked his hands through his hair one more time. "I'll meet you back here at nine o'clock."

"And until then, be careful. Livingston's men could be waiting for you at any turn."

"You're back. Did you see Eric?" Jessica asked as she slipped quietly into the room James and his father were sharing while at Aaron's house. Knowing Oliver was downstairs visiting with all the other wedding guests on the veranda, she knew it would be safe to talk. "Has he heard anything yet?"

"No, nothing." James shook his head dismally and rebuttoned the top two buttons of his shirt. He had just made himself comfortable.

Jessica's hopeful expression fell. "Nothing? Nothing at all?"

"Nothing. And I'm baffled as to why. The men we have planted in the jails have heard nothing other than the fact that Eric is supposed to be hiding out at Ben's, and if they've heard that, then surely Livingston has, too. Tony and Walt have both been into town and tried to find out what they could from some of the locals, but they haven't been able to turn up anything either."

"What about Coolabah? He's right there with him. Hasn't he heard anything?"

"We don't know yet. He was supposed to meet me last night but did not show, and our next scheduled meeting is not until tonight. I won't know until then if Coolabah's learned anything," he said and tried not to let his concern show. "Until then, all we can do is keep our eyes open and wait."

Jessica walked over to the window and stared out at the yard below. "And what if Coolabah's been found out?"

"Not you, too," James said and sighed softly. He came to stand behind her and placed a reassuring hand on her shoulder. "You are just as big a worrier as Eric is. I told Coolabah not to take any risks in making our meetings. I imagine he simply could not get free. It's not the first meeting he's missed, and besides, Livingston has no way of linking Coolabah to Eric. Other than the fact that he once worked for Ben, there's no reason for Coolabah to even know Eric."

Jessica watched as Aaron and his Uncle Thaddeus walked across the smoothly swept yard from the stables. No doubt, Aaron had just shown his uncle the new breeding mare he bought early last week. He had mentioned wanting to get his Uncle Tad's opinion about the quality of the animal. She smiled briefly and leaned against the cool windowpane. How courageously Aaron was holding up through all this. He knew the danger Eric was in and knew that time had grown short for something to happen, but he hid his anxieties so well. Even now as Buck strode up to them and pounded Tad, his youngest brother, on the back in greeting, Aaron smiled and listened intently to what the two brothers had to say. She wished she could do as well, but then most of the family attributed her many emotional outbursts and her lapses in concentration to the fact that she was about to be married. Brides were supposed to be addled and absentminded.

"What if Judge Livingston doesn't try something by morning?" she finally asked. Without realizing it she reached up to place her hand over his and held it captive on her shoulder. Her eyes were still on Aaron, but her thoughts were back on Eric.

"You know the answer to that. You send for Aaron and he comes to examine you, then he announces you are too sick to be married that day. The wedding will be postponed just like we promised."

"Then what?"

"I don't know. I honestly thought the judge would have done something by now. I don't understand what is holding him back. I don't understand it at all." What he failed to say was that he was really worried. For the first time, he was experiencing doubts. Serious doubts.

"Am I ever glad to see you," Eric said when Jacky escorted Coolabah into the clearing just minutes after nine o'clock. There was just enough moonlight for them to see each other but dark enough to hide in the shadows if the need arose. Tonight there were three lookouts in the trees, and should any one of them send out the warning, everyone was instructed to take immediate cover.

"So Jacky has told me," Coolabah said and grinned. "Nice to know you were worried about me. But I just couldn't quite make it last night. Or the night before. I was followed."

"Followed?" James asked, his eyes going from Eric to Coolabah in question. "Who followed you?"

"One of Livingston's stockmen. Night before last, I slipped off to pretend I was going to have a smoke and noticed he came out shortly after that for a breath of fresh air. I strolled off toward the stables and he took to the shadows. Just to be sure he was following me, I walked on out to take my smoke and, sure enough, he stayed behind me, though at a distance, always at a distance. He did the same thing last night. Oh, I could have lost him easy enough and come on, but I didn't want to go puttin' any suspicions on me when I really didn't have anything to report."

"Nothing?"

"Not then. I do tonight. That's why I'm here. I was up in the loft this afternoon, minding my own business, when I overheard a couple of men talking about an ambush. Tomorrow morning, when Eric leaves Ben's to go to Aaron's, they plan to ambush him."

"Where?"

"That I don't know, but I figure it will have to be close to Ben's place. They have no way of knowing what route he will take. It's certain they don't expect him to take the

463

main track, not when he's supposed to be in hiding."

"Do you know how many men will be in on it?"

"No, don't know that, either. All I heard was that there was to be an ambush and that it didn't really matter if Eric was brought back dead or alive. They'd all get paid the same," he said glumly.

"Then we'll have to go right ahead with the plans for the wedding," James pointed out. "There'll be no postponing it now." He looked to Eric. "Agreed?"

"Agreed."

"But what about Coolabah?" Jacky interrupted. "If they suspect him enough to follow him around like that, he won't be safe in going back."

"They'll suspect me more if I don't go back, and it might make them nervous enough to change their plans," Coolabah told him. "I'll be safe enough. Besides, if I'm not there to witness the men leaving with Livingston's approval, we'll lose a valuable piece of evidence against the man. I've got to go back, and the sooner I get back there the better." When he looked up to find Eric's pensive expression, he laughed. "I know, I know, you and the captain want me to be careful. You are worried about me. But you don't need to be so worried. I can handle it. I've been in worse scrapes than this before."

"Jessica, wake up," James said in a whispered voice, not wanting to wake Eric's grandmother, who slept in the bed beside her. Kneeling beside the bed, which was lightly bathed in silvery moonlight, he touched Jessica's soft, silky skin with his fingertips and fought the desire that welled up inside of him as he again whispered her name close to her ear. This time Jessica's eyes fluttered open, and she turned to look questioningly at him. Quickly, he placed his fingertip to his lips, then pointed to Milicent Aylesbury lying beside her to remind her they were not alone.

Jessica looked first to the sleeping elderly woman, then to her night wrapper, which lay draped over a chair nearby. Without saying a word, she pointed to the wrapper, and James quickly retrieved it for her, then turned his back so she could slip into it. He waited until he felt her light touch on his arm before stepping over to a darkened corner of the room and pulling her near. He wished he could embrace her, hold her close against him and feel the pulse of her body against his, but he managed to restrain his passion and leaned next to her ear instead.

"The wedding is to go on as planned. Nothing has happened yet." He paused a moment, temporarily losing his train of thought. The sweet scent of lilac soap permeated his senses and distracted him completely from what he had been about to say. She turned to look at him, her brows drawn together in question, and he turned her head back to the side so he could finish, his lips so near her ear he could easily have kissed the velvety lobe. "There's to be an ambush this morning. It's all set. They plan to try to take him on his way over here. I won't be here when everyone wakes up, but I did want to make sure you went ahead with the wedding as planned. Stuart Mays will make excuses for my absence, and I doubt anyone will really miss Walt or Tony. You need not let on that we've even talked."

Jessica's eyes were wide when she turned back to face him, her fear so overwhelmingly evident that James wanted to crush her to him. It took all the inner strength he had to walk away, knowing the next time he saw her, she would be only minutes away from finally becoming Mrs. Eric Aylesbury. He would never know her warm caress or feel her gentle kiss upon his lips. She would be another man's wife. Jessica, the only woman he ever loved, the only woman he ever would love.

He shook his head glumly and slipped back out of the room as quietly as he had entered, pausing just long enough to take one last look at her. Then he hurriedly made his way through the darkened hallway, down the stairs, and out into the star-filled night. Looking skyward, he blinked back the burning moisture that collected in the corners of his eyes, letting the cool, night air soothe his aching face. Thinking of his father and the man's undying love for Milicent Aylesbury all these years, a love that never was and never would be returned, James was filled with anguish. Sadly, he looked skyward and wondered if it was somehow written in the stars that Cranston men would never be able to have or hold their true loves, never know the joy of feeling their love returned. It was as if there was a family curse. Cranston men were doomed to suffer their unrequited love— always from afar.

Pausing in the yard, he glanced briefly back at the darkened window that opened from Jessica's room. The room that now held both women, the ones both he and his father desperately longed for but could never have. Turning away again, he knew that he loved Jessica deeply and always would. So deeply in fact, he would gladly lay down his own life for her. And if Eric Aylesbury was the only man who could make Jessica happy, then he would damn well see that Eric made it through Livingston's ambush alive. For her sake. Because above all else, he wanted Jessica to be happy.

Eric and Ben mounted their horses as if nothing troubled them, as if nothing could possibly be wrong. Both men were dressed in their finest tailored suits. Ben was the image of his father, the elder Ben Crawford. He was tall, slim, and had all the same facial features, only the younger Ben's were usually softer, less stern and far less serious. But today he looked even more like his father than usual. Knowing the extreme danger he and Eric were in, his features were a little more hardened than usual, as were Eric's.

Ben already had on a black silk top hat while Eric still wore his usual black, broad-brimmed felt hat, though he had his stove hat with him, hooked over the saddle horn in front of him. He had shaved just an hour prior to the wedding, and his jaw looked peculiarly white against all the black he wore.

To the casual observer, it looked as if they were two men headed for a wedding, completely unaware of the possibility that danger lurked nearby. They joked lightly and laughed a little too loudly, but anyone listening would attribute that to Eric's impending marriage.

As soon as they were mounted, they turned their horses in the direction James had carefully mapped out for them the night before. The path they were to take would provide a maximum of protection to the men who would be stationed at various intervals along the way, close enough to be within sight of each other, yet necessarily distant because of the large area they had to

467

cover with the few men they had on hand.

"I hope they have already spotted them," Ben muttered in a low voice just before they entered the bush at the predesignated spot. Then in a louder, more cheerful voice, he laughed. "Yes, and she'll have you on your knees scrubbing floors by nightfall, and in the morning, she'll have you keeping her beds."

"I'll be keeping her beds all right, keeping them warm, that is," he retorted loudly and laughed. Then, in a low voice, he added, "Everyone's been in place since before sunup. They're bound to have them under surveillance by now."

"We shall see," Ben said with a forced smile. "We shall see."

As they got deeper into the bush, they fell silent and kept a keen watch on the bush ahead of them. They were careful to keep directly to the path James had drawn out for them, and when they passed the huge twisted gum tree that Jacky was supposed to be hiding in, Eric frowned when he didn't see him and mentioned it to Ben out of the side of his mouth.

"Where do you suppose he is?" Ben asked, his hand going to the smooth, wooden stock of the carbine rifle that rested at the side of his saddle, just in front of his right knee.

"Don't know, unless they know exactly where everyone is and have regrouped accordingly," Eric told him, unwilling to speculate on the possibility that Jacky had been spotted by one of Livingston's men and physically removed.

Again they rode in silence, their nerves taut, their hands open and ready for action. The snap of a twig brought both their heads around in time to spot the top of

468

someone's head just before it disappeared behind a jutting rock. If it had been one of their own men, he would not have been so concerned at being spotted. Eric's blood ran cold, and his pulse pounded through his fingertips as he pressed his hand against the stock of his own rifle. They were only moments away from the attack and he knew it. At any moment a bullet could come whizzing through the trees, and if the man was a marksman, that bullet could hit its intended target.

"You saw that, didn't you?" he said softly, barely moving his lips.

"Sure did," Ben replied just as softly. Although he did not move his head, his eyes darted from tree to tree, from shadow to shadow.

"Coo-ee!" The high shrill split the cool, morning air, and both Eric and Ben reacted by dropping over to hang off the sides of their horses, putting the horses to the outside, between them and the bush, just as the first shot rang out. Ben's horse reared and fell, taking his rider down with him. Eric looked back and cried out his anguish when he saw the horse roll over on top of Ben, crushing him beneath its weight. The horse continued to writhe on the ground, stirring up enough dust and dirt to keep Eric from seeing if Ben was moving or not.

There was a loud volley of gunfire in the bush on both sides of him as he continued to hang onto the side of his horse, draped low enough to be protected on one side, though he was left completely open on the other side, now. Reaching up and pulling his rifle out of the scabbard in readiness, he waited until he was just about to pass a thick clump of golden wattle and tall green ferns before letting go of the saddle and rolling into the thicket for protection. He hoped the dust that the horse had kicked

469

up would screen his actions long enough to give him time to get himself situated. He needed a chance to get his bearings straight before anyone could fully realize what he had done.

Lying on his stomach, he raised his rifle to eye level and searched the immediate area for movement. He spotted a shaking bush several hundred yards away but had no way of knowing if it was a friend or foe. Although distracted by occasional gunshots in the distance, Eric lay there on the cold, hard earth with his eyes keenly set on the bush, his rifle carefully aimed into the center of the bush, his index finger ready at the trigger. His heart raced out of control and his left shoulder ached from having struck something hard during his fall from the horse, but he refused to concern himself with the pain just now.

While he waited, he could hear the rush of blood as it pounded in his ears, drowning out the sounds that surrounded him, and though he was very relieved to have had made it this far, he wondered just what lay ahead. He was fighting for his life and he knew it.

"Well, wot 'ave we here?"

The low, guttural voice came from right behind Eric, startling him, but by the time he rolled over on his back to face whoever had just spoken, it was too late. The man's revolver was already pointed directly at his forehead. "Who'da thought you'd pick my hiding spot for your very own?"

Eric watched helplessly as the man, kneeling only a few feet away from him, slowly pulled the rifle away from his hands and laid it well out of his reach. Then, in a loud voice, the man called out, "Hey, you men, whoever you are, I got Aylesbury here. I want all of you to stop your

470

shootin' and throw out all your weapons where I or me friends can see them, or I'll blow this bloody bloke's brains all over this place right here and now."

The gunplay ended abruptly and a strange, eerie silence replaced it for several moments. Then, one by one, rifles and revolvers dropped from the trees or were tossed out from behind large boulders with loud thuds. After another moment several men came out from their hiding places with their hands held high. Eric took a quick look around and realized that James and Sam were both among them. So was Jacky. Turning back to stare at the man who now held him captive, Eric waited to see what would happen next.

A low, wheezy chuckle came from deep within the man's barrel-sized chest, and his mouth lifted to one side as he tilted his head and met Eric's angry gaze with a look of pure amusement. "But then again, I'll probably go right ahead and blow your bloody fool brains all over the place anyway. Money's the same and it'd be a hell of a lot easier."

Chapter XXVII

Jessica leaned out of her bedroom window and carefully scanned the sunbathed countryside for a possible glimpse of Eric, but all she could really see beyond the well-cropped paddocks and the large, grassy meadows in the distance were the tall gum trees with their delicate layers of green foliage and the thick wattle and bushes, which filled in the shaded spaces beneath. There was no movement in the distance, other than what was caused by the gentle west wind as it tugged at the tops of the tallest trees.

Sighing aloud with her growing frustration, she knew that beyond those trees lay almost a mile of dense bush before it cleared off again only a few hundred yards before it neared the edge of Ben's small cattle station. With her lower lip drawn between her teeth, she glanced back at the clock on her bedside table.

Twelve-thirty already. The wedding was supposed to start at one o'clock sharp, and Eric had promised to be there well before noon. Something had happened. Something had gone wrong, terribly wrong. Did Livingston's men carry off their ambush after all? Did they somehow manage to overpower James's men and take Eric prisoner? If so, what would happen to him once he was delivered to Livingston? Or would he be killed on the spot? What if he was already— No she refused to even consider that final possibility. She shuddered and pressed her eyes shut.

Leaning heavily against the window frame, Jessica felt her insides twist and knot, causing her legs to grow shaky from the agony of not knowing. In an effort to fight the wild turmoil of the confused emotions that churned constantly inside of her, she drew in several long, steadying breaths. The later it got to be, though, the more her fears raged out of control, piercing her very soul, tearing her apart inside. Eric should have been there by now.

Keenly apprehensive, she walked away from the window and sank into the soft yellow depths of a nearby upholstered occasional chair and let her gaze wander around the room as she tried to keep from looking at the clock again. Never had time crawled by at such a snail's pace. Blast it all! If something did go wrong, why hadn't James sent someone over to let them know? Didn't he realize how worried she would be? Didn't he also realize that the wedding was scheduled for one o'clock, and when the bridegroom did not appear, there would be questions? She knew Aaron's uncles. If Eric did not come soon, they would all take out in blind search of him.

Playing idly with the lace that edged the tiny ivory cuff of her left sleeve, Jessica patted her slippered foot against the polished wooden floor and wondered what she should do if he did not show up by one o'clock. What could she do? Maybe Stuart Mays would know. After all, he was chief of that whole detective force. Grabbing great handfuls of the soft organza that made up her three full layers of skirts, she hurried out of the room in search of Stuart Mays. Her first stop was the room at the end of the hall which Stuart temporarily shared with one of the two detectives who had come with him, but when no one answered her knock, she lifted her skirts again and scurried down the hall toward the stairway.

"And where do you think you're going?" Carrie asked.

"I need to talk with Mr. Mays," Jessica said abruptly. She did not care if Carrie became curious about the reason.

"But you can't go down there like that. No one's supposed to see you until the wedding begins. It spoils everything for the guests. Which one is Mr. Mays? I'll go get him and tell him to come up to your room if it is that important to you. Just tell me which one he is. There are so many people here, I can't remember all their names."

"He's a fairly tall, slender man, about forty-five or forty-six, with closely cropped brown hair and a well-trimmed brown beard. He wears eyeglasses, but then again he doesn't always. He might not have them on." Jessica's face twisted into a frown as she thought. She remembered having seen him in the yard earlier that morning from her window but could not remember exactly what his clothing looked like, but she knew enough about the fashion in which the man dressed. "He'll be dressed in a tailor-fitted suit, probably in dark colors, and he should have a long golden watch chain drooping down out of his vest. Ask Aaron to point him out if you can't find him. Just hurry."

"I will. You go on back up there and finish getting ready. I'll be up in a minute to help you put on the veil."

474

Jessica went back to her room and barely had time to check the window again when she heard several light taps at the door.

"Come in." She sighed with relief and hurried toward the door, but to her dismay, it was Penelope and not Stuart Mays who entered.

"Just wanted to see how you were coming along," Penelope said as she closed the door and turned to inspect Jessica's appearance. Although she smiled, the smile did not quite overwhelm her face as it usually did. "You are lovely, simply lovely. But where's your veil?"

"Carrie's coming up in a minute to help me with it," she explained. Then, deciding it was not time for secrets and hoping that Penelope might know something she didn't, she added. "I sent her in search of Stuart Mays. I'm worried about Eric. He should have been here by now."

"I know. Aaron's worried, too. He and Stuart have already discussed it, and if Eric isn't here soon, they are going to ride out and see if they can find out what happened."

"Just the two of them?" Jessica's eyes widened with concern.

"No, they plan to gather together some of the uncles and cousins first."

"What are they going to say to them? Surely they don't plan to tell everyone about the detective force."

"No, of course not. The fact that Eric is not here for his own wedding is enough to cause alarm in itself."

A second knock on the door caused Jessica to jump. "Come in."

The door opened slowly and Carrie stepped inside, her brow raised in question. "I couldn't speak with your Mr.

Mays. He and a lot of the men have gone out to the stables with Aaron, and I was told not to go out there. Their meeting was for the menfolk only. I thought maybe it had to do with getting Eric ready for the wedding, but Mundora told me that as far as she knew, Eric hasn't ridden in yet."

Jessica hurried to her window and peered at the stables. She caught a glimpse of her grandfather, Buck, and Regie just before they stepped inside and disappeared into the shadows. Her heart thudded against her breast as she waited breathlessly to see if they would all come out on horseback and if so, how many would be armed. That's when she first noticed that a small cloud of dust stirred in the distance. A rider was headed toward them, just now crossing the far meadow. She caught her breath in her throat and narrowed her eyes as she tried to determine just who the rider might be, but he was still too far away to tell.

"Look, here comes someone. Suppose it's Eric?" Carrie asked, next to notice the rider. She tiptoed in order to see better over Jessica's shoulder and observed aloud for Penelope, who could not get close enough to the window to see. "Looks like a man sittin' back a ways and has got something big draped over his saddle in front of him."

"Something . . . or someone," Jessica said, her hand pressed to her throat. Then suddenly, her feet took flight and she pushed her way passed Carrie and Penelope. Down the stairs she went in a rustle of soft organza and silk with Carrie and Penelope only a few feet behind her. When they rushed out of the house, through the front door, they found that several of the women guests had gathered on the veranda and, having also spotted the

476

distant rider, stood in small groups peering out into the pasture as they murmured among themselves. Little Donnie Schiller took off in the direction of the stables to warn the men about the rider.

Jessica did not wait on the veranda with the rest of the women. Lifting her ivory-colored skirts high again, she rushed on out into the yard, in a hurry to meet the rider. By now she had recognized Jacky, and her spiraling fear had prodded her into a near frantic state because as he neared the yard, she could clearly see that the dark form draped in front of him was indeed a body. She could distinguish the fact that it had arms and legs, though the head dangled on the far side of the horse, just out of her sight. Tears spilled freely down her cheeks while she continued to run, her heart frozen beneath her breast. Silently, she prayed that it wasn't Eric.

By the time Jacky's horse hurdled the last fence, barely clearing its height because of the added burden, Jessica could see no more than mere shapes and colors. Her tears blinded her, causing her to stumble again and again in her attempt to keep going.

"Is it Eric?" she called out, blinking hard. "Jacky? Is that Eric?"

"No, it's Coolabah. Where's the doctor? Where's Mundora?"

"Here I am," Aaron called out as he hurried toward them from the stables, several men at his side. "Let's get him into the house." Turning to Regie and Deen who ran along beside him, he said, "Help Jacky get him inside. Put him on the sofa. I'll be there as soon as I can get my bag." Then stopping abruptly, he shouted to Jacky and asked, "What is it? Gunshot?"

Penelope turned around and hurried toward the house

to get the sofa ready while Regie and Deen ran toward Jacky's horse.

"Yes, sir," Jacky shouted as he dismounted. "It's a gunshot all right. He's been shot in the chest. He's loosing blood fast." Gingerly, Jacky lifted Coolabah's head and held it against his chest. Tears glistened in his dark eyes, and his voice strained to be heard when he added, "Help him, Dr. Aylesbury. Please help him. He got himself shot saving Eric's life—saving all our lives. You've got to help him."

Jacky's words whirled through Jessica's head as she stepped forward to examine Coolabah. The words grasped at her mind, slowly pulling her thoughts together, while she lifted back his eyelids and noticed the dilation. Her heart stopped. She wondered if he was already dead. Quickly, she felt his neck for a pulse and was relieved to discover one, faint as it was. "Did you say he saved Eric's life? Eric is safe?"

Though Jacky's eyes followed the men who had come to take Coolabah inside, he stayed behind to answer Jessica's questions. "Yes, he's safe. He'll be coming on just as soon as they can get a wagon to haul Ben with."

"Ben?"

"Ben was hurt. Broke both his legs when his horse fell on him. Tony went to get a flat bed to haul him over here in, and Eric decided to stay there with him until Tony could get back."

"What about the others? Where's James Cranston?"

Jacky blinked as he tried to keep his thoughts focused on their conversation. "The captain's gone with the rest of the men to arrest Livingston and see to it that he is safely hauled away to Sydney."

"Arrest him?"

"Yes, ma'am. They've got the goods on him now. One of the men who was in on the ambush sang out like a lyrebird. That, along with the evidence Coolabah found in Livingston's house this morning links the judge to plenty more than this one ambush," Jacky said hurriedly, then turned away from her. "Excuse me, ma'am. I've got to go. I've got to be with him."

Jessica stood with her hands folded over her mouth, her vision finally clear enough to see as she watched him break into a run for the house. Her mind tried to assimilate the facts Jacky had just given her so that she could fully understand everything that had happened, but there were too many things she did not yet know, but what she did know was that Eric was all right and that they had somehow gotten all the proof they needed against Livingston. Her heart soared and new tears threatened to spill down her cheeks, tears of joy. Lifting her skirts again, she hurried back toward the house to see what else she could find out.

Milicent settled into one of the tall-woven chairs that lined the veranda and leaned back to rest her weary body. All she had learned from Penelope, once she had finally found her, was that Eric was all right, delayed only by some sort of bail up, which had occurred on the way over, and that the man Aaron was busy trying to patch up had somehow saved her dear grandson's life. She had also been told the wedding would probably have to be put off until late afternoon because as soon as Aaron and Deen's wife were through with this man, they would have to work on Little Ben, who had also gotten hurt in the scuffle and should already be on his way over there.

479

Having chosen a chair that took full advantage of the afternoon sun, Milicent settled back and allowed the sun's gentle warmth to soothe her aching bones. She had been up since sunrise, and the busy morning she had spent helping Penelope had taken its toll. A chance to rest was more than a little welcome. Glancing across the rich, fertile land, Aaron's land, Milicent felt a strong surge of pride in her son. He had done well for himself. She wished Matthew had given up his stubbornness just once in his life and come out to see this place for himself. She closed her eyes for a moment as a deep wave of sadness swept over her. How she missed Matthew.

She wished he could have been with them when she, Oliver, and Glenn made the trip overland from the Hawkesbury—all of them headed for the wedding of a grandchild. What a merry time they had had on the way. Glenn Moffett, with all his wild stories about the time he and Aaron had put together the expedition into the wilderness those many years ago. And Oliver Cranston, bless his soul, still flirted with her shamelessly, despite his aging years and blurring eyesight. But then she reflected that his blurred eyesight might be a blessing, for if he managed to clearly see the wrinkles and gray hair time had bestowed on her, he might not find his flirtations worth the effort. She smiled at such a thought. And Matthew—Matthew would have been outraged by Oliver's forwardness. He would have called him down on it, and his sister Frannie would not have been there to help calm down his anger, with her being too ill to travel right now.

Matthew would have let his anger get the better of him and would have challenged Oliver to a fight before their journey was over, despite the fact that Oliver was barely

480

able to get around these days. Again sadness ached inside of her. Matthew had been gone for over a year now, and still her grief was extremely painful, almost unbearable. Time was supposed to heal all wounds, but she wondered if there would ever be enough time for her to get over missing Matthew.

Opening her eyes again, Milicent gazed across the green paddocks and rolling meadows and then let her gaze drift skyward. Again she wished Matthew could have somehow managed to see this place just once before he died. He would have finally come to understand why Aaron had been so driven to leave his family and the well-laid plans of his father in order to become a part of all this. Had Matthew been with her when they crossed the Blue Mountains and seen the powerful beauty and felt the deep feeling of awe she had felt, he would finally have known what lured Aaron to them and beyond, as she now knew.

Letting her eyes wander back to the guests milling about in the yard and in the shade of the veranda, she felt content to note how well so many lives had turned out. Her oldest brother, Ben, now stood just outside the doorway, carefully watching the main track for a sign of the wagon that would bring his oldest son. Ben had a successful dairy business and a huge family, all prospering—a family to be proud of. And Buck, who was just now stepping outside and talking with Ben, lived life the way he wanted, free to do as he pleased—always a bushman, always a rebel. Then there was Owen, though he had not been able to come. She could not forget Owen with his fine fleet of boats and his furniture manufacturing business, one of the first to be established in New South Wales. And last but never least among her brothers was Thaddeus. At the age of sixty-four, he was the youngest and the only one whose hair had never turned gray.

Tad's dark brown hair was just as thick and just as brown as it had been the day he was forced to sell Domini at the harvest fair; the day a thief had stolen the money young Tad had gotten for his beloved horse. Matt had come to the rescue. Smiling wistfully, she remembered that was also the very same day Matthew first kissed her—kissed her without asking. It was also the day she had fallen in love with him.

As the sun warmed her, Milicent found herself being slowly lulled to sleep. Though she wanted to be awake when Eric returned, she did not fight the need for sleep, and it was in her dream that Matthew visited her, as he often did. In the dream, she was finally able to share with him all that she had seen and explain to him what she had finally come to understand about Aaron.

"Grandmother? Grandmother, wake up. The ceremony's about to begin," Eric said as he bent over and gently shook his grandmother's arm.

Blinking groggily, she squinted and peered into Eric's handsome face. "How long have I been asleep?"

"I don't know, but you've been asleep ever since I got here and that was almost two hours ago." He chuckled when she glanced up into the rich, blue afternoon sky and found that the sun was well on its way across it.

"Why didn't you wake me when you first arrived?" she admonished with a purse of her lips and a tug of her wrinkled brow.

"I saw no need in it. Father had to tend to Ben's legs

482

before we could start the ceremony, anyway. We felt it would be best to let you rest."

Slowly, Milicent's gaze drifted from Eric's smiling face to the man who stood at his side. Her eyes traveled up to look at his face and grew instantly wide with wonder, for there beside Eric stood Matthew, smiling. Her trembling hand came up to cover her mouth as she leaned forward in her chair to get a better look. It was Matthew as he had been when they first met, back in England. Young, tall, and so handsome.

"Matthew?" she whispered. Her voice quivered with emotion as she put her hands down on the arms of the chair in order to push herself up. When Eric's hand came to her arm to help her, she pushed him away and got up on her own accord, feeling suddenly young again. Cautiously, she reached out a quivering hand and brought it forward in an attempt to touch the vision before her, though she knew it could cause the wondrous vision to disappear as the many visions of Matthew always did in the past. Still she had to try.

She knew Eric had spoken to her, but she could not focus on anything he had to say at the moment. Now that she was standing before the vision and could see him more clearly, what she saw made her heart stop. Her hand was only inches away now.

She looked deep into his eyes and held what she saw dear to her heart. Although some of the brooding demon, that overabundance of anger and indignation, which had so long been a part of Matthew, was finally gone, the mischief and the clear passion for life was still there. He looked a little thinner than she remembered him in his youth, but he was every bit as handsome, and at that moment he looked just as bewildered as he had the day he had happened on her while she was hiding in the woods on Lord Wyndham's property.

Slowly, she brought her hand closer, ever closer, until she finally touched him and discovered he was real. She pressed her hand harder and felt the warmth, the firmness. He was indeed real. She reached up and touched the thick, wavy wheat-colored hair and gasped at the softness. Then she trailed her hand along the gentle curve of his cheek. That's when it occurred to her, in her sleep-muddled mind, that her time had come and that Matthew was the angel heaven had sent down to escort her there. Her face drew up into a pensive frown.

"Not yet, Matthew, give me a few more hours and then I'll be ready. Today is Eric's wedding day. Eric and Jessica are getting married and I don't want to miss that. Just another hour and I'll go with you gladly."

"Grandmother? Listen to me!" Eric's concerned voice finally got through to her and she turned to face him.

"Grandmother, that's not Grandfather. That's Regie, Regie Schiller." He gripped both her shoulders and stared into her eyes as if searching for a sign that she finally understood.

Bewildered, she looked back at the young man in front of her. "But he looks just like Matthew. Almost exactly like he did when we first met. How can that be?"

Eric glanced first into her confused face then back at Regie, his face taut with indecision.

"It's all right. I know who my real father was," Regie said with a firm nod. "Tell her if you want."

"Grandmother, Regie is Mark's son. Mark fathered him back when he was married to Mother. Yes, Mark had a mistress. But because he was drowned before Regie was even born, his mother never felt it necessary to inform

484

the family about it. I only found out about it recently."

"Then he is Matthew's grandson?" she asked, her eyes searching Regie's face for every corresponding feature. He was almost an exact replica of Matthew. He had the same wintery blue eyes, the same virile, wide mouth that curled easily into a heart-touching smile. His tanned forehead was wide and his chin, strong. Yes, he was indeed Matthew made over.

"Son? I have a favor to ask of you," she said hesitantly. Her gaze dropped to her hands, now folded at her waist.

"Certainly, ma'am," Regie responded eagerly. His eyes glimmered with untold emotion. "What is it?"

"Would you please hold me for a minute? Hold me close and don't speak." When her eyes lifted to meet his, there was such raw emotion, such need, that Regie simply opened his arms and took her in. Milicent pressed her eyes shut, tight as she could get them to prevent the tears from spilling down her cheek and embarrassing her. Slowly, she brought her own trembling arms around him and held him close. She tried to swallow back the sob that had lodged in her throat, but couldn't. He even felt like her Matthew.

After a four hour delay, Eric and Jessica were finally married, outdoors beneath the shade of several huge gum trees, in the company of their family and closest friends. And when it came time for the customary kiss, even Coolabah found the strength to whoop and holler with the rest, though from his poor vantage point on the sofa, which had been pulled up to one of the front windows, he could not see as well as he would have liked. Once he had sought to stand up in order to try and join the rest of the guests outside where he would be able to see everything that went on, but found his knees were too weak to carry his heavy load. Though he was not at all sure if the weakness came more from all the Irish whiskey Eric's father had plied him with or from the loss of all that blood, he had finally resigned himself to the fact that he would have to watch the proceedings from inside. Glancing down at Ben, who slept peacefully through it all on a thick pallet of quilts, Coolabah was glad that he was at least awake to watch. Poor Ben never had been one to hold his liquor.

Outside, the sun still shown brightly, though it had dipped low into the sky, casting long shadows and reminding everyone that nightfall was only hours away.

"Congratulations," Aaron said to his son when the couple had finally turned around to accept everyone's customary praises and good wishes. Eric and Jessica were now officially man and wife, bound together forever with their open vows of their love and total commitment.

Eric graciously accepted his father's eager handshake but then, when Aaron slowly pulled his hand away, Eric grasped him by the shoulders and hugged him close. Gone was the resentment he had felt for the man who had kept his secrets for so long, secrets that had allowed him to grow up suffering such deep shame, such an overwhelming guilt for what he had come to feel for the girl who was supposed to be his half sister, when in fact she was no sister at all.

Jessica blinked back tears, causing her vision to blur, as she watched father and son embrace. She had longed for the day when the two would finally be able to push their foolish pride aside and truly forgive one another.

What a perfect day for forgiveness. Smiling, she glanced away just in time to see Carrie hurling herself through the crowd toward her.

"Jessica, you did it. You finally did it." She beamed as she hugged her friend close. "I hope you two will be as happy as Regie and I are. I can't think of anyone who deserves it more than you. I'll miss you dreadfully when Regie and I move to the Murray Valley with his family."

"But you aren't going for at least a year. We'll still have that time together. Regie said you two would wait until the rest of his family was well settled before you would make the move to join them. It really will be best for them. The land around here just is not right for growing grapes or hops. The Murray Valley is much more suitable."

"I guess so. It's just that I wanted you to be the one to help deliver my children. I was so looking forward to sharing that with you."

"Who knows, maybe you will manage to have your first before you move." Jessica smiled and raised her brows. "I'm sure Regie is willing to do his part."

Carrie blushed and pressed Jessica's hand to her cheek. "I'm quite sure that he is."

Suddenly, Jessica was surrounded by well wishers, and Eric was drawn into the crowd and out of her sight, though she could sense he was still nearby. Even Carrie was quickly pulled away and dwarfed by the crowd until Jessica could no longer see her.

"Dat was a beautiful vedding," Karl Schiller said as he pushed his way through to give her a big, German hug. His eyes were red with emotion when he boistered, "I know you two are goin' to be just as 'appy as Betty and me are."

487

"I hope so," she muttered, gasping to get her breath back. Karl had literally squeezed the air right out of her.

"She will be," Deen put in assuredly. "She married for love, and nothing makes for a happier future than knowing you are going to be able to share it with one you love."

Jessica held her arms out and embraced Deen warmly. She held onto him a moment longer than necessary as she quietly searched his glittering brown eyes. "And I see that you are happy, very happy. I'm glad."

"My joy spills through me freely," he told her and bent his head low to kiss her cheek. "And you have brought me a large part of my joy."

Jessica found she could no longer speak. Her happiness was too overwhelming. Teary eyed, she simply nodded that she understood and hugged him once more before she finally released him and allowed herself to be swept into another brief embrace. This time it was Sam who took her into his arms.

"Eric picked himself a beauty all right, a real beauty," he told her as he quickly released her. Then, in a brotherly tone, he wagged his finger at her and added, "Just you do what you can to make him happy. I know you will be wantin' to do your doctoring and help with the birthing of babies, but don't you go neglecting Eric in any way."

"I won't," she rasped out, still fighting the emotion lodged in her throat. "Eric will always come first." Then noticing Jacky standing hesitantly to the side, she sniffed and asked, "Don't I get a hug and a few well wishes from you, too?"

Jacky's eyes grew wide as if her words had been totally unexpected, but when she threw her arms around him and pulled him close, he smiled and explained. "I didn't know if you'd want for me to hug you, after all, I'm . . ."

She laughed and said, "I hug short people, too, you know. I'm not prejudiced to a man's height."

When the broad smile stretched across his dark face, she hugged him again. "Any good friend of Eric's is a dear friend of mine, and I've no objection to hugging a dear friend."

"Well, then, does that mean you have no objection to hugging me? James Cranston asked as he stepped forward, with his arms outstretched.

"I thought you had left already to help escort Judge Livingston safely back to Sydney," she said, questioningly.

"And miss your wedding? Never. I sent my men on ahead without me. I'll catch up with them on the track later." Having said that, he brought her into his arms and held her close for a long moment before finally releasing her enough to look down into her beautiful, tear-reddened eyes. Slowly, he smiled. His eyes glimmered with a strange sort of hopelessness when he spoke again. "Be happy, Jessica. All I ask is that you be happy." Then he released her completely and turned away, disappearing into the crowd of young men who still surrounded her.

Before she could think much about the strange feelings James's actions had evoked, she found herself being swept from Hiram Blackmon to Zacharia Bodine, to Dick Lawson—all taking a quick hug and making joking remarks about her dismal future as Eric's bride. Hired hands, who never would have dreamed of touching her at any other time, crowded around her for a quick hug of their own. It was tradition. But soon the throng of well wishers began to thin out, and Jessica found herself being faced by a long line of Eric's uncles. They had waited patiently for their turn to hug Eric's new bride and offer her their good-natured sympathy.

One by one they embraced her hard and made brash comments about the bleak outlook of a future tied to young Eric. One by one she laughed with them and thanked them, until she came to Buck. Buck Crawford, who was also Deen's father and her own grandfather, held back until she was finished with all his brothers. But when it finally came his turn, Buck simply held his hand out to her, and when she extended hers in kind, he grasped it and shook it firmly.

"You make a very beautiful bride," he said, his eyes leaving hers to take in every feature of her face. "I am very proud of you."

Jessica stared back at him a moment, then asked, hesitant but hopeful, "May I embrace you, Grandfather?" She was aware that Buck never hugged anyone other than his sister, Milicent, and even then Milicent hugged him first.

Buck's eyes widened, then relaxed, and something suspiciously close to a smile spread across his weathered face. "Yes, that would be nice."

When she took him into her arms and held him to her, she felt his strong arms go around her. Slowly, she closed her eyes and reveled in the feel of him. He was rock hard in her arms, though years should have softened him. She supposed it was his harsh way of life that kept him so strong, so muscular.

When she finally opened her eyes again, she noticed that many of the people in the yard had stopped what they were doing to watch. Blushing slightly, she murmured, "Thank you, Grandfather," and continued to watch him as she allowed him to pull away.

"Hey, you have another grandfather here, you know," she heard Glenn Moffett say, and she turned to be quickly taken into her other grandfather's waiting arms. She laughed when he picked her up off the floor and swung her around. Never had she done so much hugging. Never could she remember being this happy.

"That's enough," Eric finally said when he came to stand beside her again, his brows low and menacing as if he dared anyone to defy him. "You all have had her long enough. It's my turn now."

A roar of laughter swept the yard when Eric pulled Jessica into his arms and embraced her, his head dipping low to take another long and demanding kiss from his new wife. "You seem to like all this hugging just a little too much. I'll have to keep my eye on you."

"Is that a promise?" she laughed and tiptoed to take another quick kiss, laughing harder when his little-boy pout turned into a pleased smile.

"Aye, that it is. I've already told Captain Cranston that my resignation will reach his office as early as next week. And once Livingston's trial is over and after I've fulfilled my two years on Cranston's reserve list, I'll never have to worry about leaving you again."

"Ever?"

"Never."

Again he lowered his lips to hers, and she was overwhelmed by the love and the passion she felt for her husband, a passion that would surely bring them many fine children and years and years of true, devoted happiness. How lucky she was. Theirs would be a rich and rewarding life together, for whatever Eric finally decided to do with himself, wherever he eventually settled, she would be there at his side, supporting him, loving him, and doing all that she could to make him happy. Pulling free of his kiss, she smiled up into his handsome face, brimming with wifely pride, for their future was as hopeful and bright as the huge Australian sun that bathed them both with its warm, shining glory.

BESTSELLING HISTORICAL ROMANCE
from Zebra Books

PASSION'S GAMBLE (1477, $3.50)
by Linda Benjamin

Jessica was shocked when she was offered as the stakes in a poker game, but soon she found herself wishing that Luke Garrett, her handsome, muscular opponent, would hold the winning hand. For only his touch could release the rapturous torment trapped within her innocence.

YANKEE'S LADY (1784, $3.95)
by Kay McMahon

Rachel lashed at the Union officer and fought to flee the dangerous fire he ignited in her. But soon Rachel touched him with a bold fiery caress that told him—despite the war—that she yearned to be the YANKEE'S LADY

SEPTEMBER MOON (1838, $3.95)
by Constance O'Banyon

Ever since she was a little girl Cameron had dreamed of getting even with the Kingstons. But the extremely handsome Hunter Kingston caught her off guard and all she could think of was his lips crushing hers in feverish rapture beneath the SEPTEMBER MOON.

MIDNIGHT THUNDER (1873, $3.95)
by Casey Stuart

The last thing Gabrielle remembered before slipping into unconsciousness was a pair of the deepest blue eyes she'd ever seen. Instead of stopping her crime, Alexander wanted to imprison her in his arms and embrace her with the fury of MIDNIGHT THUNDER.